The Alaska
SAGA

The *Alaska* SAGA

3 Best-Loved
Historical Romances

TRACIE PETERSON

BARBOUR
PUBLISHING

A Light in the Window ©1993 by Tracie J. Peterson

Destiny's Road ©1994 by Tracie J. Peterson

Iditarod Dream ©1994 by Tracie J. Peterson

Print ISBN 978-1-63609-316-1

Adobe Digital Edition (.epub) 978-1-63609-318-5

All scripture quotations, unless otherwise noted, are taken from the King James Version of the Bible.

Scripture taken from the Holy Bible, New International Version®, NIV®. Copyright 1973, 1978, 1984, 2011 by Biblica, Inc.™ Used by permission. All rights reserved worldwide.

This book is a work of fiction. Names, characters, places, and incidents are either products of the author's imagination or used fictitiously. Any similarity to actual people, organizations, and/or events is purely coincidental.

Cover Model Photograph: Mark Owen/ Trevillion Images

Published by Barbour Publishing, Inc., 1810 Barbour Drive, Uhrichsville, Ohio 44683, www.barbourbooks.com

Our mission is to inspire the world with the life-changing message of the Bible.

Member of the
Evangelical Christian
Publishers Association

Printed in Canada.

A *Light*
IN THE WINDOW

DEDICATION

To Pam and David, Cheri, and Ryan Thibault.
To Joyce and Ray Mains,
my personal Alaska connection.
Thanks for your love and prayers over the years.
I thank God upon my every remembrance of you.

ACKNOWLEDGMENTS

The 1925 diphtheria epidemic in Nome, Alaska, would have taken more lives and spread farther had it not been for the heroic hearts of the men who shared the serum run. Their names are listed here in honor of their sacrifice and spirit.

"WILD BILL" SHANNON—Nenana to Tolovana (52 miles)
DAN GREEN—Tolovana to Manley Hot Springs (31 miles)
JOHNNY FOLGER—Manley Hot Springs to Fish Lake (28 miles)
SAM JOSEPH—Fish Lake to Tanana (26 miles)
TITUS NIKOLI—Tanana to Kallands (34 miles)
DAVE CORNING—Kallands to Nine Mile mail cabin (24 miles)
EDGAR KALLAND—Nine Mile to Kokrines (30 miles)
HARRY PITKA—Kokrines to Ruby (30 miles)
BILL MCCARTY—Ruby to Whiskey Creek (28 miles)
EDGAR NOLLNER—Whiskey Creek to Galena (24 miles)
GEORGE NOLLNER—Galena to Bishop Mountain (18 miles)
CHARLIE EVANS—Bishop Mountain to Nulato (30 miles)
TOMMY PATSY—Nulato to Kaltag (36 miles)
JACKSCREW—Kaltag to Old Woman shelter house (40 miles)
VICTOR ANAGICK—Old Woman to Unalakleet (34 miles)
MYLES GONANGNAN—Unalakleet to Shaktolik (40 miles)
HENRY IVANOFF—starts from Shaktolik but meets Seppala
LEONHARD SEPPALA—Shaktolik to Golovin (91 miles)
CHARLIE OLSON—Golovin to Bluff (25 miles)
GUNNAR KAASEN—Bluff to Nome (53 miles)
And, of course, the dogs!

My special thanks to the Anchorage Museum of History and Art; Anchorage Municipal Libraries; the University of Alaska, Fairbanks; and my husband, Jim, for their assistance with the historical research surrounding this event.

Chapter 1

J ulie Eriksson hastily donned her fur-trimmed cloak and made her way to the viewing deck of the SS *Victoria*. She strained to see the hazy blue outline of land. Nome, Alaska! After five long years, she was finally coming home. For the rest of her life, she would celebrate the seventh of October.

Squinting against the brilliance of the sun as it hit the ice floes in the Nome roadstead, Julie thrilled at the crisp, cold wind on her face. Where other passengers—visitors to her far north—shuddered at the zero-degree weather and went quickly below, Julie felt like casting off her cloak. This was her home, and never again would she leave it. She longed to soak it all up.

The deep blast of the steamer's whistle startled Julie. She remembered back to 1919, when she'd left Nome for Seattle in order to study nursing. Then, the ship's whistle had been a lonely reminder that Julie was leaving home. Now an experienced public health nurse, Julie was returning to her people to offer what skills she'd learned in order to better their lives.

Her only regret was that her mother, Agneta, had passed away while Julie was in school. Having been a sickly woman, Agneta was Julie's biggest reason for becoming a nurse. What little health care existed in Alaska was inadequate to deal with the ailments of Agneta Eriksson. Julie had always desired to bring her mother relief from her torturous bouts with asthma. Julie had learned all she could about the illness, but she hadn't returned in time to help.

Her mother's memory would live on in Julie's heart, but the empty place Agneta's death left would never be filled. With this thought in mind, Julie wondered if her father and brother would be meeting her. Their homestead was some twelve miles northeast of Nome—a short, easy trip by dogsled.

She smiled as she thought of the dogs. It had been so long since she'd driven her own team. City people in Seattle had laughed at her talk of driving dogs, unable to imagine Julie handling the demand.

Of course, some of the rural students had known only too well the love of mushing dogs, and when several had invited Julie to join them at a local winter race, she'd readily accepted. Those simple kindnesses had helped ease her homesick heart that first year.

Glancing at her watch, Julie noted that it was ten minutes till twelve. They'd made excellent time, with perfect weather for their six-day journey from Seattle. During her bleakest moments in the States, it had been hard to believe that Nome was only six days away. Most of the time the distance had seemed an eternity, and had Julie not been resolved to become a nurse, she would have gladly taken the short trip home and forgotten the loneliness that haunted her in the state of Washington.

Julie felt the ship slow as the ice floes grew larger and threatened to halt the *Victoria*'s progress. Nicknamed the Grand Old Lady, the SS *Victoria* was one of the only ships to brave the harbor of Nome this late in the year. Julie knew that even the *Victoria* wouldn't challenge the icy waters past the first of November. Insurance premiums would soar due to the risk of icebergs. In fact, after the *Victoria* pulled out of the harbor for Seattle, there wouldn't be another ship into Nome until April.

"All for Nome! All for Nome!" a man called out through a megaphone.

Julie moved toward the man. "Are we going to take the ferry across the roadstead?" she asked as the man moved past her.

"No ma'am," the man said with a tip of his cap. "The ice is too thick. We're going to walk you across."

Julie nodded. It wasn't unusual for Nome-bound ships to anchor in the ice-laden harbor while passengers walked ashore across the thick ice. Leaning against the icy railing, Julie smiled to herself. Another hour and she'd be on the sandy banks of Nome.

"Oh thank You, Father," she whispered in prayer. "I'm so happy to be home and so happy to be doing Your work." Julie glanced around to make certain no one was watching her before she continued. No sense in folks thinking she was daft.

"Dear God, make me an ambassador of Your love and goodwill. Let me help the people in this territory both with my nursing skills and my knowledge of You. And Lord, thank You so very much for allowing the years away to pass quickly and for the good friends You sent my way—friends who helped to ease my burden of loneliness and separation. Amen."

The ship came to a full stop, resting gracefully against the solid platform of ice. Julie raced back to her cabin and gathered her things. It was going to be a glorious day!

The walk across the icy harbor made Julie glad she'd bought a sturdy pair of boots in Seattle before leaving for home. Of course, they weren't as warm as native wolfskin boots with moosehide bottoms, but they got her across the ice without any mishaps.

Some of the "cheechakos," the Alaskan name for greenhorns, were trying to snowshoe or skate in city boots across the ice. If she hadn't worried about hurting their pride, Julie might have laughed out loud in amusement. The only other women on the trip were a pair of frail-looking things who insisted on being pushed across the ice in sled baskets.

Julie wondered about the handful of passengers. Always there were those who came to find their fortunes in gold, but they usually arrived in April or May and departed before the temperatures dropped below zero. There weren't many from the lower forty-eight who, upon hearing of days, even weeks, spent at fifty degrees below zero, would brave the Alaskan winter. Those hearty souls who did usually came for reasons other than acquiring gold.

Of course, some people were running from the law. Alaska provided a good place for criminals to escape from those who might put them behind bars. Others might have family or friends who'd beckoned them north.

Julie surmised the two women in the sled baskets might be mail-order brides. They weren't familiar faces, nor did they appear to be saloon girls. She felt sorry for them as she watched them shivering against the cold. She wondered if they'd ever bear up and become sourdoughs, as those who made it through at least one Alaskan winter were called.

Nearly losing her footing, Julie decided to forget about the other passengers. She was nearly a visitor herself, and she hastened to remember the little things she'd forgotten while enjoying the conveniences in Seattle. She kept her eyes to the ice, determined to keep her suitcases balanced and firmly gripped in her ladylike, gloved hands. *Useless things, city gloves,* Julie thought. She'd be only too happy to trade them in for a warm pair of fur gloves or mittens. *Not that it hasn't been fun to play the part of the grand lady.* Given that Nome streets in winter were always in some state of mud, ice, or snow, Julie knew it would be wise to forget about dressing up. *No,* she reasoned, *sealskin pants, mukluks, heavy fur parkas, and wool scarves will be of more comfort to me here.*

The wind whipped across her face and pulled at her carefully pinned black hair. Having spent most of her time indoors in Seattle, Julie's pale skin made an impressive contrast to her ebony hair and eyes.

Julie had her Eskimo grandmother to thank for the rich, dark color of her eyes and shining hair. Having left her Inupiat Eskimo village, Julie's grandmother had married a Swedish fur trapper and moved to Nome. Their only child, Lavern Eriksson, had been born in 1865, some thirty-six years before the famed ninety-seven-ounce gold nugget was taken out of Anvil Creek near Nome.

It was the rumor of gold as early as 1899 that had brought Agneta's family north. While others were eager to make their fortunes, Julie's parents had found a fortune in love. Agneta and Vern had married after a brief courtship and soon Julie's brother, August, had been born. In 1902, Julie's birth had completed the family.

Julie scanned the banks again for a familiar face. She was about to give up hope when her brother's face came into view. His hand shielded his eyes, but Julie easily recognized his easygoing looks.

"August!" she shouted across the ice as she picked up her pace. Her brother pushed through the crowd and rushed across the frozen harbor to greet Julie.

"I can't believe you're finally here," August said as he pulled Julie into his muscular arms.

"Me either," Julie said as she enjoyed the first hug she'd had in five years. She'd nearly forgotten the feel of supportive arms.

"Here," August said as he took hold of her bags. "Let me carry those. I suppose the rest will be brought ashore sometime later?"

"Actually the *Victoria* is unloading immediately. The ice is much worse than they expected, and they want to get on their way."

"Great," August said as they came onto firm land. He put the bags down and asked, "Did you bring much back from the States?"

"Well, there are quite a few supplies for Dr. Welch, and of course the things you and Father requested. Not to mention the dozen or more things that friends wired me to bring back from Seattle. I'd say maybe eight or nine crates," Julie said with a grin.

"That many?" August questioned as his eyes grew wide. "It's a good thing I brought a twelve-dog team."

"You needn't worry," Julie said as she linked her arm through August's. "At least half the crates are for Dr. Welch. They're marked with bright red crosses, so we won't have to spend time figuring out which is which."

"What a relief," August said with a laugh. "Look, you wait here, and I'll go get the dogs." Julie nodded and watched as August walked through the bustling crowd of people. It was good to be home.

An hour later, Julie was helping August load the last of Dr. Welch's supplies into the sled.

"I'll come back for our things after we drop these off at the Doc's. Do you want to drive the sled?" August asked.

"No, you go ahead. I'm just going to walk and enjoy being back," Julie replied.

"Whatever you want," August said and took to the sled. "Let's go. Hike!" he called, and the dogs set out as if the sled basket were empty. They were a hearty, powerful breed of animal, well suited to the work and cold.

Julie trekked behind August, familiarizing herself with the few shops. The post office bustled with activity as the postmaster unloaded the incoming mail. Nome hadn't changed that much during her five-year absence. The Northwestern Commercial Company remained with a number of buildings that lined the main street of town, and folks could still get a meal at the Union Restaurant for four bits.

Up ahead, August had brought the dogs to a halt outside the twenty-five-bed hospital. Julie joined him just as Dr. Welch popped his head out the door.

"You're certainly a welcome sight," Dr. Welch said as he opened the door wide to receive August and Julie. "Let me grab my coat and I'll give you a hand."

August waved him off. "That's all right, Doc. I can handle it."

"In that case," Dr. Welch said with a shiver, "I'll speak with your sister while you unload the sled. You can bring everything around back. I'll have Nurse Seville show you where to put things."

August nodded and drove the dogs to the back of the hospital.

Julie followed the middle-aged man up the stairs and into his office. "I was able to obtain almost all the things you needed from the hospital in Seattle."

"That's a relief," Dr. Welch replied as he offered Julie a chair. "How was your trip?"

"Perfect," Julie answered and took a seat. "Of course, the destination alone made it that. I wouldn't have noticed if they'd stuck me in the galley washing dishes. I was coming home, and that made everything else unimportant."

Dr. Welch smiled and nodded. "I can well understand. Would you like something hot to drink?"

"No, I'm fine," Julie replied as she pulled off her gloves. "As soon as August finishes unloading the sled, we'll need to be on our way home."

"I'm afraid I must insist that you stay at least a day. Preferably two. As this area's public health nurse, you will report directly to me. Our combined reports will then go via mail to the proper officials. There's a great deal we'll need to cover before you can actually begin your work."

"I understand," Julie said thoughtfully, "but I have been working without much time to call my own. I need to go home and see my father, and I need time to rest."

"I confess, I haven't given much thought to your needs. Usually people go to Seattle for a vacation. It's odd to think of someone coming to Alaska for a break. I'm just so relieved to have an extra helping hand with the outlying population," Dr. Welch said as he took a seat across from Julie. "You will actually do many jobs that are often reserved for doctors in more populated regions. Especially as you venture out among the villages."

Julie nodded. "If August agrees," she stated as her brother walked into the room bringing a package, "we'll stay in Nome for one night. Then I really must take a short rest." Both Julie and Dr. Welch looked at August.

"There's no way I can stay. I'm needed to help with the dogs," August replied, reminding Julie of her father's sled dog kennel. "But I can leave part of the team for Julie to mush home tomorrow. I'll need to borrow another sled, however."

"There's one here standing ready for Nurse Eriksson's use," Dr. Welch offered. Julie smiled to herself. It was the first time anyone in Nome had called her that.

"Well, Julie?" August looked at his sister and waited for her approval.

Julie nodded. "I think I can remember the way home," she said with a laugh.

"If you don't"—August grinned—"the dogs sure will. Especially if it's close to dinnertime."

"It's agreed then," Dr. Welch said. "Julie, you are welcome to sleep in the back room. There's a stove and plenty of coal. It's well protected from the wind and shouldn't get too cold."

"Once you get past twenty degrees below zero, it's just about the same. Cold is cold," Julie said like a true Alaskan.

Turning to August, Dr. Welch gave him instructions on where he could leave Julie's dogs and sled gear. "Oh, here. I almost forgot," August said as he handed Julie the package he'd been holding. "These are the things you asked me to bring. I was going to have you change before the trip home."

"You remembered!" Julie said with a note of excitement in her voice. "My sealskin pants and parka!"

August smiled as he secured his parka hood. "I'll tell Pa you'll be home tomorrow. Now if you'll both excuse me, I'll finish unloading the sled and be on my way."

Julie put the package aside and threw herself into August's arms. "Thank you, August. Please tell Pa I love him and I can't wait to see him again." August gave Julie a tight squeeze and was gone.

Loneliness seeped into her heart, reminding Julie once again of the isolation she'd known in Seattle. She tried to shake the feeling, convincing herself that because she was home, she'd no longer be lonely.

As she turned from the door, she could hear the dogs yipping outside, anxious to be on the trail. She understood their cries. She too longed to be making the trip home.

Chapter 2

The next morning at breakfast, Julie couldn't contain her excitement. "I can't believe I'm finally home. I can hardly wait to see my father."

"I would've gotten about as much accomplished if I'd sent you on home with your brother. I suppose I should have realized the importance of your spending time with your family," Dr. Welch said as he and Julie accepted a stack of hotcakes from the Union Restaurant's waitress.

Julie laughed in animated excitement. "I feel just like a little girl at Christmas," she said as she poured warmed corn syrup on her cakes.

"We still need to pick up a few things for your trip home," Dr. Welch reminded her.

"Umm," Julie nodded with her mouth full. Taking a drink of hot coffee, she added, "I appreciate the supplies you've already loaned me. I'll only need to pick up food for the dogs. It's always wise to keep your transportation well cared for, just in case we get stuck on the trail."

"I heard tell a blizzard is due in," Dr. Welch said between bites. "I'm afraid you'll have to really move those dogs to get home before the storm catches up with you."

Julie glanced out the window. The skies were still dark, making it impossible to get any bearing on the incoming storm. "I'd nearly forgotten about the darkness. How many hours of daylight can I count on this time of year?"

"I wouldn't expect more than seven—especially if that storm moves in as planned. The sun won't be up for another hour or so," Dr. Welch said, glancing at his pocket watch.

"I don't dare wait that long," Julie said thoughtfully. "I'll mush out in the dark. The dogs know the trail in their sleep, and I won't need more than two or three hours at the most, if the trail is clear."

"Are you sure you're up to it?" Dr. Welch questioned. "I don't intend to lose my first public health nurse. I've waited too long for help."

Julie smiled. "Don't worry about me," she reassured. "I've never been one to take unnecessary risks. I'll be fine if I can move out right away."

"Then I'll pay for this meal, and we'll go secure some food for your dogs," Dr. Welch said as he rose from the table.

Julie hurriedly forked the last of the hotcakes into her mouth and pulled on her parka. The warmth of the coat made her feel confident that she could face the trail without danger.

Julie affixed the dog harness to the sled, remembering to anchor the sled securely before attaching any of the dogs. Reaching for her lead dog, Dusty, Julie gave the strong, broad-chested malamute a hearty hug. "Good dog, Dusty. You remember me, don't you, boy?" she questioned as she led him to the harness.

Dusty yipped, and soon the rest of the dogs perked up and began dancing around as Julie talked to and petted each one. Within minutes, they were once again good friends.

After harnessing Dusty in the lead, Julie secured her swing dogs, Nugget and Bear. Two team dogs, Teddy and Tuffy, came next, with two wheel dogs, Cookie and Sandy, rounding out the sled team.

Julie checked the lines and then rechecked them. It had been at least five years since she'd had to be responsible for such a job, and she was self-conscious about doing it right. The wind picked up, reminding her of the expected snow.

"Well, boys," Julie said as she checked the ropes that held her sled load. "I think we'd best be on our way." She left the dogs long enough to go inside and bid Dr. Welch good-bye, promising to return in two weeks.

Taking her place at the sled, Julie paused for a moment of prayer.

"Dear Lord, please watch over us and deliver me safely to my father and brother. Amen." She pulled up the snow hook and tossed it into the sled basket.

"All right, team. Hike!" she called, grabbing the bar tightly. She ran behind the sled for a few feet before taking her place on the runners. Soon she'd be home!

Once the dogs made their way out of Nome, they followed a trail that paralleled Norton Sound. Julie was relieved that, because the wind had been surprisingly calm through the night, the trail hadn't drifted much.

Julie barely felt the cold, even though the temperature had dropped to fifteen below. She was so well bundled beneath the layers of wool and fur that when snow started to fall, she barely noticed.

An hour later, however, the snow had worked into a blizzard with fierce winds blowing off the sea. Julie knew the dogs would stay to the trail unless something barred their way, so she moved on without concern.

The wind and ice pelted down ruthlessly, causing Julie to nearly lose control of the sled once or twice. The snow drifted and blew, almost obliterating the trail. Julie reassured herself by remembering that the dogs would be able to find their way through. Nonetheless, she found herself whispering a prayer. It wasn't until Dusty abruptly brought the team to a stop that Julie began to worry.

She couldn't call to the dogs above the blizzard's roar, and the blowing snow made it impossible to see up ahead. Julie wondered why Dusty felt it necessary to stop. She grabbed the snow hook and, after securely anchoring it in the ice-covered snowbank, made her way along the sled.

Taking hold of the harness, Julie made her way down the line past each dog. Finally coming to Dusty, she took hold of the tugline. "What is it, boy?" she questioned as she strained to see down the obscured trail.

Dusty whined and yipped but refused to move forward. Julie turned to move back down the line of dogs when someone grabbed her arm from behind. Her scream of surprise was lost in the muffling of scarves and blowing wind. She turned. A pair of ice-encrusted eyes stared at her.

For a moment Julie did nothing. Her pounding heart obscured all other sounds. She was surprised that the dogs remained relatively calm, and because even Dusty seemed at ease with this person, she began to relax.

The man let go of Julie's arm and motioned her to the sled. Julie nodded while the man took hold of Dusty's harness. Julie pulled the snow hook and grabbed onto the sled bar. The team barely moved as the stranger helped them down a steep embankment and across a solid sheet of ice.

The dogs couldn't get good footing against the slick surface, but the man moved them across with little difficulty. The snow let up just a bit, and Julie could see the stranger urging Dusty up the opposite bank. Whoever he was, Julie was grateful.

The dogs were struggling to get up the bank. Julie knew she should get off the sled and help push. She gingerly took one foot off and then the other. The ice offered no traction, and when Julie pushed forward, her feet went out from beneath her.

Smacking hard onto the ice, Julie lay still, struggling to draw a good breath. Tucking her legs up under her, Julie managed to get to her hands and knees. Just then she felt the firm grip of the man as his hands encircled her waist. Within moments, Julie was up on her feet and, thanks to the stranger, soon up the embankment.

Standing at the top to catch her breath, Julie thanked God for answering her prayers for safety by providing help from a stranger. She quickly resumed her place on the runner of her sled, ready to set out again.

The stranger moved forward. Julie could barely see the outline of another dogsled team. They would now progress together, Julie realized as the man waved her ahead. She felt much better traveling through the storm with a companion.

They progressed slowly, but evenly. Snow fell heavily at times, and the wind threatened to freeze Julie's eyes closed. Just as quickly, the wind would let up and visibility would improve. In spite of the questionable weather, Julie felt confident that nothing would hamper her trip home. She'd put the entire matter in God's hands, and she refused to take it back.

No sooner had this thought crossed her mind than the teams approached a river. Julie waited patiently while the stranger moved his dogs onto the ice. She watched silently as the man expertly maneuvered his animals across the river. It would only be a few more minutes before he'd signal her to start down the embankment.

Then the unthinkable happened. The stranger's lead dog disappeared into the river. Julie watched in horror as the stranger moved ahead of the team to pull his dog from the water. A sudden stillness in the wind carried the sound of cracking ice just before the stranger joined his dog in the water.

Julie had to act fast. She worked her dogs down the riverbank and onto a ledge of even ground. Fearful that the ice would give way and cause more harm, Julie tied a line around her waist and secured it to her anchored sled.

Cautiously, she worked her way across the slippery ice to the place where the stranger's dog team waited for their leader. The stranger was holding on to the edge of the ice, but it was impossible for him to get out. He'd cut the lead dog from the harness and was trying to boost him out of the water.

Julie reached down, took hold of the dog's thick, rough fur, and pulled him forward. The dog seemed fine as he found his footing and shook out his heavy coat. Untying the line from around her waist, Julie motioned the stranger to secure it under his arms.

Following the rope back to her own dogs, Julie took hold of Dusty's harness and pulled him forward down the bank of the river. "Forward!" Julie called against the wind. The dogs worked perfectly, pulling against the added weight of the stranger. Julie kept looking over her shoulder as she encouraged the dogs to pull. When she saw the man roll up onto the ice, she stopped the dogs and quickly crossed the ice to help the man to his feet.

Julie reached out her hand and helped the man stand. He seemed unharmed, yet Julie knew the possibility of hypothermia was great. She motioned to the man to take off his parka, but he shook his head and pointed up the embankment.

She reluctantly agreed to follow the man as he loaded his lead dog into the sled basket and led his dogs away from the broken ice. Julie retrieved her team and, feeling more confident of her abilities, urged them up the riverbank. At the top of the embankment, she could see why the man had motioned her on. A light flickered brightly in a cabin window.

With so much of the Alaskan winter months spent in darkness, all travelers looked for that welcoming beacon: a light in the window. Relief poured through Julie as she realized that shelter was so near. She moved her dogs forward and then realized that the cabin she was nearing was her own home. The dogs began to yip and howl as Julie mushed them on. They were home at last!

As Julie stopped in front of the cabin, two bundled forms made their way from one of the outbuildings. Vern and August Eriksson both motioned Julie to the house while they worked together to care for her dogs.

August left Julie's dogs to his father's care and went to the stranger. He motioned him to follow Julie. The stranger pulled August to the sled basket and revealed his water-soaked dog. August nodded and pulled the dog into his arms. He moved quickly to the outbuilding where Julie knew her father kept the sick or weak dogs.

The stranger reached into the sled basket, pulled a canvas pack out, and made his way toward the house. Julie went ahead of him and opened the door. A warm wave of air hit her eyes as she walked into the cabin. Quickly, she made her way to the fireplace.

With no thought of the man behind her, Julie pulled off her heavy fur gloves and scarves. She pulled the parka over her head and tossed it to the floor. Thick black hair tumbled around her shoulders as Julie worked to loosen the laces of her mukluks. Kicking the heavy boots aside, she unfastened the catch on her sealskin pants and let them drop to the floor.

Beneath her sealskin pants, Julie wore heavy denim jeans. She felt them to see if they were wet. Finding her pants in good shape, she straightened up, brushing back the hair from her face. Staring at her from across the room was the stranger.

The shocked expression on the man's face nearly caused Julie to laugh out loud. Her black eyes danced with amusement, and a grin formed at the corner of her lips.

"I'm Julie Eriksson, and this is my home," she offered, extending her hand. She immediately liked his rugged looks.

The man broke into laughter as he took Julie's hand. "I'll be," he said, and his shocked expression changed to admiration. "I must say that's the first time a woman saved my life. I figured you were a man. I mean, well. . ."

He fell silent as he dropped Julie's hand. "Of course," he murmured as he stepped back and allowed his eyes to travel the length of Julie's slim frame, "that's obviously not the case."

"I believe I owe you thanks as well," Julie said, growing uncomfortable under the stranger's scrutiny.

"I think we're more than even. By the way, I'm Sam Curtiss."

"Lucky Sam?" Julie questioned, remembering the nickname from things her brother had told her of his best friend.

"The very same," Sam said with a grin. "Although I think I owe my survival today to more than luck."

Julie nodded. "No doubt."

Sam shook his head. "So you're August's little sister," he said as he took a seat and kicked off his boots.

"I'm also a nurse," Julie said, taking a step forward. "And as such, I know that you're in danger of hypothermia. You should get out of those wet clothes and into something warm and dry."

Sam raised his eyebrows and crossed his arms against his chest. "Yes ma'am," he said as he leaned back against the chair, "I'd say I owe this encounter to a great deal more than luck."

Chapter 3

Sam refused to take his eyes off Julie while they waited for Vern and August to return from caring for the dogs. He was captivated by this woman as he'd never been by any other. She was so graceful and fluid in her motions, yet the knowledge that she had saved him out on the ice gave Sam a heartfelt respect for her.

As Julie moved about the room and tried to avoid his gaze, Sam couldn't help but smile. She was uncomfortable in his presence—that much was obvious—and Sam wondered why.

Julie ignored Sam as she went about the cabin, reacquainting herself with the home she'd left so long ago. Vern and August, true to their Swedish ancestry, hadn't changed things except to add a portrait of Julie that she'd mailed them while at school in Seattle.

Julie circled the room, touching the things her mother had loved, cherishing the memory of days spent in her company. The house seemed empty without her. She grimaced as she remembered the day months earlier when the telegram had arrived. Because it was February, passage to Nome had been impossible.

Julie blamed herself for not being at her mother's side. Her schooling had been complete in time to return to Nome before ice isolated it from the rest of the world. But because Julie had decided to become a public health nurse, there were certain additional requirements she had to meet.

When word reached her of her mother's death, Julie had had no other choice but to stay on at least until April, when the ports reopened. By then, her mother's body would have long since been cared for, so Julie decided to finish her government training and return in the fall as a fully certified public health nurse.

Julie glanced up to find Sam's eyes fixed on her. His presence made her feel awkward. For the last few years, Julie had spent most of her time with women. Outside of the men she'd helped care for, Julie hadn't allowed herself the luxury of gentlemanly companionship.

The silence grew unbearable, but just as Julie began to fear she'd have to start talking with Sam, the front door burst open in a flurry of snow and fur.

"Father!" Julie ran across the room to embrace the elder Eriksson.

"Julie, it's so good to have you home. Let me look you over," Vern said as he put his daughter at arm's length. "You look more like your mother every day, God rest her soul. Of course, I see a bit of your grandmother Eriksson as well."

"Oh Father," Julie said with a smile, "come get warm by the fire. Here, let me help you with your parka."

"You're just like your mother. She was always fussing and worrying about me, even when she was. . ." Her father's words trailed into silence.

Julie took the parka as her father pulled it over his head. "Even when she was dying?" Julie finished her father's words.

"Yes." Vern Eriksson seemed to age with the statement. "It hasn't been a year, and it seems forever. Wish it didn't have to be so for your homecoming."

"I thought I'd die for want of home," Julie stated evenly. Her voice strained slightly. "I'd rather it not be this way, but I've still got you and August." The young woman threw herself into her father's open arms. Her eyes grew misty.

"I see you brought Sam home with you," August said as he threw his coat aside.

"I think it was more the other way around," Julie said. "That blizzard hit hard, and I was still at least an hour from home. Sam appeared out of nowhere and, well, here we are."

Julie studied Sam for a moment. His brown eyes were so intense in their evaluation, however, that she quickly looked away.

"Don't you dare believe her," Sam's deep voice boomed out. "She saved my life. Pulled me out of the Nome River when the ice gave way."

"Are you all right, Sam?" Vern questioned with the voice of a concerned father.

"I'm just fine, Vern. Julie's quick thinking and my sealskin pants kept me from getting too wet. That daughter of yours is quite a dog driver. You ought to be proud of her."

"We are, to be sure," Vern said as he squeezed Julie's shoulders. "I'll bet you two could use something hot. Why don't you kick back, and August and I will get something on the stove."

"I'd like to unpack first," Julie said as she picked up her mukluks.

"Your things are already in your room," August offered. "I could pretty well figure out which crates were yours and which weren't."

"Thanks, August," Julie said as she walked over and kissed him on the cheek. "I could get used to being cared for," she said with a smile.

"Somebody as pretty as you ought to be cared for," Sam offered seriously. There was only the slightest hint of a smile on his lips. Julie blushed crimson, uncertain what she should say.

"Don't let her looks deceive you, Sam. She's wild enough to handle when she's got her steam up. I remember the time we were going to have to shoot one of the pups and—"

"I don't think Sam needs to hear about that," Julie interrupted as she shifted uncomfortably. She looked almost pleadingly at Sam, melting his heart and any protest he might have voiced.

"All right, all right," Vern said with a chuckle. "I guess anyone who's worked as hard as you have today deserves extra consideration. Go ahead and do what you need to. August and I will get lunch."

"Sam, you might as well put your things in my room. From the looks of the weather, you're going to be here tonight," August added.

Julie's head snapped up and turned to face Sam. *He's staying the night,* she thought as she met his laughing eyes.

A smile played at the corner of Sam's lips, and Julie was shocked to realize she was paying attention to them. It was even more shocking to wonder what it would be like to kiss those lips.

Julie lifted her gaze to Sam's eyes and found they had sobered considerably under her scrutiny. *What was he thinking? Did he know what she was thinking?* Julie felt her cheeks grow hot and dropped her gaze.

"I think I'd better get busy," she muttered and left the room. Why did he make her feel so strange? Julie chided herself for even caring. She was a nurse now, and her mother's dream for her was finally realized. There was no way Julie was going to jeopardize that dream by getting involved with a man. Even if the man was the handsome Lucky Sam Curtiss.

Julie marveled that her room hadn't changed in her absence. Her bed was still made up with the crazy quilt her mother had given her for her fourteenth birthday. Julie reached out and stroked the quilt as if it somehow allowed her to touch her mother.

"Remember, Julie," she could hear her mother say, *"God only lends us to this world for a short time. What we do with that time, what we leave behind, is our representation of our love for Him. It doesn't matter that we make the most money or have the finest homes. What matters is that we can stand confidently before our Lord and King, knowing that we lived as He would have us live and gave Him our best."*

This quilt was only a small part of what Agneta Eriksson had left behind, Julie realized. She'd lived her life for God and had brought both her children to an understanding of salvation. Surely God had welcomed her as a faithful servant.

Julie sat down on the edge of the bed and sighed. She loved the simplicity of her room. A picture of Jesus praying, a small mirror, and a cross-stitched sampler were the only ornaments decorating the walls, while delicate, flower-print curtains framed her window. A small desk and chair completed the room.

Julie stretched out on her bed and listened to the wind howling outside her boarded window. The pulsating rhythm soon put her to sleep, leaving her to dream of penetrating brown eyes and a man she feared would change her destiny forever.

———— # ————

"Julie," Vern called softly as he gently shook his daughter. "Wake up. Dinner's on."

Julie wiped her eyes and sat up. "It's sure been a long time since I've had a wake-up call like this."

Vern smiled and Julie noticed the wrinkles that lined his face and the gray in his beard. *When had he grown old?* she wondered.

"Come on. The food will be cold by the time you make it to the table."

"I'll be right there," Julie said as she got up. "Just let me brush out my hair and change my shirt."

"All right, but it won't be easy to hold back August and Sam. They look mighty hungry," Vern said with a laugh.

"I'll hurry," Julie promised and went to her closet.

The clothes that hung there were those she'd left behind when she'd gone to Seattle. They seemed foreign to her. Finally settling on a navy print with long sleeves and a softly rounded, feminine collar, Julie dressed hastily and dug her hairbrush from her unpacked baggage.

Studying her reflection in the mirror, Julie thought she'd aged a great deal since leaving home. Maybe it was the trials of nursing duty or the loss of her mother, but she looked older than her twenty-two years.

She brushed back her dark hair and decided to let it fall just below her shoulders. There'd be plenty of time to pin it up when she was back at work. For now, Julie was determined to enjoy being a civilian without any obligation to a uniform or dress code.

She finished buttoning the cuffs on her sleeves as she made her way to the table. "Sorry to have kept you waiting," she said, taking her place.

"It was well worth it," Sam said with admiration in his eyes.

"Shall we say grace?" Vern asked and waited for everyone to bow their heads. "Father, we thank You for Julie's safe return, and we praise You for bringing Sam and her through the storm. Thank You for the bounty You've placed before us. Bless this house and all who pass here. Amen."

Julie whispered, "Amen," and lifted her head.

Across the table, Sam lifted a plate of bread and handed it to Julie. When their eyes met, she swallowed uncomfortably and accepted the plate. Sam offered a broad grin before turning his attention to the reindeer steaks that Vern passed his way.

"So," Sam began the conversation while Vern and August occupied their mouths with food, "your brother tells me that you're about to embark on a new career. How soon will you have to report to work?"

"I, uh," Julie stammered, trying to think of what to say. "I told Dr. Welch that I needed a rest. I've been working almost nonstop since I left Nome in order to study nursing."

"That's true, Sam," August said as he paused to take a drink. "My sister never does anything halfway. She completed her courses at the top of her class. She was suggested by none other than the hospital administrator for her position as a public health worker."

"I'm impressed," Sam replied with growing admiration.

It was exactly what Julie didn't want. She tried desperately to steer the conversation in another direction. "I know the need of the people in the villages. My mother was a good example. A doctor can only do so much. As a nurse, I can travel from village to village, and as a native, I'm already known to many and related to a great many more."

"Your mother would be proud," Julie's father said with a smile.

"I only wish I could have finished soon enough to help her." Regret darkened Julie's voice.

"Regret will only grow bitterness, Jewels," Vern said using his daughter's nickname.

Julie nodded. "I know. I'm not going to let it tarnish Mother's dream for me. I want to share more than medicine with the natives."

"Just what did you have in mind?" Sam questioned.

"Well," Julie began slowly as she put her fork down, "I would like to share the Gospel with them. Mother and I talked many times about caring for more than wounded bodies. We felt that there was a need to care for their wounded spirits as well."

"Do you think folks in the villages will accept your ideas? They might not think too highly of a woman showing up to offer a cure for what ails them."

Sam's voice was lighthearted, but Julie resented his interference in her dreams. Instead of answering, she turned her attention back to the meal.

Vern realized Julie's silence was her way of dealing with things that hurt her. "I believe if the Lord lays a ministry upon your heart, He'll also open the necessary doors," he stated quietly. "Julie's felt this call for a long time. I have to believe that because she's gotten this far, God has been in it from the start. She'll do just fine."

Julie flashed a grateful look in her father's direction before allowing herself to look at Sam's face. She expected to find sarcastic laughing eyes staring back at her, but instead Sam's face seemed sober, almost apologetic.

The conversation took many turns after that, but Julie sensed that Sam wanted to say something more. When dinner was over, Julie insisted the men allow her to clean up the mess. She waited until all three had moved to the front room before she got up from the table.

The wind was still howling outside, and Julie knew without the benefit of an open window that the blizzard was raging. Part of her hated the long, dark winters when windows were boarded up to insulate against the cold, but another part of her loved the raw wildness of it. Days, even weeks, would pass when the only people she would see were those who shared a roof with her. This isolation was part of the region's attraction, and Julie knew she could never leave it for good.

"Still mad at me?"

Julie looked up from the dishes and met Sam's dark brown eyes. "I wasn't mad at you."

"Good," Sam replied, sounding relieved. "I'd hate for you to think lowly of me, especially when I think so highly of you." Julie's puzzled expression amused Sam. "You don't think a guy like me could think highly of a woman like you?"

"I don't know," Julie whispered. "I guess I never thought about it."

"Too busy with your studies and all?"

"I suppose," Julie answered.

"Well then, it's about time you heard it from someone who cares enough to be honest with you," Sam said as he put his hand on Julie's shoulder.

Julie grew painfully aware of Sam's closeness. She had no experience with this. What should she do? Before she could do or say anything, however, Sam leaned down.

"I think I've looked for someone like you all of my life."

His breath was warm against Julie's ear, causing her to shudder. She needed to move away from him, but in order to do so, she'd have to turn and face him. Making her decision, Julie turned quickly and found herself in Sam's arms.

"Don't. I mean, I. . . ," Julie stammered. Why couldn't she say what she wanted to say? Then again, what was it she wanted to say?

"Don't be afraid of me," Sam whispered as he lifted Julie's face to meet his. "I'd never hurt you, Julie."

Julie felt her breath quicken at the sound of her name on Sam's lips. She could feel her heart in her throat. "I know," Julie managed to whisper just before Sam lowered his lips to hers.

The kiss lasted only a moment, but when Sam pulled away, Julie realized she'd wrapped her arms around his neck. Frozen in the shock of what she'd done, Julie met Sam's surprised stare.

"Sam," August's voice called out from the front room, "we've got the chessboard set up. If you're going to play, you'd best get in here."

The tension was broken by the sound of her brother's voice, and Julie quickly dropped her arms and moved around Sam. "I'd better get back to work," she said as she left the kitchen with Sam staring silently after her.

Chapter 4

The raging wind and snow left Sam little doubt he'd be staying with the Erikssons through another day. He smiled to himself as he dressed for breakfast. Julie would be there! He could hear her now as she moved around in the room next to his.

Maybe he'd been away from women too long, or maybe he'd been too selfish as a young man to notice, but the existence of a woman like Julie Eriksson was a welcome surprise to him.

Julie beat Sam to the kitchen, where Vern had already stoked the fire in the stove. August had another fire burning brightly in the front room, and several oil lamps had been strategically placed to offer the maximum light.

Julie knew better than to open the door, although a look outside was exactly what she desired most. She could hear the wind and knew the storm hadn't let up. How much snow would this blizzard leave behind? Two, maybe three feet? Julie thought of her upcoming job and wondered how much difficulty she'd have maneuvering the snow-packed trails. Maybe she'd grown too soft for the demands of her duties.

"Good morning," Vern said as he came in from one of the back rooms. "How did you sleep?"

"I was nearly asleep before I finished undressing," Julie said with a laugh. "I was just thinking that maybe I'm not cut out for life in the wilds after five years of civilization."

"Nonsense!" Vern exclaimed. "You have Eskimo and Swedish blood in your veins. That combination will overcome any obstacle in your way. You can do it, Jewels. I have confidence in you."

"So do I," Sam said as he stood leaning against the frame of the door. "I think you're more than able to meet any challenge. Of course, you'll find one or two unexpected surprises along the way, but you're one tough gal. I pity the obstacle that stands in your way."

"That's for sure," Vern chuckled as he motioned Julie and Sam to the front room. "Breakfast will be ready in a little while. You two relax in front of the fire, and I'll call you when it's time."

"I wouldn't dream of it," Julie protested.

Her father wouldn't have any part of it. "I'm still in charge here," Vern said in mock sternness. "Now scoot."

Julie shrugged her shoulders and made her way to the front room. Plopping down on the sofa, she stretched her feet out to absorb the warmth of the fire. Flames snapped and crackled as the logs shifted in the grate.

"You make quite the perfect picture sitting there," Sam said as he took a seat at the opposite end of the couch.

Julie felt the full impact of Sam's stare, and without looking at him she replied, "I wish you wouldn't talk like that."

"Why?"

"Because I'm already humiliated enough. You aren't helping matters one bit," she answered simply.

"Humiliated? Why are you humiliated?" Sam asked as he leaned toward Julie.

She grimaced. "I don't know how you can ask that. I'm totally ashamed of the way I acted last night."

"You mean when August beat you at chess?" Sam teased. Julie couldn't hold back her smile. "That's better," Sam added.

"What is?" Julie asked innocently.

"The smile. I love it when you smile," Sam said softly.

Julie shook her head. "I don't understand you, and I don't know how to deal with you," she said honestly.

"Go on," Sam urged.

"Go on?" Julie questioned as she finally looked Sam in the eye. "What do you expect me to say?"

"I expect you to face up to your feelings. You don't have any reason to feel embarrassment. Especially not on account of our kiss."

Julie put her face in her hands and moaned. "I can't believe I'm sitting here talking to you about it. I get kissed for the first time. . ."

"The first time, eh?" Sam questioned with a teasing grin. "So I was the first man to kiss you. I think I like that."

Julie groaned. "Let's just forget it. Please!"

"I don't intend to forget it," Sam said firmly.

"Don't intend to forget what?" August asked as he bounded into the room.

Julie fell back against the couch and rolled her eyes. Sam only laughed. "I don't intend to forget that your sister saved my life. I'd like to do something nice for her. Something special."

"You've already done plenty," Julie said as she got to her feet.

Knowing that August couldn't see him, Sam made a face, nearly causing Julie to laugh. "I think I'll see if Pa needs any help," she said, struggling to keep a straight face.

———*H*———

Breakfast passed quickly with the men sharing all the news they could think of. Julie remained silent until the subject of the dogs came up.

"I'll need all the help I can get with the dogs this morning," Vern said as he finished a huge bowl of oatmeal. "That storm's wreaking havoc with everything, and I've got to get treatment to the sick dogs and food to all of them."

"I'll be happy to help," Sam said, pushing his chair back from the table.

"Me too," Julie agreed. "In fact, why don't I take care of the sick ones. That's my field of interest."

"That sounds great," Vern said and smacked his hands down on the table. He'd made that gesture often throughout Julie's childhood, and it always signaled that he was ready for action.

Julie hastily finished her oatmeal and got to her feet. "I'll be ready as soon as I get my coat and mukluks."

"Then the rest of us better get with it, or Julie will have everything done before we get out there," August added.

"Sounds good," Sam said and reached over for his own mukluks.

By the time Julie came back into the kitchen, the men were ready to go. Securing her parka, Julie followed her father and brother, with Sam bringing up the rear. When Vern opened the back door, a gusty wind sent them all back a step, putting Julie squarely into Sam's arms. Despite Julie's push to break away, Sam's grip remained firm. Deciding not to take the action personally, Julie continued to follow her brother into the snow.

"You come with me, Julie. I'll show you what I need done," Vern yelled above the wind. Julie nodded and felt Sam release her as she moved away to go with her father. She watched as Sam went with August to where the dogs were kept behind the house.

Vern ushered Julie into the outbuilding. While it wasn't warm, the building provided welcome relief from the blowing snow.

"Here," Vern said as he pulled Julie to the medicine cabinet. "I still keep all my concoctions and tonics in here. We're blessed to have only five dogs with any health problems. One is Sam's lead dog, Kodiak. He's getting a little extra care after the soaking he got in the Nome River. Other than that, he'll be fine and doesn't really need anything."

"Do you want me to feed him?" Julie asked.

"Yes," her father replied. "I've got a drum of dried fish over in the corner and a barrel of my own special blend for the sick dogs."

"What's wrong with the others?" Julie questioned as she pushed back her parka hood.

"Buster tangled with a trap. He's in the pen along the south wall. I had to put twenty-two stitches in his hind leg. That ought to be easy for you to take care of. The rest have a bowel infection. I have a list on the table of what I've been giving them and how much food they're getting."

"Sounds simple enough. I'll start with Buster."

"If you're all right with all of this, I'll go help the guys with the regular feeding and watering," Vern replied and opened the door. "It's mighty bad out there. If you come looking for us or want to help, be sure to tie a rope to the post outside and then to yourself."

"I will," Julie promised and turned to examine Buster as her father closed the door behind him.

———— # ————

Julie worked for nearly an hour with the sick dogs. She offered each one a tender hand and a soft, soothing voice. The dogs whined and licked at Julie's hands as she stroked their fur.

"You're a good bunch of dogs," Julie said as she dished out their food into individual tins. The dogs cocked their heads first to one side and then the other, as if trying to understand what she was saying.

After giving each dog his ration of food and water, Julie pulled her hood up and dug her mittens out of her pocket. Kodiak yipped and whined for extra attention, and Julie couldn't resist the look on his black-and-white face.

Putting her mittens on the hard dirt floor, she knelt beside the happy dog. "You're just like your master," she said as she rubbed the dog vigorously. "What is it with you two?" Kodiak licked her hand and then, without warning, gave Julie a hearty lick across the lips.

"You *are* just like him!" Julie exclaimed and got to her feet. She wiped her face with the back of her parka sleeve, picked up her mittens, and went in search of her father.

The wind refused to subside. Standing beside the sick-dog building, Julie couldn't see the house, which stood less than twenty feet away. The snow mixed with pelting ice, and Julie winced as it stung her unprotected face.

Forgetting her father's warning about tying herself down, Julie felt her way along the building, knowing that the dogs were just to the north. She strained to listen for any sound of conversation or noise as the men worked with the dogs, but the howling wind blended every sound into one massive roar.

Julie felt her eyelids grow heavy with ice as she moved past the edge of the building and, with outstretched hands, walked in the direction of the dogs.

Taking ten gingerly placed steps, Julie again squinted her eyes against the ice and snow in order to get her bearings. She couldn't see anything but snow. She called out to her father and brother, but the wind drowned out her voice. Fear gripped her heart, and Julie scolded herself for being so helpless. Bolstering her courage, Julie pressed forward. The dogs had to be just within reach.

After struggling against the storm's pressing power for more than twenty minutes, Julie admitted to herself that she was lost. Angry with herself for not heeding her father's instructions, Julie began to pray.

"Lord, I know I've done the wrong thing in not listening to my father. Please forgive me and help me find my way out of this storm." Just then Julie thought she heard the yip of a dog and moved rapidly in the direction of the sound.

She pushed back her parka in order to better hear and instantly regretted the action. Pulling the hood back into place, Julie wandered aimlessly, searching for any kind of landmark that would distinguish her whereabouts.

Cold seeped into her bones, bringing excruciating pain to her legs. Julie regretted having not dressed more appropriately for the outdoors. She'd remembered her mukluks and parka, of course, but she hadn't thought to bring along her scarves or to wear sealskin pants. Now she was paying the price.

Desperation caused an aching lump to form in her throat, but Julie knew crying would only ensure worse problems. A heavy gust of wind took her by surprise, knocking her into a snowbank. Sitting in the snow, Julie suddenly realized how tired she was. Her mind felt muddled from the strain.

"If I rest for a minute," Julie said, rubbing her mittens against her frozen face, "then I'll feel clearer-headed and be able to go on." Something inside her warned Julie that this wasn't wise, but she couldn't fight the need to rest.

Looking up, Julie realized she was snow-blind. There was nothing to indicate that civilization was anywhere nearby. When she moved to shift her weight, Julie heard a crunching sound come from within her parka. Ice had formed on her back and chest from the sweat of her search.

An alarm went off in her mind. That crunching sound meant that she was freezing to death. "Yes," she thought aloud as she got to her feet. "This is the way you freeze. You have to keep moving, Julie. You can't rest, or you won't wake up! Oh God, send someone to find me. Please, God, rescue me before I die."

Stumbling in her blindness and pain, Julie fell against the trunk of a tree. She leaned against it for a moment, licked her lips, and forced her mind to focus on moving. "I don't want to die," she whispered over and over. "I want to live."

Julie wrapped her arms around the trunk and sank into the wet snow. *It isn't at all unpleasant,* she thought. *If a body has to die, freezing to death is at least a simple way to go.* She felt sleep come upon her; they called it "the white death." *Funny,* she thought, *they also call tuberculosis white death because of the thick, white substance that patients cough up from their lungs.* Why had she thought of that? It was strange that something so insignificant to her life as TB should come to her mind now. She'd never need to worry about such diseases again. Not now that she was nearly dead.

"Good boy, Kodiak. You found her. Julie! Julie, wake up." Sam's face floated only inches above hers. "Julie, stand up. Walk with me." Sam was pulling her to her feet.

Julie tried to concentrate on his words as Kodiak whined at her knee. She even attempted to give him a smile. "I'm glad you found me," Julie whispered. She tried to walk but stumbled and fell against Sam.

Sam easily lifted Julie into his arms and pulled his way back to safety on the rope he'd secured around his waist. Was he too late? There was no way to tell how long she'd been sitting in the snow. Sam gritted his teeth and prayed that she would live. *She has to live,* Sam thought as he moved quickly to the house.

Chapter 5

Julie heard the men rushing around her. She felt her father pulling off her parka, while Sam and August worked to unlace her mukluks. She was dazed and groggy from the cold, and only the pain in her feet reminded her that she'd come terribly close to freezing.

"We've got to get her warmed up," Sam said as he rubbed Julie's feet.

"I'll build up the fire and heat some rocks to put in bed with her," August offered. "We can pack them around her blankets."

"Let's get her to her room," Vern suggested.

"Lead the way," Sam replied as he got to his feet and lifted Julie before August or Vern could move.

Vern nodded and August went to the fireplace. Sam followed Julie's father, ever mindful of Julie's near-lifeless body.

"Put her on the bed," Vern said as he pulled back the covers.

"We'd better get her out of these clothes," Sam said, without any concern for the propriety of the situation. "They're still frozen, but when they thaw, she'll be soaked."

"You're right of course," Vern answered with a worried look on his face.

Sam was already unfastening Julie's belt as Vern prepared to pull the icy denim jeans from his daughter's half-frozen frame.

Pulling off the pants, Vern leaned over and felt the heavy woolen long johns that Julie had wisely thought to wear.

"These are dry," he said with a sound of relief.

"That's good," Sam said and added, "but this shirt was sweat-soaked. It was frozen solid, but it's already starting to melt. I'd suggest you get her a dry one. I'll leave the room so you can change her privately."

Vern nodded. "I'll take care of it now. You might want to help August."

Sam reluctantly left Julie's side. His brown eyes betrayed the concern in his heart. *Dear God*, he prayed silently, *You must save her!* Pausing at the door, Sam shook his head and took a deep breath before adding, *Thy will be done.*

August was lining stones in the fireplace when Sam entered the front room.

"How is she?" August questioned anxiously. He glanced up and met Sam's worried expression. "Is she going to make it?"

"I don't know yet," Sam said as he handed rocks to August. "She's pretty cold and her pulse is real slow. I wish I had my duck down comforter. It's of little use to anyone back at my cabin."

"We've got a goose down mattress on Pa's bed," August said hopefully. "Could we make use of it?"

"We might be able to cut it open at one end and slide Julie inside," Sam replied in an eager tone. "Would your father mind?"

"Not if it's going to save Julie's life," August said, dusting his hands off as he got to his feet. "It belonged to my mother. It was her most beloved possession. She always said it was like sleeping on a cloud. She wouldn't even use it for everyday. Come on." He motioned. "Let's go get it."

Sam helped August remove all the bedding, and together they pulled the mattress off the bed.

"I can manage this," Sam said as he hoisted the mattress on his back. "You get some of those rocks. Get the flattest ones and we'll put them under Julie. The rest we can put over and around her."

"That ought to warm her up," August said and went to retrieve the rocks from the fire.

Julie moaned, speaking in her delirium. "Tried to find the way," she whispered. "Papa!"

"I'm here, darling," Vern said as he finished buttoning the dry flannel shirt he'd just clothed his daughter in. He patted Julie's arm and talked loudly to her.

"You can't sleep now, my Jewels. It's time to wake up. Come on, we're all waiting for you."

"Too tired," Julie whispered. "Let me sleep."

Just then Sam entered the room, bringing in the feather mattress.

"If you don't object, I'd like to cut this open and put Julie inside. I think the goose down will warm her faster than the wool blankets."

"That's brilliant, Sam," Vern said as he pulled a knife from its sheath on his belt and handed it to him. "Be my guest."

Sam sliced the end of the mattress open just as August came in with a tray of warmed rocks.

"This is going to be a real team effort," Sam said as goose feathers puffed out of the open end of the mattress. "Vern, if you can hold this, I'll lift Julie while August arranges the rocks on her bed. After he's finished, we'll put the mattress on the rocks and put Julie inside it."

The father and son nodded. Sam went to Julie's bedside. She looked so pale and helpless. Her dark hair spread out around her, making her face seem unnaturally white.

Sam thought she looked beautiful, more beautiful than any other woman he'd known. He'd lost his heart to her and prayed that she'd live long enough for him to share a place in her heart.

Cradling Julie as though she were a child, Sam stepped back and let August and Vern work. It was only a matter of seconds before they were ready to put Julie inside the mattress. Together, they eased her down into the goose feathers.

"Now, August, how about some more of those rocks? We can pack them all around the sides and put some on top as well," Sam said as he pulled the mattress up to meet just under Julie's chin.

Julie murmured incoherent words as the men worked around her.

"I'll get some coffee on the stove and warm some cider. That way we can start getting her insides warmed up as well," Vern suggested. "Sam, would you mind staying with her?"

"You know I wouldn't. Go on. I'll be here, friend," Sam replied, and Vern hurried from the room.

When Vern returned, he took turns with Sam and August forcing warm fluids into Julie's mouth. The passing hours filled the men with apprehension. Were they doing enough or had they forgotten something?

———— # ————

As warmth entered Julie's body, she felt as though the blood were thawing in her veins. Pain roused her to consciousness. When she opened her eyes, Sam's face stared back at her.

"Hello," Julie said nonchalantly.

Sam smiled broadly. "Hello, yourself. How do you feel?"

"Buried alive," Julie said as she tried to sit up.

"You stay put, Jewels," her father spoke authoritatively. "You nearly froze to death."

"I remember," Julie said as she fell back against the pillow.

"You gave us a bad scare, little sister," August said, leaning over the foot of Julie's bed. "I think you aged me ten years, and I'm positive you did the same to Sam."

"That's for sure." Sam laughed.

Julie shook her head at the three men.

"How long did it take for you to find me?" she asked.

"That depends on how long you were with the dogs," Sam answered.

"It couldn't have been much more than an hour. Maybe half again as much."

"Well, let's see." Vern figured in his head. "We started around nine. That would've made it ten or ten thirty when you left the building. We didn't find out that you were missing until noon. After that we took turns looking for you. Sam and Kodiak found you just after two."

"Kodiak?"

"That's right. When we weren't having any success finding you, we decided to get help from the dogs. Since you'd been working with Kodiak, we put him onto your scent, and he helped Sam locate you."

"Is he all right?" Julie questioned weakly.

"Who? Sam?" Vern teased.

"No, no. Kodiak. He didn't get too cold, did he?"

"You stop worrying about that dog. He's doing fine," Vern chided. "We need to know how you feel."

"I hurt," Julie answered honestly. "I suppose that's a good sign. I feel like I ought to be issuing a lot of thank-yous." She looked at the three men who watched her so intently and added, "I thank God for all of you."

Vern's eyes grew misty. "Come on, August. Let's get some more rocks heated. Sam, you make sure she drinks more of this hot cider."

"I will," Sam promised as Vern and August disappeared out the door.

Julie looked at Sam. He hadn't shaved, and the shadow of stubble on his face only made him more handsome. "Thank you for saving me," she whispered.

"You've already thanked me," Sam stated as he helped her to drink the cider. "Several times."

"I did? When?"

"When I found you. When you were lying here muttering in your sleep. In fact," Sam said with a self-assured grin, "you said quite a few interesting things."

Julie swallowed hard to steady her nerves. "I did? Well, I imagine the cold affected my mind."

"Oh, I don't know about that," Sam said in a thoughtful way that made Julie wonder what she'd said.

"Just who are you, anyway?" she questioned, causing Sam to burst out laughing.

"What a question! You know full well who I am. Your brother and I have known each other for seven years."

"I know all that," Julie said as she stared at the ceiling to avoid losing herself in Sam's eyes. "I want to know, well, I want to know more."

Sam laughed. "All right. Where would you like me to begin?"

Julie's forehead furrowed slightly as she considered what she wanted to ask. "I suppose at the beginning," she finally answered. "Where were you born?"

"Sacramento, California, in 1889—although we weren't there long enough for the ink to dry on the Bible entry. My father was bent on finding gold. He was always late to everything, including the gold rush."

Julie laughed. "Unlike his son, who seems to make a habit of arriving right on time."

"My father had big dreams. He was one of the reasons I came on up to Nome after my mother died," Sam answered.

"Is your father dead as well?"

Sam nodded. "He got into a fight over a claim. The man took a knife out and killed him then and there. They strung the killer up not twenty feet from where my father lay dead and hanged him. My mother was never the same after that. She was left with three children and had no idea how to support them. The miners were good to her, however. They took up a collection and gave her three hundred dollars."

"What happened after that?" Julie asked, fascinated with Sam's story.

"She moved us around. Sometimes she did laundry for other miners. Other times she'd cook and run a boardinghouse. When my sister married and moved off, I was thirteen and my younger sister was nine. Ma moved us to Seattle, where talk of the gold rush to Nome and the Klondike was all I ever heard tell about. It got in my blood, and I promised myself that I'd one day make the trip to Nome and find the gold that had eluded my father."

"Sounds interesting," Julie said, "but why did it take you so long before you came to Nome?"

"I couldn't leave my mother and sister, and they didn't want any part of it. My mother was getting old, so I went to work. I did a little bit of everything but finally stayed with shipyard work. My sister married at sixteen and offered to take my mother back East with her, but Ma wanted to stay close to where my father was buried. She made me promise to bury her in California, so I stayed on."

"You never married?" Julie asked boldly.

"No," Sam said with a smile. "I never found the right woman. My mother died not long before my twenty-eighth birthday, and right after I got her buried alongside my father, I boarded a ship for Nome and never looked back."

"It must have been lonely for you," Julie said thoughtfully. She knew how the loss of her own mother had left an unfillable hole in her heart.

"Yeah, I guess it was in some ways. Of course, I had the comfort of knowing she was saved. I'd see her again, and that made it a lot easier to deal with."

Julie's eyes opened wide. "So you're a Christian?"

Sam grinned. "Yes, I am."

"Tell me how you came to know God," Julie said as she shifted her weight.

August and Vern came in with a tray full of rocks. "Sam, you take the rocks from the bed while we put these hot ones in their place," Vern said, using tongs to place hot rocks around Julie's covered feet.

August held the tray while Vern positioned each rock. Sam put the cooled rocks in a pile on the floor, and when he reached beneath Julie to retrieve the rocks which August had placed underneath her, the girl began to laugh.

"I thought this mattress was a little lumpy. Now I see that it was just that I was sleeping on rocks."

Sam bent over her and reached across to get the last of the stones. He gave Julie a wink and quickly handed the rocks to Vern.

"We'll warm up another batch, Sam. How are you doing, Jewels?"

Vern asked as he put a hand to his daughter's forehead. "You feel much warmer. That's a good sign. Let's just hope you don't suffer from frostbite."

"Please don't worry, Papa," Julie said and pulled her arm out from the mattress to touch her father's hand. Feathers flew everywhere, causing Julie to sneeze. It was only then that she realized they'd stuffed her inside the goose down mattress. "What a wonderful idea! Who thought to put me here?" she asked.

"It was Sam's idea," August replied. "Sam was determined to save your life, and he usually gets what he wants. They don't call him Lucky Sam for nothing."

"Lucky Sam," Julie echoed as she looked up and met Sam's eyes.

"That's right, and so's the part about getting what I want," Sam declared.

Vern and August laughed as they left the room, but Julie bit her lower lip and stared thoughtfully at the man who remained at her bedside.

Sam returned the look and then spoke. "Now, where was I? Oh yeah, you were asking me how I came to know Christ. Well, my mother was saved, my sister too. I always tagged along with them to church on Sunday, at least whenever I could. When I was seventeen, I took a job on a fishing boat. We were pretty far into the Pacific one day when a storm blew up and destroyed the ship. I was left clinging to a piece of the craft while the storm tossed me back and forth.

"I began to pray like I'd never prayed before. I asked God to save me, and I didn't mean just my worthless hide. I prayed for redemption, and I prayed for deliverance. Some people come to God in a quiet way, but I came to Him in a flash of lightning on the stormy Pacific. Right after I asked Jesus into my heart, a wave came crashing down over my head, and I kind of figured I'd been forgiven, redeemed, and baptized all at once."

Julie laughed. "What happened next?" she questioned as she caught her breath.

"He saved me. The storm calmed just like the time in the Bible when Jesus stilled the waves. I was found by another fishing vessel about an hour later."

"How fascinating," Julie said with true admiration in her voice.

"Yeah, I guess you could say that," Sam said thoughtfully. "I'm just mighty glad God never gave up on me. He's been a powerfully good friend to have alongside all these years."

Julie liked the open way in which Sam talked about God. It was exactly the way she felt about Him. He was so much more than a figurehead, sitting out there somewhere in heaven. God was a good friend and a constant comfort. Julie felt her thoughts blending to include her admiration of Sam. Had God sent Sam into her life for more than friendship? Already he'd saved her life twice, and whenever she was with him, the aching loneliness she'd known for so many years was absent.

Julie grew suddenly distant, and Sam put his hand out to touch her face.

"Don't," Julie whispered. Instead of getting mad, as Julie had anticipated he would, Sam just shrugged his shoulders and got to his feet.

"I think I'll go find us something to eat," he said and left Julie to contemplate her conflicting emotions.

Chapter 6

Julie recovered quickly from her brush with death. She hadn't suffered any permanent damage, although her pride was sorely bruised. The day after her ordeal, she felt good enough to be up and joined the men in the front room for games of chess and checkers.

"Sometimes," Vern began as he lit one of the oil lamps, "I think I'll be glad when they string electricity this far. Other times, I'm just as glad not to have it to mess with. When the wind picks up past twenty knots, the lines blow down anyway, and then you have to dig the lamps back out."

"Yeah," August agreed as he moved his bishop to threaten Sam's queen, "but staying at the hotel in Nome sure spoils a fellow."

"When did you stay at the hotel in Nome?" Julie asked curiously. "I can't imagine either one of you leaving the dogs long enough."

"It was something your mother wanted to do," Vern answered.

Julie looked up from the table. "Mother? She always seemed to enjoy it here. I never heard her mention a preference for life in Nome."

"Oh, she wasn't partial to Nome. It was just that she knew we'd never lived in a place with electricity or telephone."

"Well I'll be," Julie said as she shook her head. "I never would have thought it."

"I never would've thought an old sourdough like you would have forgotten how to take care of herself in the snow either," Vern said as his eyes narrowed ever so slightly. "Julie, you can't be out there on the trail without paying attention to your surroundings."

"Nor to the survival skills that you've no doubt known all of your life," Sam added.

Julie felt as though she were a small child being taken to task. "I know I was foolish. I've readily admitted it, and I've even taken to reading some of Grandfather's books about surviving in the North," Julie said, alluding to books that her mother's father had brought with his family during the gold rush.

"Books can't teach you everything. Besides, you've lived it almost all your life. You need to sit back and pay attention for your own good," Vern said seriously, adding, "August and I will work on your memory."

Julie smiled and jumped three of her father's checkers. "Crown me."

———— # ————

The day passed pleasantly, and as long as they sat in her father and brother's company, Julie didn't feel uncomfortable around Sam. She even enjoyed hearing about his exploits. Sometimes his stories involved August, and Julie shook her head in disbelief.

"I'm amazed that August never brought you home before I left for the outside," Julie stated, calling the lower forty-eight by the term used by most people in the northern territories. She remembered the five years she'd listened to people in Seattle call Alaska "the frozen North" or "Seward's icebox." Julie just called it "home" and longed for it with all her heart.

"And I suppose that's as much a reason as any," August was saying as Julie stared blankly into space.

"Uh, sorry," Julie said as she cleared her thoughts. "What were you saying?"

"You asked why Sam had never come home with me," August replied.

"And?" Julie questioned over Vern and Sam's chuckles.

"And, I told you. Sam was working a claim that took all of his energy. He didn't dare leave it unoccupied."

"Yeah," Sam agreed. "I was fortunate to have August's help. I don't think I left the claim for the first three years."

"Do you still work it?" Julie asked, suddenly realizing that she knew very little about Sam's current life.

"No," Sam replied as he put August in check. "I sold the claim to the Hammon Consolidated Gold Fields. Mr. Summers, the superintendent, came out to offer me an impressive amount of money for the claim. I'd already made plenty off the mine and was thinking of selling anyway. By the time we'd finished settling, I had more money in the bank than I'd ever need to use."

"You could've sent it to your sisters," Julie said innocently.

Sam's brow wrinkled, and behind his beard stubble, Julie could see him grit his teeth. "They're dead."

"Both of them?" she questioned.

"Yes," Sam replied sadly. "My youngest sister was killed in an accident, and my older sister died during the influenza epidemic."

"How awful," Julie replied.

"We lost an awful lot of folks up here as well," August said as he conceded defeat to Sam. "Especially the Eskimos and Indians. They can't stand up to some of the diseases that accompanied the white man north."

Sam nodded and began to reset the chessboard. "I know. I remember reading in the *Nome Nugget* that the influenza epidemic left more than ninety-one flu orphans."

"That's true," Julie replied, remembering the awful time. "Poor things. Some of them are still quite young."

"It's always amazing who lives and who dies in a situation like that," Sam said, sitting back. "I always wonder what God's overall plan is when I see a family of youngsters left without their folks."

"Me too," Julie agreed. "And I have a real hard time when children are the victims of sickness. I've had to nurse dying children," she added, remembering her days in the Seattle hospital. "I don't think I'll ever get used to it." Her words sobered the atmosphere considerably.

"Yet," Vern finally spoke, "we have to trust God's wisdom. He always knows best. I know when your mother was dying, she kept reminding me of Job and how much he endured. 'Curse God, and die,' Job's wife told him. Agneta used that example whenever I grumbled too much about the injustice of her condition. She loved to remember Job's patience and strength whenever her own gave way to the sickness. Her favorite verse was Job 13:15: 'Though he slay me, yet will I trust in him.' I admired her loyalty. It strengthened my faith."

"I can well imagine," Sam said with a thoughtful look toward Julie. "A woman of strong faith is one to be cherished. I don't think God intended for any man to live alone."

"You know," Vern said as Julie won the checkers game, "I believe the Bible says that two are better than one."

Sam nodded. "It sure does. It's in Ecclesiastes. 'Two are better than one; because they have a good reward for their labour.'"

" 'For if they fall, the one will lift up his fellow: but woe to him that is alone when he falleth; for he hath not another to help him up,'" Julie recited the verse from somewhere in her memory.

Vern reached for his Bible and flipped through its pages to Ecclesiastes 4. He continued reading from verse eleven. "'Again, if two lie together, then they have heat: but how can one be warm alone?'" Julie glanced up at Sam and found his eyes on her.

"That's true," August added. "I remember times when the weather was like this, and Ma would put us all together in bed with you and her."

"I remember that too," Julie said, forgetting about Sam's fixed stare. "I loved it. I always felt safe and warm. It was so hard to leave and go to Seattle. It was like you were all here together in one safe haven, and suddenly I was left out."

"You were never left out," August said with a smile. "Ma always remembered you in prayers, and Pa talked about you constantly."

Vern nodded and reached across to affectionately squeeze Julie's shoulder. "That's true. Even in Seattle, you were an important part of our family. Almost as if you were never separated from us."

"That's sure not how it felt in Washington," Julie responded. Forgetting about Sam and how he might perceive her, Julie continued. "I remember watching Nome disappear as we steamed to the south. I wanted to jump overboard and come home. I was so lonely. School left so little time for any kind of social life, and I didn't get to attend church regularly because of my hospital duties." Julie needed to say more, but it was difficult to continue, so she fell silent.

"Didn't you have any friends among the other students?" Vern asked.

Julie thought for a moment. "I suppose there were one or two whom I felt comfortable with. We studied together and often worked together, but it wasn't like having a real friend. I suppose that's my own fault though. I didn't want to be close to anyone."

"Why was that?" Sam asked.

"I guess I was worried about having ties in Seattle. I didn't want anything to hamper my homecoming. I suppose I created my own prison."

"Oftentimes we do," Vern said as he closed his Bible. "Everyone is different, and how they handle their fears varies. I wish I could have saved you the loneliness."

"Truth is," Julie said without thinking, "I still feel empty at times. I have my faith in God and my family, but, well. . ." She paused for a moment. "I don't know. I guess I'm just anxious to be at my job." Getting to her feet, Julie was just as anxious to drop the subject. "Now, if you'll all excuse me, tomorrow is October twelfth and that means it's August's birthday. I'm going to see what I can whip up in the kitchen."

August grinned. "I figured everybody would forget."

"Just why do you think I braved the weather to come this way?" Sam said and laughed. "Besides, why do you think I let you win at chess yesterday?"

"Well, if it was a birthday present, you should have let me win today as well. I'm a bit humbled by the entire experience," August said as he got up, stretched, and looked at his watch. "I guess I'd better go check on the dogs."

"That'd be a good idea," Vern said. "Let's go."

"I'll lend you a hand," Sam offered.

"No." Vern waved him off. "Somebody has to keep an eye on *her*," he said pointing at Julie.

"Me?" Julie questioned as she pointed to herself. "I don't need a keeper. I'll be just fine. I promise to behave myself and stay in the kitchen."

Vern smiled at his daughter. "I'd feel better if Sam kept an eye on you."

Julie rolled her eyes and shrugged her shoulders before she let the men go. *Who was going to keep an eye on Sam?* she wondered.

———— *#* ————

By the time the sun began to set, the weather had calmed, and the temperature had risen significantly. The silence left in the wake of the roaring wind was unsettling.

Julie bundled up against the cold and waved off her father's protests. "I'm just going outside to look things over. There's no wind, no snow, and I'd best get used to the elements. I have a job to report to in little over a week," she said, more harshly than she'd intended.

Vern nodded. "I can't help worrying. I love you, Jewels."

Julie's expression softened as she reached out to put a reassuring hand on Vern's arm. "I love you too, Papa. Please don't worry. I was very foolish the other day. I realize my mistake, and I won't make it again."

Vern embraced his daughter momentarily and then opened the back door for her. "Have fun," he said. Julie knew it was his way of giving her his blessing and confidence.

Julie walked out into the darkness. She turned back and saw the cheery glow of light shining from the house. Out on the nursing trail, there would only be the lighted windows of strangers to look forward to. Was she doing the right thing? Was she really cut out for the solitary existence her job required?

"You're mighty deep in thought," Sam said as he came from somewhere out of the blackness.

"I was just thinking about my work."

"Apprehensive?" Sam questioned.

Julie looked rather quizzically at Sam. "How did you know?"

"Just something I felt."

"Well," Julie continued before Sam could get personal, "I'm sure everyone has second thoughts. I'm just settling mine, that's all. How about you? What brings you out tonight?"

"I just bought two new dogs from your father. We staked them out with my team this afternoon, and I was checking up on them. They fit right in," Sam said as he moved closer to Julie. "I figure we'll leave sometime in the morning."

"Oh, so soon?" Julie questioned.

"Disappointed?" Sam asked with a grin.

Julie moved away from Sam and noticed the sky. "Look!"

Overhead, the sky filled with pulsating light. Green, pink, and white lights streaked the night blackness, and the heavens exploded with northern lights.

"The aurora," Sam said as he came to stand directly behind Julie.

"I'd nearly forgotten," Julie said. She felt a trembling in her body at the nearness of Sam.

For a long time neither Julie nor Sam said a word. They watched the dancing lights as the colors faded, then radiated and grew brilliant again. The stillness of the windless night made the cold easily tolerated, but Sam moved closer to block the chill from Julie's back.

Julie decided she had to deal with Sam. He wasn't going to go away, and even though he planned to leave the next morning, it was necessary to tell him exactly where she stood.

"Sam," Julie said as she turned to face him. She hadn't realized just how close he was. Sam reached out and quickly pulled Julie into his arms. "Wait just a minute," Julie protested. "You can't keep doing this."

"Oh yes, I can, and I intend to do it often after we're married," Sam said, refusing to let Julie loose.

"Married? I'm not going to—" Her words fell into silence as Sam lowered his mouth to hers. Julie expected the same brief type of kiss Sam had given her in the kitchen, but instead his mouth was firmly fixed on hers in a deeply passionate kiss. Julie had set out to concentrate on not responding, but easily lost that thought as Sam aroused feelings inside her that Julie had never known existed. Giving in, Julie allowed Sam to pull her tightly to his chest as her arms went around his neck.

When Sam pulled back, Julie felt herself gasp for air. "You'll never stop feeling lonely until you give in to your heart and marry me. Remember, two are better than one," Sam whispered.

"But, I prayed about working as a nurse. I know it's my destiny." Julie forced the words from her muddled mind.

"And you are mine," Sam said before silencing Julie's protests with his mouth.

Chapter 7

On the first day of November, Julie reported to Dr. Welch at the two-story Maynard-Columbus Hospital. The whitewashed clapboard building offered the most thorough medical help in northwestern Alaska and had seen more than its share of action.

After meeting with Dr. Welch for a few days, Julie's confidence returned. Dr. Welch was habitually happy. He was at his best when he was working in and around his patients, and his nurses enjoyed his vibrant love of life. Emily Morgan, training to take over as head nurse at the hospital, told Julie that it was Dr. Welch's devoted wife, Lula, who'd made the gray-haired doctor so content.

"You know," Emily said as she showed Julie to a small office, "she married him right after his internship in Los Angeles. She's worked alongside him for many years."

"Yes, I know," Julie said as she slipped out of her parka. "I'm quite familiar with both the doctor and his wife. I was born in Nome."

"I didn't know you were native to Alaska," Emily said. "Oh, by the way, this is Nurse Seville," she added as a rather plain-looking woman came into the office.

"Glad to meet you," the woman said, extending her hand. "I'm Bertha."

"It's nice to meet you as well," Julie said and shook the woman's hand. "I'm Julie Eriksson."

"Well, it's quite a challenge you've carved out for yourself. I've made calls with Dr. Welch to the nearest Eskimo settlements, and I've never really enjoyed the sled travel. Although I must say, Doc enjoys every bit of it. But you'll be out there on your own, driving your own team and facing the elements. I admire your spirit," Bertha said honestly.

"Thank you," Julie answered just as Dr. Welch entered the room.

"Are you ready to go?" he questioned as he took a seat behind a paper-laden desk.

"I sure am," Julie responded. "I came to say good-bye and see if there were any last-minute instructions."

"Take good care of your dogs," Welch answered firmly. "Of course, take good care of yourself as well. Keep detailed records, and let me know if there's anything that needs my attention."

"I will," Julie promised and picked up her parka. "I'd best be on my way. My first stop is nearly two hours away."

"At least the weather's been good. Unseasonably so, if you ask me," the veteran doctor replied. After nearly twenty years in Alaska, he spoke with authority.

"Well, remember me in your prayers," Julie said as she pulled on her coat.

"That we will," Nurse Morgan replied.

Moving out on the open trail, Julie had plenty of time to think. Too much time. She'd been working for nearly six weeks, and during that time, she'd seen just about everything.

She'd delivered babies, set broken bones, stitched up wounds, and dealt with a multitude of other ailments. Overall, her experience had been a good one, but always there were the hours alone on the trail when the only thing she could think about was Sam.

How could one man affect a woman so much that she questioned her purpose in life? Ever since Sam had kissed her and told her he intended to marry her, Julie had been confused.

When Julie was younger and there had been only her mother's driving desire to see her daughter become a nurse, she'd felt certain of her destiny.

But Sam was just as strong in maintaining that Julie was his destiny.

Julie stopped the dogs for a brief rest. There were only three to four hours of light a day as Christmas drew near. Usually she woke up in the darkness and moved out, only to spend the daylight hours inside a sod igloo, delivering a baby or tending to some other medical need. She was enjoying this rare opportunity to travel during the daylight hours.

Julie checked her compass and pulled out a small map from inside her parka. If everything went according to plan, she'd be in the next village within two hours. Carefully replacing the compass and map, Julie checked her dogs and took her place at the back of the sled.

"Let's go," she called out, and the dogs immediately picked up a nice trotting pace.

Julie alternated running behind the sled and riding the runners. She'd gradually regained her muscular arms and running legs. Physically, she'd never felt better, but emotionally, she was drained.

"God, please help me," she prayed. The winter sky's pale turquoise color was already giving way to the coming darkness. In the distance, Julie saw the telltale signs of a snowstorm. She called to the dogs to pick up the pace before turning her mind and soul back to God in prayer. "Lord, I don't understand why You sent Sam into my life at this time. I thought I knew what You wanted me to do, but how can I do that and care for a husband? And if You don't want Sam to be my husband, then why did You allow him to complicate things for me?" Julie realized how selfish her prayer sounded and fell silent.

She watched the frozen wasteland pass by her moving sled. The horizon stretched out forever, and yet, just ahead Julie would thrill to the light in the window of some thoughtful villager, and once again she'd be safe.

The dogs seemed to sense the end of the journey and hastened to the place where they would receive fresh tom cod and tallow. *They are smarter than human beings*, Julie thought. *They never press on in a storm when they know it's dangerous, and they're content to do their work and take their rest. If only I could be the same.*

Blackness fell long before Julie reached the small Eskimo village. She kept watch through the darkness as the dogs, confident of their trail, pressed on.

Visions of Sam filled her mind, and for a moment Julie allowed herself to wonder what it would be like to marry Lucky Sam Curtiss.

"Surely I'd have to give up my nursing," Julie mused. "He would expect me to give him my undivided attention. And there would be the possibility of children. A man like Sam would probably want a dozen or more," she added sarcastically. "But then, I hope to one day have a big family too.

"Why did he have to come?" Julie yelled into the darkness. She hadn't noticed that they were nearly upon the village, and only when Dusty brought the team to a stop did Julie realize why.

"Good boy, Dusty. I was daydreaming again," Julie said as she planted the snow hook.

A middle-aged Eskimo man appeared with his two sons. She recognized the man as George Nakoota. She had tended his youngest child during a bad bout of tonsillitis during her first visit to the village.

"There's warm food inside for you," George said as he helped Julie unload her sled. "The boys and I will take care of the dogs." Julie nodded and went inside. As long as the dogs were fed and bedded down, she could rest.

George's wife, Tanana, helped Julie out of her parka and mukluks. "George heard you coming from far off," Tanana said as she placed the parka over a chair by the oilcan stove.

"I don't see how George can hear these things from so far away," Julie said. "He's always saying that he can hear any storm or animal coming for fifty miles. Those are mighty perceptive ears."

"George does not listen with his ears. He listens with his soul. George and the land are close, like old friends."

"The soul can tell a person a great deal, if we choose to listen to it," Julie agreed. "Have you thought about what I told you when I was here before?"

"I remember when your father used to visit with George and tell him about white man's God in heaven. George said it made nights pass faster with stories from your Bible."

"But they're more than stories, Tanana." Julie hoped her old friend wouldn't be offended by her boldness. "I know you're skeptical of the things that white folks bring to your people—the sickness and disease, the mining operations and such—but honestly, Tanana, God has a great deal of love for you and your people."

"I know that," Tanana agreed, "but He loves me in the Eskimo way."

George came in, bringing the rest of Julie's gear. "Your dogs are looking good, Julie. You've been taking good care of them."

"The people have all been so good to me," Julie said as she sat down at the small crude table where Tanana was dishing up hot food. "They feed the dogs and me and always give us a warm place to sleep. I have no complaints."

"Any trouble with animals?" George asked as he joined Julie at the table. "I noticed that Dusty looked a bit chewed-on."

"He was." Julie nodded. "You've got eyes that are every bit as good as your ears, George. He got into a fight with a village dog. The other dog looks worse, so we count it a victory for him. I'd appreciate it if you didn't tell him otherwise."

George laughed. "You spoil him. He'll grow fat and lazy and never run fast, but I won't tell him."

———— # ————

Julie stayed on in George's village for two days. She treated several bad colds and looked in on George's mother, who'd suffered from an infected wound on her hand. Julie was preparing to leave when George's oldest son came running.

"My father's been hurt," he said breathlessly as he pulled at Julie's arm.

"What happened?" Julie asked, pulling her medical bag from the sled.

"The dogs were fighting, and he tried to pull them apart. His arm is pretty bad."

Julie followed the boy on a dead run to the opposite side of the village where George had been carried to his house. When Julie walked into the house, George had already been placed on the small kitchen table. His arm was a bloody mangled mess, and Julie wasn't sure that she could save it.

She motioned George's son to hold a cloth to his father's arm. "Put pressure here while I prepare my instruments. Tanana, I'll need some hot water. George, George, can you hear me?" Julie questioned as she leaned down.

"I hear you," George said between gritted teeth.

"I'm going to clean your arm and see what's what. I'm going to do a lot of stitching, and I'd just as soon you not have to be awake for it. I've got some chloroform, and I'm going to put you to sleep," Julie said as she prepared a place for her instruments.

"Julie," George whispered weakly.

He was losing a great deal of blood, and Julie knew she'd have to hurry. "What is it, George?"

"You gonna pray for me?"

"Of course," Julie said with a smile.

"Your pa has talked to me before"—George paused and drew a deep breath before continuing—"about eternal life. I think I need to have that about now."

George was always good-natured, even when he was bleeding to death, Julie decided. Nevertheless, she continued as if George had nothing more complicated than a splinter. "John 3:16 says, 'For God so loved the world, that he gave his only begotten Son, that whosoever believeth in him should not perish, but have everlasting life.' You must believe that God sent His Son to save your life. Do you believe that, George?" Julie asked as she washed her hands in carbolic acid before pouring a great amount into a bowl for her instruments.

"I believe," George whispered.

"Then pray with me, George," Julie said as she took fresh water from Tanana. "Dear Father, George knows he's a sinner, and he wants Your forgiveness." Julie paused to wave George's son away and poured water over his father's arm.

George bit his lip but refused to cry out. "I'm a sinner, God. Forgive me," he said and looked up at Julie.

Julie nodded and continued, "George wants to accept Your Son, Jesus, so that he might have eternal life."

"I want eternal life," George murmured. "I want Your Son, Jesus."

"And, Lord," Julie said as she poured disinfectant over the mangled limb, "help me to mend George's arm. Amen."

George nodded, too weak to speak. Julie poured a liberal amount of chloroform on a clean cloth. "I'm going to put you to sleep now, George." She placed the cloth over George's nose and mouth.

Instantly, George was rendered unconscious, and Julie flew into action. She picked her way through the strips of flesh, cleaning each one thoroughly and moving on to the deep gashes.

Tanana held a lantern to one side. Periodically, Julie felt for George's pulse and respiration. He was doing well, and Julie felt confident that his relative good health and God's direction would see her through the situation.

After two hours, Julie stood back and assessed her work. Barring infection, George would retain full use of his arm. She decided to stay on in the village until she felt confident that the wounds were free from contamination.

Dragging her weary body to bed, Julie thanked God for His direction. She fell asleep listening to George's rhythmic breathing.

———#———

With George well on the way to recovering and Christmas only three days away, Julie readied once again to return to Nome. She was determined to be home for Christmas, but she hadn't managed to do any Christmas shopping yet.

She was rechecking the dogs' harness when Tanana approached her. "You have my gratitude for saving George's life. I thanked your white God too."

"He can be your God as well, Tanana," Julie said as she turned from the dogs.

Tanana nodded and held out several packages. "I'll think about your words, Nurse Julie. These are for you. They are payment for George. I know your Christmas is coming soon, and maybe you will need things for your father and brother. I have made two pairs of sealskin mukluks. They have fox fur inside to make them extra warm."

"Thank you, Tanana. I'll give them to my father and brother for Christmas and tell them that you made them."

The woman smiled broadly and backed up a step. "You are welcome here anytime. We'll look forward to seeing you after your celebration."

Julie nodded and rallied her team. "Hike!" she called out and held onto the sled handle as the dogs, eager to be on the trail, moved out.

———— # ————

Nome looked the same as when Julie had left. She knew she ought to go directly to Dr. Welch's office at the Merchants and Miners Bank of Alaska, but keeping in mind that it was Christmas Eve, she took time, instead, to do a bit of shopping.

She searched through several shops, looking for just the right gifts for Vern and August. She finally settled on some tools for her father and a guitar for August. She smiled as she brought the items out to her sled. August had always wanted to learn to play the guitar, and now Julie would hound him until he could play her a tune.

Julie wrapped the gifts safely inside a large fur pelt and loaded them onto the sled. She started to walk down the street to the hospital when something in the store window caught her attention. A handsome, ivory-handled knife was prominently displayed.

Julie went inside and asked to see it in order to better study the detail of the carving. A talented craftsman had skillfully transformed the ivory into an intricate piece of art. The outline of a dog driver with his sled team was highlighted on the handle of the knife.

Impulsively, Julie purchased the knife for Sam. She hadn't seen him in seven weeks, but the urge to buy him a Christmas gift over-ruled her better judgment.

Adding the knife to the other gifts on the sled, Julie went in search of Dr. Welch.

Chapter 8

Julie found Dr. Welch, and after quickly exchanging her paperwork and personal assessments of the villages she'd visited, she bid him a Merry Christmas and received permission to go home for the holidays.

"You know," Dr. Welch said as he followed Julie outside, "we're having a bit of a Christmas Eve party, and I know Lula would love for you to join us."

"I've never been one for parties," Julie answered honestly. "I'm just a home girl. I want to be with my family."

"I understand," Dr. Welch said with a smile. "You have a well-deserved rest, and I'll see you the day after New Year's."

"I'll be here," Julie replied with a wave.

Making her way to the dogs, Julie started thinking of Sam. Would he make an appearance on Christmas, and if he did, would she be happy to see him? She tried to forget about him and concentrate on getting home, but nothing could get him out of her thoughts.

Julie looked over each of her dogs, checking their paws and bellies for signs of freezing. They were tired and deserved a good rest, but Julie had no alternative but to drive them home.

"Your team looks a bit spent."

Julie smiled before straightening up to meet Sam's bearded face. "I'll give you that much," she said, pushing her parka hood back. Her black hair had been neatly braided when she'd started out that morning, but now wisps of it blew around her face.

"Is that all?" Sam said with a grin. "I haven't seen you in nearly two months. I was beginning to think I'd scared you off. Thought I might have to come find you."

Julie put her hands on her hips. "Same old Sam."

Sam laughed and watched Julie as she finished with her dogs. "I've been thinking about you," he said. "Now that I know what it is to have you in my arms, I couldn't stop thinking about it."

Julie stiffened slightly. She was unprepared for Sam's boldness. How should she react? Nervously, she shifted from one foot to the other. "I certainly hope you don't plan to repeat the scene here in the middle of Nome's Front Street."

"Why not?" Sam said as he took a step toward Julie.

"Oh no," Julie said, backing up. "You can't mean it. I have a reputation to preserve, if not for myself, for my career."

Sam stopped and shook his head. "I'm never going to do anything but honor and love you. I would throttle any man, or woman, for that matter, who might blemish your reputation. However, I think your dogs have earned a rest. Let's take them over to my cabin. I'll hitch my dogs, and we'll give yours a break. There's a snow building up, and I don't want you out here alone. I'll take you home."

"No," Julie protested. "My dogs will be fine. It's only another twelve miles. I couldn't ask you to—"

"You didn't ask, and I am telling you," Sam said as he pointed to the sled. "I expect you to get in the basket while I drive these dogs to my house. If you don't get in on your own, I'll put you there myself. Then we'll just see how your reputation withstands the talk."

"I will not," Julie said as she moved to the back of her sled. She thought to jump on the runners and order Dusty into action, but Sam outmaneuvered her and took hold of Dusty's tugline.

Sam raised a questioning eyebrow and waited for Julie to respond. Julie matched his stare. Her breathing quickened as a smile played at the corner of Sam's lips. He waved his hand in front of him and motioned Julie to the sled.

"All right," Julie said and carefully climbed into the sled basket, narrowly avoiding the gifts she'd purchased. "I give up. You win. Take me home."

Sam laughed and dropped the tugline. He walked down the side of the dog team and leaned over Julie. "That's a good girl," he said and dropped a kiss on her forehead.

Julie squirmed away, blushed, and pulled her hood back in place so that Sam couldn't see her face. She wondered who all in Nome had seen Sam's actions, but before she could glance around, Sam moved the dogs out.

While Julie enjoyed the ride to Sam's house on the outskirts of Nome, she was also nervous. Just knowing that Sam stood on the runners behind her made Julie apprehensive. She tried to concentrate on the excitement of seeing her father and brother and celebrating Christmas.

When Sam stopped in front of the two-story clapboard house, Julie was impressed. It wasn't the type of place she'd pictured Sam in.

"We're home," Sam said in a jovial way. "One day I'll say that, and it'll be true."

Julie tried to appear unaffected by Sam's words, but when he reached down to help her from the basket, she nearly jumped out the opposite side of the sled.

"I wish you'd stop," she said and pushed back her parka hood to better see Sam. "I don't know why you insist on doing this, but I want to go home, and if you aren't going to behave, then I'll drive myself." She was determined to stand her ground.

"You're tired, Julie," Sam said, ignoring her protest. "Why don't you go inside and make yourself comfortable?"

"I can wait out here," Julie said anxiously.

"I know you can wait out here. I know you can drive dogs through bitter cold and horrible blizzards. I know too that you have a mind of your own, but I'm every bit as stubborn, and I'm telling you to go in the house and warm up." Sam's words were stern, yet Julie knew they were given out of concern for her welfare.

"I'm touched that you care, Sam, but—"

In three long strides, Sam was at Julie's side. He hoisted her over his shoulder as if he were carrying a sack of grain.

"Put me down," Julie yelled and pounded against Sam's back.

"I'll put you down when we're in the house. We're wasting what few daylight hours we have because you can't cooperate," Sam said as he carried Julie into his house.

Once they were inside, Sam put Julie down. She expected him to try to kiss her again, so she moved quickly away. "All right, you've had your way," she said with a trembling voice.

"Not hardly," Sam said with a grin. "I haven't married you yet." He turned with a laugh and walked out the front door.

Once he was outside, Sam stopped laughing. He'd come very close to pulling Julie into his arms and was still trembling himself when he went to unharness the dogs.

He thought about what he'd done as he fed and watered Julie's team. Sam had never imagined that he'd see Julie in Nome. It had been his plan to question Dr. Welch about her schedule and surprise her for Christmas. But the surprise had been his when he found her standing on Front Street preparing to leave town.

Sam rubbed his beard and sighed. She was a beautiful woman, but more than that, she was intelligent and self-confident, although a bit too stubborn. She was exactly everything that he'd prayed for, everything and more.

"Thank You, God, for sending Julie into my life. I feel sure she's the one You would have me marry. I've prayed so long for a Christian wife, and if Julie is the right one, Lord, then I pray You will help her to see me as the man You have chosen for her. Above all else, Lord, protect her from harm. In Jesus' name, amen."

Sam glanced back at the house. The woman he planned to marry was sitting inside the home he hoped to one day share with her. He would have loved nothing more than to go inside and share her company in the comfort of his home, but he knew it would only make Julie more uncomfortable, so he put the thought aside.

Sam finished harnessing his eager dogs to Julie's sled. He gave his lead dog, Kodiak, a brief pat on the head before going inside to retrieve Julie.

"You're anxious to be on the road, aren't you, boy?" Kodiak whined as though answering, and Sam laughed. "I'm going. I'm going. I just have to go get our girl, and we'll be off."

Sam bounded up the front steps and peered cautiously through the doorway in case Julie planned to throw anything at him. The sight that caught his eye caused Sam to stop in his tracks. Julie lay innocently sleeping on the couch.

Sam called her name, but Julie slept too deeply to hear him. He approached her sleeping form and gently stroked her cheek. It was rosy from the wind, but soft—just as he remembered from the time he'd last kissed her.

Avoiding the memory, Sam went outside and made a place in the basket for Julie. Once he'd placed several blankets in the basket, Sam went back inside. He threw several of his own things into a pack and loaded it onto the sled. Finally, Sam trudged through the snow to the house of his neighbor, Joe Morely, a bachelor who often traded favors with Sam.

Sam let Joe know he'd be gone for several days and asked if he'd mind tending the dogs. After receiving Joe's promise to watch over the house and animals, Sam went back to his house.

Julie slept soundly as Sam lifted her into his arms and carried her to the sled. The cold air caused her to stir and nestle her face against his chest, but she slept on, dreaming of warm arms and a man named Sam.

Chapter 9

J ulie woke up just as Sam led the dog team down the embankment of the Nome River. She couldn't believe that he had packed her into the sled to sleep away the miles between Nome and the Eriksson homestead. Wiping sleep from her eyes, Julie worked her way out of the covers and sat up.

The sky was gray and heavy with snow. Julie knew it would only be a matter of time before those clouds would open up and dump another white blanketing on the Alaskan coastline.

"We're nearly there," Sam said as he moved out on the river ice.

"I hope we're not about to repeat scenes from our last shared trip across the Nome," Julie called up from the basket.

Sam laughed good-naturedly. "You'd better mind your manners, or I'll make you get out and walk, and we both know your ability on ice is questionable."

Julie laughed. "I can manage."

"No doubt," Sam said as he reached the opposite bank. He jumped off the runners and pushed as his ten-dog team pulled. Within seconds they were over the top.

In the fading light, Julie could see the welcoming sight of her home. She would be home with her family for Christmas. In the distance the dogs yipped and howled as Sam's team drew near, alerting Vern and August to their arriving visitors.

Sam halted the sled at the back door and helped Julie from the sled. "You go on in, and I'll unload the basket and take care of the dogs."

Julie started into the house but remembered her gifts. "I need to unpack some of it myself," she said as she turned back to the sled.

"I can take care of it," Sam insisted.

"Look, I'm not just being stubborn this time," an exasperated Julie tried to reason. "I have to take care of some of it myself. It is Christmas Eve, after all."

"I see," Sam said with a grin. "Anything for me?"

"That's a rather presumptuous question," Julie replied. "You'll just have to wait and see." She took a step back and crossed her arms against her body.

"I'm not good at waiting," Sam teased. "Especially when I want something and set my mind to get it."

Julie pretended not to understand his meaning. "You must have caused your family a great deal of trouble on Christmas morning."

"I was a perfect child." Sam grinned.

"I'm sure."

"Sure of what?" August asked as he came out the back door.

"Oh, never mind," Julie said with a sigh. "Would you mind helping Sam with the dogs while I get some of my gear?"

"You can just leave it all, and we'll bring it in," August said.

Sam laughed as Julie rolled her eyes. "Don't even start, August. She's got Christmas presents and doesn't want any of us to see them."

"Oh," August replied and went to unharness Kodiak.

Julie turned to Sam. "Now, why can't you be more like him?" Sam shrugged his shoulders and went to help August.

Julie managed to get her gifts inside without running into her father. She was coming out of her room when Vern came in search of her.

"Jewels!" he said as he embraced her. "Good to have you home."

"Good to be home. I wanted to let you know about George Nakoota. He tangled with his dogs and had his arm ripped up pretty bad. I stitched him up, and it looks good for a full recovery."

"He was blessed to have you there," Vern said as he walked with Julie to the kitchen. "He probably would have died if you hadn't been. That village is nearly fifty miles from Nome, and he would have bled to death before he got proper care."

"Well, he's doing fine now, and I know he'll follow my instructions on how to care for the wounds. My biggest frustration with many of the Eskimos is their curiosity. I'll stitch something closed and bandage it up, and before I can recheck it, they've unbandaged it so they can see my handiwork."

Vern chuckled just as Sam and August came in through the back door. "You know where curiosity will get you," Vern added.

"Yeah," Sam answered with a grin. "No Christmas present."

Julie had brought extra sugar and eggs with her from Nome. She was determined to bake something nice for Christmas, so she cleared the men from the kitchen.

Darkness fell by two o'clock, but Julie refused to let it dampen her spirits. It was Christmas Eve! She baked a cake and rolled out sugar cookies, a tradition started by her mother to pass the anxious hours.

As Julie used each of her mother's cookie cutters, she remembered with fondness the stories her mother would tell about them. The star was for the Bethlehem star that announced the birth of Christ. The Christmas tree, an outline of an evergreen, reminded them of everlasting life in Christ, and the shape of a bell was to bring to mind the joyous music in heaven whenever a sinner accepted Christ.

Taking a final batch of cookies from the oven, Julie put them aside to cool and turned her attention to the finishing touches on a chocolate cake. Setting out a stack of plates and forks, Julie went to the front room to retrieve the men.

"Who'd like some cake?" Julie asked as she entered the room.

"Cake? We should have Julie home more often," August said, deserting his chess game with Sam in order to take his sister's arm.

"I'd love some, Julie. Lead the way."

"Yes," Sam said as he rushed to take Julie's other arm. "Lead the way."

Vern laughed and got to his feet. "I guess I'll just bring up the rear," he said and followed the trio into the kitchen.

They gathered around the table, praising the towering chocolate confectionery. Julie cut the cake and heaped huge slices on each plate.

"Let's have the blessing," Vern suggested as Julie placed a pot of coffee on the table and went for cups.

Julie took a seat at the table. The men joined her, and Vern led them in a short prayer.

"Father, we thank You for the birth of Your Son, Jesus, and the free gift of salvation which You gave to us through Him. Thank You for this gathering of loved ones as we celebrate that birth. Amen."

"What say we share our gifts now?" Vern suggested after a bite of cake. "Umm, Jewels, this is excellent."

"It sure is," August agreed. "And I agree with Pa. I'd like to exchange gifts."

Julie shrugged her shoulders. "I guess that's fine by me."

"Then I suggest everyone get their Christmas gifts, and we'll move to the front room," Vern said, adding, "Oh, and Julie, please bring the cake and coffee."

"I'll help her," Sam said as he got to his feet. "I'm trying to stay in Julie's good graces." He picked up the cake and coffeepot and moved to the front room.

Julie followed Sam with the coffee cups and then excused herself to retrieve her gifts. She unwrapped the fur bundle that she'd placed on her bed and revealed the guitar. The knife and tools were in separate boxes, so Julie rewrapped the guitar, tucked it under one arm, and grabbed the other gifts with her hands.

She joined the men in the living room and was surprised to find someone had decorated a small Christmas tree and placed it on a table in the center of the room. Beneath it were several wrapped packages of different sizes.

"How wonderful," Julie said as she placed her own gifts on the table. "I remember the last time we did this."

"It was the year before you left for Seattle," August said, taking a package from beneath the tree.

"Yes," Vern remembered, "and your mother was still here. I remember she made the most wonderful meal. I wish she could be here to enjoy this evening, but in a way, I guess she is."

"She sure is, Pa," Julie said as she took a seat on one of the overstuffed chairs opposite the couch.

"Here," August said, handing his package to Julie. "I got this for you. Merry Christmas."

Julie opened the package to reveal a black lacquer jewelry box with beautiful red ornamentation. "Thank you, August. It's incredible." She opened the box to reveal a red velvet interior and added, "I've never seen anything like it."

"It's Japanese," August said proudly. "The guy I bought it from was trying to raise money to get home. He said it was one of a kind."

"Well, I haven't much in the way of jewelry, but I'll cherish it always," Julie said appreciatively. "That large bundle of fur over there is yours. But I need the wrapping back." She laughed.

August unwrapped the fur to reveal his gift. "A guitar! What a great idea, Jewels. Thanks," he said as he took the guitar out and began tightening the strings. "You didn't know I'd been taking lessons, did you?"

"Then you already have a guitar?" Julie asked disappointedly.

"No. I've been using Sam's."

"Sam's?" Julie said, turning questioning eyes to Sam. "You truly are a man of surprises, Mr. Curtiss."

"You don't know the half of it, Miss Eriksson," Sam said with a laugh.

"Well, with both guitars here it would be a nice touch to our celebration if you'd both play us some Christmas songs," Vern proposed.

"Oh yes, please!" Julie begged.

"Maybe after all the gifts are opened," Sam said and went to the table. "I have a gift for August as well."

He handed August a small package, which, when opened, revealed a dog harness. Vern and August exchanged curious glances, and Julie laughed as Sam cleared up the mystery.

"Kodiak sired a litter of pups last fall, some of the best-quality dogs I've seen in a long time. I'm giving August his pick of the litter," Sam announced. "You've been a good friend, August." The men exchanged a heartfelt hug.

"A very generous gift indeed, friend," August stated, knowing Sam could sell any one of his dogs for better than a thousand dollars. "Thank you, Sam."

"You deserve it," Sam replied and took a seat by the fireplace.

"Well, I have a gift for my daughter," Vern said. He pulled several packages from beneath the tree and brought them to Julie.

"I feel like a little girl again," Julie said as she hurried to open each one. She immediately recognized the gifts as pieces of her mother's prized jewelry collection.

"Jewels for my jewel," Vern said and planted a kiss on Julie's forehead. "These were your mother's favorites."

"Yes, I know," Julie said with tears in her eyes. She held up a necklace against her white blouse. The gold of the chain and brilliance of the ruby settings looked good against Julie's dark hair.

"This was always my favorite one," Julie added as she replaced the ruby necklace, "because you gave it to her for Christmas not long after I turned sixteen. I thought it was the most romantic gift in all the world." She wiped at her eyes before looking into the other packages.

"Those pieces were some I thought you would enjoy. I thought I'd save the rest until you marry," Vern stated, wiping tears from his own eyes as well.

"Thank you, Papa," Julie said as she got up to retrieve her father's gift. "I'm afraid my present pales in comparison." She handed her father the package.

"I've already got the best gift in all the world. You've come home to Alaska, and that's enough for me."

As Julie watched her father unwrap the tools, she wondered if she should give Sam his gift. If she did and he hadn't gotten her anything for Christmas, he might feel bad. He might also take her gift the wrong way and think it was a promise of something more than friendship.

"Well, would you look at this," Vern said as he held up a new hammer. "I can't believe it, but they're exactly what I need. I was planning on buying all of these." Julie watched as he tested the blade of the saw and examined the chisel set. "Perfect!" Vern declared, and Julie leaned back, feeling quite satisfied.

"Oh, I nearly forgot," Julie said as she got up and rushed to her room. She came back with the bundle that Tanana had given her. "These are from George's wife, Tanana. She thought I might not get a chance to do any Christmas shopping, and so she made these mukluks for me in pay for sewing up George."

"Anything that woman makes is a prize to be sure," Vern said as he undid the rawhide strip that tied the package shut. He examined the mukluks before passing one pair to August. "It also helps that she knows our sizes."

"Well, this has been a fine Christmas," Vern said as he stretched out his feet.

"Wait," August said as he went to the tree. "There's another gift here. Who's this one for?"

Julie swallowed hard. It was now or never, she decided, and quickly answered. "That one is for Sam."

Three pairs of eyes turned in surprise at her, and Julie wished she could crawl beneath the chair. "I never had a chance to properly thank him for all he did for me. Merry Christmas, Sam," she said quickly to break the tension.

"Well, I must say this is a surprise," Sam said as he accepted the package from August. He unwrapped the brown paper to reveal the knife and sheath. "It's exquisite," he murmured as he examined the craftsmanship. "I've never had one as fine. Thank you, Julie."

She blushed under the intensity of Sam's eyes. The silence was unbearable, and Julie searched her mind for something to say. "How about those songs, now?" she finally questioned.

"Yes," Vern agreed, "now would be the perfect time." He leaned his head back and closed his eyes.

"I'll get your guitar, Sam," August offered and went to his room.

Sam studied the knife before sheathing it and looping it onto his belt. He was more than touched at Julie's extravagant gift. It signaled a change in their relationship. Had Julie come to approve of the idea of marriage? He couldn't wait until a time revealed itself when he could be alone and offer his own Christmas gift.

After several hours of listening to Sam and August, as well as joining in on all the songs they could think to sing, Vern suggested they read the nativity story. Everyone readily agreed, and while Sam continued to strum the haunting melody of "Silent Night," Vern, August, and Julie took turns reading the second chapter of Luke.

When they'd finished, Vern offered a prayer and got up to stretch. "I think I'm going to retire, but before I do, I'd like to say something. I wasn't looking forward to this holiday. It was always Agneta's favorite, and I knew that it wouldn't be the same without her. But I was wrong. The celebration of Christ's birth isn't a matter of the house you live in or the people who share your table. It's a matter of the heart. If the Lord lives here," Vern said as he patted his chest with his hand, "then Christmas is a matter of everyday life. Agneta would want it that way too. Good night."

Julie watched her father walk from the room. She admired his strength and, in it, found more courage for herself.

"Unless you need help cleaning up, I'm going to bed too," August said as he ran a gentle hand over the guitar. "This is a swell gift, Jewels. I'm going to enjoy it for a long, long time."

"I'm glad you like it," Julie said, getting up to embrace her brother. "You go ahead to bed. I can manage all of this just fine. Besides, I want to see if the aurora makes an appearance tonight." August nodded, gave Sam a single-fingered salute, and took his leave.

Julie knew that Sam's eyes were on her even before she turned around. What would she say to him? How could she deal with the feelings her heart would no longer let her deny? She cared for Sam, that much was true. But how would it fit in with her nursing? Was it really love she felt or merely infatuation? Taking a deep breath, she turned to meet his eyes.

"Do you have to clear these things away just yet?" Sam asked as he came across the room.

"No," Julie whispered. "I suppose they can wait."

"Good, because I can't," Sam said and took Julie in his arms. His kiss was as gentle as the first he'd ever given her, but the feelings he evoked in Julie's heart were so much greater.

After what seemed an eternity, Julie pushed away. "I can't breathe," she laughed, trying hard to push aside the passion she was feeling.

Sam allowed her the space and led her to the couch. "I want to talk to you," he said as he sat down beside her. "I have a Christmas gift for you."

"You shouldn't have," Julie said in a barely audible voice. Having Sam so close completely muddled her thoughts.

Sam reached into his pocket and pulled out a small box. He opened it for Julie and revealed a ring of gold, with a small diamond. "Julie," he whispered, "will you marry me?"

Julie stared dumbfoundedly at the box. He'd actually proposed. None of his presumptuous attitudes or the self-assured cockiness that he'd delivered before, just the plain and simple heart of the matter. A marriage proposal!

"I don't know what to say."

"Say yes," Sam said as he took the ring from the box and slipped it on Julie's finger.

Julie stared at the ring for several minutes. It was a bit big, but it was exactly what Julie would have hoped for in a wedding ring.

"We've only known each other a couple of months," Julie said, searching for a way she could avoid dealing with the issue.

"We both know it's right," Sam said as he pulled Julie against him. "I love you, Julie, and whether or not you'll admit it, I know you love me."

Julie trembled in Sam's arms. Her breath caught in her throat and made it impossible to deny his statement. Did she love him?

"I don't know what I'm feeling," Julie finally answered honestly. "I won't deny the chemistry between us, but Sam, you weren't in my plans."

"What about God's plans?"

"But I thought I knew what God's plans for me were," Julie said, daring to look into Sam's piercing brown eyes. "I thought I knew exactly what I was supposed to do."

"And now?" Sam questioned.

"Now," Julie said as she took off the ring. "I feel confused. I can't marry you, Sam, unless I know for sure it's what I'm supposed to do." She handed him the ring, expecting an angry retort. Instead, Sam surprised her.

Closing his hand around Julie's fingers and the ring, he spoke. "Keep the ring. I feel confident that God has sent you to be my wife. One day, you'll know it too, and you'll come to me wearing it, and I'll know your answer." With that, Sam placed a light kiss on Julie's forehead and got up. "Good night, love," he said and left Julie to contemplate her feelings.

Julie held the ring tightly and prayed. "Oh God, what am I to do? I thought the way was so clear. You had shone a light of understanding on the path that I was to take, and I felt confident that I was making the right choice. Now. . ." She paused and looked at the ring. "Now, I just don't know. I'm so afraid, and I need to understand what I'm to do. I want to serve You, Father. I want to bring glory to You. Can I do this as Sam's wife?"

Several minutes passed. With the ring still in her hand, Julie retrieved her father's Bible and opened it to Joshua 1:9: "'Have not I commanded thee? Be strong and of a good courage; be not afraid, neither be thou dismayed: for the Lord thy God is with thee whithersoever thou goest.'"

"I won't be afraid," Julie said as she reread the verse. "You have commanded me to be strong and with Your help, Father, I will be." Peace filled Julie's heart. "I don't know what the answer is regarding Sam, Lord. But You do, and I am Your servant, seeking to know Your will. Open my heart to Your direction so that my own plans won't thwart the divine ones You have ordained for me. Amen."

Chapter 10

January 1925 started out cold, with the mercury dipping to thirty below zero. Julie took extra precautions to maintain warmth and safety on the trail by carrying more blankets, additional food, and dry fuel for fires.

She had read several articles in the *Nome Nugget* of the army's findings while experimenting with temperature in the far North. Apparently, it wasn't enough to calculate the outside temperature when determining how dangerous conditions were. The speed of the wind had to be considered as well. The army had concluded that, while a fifteen-degree temperature seemed warm to the natives of Nome, if the wind were blowing at ten to twelve miles an hour, it would feel more like forty below zero. Something called windchill, Julie remembered, and it could create problems for a person on the trail.

The snow had been sporadic that winter, and Nome's streets weren't buried as deeply as they usually were at the first of the year. Julie knew that however good conditions were in Nome, she had no way to tell what would greet her as she moved out across the less traveled trails.

"We haven't had any traffic from the west or north," she said as she finished her coffee one morning with Dr. Welch and his wife. "So I have no way of knowing what the trails are like."

"I wish I could go with you," Dr. Welch replied honestly. He loved to drive his dogs and found city life a bit stifling at times.

"Actually, I wish you could too," Julie said with a smile for Dr. Welch's wife. "I love to watch your husband at work, Mrs. Welch."

"Now, Julie, I think we've been friends far too long to continue with the Mrs. Welch title. Just call me Lula; all my friends do."

"I like to call her Lu," Dr. Welch said with a fond smile for his wife, "among other things."

"You're being quite impossible today, Dr. Welch," Lula said with a teasing note to her voice. "You're probably better off with him staying in Nome, Julie. I have a feeling he'd want to wander off and do some ice fishing or visit, if he went on the trail."

Julie laughed and glanced at her watch. It wouldn't be light for another three hours, but the trail beckoned. "I'm going to have to be on my way. Thanks again for the coffee, Lula," she said, trying the name for the first time. "I should be back in a few weeks."

Just then a loud knock at the door caught their attention. "A doctor's house is an open arena," Lula said with a smile. "I'll just see who that might be."

Lula Welch opened the door to reveal an Eskimo man. "I have sick children," he said in a worried way that caused Dr. Welch to jump to his feet.

"What seems to be wrong?" he questioned the man, as Lula brought his fur parka.

"They're burning with fever, and their throats are sore," the man answered.

"How old are they?" Dr. Welch questioned. Lula brought his medical bag and set it on the table.

"One's three, and my baby is only one year old. Can you help them, Doctor? I don't have much money, but I can work hard for you."

Dr. Welch waved the man's concerns away. "Nonsense. We'll discuss such matters later. First, let's see if we can figure out how to help the little ones." He planted a kiss on Lula's temple and turned to Julie. "You can always send me a radio message through the army signal corps, should you need anything or have a problem."

"I'll keep that in mind," Julie said. She pulled on her parka and secured the hood. "Would you like me to drive you to the settlement?"

"No," Dr. Welch said, shaking his head. "There's not so much snow as to impede a good walk, and I need the exercise. Thanks anyway." With that, Dr. Welch hastened into the darkness with the fearful father.

"I guess I'd better be on my way as well," Julie remarked. "I'll be in touch. Thanks again for the coffee."

"We'll look forward to seeing you when you get back," Lula said as she followed Julie to the door. "Be careful."

"I will be," Julie promised and took herself out into the darkness.

The town was quiet, even though there was plenty of activity. Julie felt an emptiness as she watched couples making their way into nearby shops. Maybe she wasn't cut out for public health nursing after all. While she loved nursing and working with the Eskimos, the long, lonely hours on the trail were difficult.

Images of Sam filled Julie's mind. She thought of the ring that lay securely at the bottom of her knapsack. It was a symbol of Sam's devotion. Would she ever be able to put the ring on and give Sam the answer he longed to hear?

In the back of her mind, Julie remembered the verses from Ecclesiastes that her father had read. *"Two are better than one. . . . For if they fall, the one will lift up his fellow: but woe to him that is alone when he falleth; for he hath not another to help him up."* Loneliness penetrated her heart.

Julie consoled herself with the idea of stopping at home before pushing west. Maybe she could talk to her father about Sam's proposal and her loneliness. He could offer her some idea of what she should do.

Julie checked the tarp covering her supplies, and when she was certain that everything was secure, she took to the back of her sled.

"Were you planning on leaving without saying good-bye?" Sam questioned as he placed his hands on Julie's shoulders.

Julie turned. Dim light illuminated Sam's bearded face. His hair had been neatly cut and his beard trimmed. He was quite handsome,

Julie decided. She could do much worse.

"I can't always be looking over my shoulder for you, every time I'm about to go on my route," Julie said, trying to distance herself from the emotions Sam stirred within her.

"I thought you were avoiding me," Sam countered. "I don't suppose you've given much thought to my proposal."

"I've, uh, well," Julie stammered, "I've been busy with my nursing. Since the first part of the month, I've been working with Dr. Welch and haven't even managed to get home. I also have several villages to the northwest to attend to, so you can see I've been very busy."

"That doesn't answer my question," Sam remarked.

"I think it should," Julie said nervously. "I've been too busy to see my family. Doesn't it seem reasonable that I've been too busy to consider your marriage proposal?"

"No," Sam said firmly. "It doesn't."

Julie's mouth opened in surprise. She had banked on Sam's good nature making him drop the issue. Instead he remained a determined force to be reckoned with.

"Do you have any idea what my nursing means to me?" Julie asked seriously. *Perhaps*, she thought, *if Sam knew what my responsibilities mean to me, he'd understand my hesitation.*

"Do you have any idea what you mean to me?" Sam said as he moved closer. His warm breath formed frosty white steam in the morning cold.

"That's not fair, Sam. I asked you first."

"If I answer you, will you give me an answer?" Sam questioned. "I think it's only fair."

"I imagine I mean something quite special to you. After all, you did ask me to marry you," Julie stated evenly. "Now, I've answered your question. Will you answer mine?"

Sam chuckled. "Your father was right. You are something else when you have a full head of steam. Sometime, you'll have to tell me what happened when your father wanted to shoot that pup. No doubt you didn't cut him any more maneuvering room than you are me."

Julie smiled ruefully. "My father told me that pup was good for nothing but taking up space and eating. He said he couldn't be expected to pull his own weight, much less that of a sled. I told him I wasn't all that different. I was too young to bring in any wealth to the family, and certainly I wasn't capable of pulling my own weight. I put myself between the pup and my father's leveled gun and told him he might as well do away with both of us, because the weak were worthless when it came to surviving in the North."

Sam smiled at her determination. "I guess I don't have to ask what happened."

"My father relented. Told me I was spoiled and," Julie added with amusement, "he made me take care of the pup."

"How'd it work out?"

"My father knew best," Julie said sadly. "The pup got in a fight with some of the other dogs. They killed him."

"I'm sorry," Sam replied honestly.

"I learned a good lesson," Julie said as she shook the image from her mind. "Never once did my father tell me, 'I told you so.' He put his arms around me and let me cry. Then he shared the words of Proverbs 1:8: 'My son, hear the instruction of thy father, and forsake not the law of thy mother.' He told me it counted for daughters as well."

"Your father is a wise man," Sam said softly.

"Yes, he is," Julie agreed, "and that's exactly why I need to talk to him before I can give you any kind of an answer."

"I see," Sam answered thoughtfully. "I suppose it wouldn't help if I told you that I've already talked to him about it."

"What?" Julie's head snapped up.

"I talked to your father before I ever asked you to marry me," Sam replied. "I wouldn't have dreamed of approaching you with a proposal unless I was certain your father approved."

"And did he?"

Sam smiled and reached out a hand to push back Julie's hood. "He told me it was up to you."

"That's it?" Julie questioned as she took a step back to avoid Sam's touch. "He didn't say anything else?"

"Should he have?"

"I don't know. I guess I just wondered if he—"

"If he had an answer for you?" Sam interrupted. "I didn't ask your father to marry me. I only sought his blessing. It's you I want an answer from."

Julie turned away from Sam and rechecked her sled harness. Part of her wanted to tell Sam no, but no matter how she tried, Julie couldn't form the word. Why couldn't she simply refuse to marry him and let him slip from her life? "I don't have an answer for you, Sam," she finally said.

"Do you know when you might?"

Julie straightened up slowly, avoiding his eyes.

"Look at me, Julie," Sam said as he reached out and turned her to face him. "This should be a happy experience for both of us. It should be a wonderful and joyful event for two people who love each other. You do love me, don't you?" It was more a statement than a question.

Julie took a deep breath to steady herself. That was the important question. Did she love Sam?

"I—"

"Say, aren't you Julie Eriksson?" a voice called out from behind Sam. Julie recognized the bulky form of her father's longtime friend, Jonah Emery.

"Hello, Jonah," Julie said sweetly, grateful for the reprieve.

"I heard you were back in these parts as a nurse. Say, I'll bet your papa is mighty proud."

"I'll say he is," Sam joined in.

"Why, Sam Curtiss, I should have known that towering frame belonged to you. Well, I'll let you two get back to your discussion," Jonah said with a wave. "You be sure and tell your pa hello from me."

"I will," Julie promised and watched as Jonah moved down the street to one of the small cafés.

"I'm still waiting for my answer," Sam said as Julie turned back to face him.

"I can't give you an answer."

"Then when, Julie?"

She thought for a moment. "I'm going to be gone for a month, maybe more. I'll have an answer for you when I return."

Sam grinned and pulled Julie into his arms. "Then let me give you a reminder to take on the trail," he whispered and lowered his lips to kiss her.

Julie stepped back breathlessly, even though the kiss was brief. She looked apprehensively up and down the street to see if anyone had seen Sam kiss her. When she turned back to reprimand Sam for his behavior, he was gone.

Balancing between relief and disappointment, Julie quickly wrapped several scarves around her face and secured her hood. She could only pray that God would provide her an answer to Sam's question.

"Let's go, boys!" she called out and held on tightly as the dogs fairly burst from the start.

From the dark haven of the entryway to a store, Sam watched Julie move down the street and out of sight. It was hard to let her go without demanding that she accept his love and affection, but Sam had made God a promise. "Thy will be done," Sam whispered in the darkness. "Thy will be done."

Chapter 11

Troubled by her promise to Sam, Julie forgot about going home. She mushed out of Nome on trails that took her west along the ice-packed Bering Sea. The coastline trails were easy to follow, and they often moved off the banks onto the frozen sea itself. This helped drivers avoid heavily drifted snow and hidden obstacles.

Out on the ice, Julie had new concerns to keep her mind on. The wind and pressure often caused the ice to form what the natives called "spears." These ice needles jutted upward from the frozen trail and could pierce the padding of a dog's feet. Whenever spears were evident, Julie took time out to put coverings on the paws of each of her dogs. So far, they'd avoided injury.

As the dimly lit skies gave way to sunlight, Julie pushed back her parka hood. She could tell by the dogs' breath that the temperature had risen. A good driver always paid attention to the degree of whiteness that showed in a team's exhaled breath. Little things like that often saved a driver's life, and Julie, ever mindful of her near-death from the blizzard, paid special attention to such details.

The ice and snow stretched for miles, and the glare of reflecting sunlight caused Julie to shelter her eyes by replacing her hood.

The team moved at a nice trot, and Julie felt exhilarated as she made her way down the coastline. The hills and mountains in the distance, however, reminded her of the dangers that came with isolation.

One mistake could be her last.

Thinking about mistakes, Julie considered Sam's marriage proposal. "Lord," she prayed, "I don't know what to do about Sam. He says he loves me, but I don't know if I love him. I suppose I shouldn't be so worried about it—after all, Sam is a Christian."

The miles passed in a blur as Julie continued, "I don't know what to do! My job as a public health nurse takes me out on the trail for weeks, even months at a time. How can I be a good wife to a man while I'm hundreds of miles away inoculating children and teaching mothers about hygiene? Sam deserves more than a pittance of attention every few weeks. I'm sure a man with his zest for living would expect a great deal more, Father. I know he would, and I'd feel obligated to give it to him and leave my job. Since I can't do that, it must be wrong for me to accept his proposal."

That conclusion didn't last long. Unsettled feelings in Julie's mind told her that the issue was far from being resolved.

Sam's never suggested I leave my work as a nurse, she reasoned. *Even when he bids me good-bye, he never causes a scene about my work or says that I ought to be safe at home. Maybe Sam is more sympathetic to the needs of the people up here. Maybe Sam would want me to continue working as a public health nurse, even after we were married.*

"So the answer must be yes," Julie said aloud, but again the feeling that the issue wasn't settled came to haunt her.

"Do I love him?" she asked.

She thought of the way he smiled and the laughter in his brown eyes. The vision of Sam's muscular shoulders and towering frame came to mind. Julie admitted to herself that she was attracted to Sam as she'd never been to another man. *Attraction isn't love,* she reminded herself. *But is it part of love?*

Julie's mittened hands twisted at the sled bar. She couldn't settle on any answers to her many questions.

Please, Lord, I promised him an answer. Please show me whether or not I love him. I must know that before I can answer his proposal because I simply cannot marry a man I do not love.

The daylight hours passed much too quickly. In the distance, Julie saw the flickering light of a lantern hanging on a pole outside a sod igloo. She sighed in relief, eager to rest after only two short stops on the trail.

The village wouldn't recognize their new public health nurse, but Julie knew she'd be warmly welcomed. She halted the dogs as several Eskimos appeared.

"I'm Nurse Eriksson from Nome," Julie offered by way of introduction.

"We're glad to have you," an older man said as he extended his hand. "We have sickness in our village. It is good you have come."

"If you will lend me a warm place to work," Julie said as she reached for her gear, "I'll be glad to examine your sick."

The man nodded and pointed to the sod igloo. "You use my house. I have no wife. I will stay with my brother and his family while you work. Come."

"Thank you," Julie said as she followed the man. "What should I call you?"

The man turned and smiled, revealing several missing teeth. "Call me Charlie," he said and showed Julie inside the shack.

Julie was appalled by what greeted her. The igloo was filthy and very small, leaving her to wonder if these conditions were common in the rest of the village. She noticed the small oilcan stove and turned to Charlie.

"Is there fuel for the stove?"

"Sure," Charlie replied. "I get you nice fire. Plenty warm in here with big fire."

"I'll need water too," Julie said as she pulled her parka off. It was chilly, but not unbearable, and once she began to clean the room, her body would warm considerably.

"I get you plenty snow, and we melt on big fire. You can have much hot water."

Charlie seemed so pleased to offer Julie his home that she didn't want to hurt his feelings by rearranging everything. "Would it be all right," she began, "if I clean this table so that I can examine the patients?"

"Sure, sure," Charlie said with his broad toothless smile. "You have plenty fire, plenty water, and plenty clean. Sure."

Charlie disappeared out the door, and Julie could hear him talking excitedly to the villagers. He reappeared and within minutes had a nice fire going in the stove as well as several pans of snow melting on top of it.

Julie rolled up the sleeves of her heavy flannel shirt. While nurses in Nome's hospital wore a recognizable uniform, Julie wore what best suited the climate and elements she would have to combat; warm flannels and wools along with furs and skin pants were of much more benefit to her near the Bering Sea than starched aprons and freshly pressed dresses. She was just pinning up her hair when a young woman burst through the door with her infant child in hand.

"My baby is sick," she cried as she held the infant up to Julie.

Julie reached for the child. His burning skin told her that he had a dangerously high fever.

"How long has he been sick?" Julie questioned the mother while examining the baby.

"He's had a bad cold for two days. He breathes so hard I can't rest for fear he'll stop breathing," the little Eskimo woman said as she twisted her hands.

Julie could hear the labored, shallow breathing of the infant. He was perilously close to death. But why? Julie couldn't find any obvious reason for the baby to be so ill. "I must look in his mouth," Julie told his mother as she pulled a tongue depressor from her bag. "I won't hurt him, but he won't like it." Julie doubted that the lethargic baby would fight her, but she felt better warning the mother about her actions.

The light was so poor that Julie could scarcely see past the child's tongue and gums. "I need more light," she called to Charlie and waited until he brought her a lantern.

"Plenty light for the nurse," Charlie said and went back to his self-assigned task of melting snow at the stove.

Julie positioned the light to give her a good view into the child's mouth. She pried the tiny mouth open and gasped. The back of the child's swollen throat was covered with gray-white patches of dead mucous membrane, the unmistakable calling card of diphtheria. Julie looked up sympathetically at the frantically worried young mother. How could she explain to the woman that her baby would probably die that night?

"Are there any others in the village with this sickness?" Julie asked.

"Yes, there are two other children with sore throats and high fevers," the woman answered. "Can you make my baby well?"

Julie felt the pain displayed in the woman's eyes. "No, I'm sorry. Your baby is very sick, and I can't help him. We've waited too long, and I don't have the medicine I need to help you."

The woman's anxious face fell into complete dejection. She grabbed up her baby and began to wail. Charlie came from the stove and asked Julie what was wrong with the baby.

"It's a white man's disease called diphtheria," Julie said as the crying mother rocked back and forth, cradling her dying child. "I need medicine from Nome in order to save the people from getting the disease. The ones who are already sick may not have enough time left for me to get back and help them. Charlie, I'm going to need your help. Do you have a village council?"

"Sure, sure," Charlie said, repeating what appeared to be his favorite word. "We got plenty people on council."

"I need you to call them together. This disease is very contagious. That means it spreads quickly. Charlie, we mustn't let anyone come into the village or leave it. Do you understand? I have to go back to Nome and get the antitoxin."

"Sure, Charlie understand plenty good," the old man said with a grave nod. "I keep people here, and nobody else come in."

"Good," Julie replied. "Charlie, I need to have the dogs ready to leave in ten minutes. Can you have them ready for me?"

"Sure, but you plenty tired. You need rest to travel," Charlie answered in a way that reminded Julie of her father.

"Yes, Charlie, I know. But if I don't get the medicine and get right back to the village, many of your people will die. I have to try."

"You try then," Charlie said and patted Julie on the back. "But you don't take the ice. Big wind blowing off the water is making it soft. It might be gone in the night."

"Thank you, Charlie. I'll stick to the land trail," Julie promised.

After speaking with the council about quarantining the homes of the sick and leaving instructions on how to ease the sufferings of those with the disease, Julie repacked her supplies and readied her sled.

Starting with Dusty, Julie lovingly patted her dogs and checked them for any signs of stiffness or injury. Eager to be back on the trail, the dogs seemed to understand the importance of their mission.

Julie moved her team out and ran alongside the sled for quite a distance. She wanted to ensure that she stayed warm, so she only rode the runners when fatigue threatened her with exhaustion. In record time, she saw the lights of Nome and breathed a prayer of thanksgiving.

Julie pushed the dogs to Dr. Welch's house. Mindless of the hour, she pounded on the door. Surprisingly, Dr. Welch himself appeared at the door, fully dressed.

"Julie, come inside. What is it?" Dr. Welch questioned as he ushered the girl to a seat by the stove.

"Diphtheria! The Sinuak village has several cases. One will certainly not make it through the night, and the others I doubt I can help either. I came back for antitoxin."

Dr. Welch looked old beyond his years. Julie worried for his health as he ran a hand through his graying hair and sat down at the kitchen table. "I haven't got any. At least not enough."

"How much do you have?" Julie questioned in a worried tone that matched the doctor's.

"We only have 75,000 units, and I already have cases of diphtheria appearing here in Nome. The two children I was called to care for are dead. I didn't know then that it was diphtheria, as I couldn't get a look inside their mouths. However, little Richard Stanley is also sick, and I saw quite well the patches on his throat. It's diphtheria, all right."

"What are we to do?" Julie asked as she joined the doctor at the table.

"I don't know," the doctor answered bluntly. "It takes 30,000 units of antitoxin to treat one sick person. I've already got at least four who are sick with the disease and hundreds of others who are exposed."

"To make matters worse," Lula Welch said as she appeared in her nightgown and robe, "the serum we have on hand is over five years old. We'd hoped that the Public Health Department had sent some with you when you returned from Seattle, but they must have been short on it themselves. We didn't receive a single unit."

Julie sat back and took a deep breath. "So we don't know if the serum on hand is effective?"

"That's about the whole of it," Dr. Welch said and put his head in his hands. "We must be prepared to deal with a full-scale epidemic. Diphtheria will only take a matter of days to spread like a flame on dried kindling. The entire peninsula is in danger of epidemic. God help us."

"Yes, He's our only hope now," Julie agreed. "He's our only hope!"

Chapter 12

Julie stayed at the Welch home, and that morning word came that little Richard Stanley had passed away in the night. There was nothing left to do, Dr. Welch decided, but to call upon the mayor and announce an epidemic.

Sitting in the office of the *Nome Nugget*, all eyes of the city council turned to the publisher, George Maynard. As well as operating and publishing Nome's only newspaper, George Maynard was also the town's mayor.

"Diphtheria? Are you sure, Curt?" George questioned Dr. Welch. "We haven't had diphtheria in these parts for over twenty years, and with the ports all frozen up, how would we get the serum now?"

"I can't tell you the hows and whys, but facts are facts. I wish it weren't so, but the truth of the matter is I've already got three dead children to prove my diagnosis. I'm getting more reports of people taken with fever and sore throat. Frankly, George, it's going to get a whole lot worse before it gets better."

"But don't we have an injection for that kind of thing?" the mayor asked with a hopeful expression.

"We do, and we don't," Dr. Welch explained as he rubbed his eyes with the backs of his hands. "There is an antitoxin, but Nome doesn't have it."

"What are you saying?" M. L. Summers, superintendent of the

Hammon Consolidated Gold Fields, questioned.

"I'm saying we have an epidemic, and people are dying. Furthermore, there is a cure, but we don't have it within reach. I have a small amount of antitoxin, but it's over five years old and probably ineffective. There's certainly not enough to stave off an epidemic."

"What do you suggest we do, Doc?" Sam asked as he moved forward from the back of the room.

"We have to quarantine the sick and keep people from spreading the disease. The first order of business is to close the schools and the movie theater," Dr. Welch said as he leaned back in his chair. "As this region's director of public health, I would also like to have a board of health formed to enforce the quarantine. We can't have anybody coming in or going out of Nome."

"Summers, you could take that job on, couldn't you?" Mayor Maynard asked.

"Certainly," Summers answered, feeling honored to be put in the position.

"I'll run a quarantine notice on the front page," Maynard said as he jotted down notes on a pad of paper.

"Thank you," Dr. Welch replied.

"What else can we do?" Sam questioned.

"The biggest problem we have on hand is how to get the antitoxin. I haven't any idea where there might be a supply large enough to help us. It might be in Fairbanks or Anchorage. Then again, it might be as far away as Juneau or Seattle. Regardless, when we locate the serum we'll have another problem on our hands: How do we get it here?"

"If we can locate serum in either Anchorage or Fairbanks," Mayor Maynard began, "there might be a pilot daring enough to fly it to us." Everyone looked skeptical at the suggestion. Flying was new enough to the States, but in Alaska, it was almost unheard of, especially in the winter.

"That might work if it were summer, but I don't think we can afford to risk it in the middle of winter. There's no way of knowing if those engines can handle thirty or forty below zero," one of the other council members said. Murmurs filled the room as the men concurred that flight might be a bad notion.

"Look," Sam said, suddenly getting an idea, "what if we used dog teams? We know they can make it through on the mail routes from Fairbanks. If Fairbanks has the serum, we could start it west and send someone out to meet it. Maybe even relay it across the territory."

"But that will take nearly a month," the mayor argued.

"Not if we send Leonhard Seppala," Summers said, getting to his feet. "You all know he's the best musher in Alaska. His Siberian huskies are faster than any other team around these parts." The council members nodded as Summers continued. "Seppala works for me, and I would gladly allow him the time to perform this courageous act."

"Yeah, those little plume-tailed rats might just pull it off. So we start someone out from Fairbanks with the serum and—"

"So far there is no serum," Sam interrupted the mayor. "We have to send out a radio message and find the serum before we can move it to Nome."

"Sam's right," Dr. Welch said with a nod of his head. "We have to locate the serum first and then worry about how to get it here."

"Whatever it takes," Maynard said as he pounded his fist on the table. "No matter the cost. We all remember the influenza epidemic of 1919."

"Yes, and it didn't help much that the outside had already had its death tolls from it the year before," Welch added. "We were no better prepared for that epidemic than we are for this one."

"Dr. Welch, you give a message to the US Army Signal Corps' radiotelegraph station. We're behind you one hundred percent. Just let us know what we need to do," the mayor replied.

"I'll take you there, Doc. My team's right outside the door," Sam said as he got up to retrieve his parka.

"Very well, gentlemen. I will rely upon you to work with our new board of health director and the mayor as we strive to take control of this nightmare." Dr. Welch got to his feet and followed Sam to where the coats had been haphazardly thrown to one side.

"I'll keep all of you informed," Welch promised and followed Sam out the door.

———— *#* ————

"This must go priority to Juneau, Fairbanks, Anchorage, and Seward," Dr. Welch instructed as he handed a piece of paper to the sergeant who manned the radiotelegraph station.

Sergeant James Anderson took the paper and read it, paling slightly as he finished its contents. "Looks like we're in for it, huh, Doc?"

"That it does," Dr. Welch said as he cast a side glance at Sam.

Sam was deep in thought over concern for the town of Nome, but especially for Julie. He wished it were possible to make the serum appear on the next mail delivery, but wishing wouldn't make it so.

"I'll notify my superiors, and we'll have a man stationed here twenty-four hours a day until we receive an answer," the sergeant said as he prepared to telegraph the message.

Sam watched the man put on his headset. Turning the dial to adjust the frequency, the man began the message.

"-./—/—/. -.-./.-/-./.-../.-./-../../-./-./—." The radio key clicked out the words "Nome, calling."

The room seemed shrouded in silence against the rhythmic tapping of the telegraph key. Sam and Dr. Welch stood to one side as the sergeant tapped out the call again. He paused and waited to see if anyone would pick up his signal.

Within seconds the answer tapped back. "Fairbanks, calling. Go ahead, Nome."

The sergeant turned and nodded to Dr. Welch. "It's Fairbanks. I'll relay the message."

The sergeant's finger tapped out the message with expert ease. "Nome, calling. We have an outbreak of diphtheria. No serum. Urgently need help."

Sam and Dr. Welch breathed a sigh of relief. Just knowing that the rest of the world would learn of their need gave them hope.

The sergeant continued to radio the message to Anchorage, Juneau, and Seward. "I'll let you know when I get anything in," Sergeant Anderson said as he took off his headset.

"Thanks, Sergeant," Sam said and offered his dog team to Dr. Welch.

For days, time stood still in Nome. The only thing that didn't slow was the diphtheria. Three children were dead, ten new active cases were revealed, and more than fifty people reported they'd been exposed. Dr. Welch could only use what little serum he had on hand. Soon not a single unit remained.

Finally, on January 25, a message was received in Nome. Anchorage had 300,000 units of serum at the Alaska Railroad Hospital. It could be packaged and loaded on the number sixty-six Anchorage-to-Fairbanks Passenger Special and received at the Nenana railhead within two days. The Star Route of the interior mail delivery operated by dogsled from Nenana and could carry the serum as part of its load.

Dr. Welch gave the go-ahead, and Sergeant Anderson wired the message to Dr. Beeson in Anchorage to proceed with the shipment.

"I suggest we call a city council meeting," Dr. Welch said as the sergeant finished his message. "This presents a whole new problem."

Within an hour, everyone had gathered for the meeting. Julie stood to one side of the meeting hall, while Sam kept a determined gaze on her from the opposite side of the room. It was the first time he'd seen her since she'd left for her routes. She'd done nothing to let him know of her hurried return to Nome.

It was also the first time Sam had seen Julie in a dress. Self-consciously, Julie smoothed the white uniform, mindful of the way it displayed her more feminine qualities. She was wearing her uniform because she'd been helping at the hospital with the non-diphtheria patients. Dr. Welch had wisely kept the hospital quarantined for those patients whose ills did not involve diphtheria and required surgery or detailed medical help. Nurse Seville had been dispatched to the

Sinuak village to work with the natives while Julie stayed on in Nome.

"I know you've all been waiting for good news," Dr. Welch began, "and finally I have some to report. Anchorage has 300,000 units of serum, and they've started it north to Nenana on the train." A cry of excited voices went up. Dr. Welch waited until the crowd had quieted before continuing. "We must decide how we are to get the serum from Nenana to Nome. Anchorage advises me that it will arrive in Nenana tomorrow."

"Leonhard Seppala has agreed to go after the serum," M. L. Summers announced.

"The arrangements have already been made to start the serum west after Nenana," Dr. Welch declared. "Several relay teams will work it down the Tanana and Yukon Rivers. Perhaps we could have Seppala meet the serum, say, at Nulato?"

"That's over six hundred miles round trip," Sam advised. "It would be a hardship for one man and one team of dogs."

"Seppala suggests he take a team of thirty or so dogs," Summers expounded. "He would drop dogs off at the various roadhouses and cabins along the route and pick them up fresh on the way back. That way he could mush night and day. He believes it would only take a return trip of three, maybe four days."

"Three or four days?" one of the other men questioned. "That would average nearly one hundred miles a day! Seppala's huskies are good, but they're not indestructible."

"Have him stand by," Dr. Welch said as he contemplated the matter. "I'm still awaiting word from the governor. I'm not authorized to make the decision on my own."

The men nodded and settled down. Julie took the opportunity to slip quietly from the room in order to avoid Sam, but he was prepared for her action and followed her out. Julie was halfway down the hall and heading for her parka when Sam caught hold of her arm and whirled her into his arms.

"You look incredible," he whispered against her ear.

Julie thrilled to his touch, melting at once against his lean, muscular form. How often had she dreamed of this during those lonely nights spent out on the trail.

"You know," Sam said with a teasing smile, "I never purchase a sled dog sight unseen. I always go over them with a well-trained eye, just in case there are any hidden defects. But you, I was ready to take sight unseen, buried under pounds of furs and leather. Boy, was that a good call!"

"I beg your pardon," Julie said indignantly and pushed away. "Are you comparing your marriage proposal to purchasing a dog?" She clamped her hand automatically over her mouth, grimacing because the very subject she'd hoped to avoid was now open for conversation.

"You know I didn't mean it that way. I just can't believe how beautiful you look in that dress. Now come here, and give me a kiss."

Julie shook her head and backed away. "Remember the quarantine," she said firmly.

"I do," Sam said as he moved forward.

"No close physical contact," Julie reminded.

"Uh-huh," Sam agreed, all the while moving forward at a steady pace.

"You aren't going to break the rules," Julie asked as she came to a stop against the wall, "are you?"

"Yup," Sam said and pulled her against him tightly. "If love could kill a man, I'd already be dead," he said as he lowered his mouth to Julie's and kissed her soundly.

Julie's mind went blank as her senses came alive. What was the cologne Sam was wearing, and why hadn't she noticed before how soft his beard was?

Voices down the hall brought Julie back to her senses. She pushed at Sam with both hands and gasped for air. "I've got to get back to work," she said and maneuvered under his sinewy arms.

"We can, uh, talk later," she said, pulling on her parka and acknowledging Dr. Welch as he approached.

Sam grinned at her embarrassment, but let it go at that. He'd have plenty of time later.

Chapter 13

B y the morning of January 30, Leonhard Seppala had been given the go-ahead and had moved his huskies out across the trail to press ever closer to the serum.

The people of Nome were frantic. There had been five deaths, twenty-two active cases, and thirty-some suspected cases of diphtheria. All they could do was wait and make those who were ill as comfortable as possible.

Julie was working with Dr. Welch when Sergeant Anderson arrived with a message from Territorial Governor Scott Bone. He was requesting that more relays be set up between Nulato and Nome, as the army reported a severe change in the weather.

"This isn't good," Dr. Welch said as he motioned Julie to follow him. "Sergeant, round up as many of the council members as you can. Julie, you go along with him and get whoever will come with you to join us at the bank. We need more drivers!"

Julie nodded and raced down the hall behind the sergeant, pulling her coat along with her as she stepped into the street. They took opposite sides of the street and worked their way down the storefronts, calling out to those inside as they went.

By one o'clock, a nice crowd had gathered at the bank. Outside the skies had turned overcast, and the wind had picked up. A storm was moving in from the northwest, and Julie was thankful that she wouldn't be required to drive her team out in the blizzard.

"If I may have your attention," Dr. Welch announced. "I have received word from the governor. He has requested we arrange for more relay points along the mail route. The weather forecast has the interior of Alaska turning into a dangerous situation. The suggestion is that more men can travel fewer miles and the risk to life would be reduced significantly."

"But Seppala's already on his way," M. L. Summers declared.

"Yes, I know. He'll no doubt catch up to the serum at one point or another, but instead of having to turn right around and travel all the way back to Nome, he'll only have to make a portion of the journey. I need volunteers to go out along the lines of the mail route and position themselves at the roadhouses."

Several hands went up, including Sam's. Julie caught her breath. What if the storm grew so bad that Sam's life was threatened? Could she stand to see him go, risking his life and the possibility of never returning, without declaring her love?

Her love? Julie tested the thought again. *Yes,* she thought excitedly. *I do love him. I really do, and to lose him now would be devastating.* She didn't hear the rest of Dr. Welch's speech. Her mind was intent on how she could share her heart with Sam. She couldn't throw herself into his arms and tell him, or could she?

The meeting broke up, and Julie recognized Gunnar Kaasen and Ed Rohn, as they had both agreed, with Sam, to participate on the serum run. She waited nervously for Dr. Welch to finish instructing the three men so that she could talk to Sam.

After several minutes, Julie thought better of talking to Sam in public and made her way down the hall. There hadn't been all that much snow, she reasoned, so she'd walk to Sam's house on the edge of Nome and wait for him there.

Julie was concerned to see that the storm was skirting to the east of Nome. It was headed directly toward the path the serum would have to take, so she prayed that it would pass quickly and blow itself out into Norton Sound before it could cause harm to the dog teams. She hurried to Sam's house and went inside to wait for him.

Minutes later, Sam arrived. He was busy with the dogs outside the back door, but Julie knew he'd have to come inside to get provisions before leaving. Nervously, she twisted her hands, wondering what to say when he finally appeared.

Outside, the wind howled, and while it hadn't yet begun to snow, Sam recognized the dangerous look of the storm. He quickly harnessed his best dogs to the sled, deciding to take eight strong malamutes, then made his way into the house.

Julie almost laughed at the shocked expression on Sam's face as he came rushing through the back door, nearly knocking her to the floor.

"Oh Sam," Julie said as her voice cracked. She was quite frightened for him and threw herself into his arms, just as she'd thought she couldn't do.

"What's all this about?" Sam questioned as he pulled away just enough to see Julie's face.

"I'm so frightened for you, and I just couldn't let you go out there without telling you. . ." Julie's words faded as she lowered her head.

Sam lifted her face to meet his gaze. "Telling me what?"

"That I love you," Julie said and broke into tears. "Oh Sam, I love you so much it hurts."

Sam laughed out loud and whirled Julie in a circle. Julie sobbed all the harder as she thought of how she'd come to love Sam's boisterous laugh and wondered if, after today, she'd ever hear it again.

"Now stop that," Sam said as he held Julie's trembling body against his own. Her tears pained him in a way he'd never known. "Don't cry, Julie. Everything is going to be all right. You'll see."

"But the storm is coming up too fast, and you have to go so far to get to your point on the relay. I couldn't bear it if I lost you now," she cried.

"Nothing's going to happen to me, silly. I've got too much to live for now that I have you. Did you really mean it? Do you honestly love me?"

Julie rolled her still-damp eyes. "How can you ask that? I thought you knew I loved you before I knew."

"Then everything is going to work out. God sent you to me, and He won't separate us now," Sam said confidently.

"Can we pray?" Julie asked as she wiped at her tears with the back of her hand. "I mean, together?"

"Oh Julie," Sam's face sobered as he spoke, "I'd love to pray with you. Come on." He led the way to the front room where Julie had previously fallen asleep. He stopped and knelt in front of the small table that held his Bible. "Come here," he motioned, and Julie felt a sudden peace.

Kneeling beside him, Julie felt Sam take hold of her hand in his. With his free hand, Sam began to turn the pages of the Bible. Julie reached up and stopped him.

"May I?" she asked with huge, saucer eyes.

"Of course," Sam replied and let Julie turn to Psalm 121.

"'I will lift up mine eyes unto the hills,'" Julie read, "'from whence cometh my help. My help cometh from the Lord, which made heaven and earth. He will not suffer thy foot to be moved: he that keepeth thee will not slumber. Behold, he that keepeth Israel shall neither slumber nor sleep.'"

She paused for a moment, then lifted her gaze from the Bible and recited the words while looking into Sam's dark eyes. "'The Lord is thy keeper: the Lord is thy shade upon thy right hand. The sun shall not smite thee by day, nor the moon by night. The Lord shall preserve thee from all evil: he shall preserve thy soul. The Lord shall preserve thy going out and thy coming in from this time forth, and even for evermore.'"

"Amen," Sam replied when Julie had finished.

"Amen," Julie echoed. "I feel much better giving you over to the Lord than just worrying about you and struggling through it alone."

Sam helped Julie to her feet and kissed her gently on the lips. "I love you, Julie. You've made me a very happy man today, and when I get back and this epidemic is behind us, I'll expect an answer to my proposal."

Julie nodded, and after one last hug, she rushed from the room and hurried back to work.

---#---

By five thirty, Dr. Welch was sending an exhausted Julie back to the hospital to rest. She had taken to sleeping in the same room she'd occupied her first night in Nome, and after being up and working for over twelve hours, Julie was ready to relax.

Julie made her way through the deserted streets, wondering about the serum that would save the lives of many and whether Sam was safely to his destination. She paid little attention to anything else, until a whining sound at her feet brought Julie's full attention to the source.

"Kodiak!" she exclaimed as she reached down to the dog's obviously cut harness. She felt her heart skip a beat as she recognized blood on Kodiak's fur. Pulling him into better light, Julie could see that he'd been injured.

Scooping the dog into her arms, Julie made her way to the hospital. Mindless of Nurse Morgan's protests, Julie took Kodiak to her room and flipped on the lights.

"What happened to you, boy?" Julie asked as she examined the dog. He was suffering from cuts on his face and neck but otherwise looked to be in decent shape. But if Kodiak had been cut loose from the harness, Sam was in trouble.

Bedding the dog down in her room, Julie pulled the pins from her nurse's cap and tossed it to the table. She slipped out of her uniform and donned heavy wool long johns and denim jeans before pulling on reliable sealskin pants.

She tucked a heavy flannel shirt into her pants and pulled on thick wool socks and her mukluks. Throwing together a bag of supplies, including her medical bag, Julie gave Kodiak her promise to find Sam, locked the door behind her, and went to harness her dog team.

Julie searched unsuccessfully for someone who might help her. She caught up with Dr. Welch at one of the quarantined homes and begged for his help.

"I can't leave Nome, Julie. You know these people are dying," Dr. Welch said firmly. "Try to find someone else to help you. If Sam is hurt, bring him to the hospital, and then I can better serve him."

"I understand," Julie said in a resigned tone. She went in search of anyone who might accompany her, and when no one offered to help, Julie made the decision to go alone.

She packed extra ropes and blankets on her sled, uncertain of what she might need or how far she'd have to go to find Sam. Against her better judgment, Julie retrieved Kodiak from her room.

"I'm sorry, boy," she said as she brought the dog out into the sub-zero darkness. "I need you to help me find Sam." Kodiak yipped as if he understood and paced back and forth until Julie finished hanging two lighted lanterns from her sled.

She had planned on harnessing Kodiak to her own team but realized he would be of more help if she allowed him to run free. "All right, boy," she called out to Kodiak. "Find Sam."

She moved the team out behind Kodiak and was surprised to find that the wounded dog responded as though he were in perfect condition. "Dear God," Julie breathed as the wind assaulted her face, "please help me find Sam, and please let him be alive and safe."

Cold numbed Julie's face as she struggled to fix her parka hood. How far would she have to go in order to find Sam? Should she take the time to get her brother and father's help? As Kodiak picked up the pace, Julie decided against any detours. A delay could mean death.

The trail was overblown with snow. Steep, icy embankments lined the Bering side, and darkness made it impossible to see. But Julie was sure of her dogs and pressed on.

After an hour, Kodiak began to yip and slow his pace. Suddenly, the dog howled and danced around. Julie stopped the team and buried the snow hook.

"Sam! Sam!" she called out and listened in the silence for a reply.

Kodiak sat at the side of the embankment and whined. Julie grabbed one of the sled's lanterns and peered over the edge. At the bottom of the embankment rested Sam's overturned sled.

"Sam!"

Julie returned to her sled and pulled out two lengths of rope. She secured them to the sled and threw them down the embankment. She also retrieved several blankets from the sled and tossed them after the ropes. Then, taking her medical bag and lantern, she gripped the rope and worked her way down the embankment.

When she reached the bottom of the icy slope, Julie was stunned by what she saw. Several of Sam's dogs were dead. Her heart beat faster as she righted the sled, praying that it wouldn't reveal Sam's dead body. The sled turned over with a thud and exposed nothing more than an indentation in the snow.

"Sam, where are you?" Julie called into the night. The yips of several dogs sent her in search of their source. A few yards away, Julie found the rest of the team faithfully surrounding Sam's lifeless form. He'd been able to cut the dogs loose from the tangled harness before he passed out in the snow.

Julie positioned the lantern to offer the best light and spread a blanket beside Sam. The dogs seemed to know that their job was done, and they allowed Julie to work without interference. She gently rolled Sam onto the blanket.

"Oh Sam," she whispered as she saw the matted blood in his hair. Examining more closely, Julie found a nasty cut along Sam's hairline. She felt quickly for a pulse to assure herself that he was still alive.

Finding a steady pulse and realizing that the bleeding was minimal, Julie wasted no time tending the wound except to wrap it with a length of bandage. She examined Sam's sled basket to see if it was in good enough shape to use. The runners and the basket's side were broken, but the damaged sled would work well enough to get Sam up the embankment.

Working the ropes around the sled, Julie prayed for strength. She had to take off her mittens for several minutes at a time in order to tie the ropes securely. Fearing frostbite, she worked quickly to finish with the ropes.

When she felt confident that the sled was secured, Julie positioned the basket beside Sam's still form. Wrapping the blanket around Sam, Julie rolled his body into the basket and tied him securely in place. The dogs who'd survived the accident scurried up the embankment behind Julie as she prepared to pull Sam up.

Realizing Sam's dogs could help, Julie pulled out an extra harness and added them to her team. Then she pulled the snow hook and took hold of the harness.

"Come on, boys. Let's go," she called as she pulled them forward. The dogs strained against the basket but pulled eagerly as if they sensed the life-and-death issue at hand.

As the basket with Sam's battered body appeared over the top of the embankment, Julie quickly secured the snow hook and went to him. He was still unconscious.

"Please, God," she prayed as she packed Sam in blankets. "Please help me to get him home."

Julie knew the basket containing Sam's body was useless for the trail. Using all her strength, she lifted first one end of the broken basket and then the other until she'd managed to place it solidly atop her own sled. Convinced that Sam was as safe as she could make him, Julie moved the dogs out and headed for Nome.

Chapter 14

Julie paced anxiously while Dr. Welch inspected Sam's wounds. She tried to remain objective, reminding herself that she could only help if she kept her fears under control.

"There's quite a bit of swelling," Dr. Welch said as he finished his examination of Sam, "especially his left eye. We'll watch him closely. Hand me some gauze, please."

Automatically, Julie performed her duties as she would for anyone else, but her heart kept reminding her that this wasn't just anyone else. This was the man she loved. What would she do if he didn't make it? Julie watched Dr. Welch stitch up Sam's head wound.

"Why doesn't he wake up? He should be awake by now." She knew she sounded frantic.

"Julie, you're a nurse. Get ahold of yourself or leave the room. You know these things, especially when they involve concussions, are very unpredictable."

"I know," Julie replied. "I just wish it didn't have to happen to Sam."

"We've done all we can," Dr. Welch said as he tied a bandage in place. "Now, we'll have to wait and see what happens. Come along."

Julie nodded and went to the sanctuary of her own room. As soon as she closed the door, she fell to her knees and threw herself against the bed. "Dear God, I love Sam so very much. Please help him." Julie stayed on her knees praying for over an hour. When the clock chimed eleven, she rose and went down the hall to where Sam lay motionless.

Sitting beside his bed, Julie held Sam's hand and felt for a pulse. Finding it steady and strong, she exhaled deeply. She patted Sam's hand gently and spoke to him as if he were wide awake.

"Sam, I wanted you to know that your dogs have been cared for. I treated them as if they were my own. Kodiak had some nasty cuts, but I washed them out and put salve on them. He'll be just fine. I knew you'd be worried about the dogs, so I wanted to tell you." She grimaced as she leaned closer. Sam's left eye looked painfully swollen, and Julie offered up a prayer for his healing.

"I love you, Sam. Please wake up. Please be all right," she whispered as she held his hand against her face.

Julie sat in the soft light and watched Sam's chest rise and fall in even, rhythmic breathing. She lost track of time, needing to know that Sam was alive, even if he wasn't conscious.

"Julie?"

Julie roused herself, startled to find that she'd fallen asleep.

"Julie?" The strained, husky voice belonged to Sam.

"Oh Sam!" Julie said, with tears streaming down her face. "You're awake. Oh, thank God."

"Where am I?" he asked weakly.

"The Nome hospital," Julie answered and rinsed out a cloth in cool water. She placed it against Sam's forehead.

"I hurt," Sam said with a sheepish grin. "I guess I took a bit of a fall."

"Just a bit." Julie returned the smile.

"Who brought me in?"

"I did," Julie answered, and nearly laughed at the surprised look that crossed Sam's face. "I tried to get someone to help me, but with the epidemic and the serum run, well, people were just preoccupied."

"How did you find me?" Sam asked as he tried painfully to sit up.

"Stay put," Julie said, with firm hands upon Sam's shoulders. "You took a nasty hit on the head, and you need to rest."

Sam fell weakly back against the pillows. "All right."

"Kodiak found me," Julie said abruptly.

"Kodiak? Is he okay?"

"He's fine. He's cut up a bit, but he led me to you and helped to pull us back to Nome."

"What about the others?"

"There were four dead when I got there," Julie said softly. "I'm sorry, Sam. I know how you love your dogs."

"I remember cutting them loose from the harness, but after that—nothing."

"The dogs saved your life," Julie added. "They were keeping you from freezing to death when I found you."

"They're a good bunch," Sam said, sounding tired.

"You'd better rest now. I'll check in on you from time to time, and Dr. Welch will be back in the morning," Julie said and got to her feet to leave.

Sam took hold of her hand and pulled her down. "Kiss me," he said, refusing to let go of her.

"Same old Sam," Julie said, and pressed her lips gently against his.

Sam smiled up at Julie. "You wouldn't have me any other way," he murmured.

"No," Julie said, "I suppose I wouldn't." She gently let go of Sam's hand. "Now, sleep."

———— # ————

Julie divided her time between Sam and the diphtheria patients. She was glad to see Sam's body healing so quickly, but worried as he became more moody and distant.

"I've brought you a special lunch," Julie said as she brought Sam a tray she'd prepared for him.

"I don't want it," Sam said and continued reading the newspaper that she'd brought him that morning.

"Sam," Julie said as she put the tray on the table beside his bed, "why are you doing this to me?"

"What do you mean?"

"Do you still love me?" Julie asked directly.

Sam's grim expression softened a bit. "This has nothing to do with you. Of course I still love you."

"Then what is this all about? Why are you so angry?" Julie demanded. "It's more than enough that I deal with dying children day by day. It's almost too much to bear that, with all the schooling and training I've received, I still can't help them. Now you're acting strange, and I haven't a clue what it's all about."

"This," Sam said as he threw the paper down, "is what it's all about."

Julie noticed the headlines. They were bold reminders that the life-saving serum was ever closer to Nome. "I don't understand. You're upset because the serum run is nearly complete?"

"I don't expect you to understand," Sam said and folded his arms across his chest. "It's just that I wanted to be part of it. I wanted to help bring the serum to Nome. Instead I'm here in this hospital like a useless lump of coal."

"Sam Curtiss, I don't believe you. You were nearly killed, and now you're feeling sorry for yourself?"

"I told you I didn't expect you to understand. Now just let me alone. I'll deal with it myself."

"I will not," Julie said firmly. "Would you walk away from me if I were behaving this way?"

Sam grinned sheepishly. "You have acted this way and, no, I didn't leave you alone."

"Well, then," Julie said and pulled a chair up to Sam's bedside, "I'm just as stubborn as you are and," she paused and smiled lovingly, "I care just as much."

Sam shook his head. "I've always been lucky, fortunate, blessed, whatever people want to call it. I usually get what I set my mind on, and it's hard not to go on getting my way."

"I'm certain that, for a man like you, missing out on something important is very difficult, but God has all of this in His perfect plan.

Sam, it doesn't matter that you won't be the one to bring the serum into Nome. What matters is that the serum gets here safely without any more loss of life."

"I know all that. Believe me, I've reasoned it out in my head, but I wanted to do this. Not just for me, mind you." Sam paused and seemed to struggle to put his feelings into words. "But for God. He's done so much for me, and I wanted to offer Him a small token of thanks."

"You do many things that offer God thanks, Sam. You are a positive asset to God's family, and you simply need to keep in mind that whatever you do, you are doing the work of God."

"Colossians 3:23, huh?" Sam said reluctantly.

"'And whatsoever ye do, do it heartily, as to the Lord, and not unto men,'" Julie quoted. "My mother was fond of that verse. She told me that anything a person did was a mission for God so long as they committed their ways to Him."

"Kind of humbles a guy," Sam said with a grin.

"It doesn't matter that you didn't run the serum, Sam. It doesn't matter what you do, so long as you do it for God and do it for His glory. I'd love you whether you raised dogs or panned gold. It doesn't matter to me what you do with your life so long as it's committed to God's will and I'm part of it," Julie said with all her heart.

Sam wrapped his arms around Julie. "You will always be a part of my life," he whispered against her ear. "Just as God will always be at the center of it. I'm glad you had the strength of faith to speak directly with me. We're going to be good for each other, because when one of us falls, the other will lift him up."

"Two are better than one," Julie murmured.

"Yes," Sam said. "Reminds me of Genesis 2:18: 'And the Lord God said, It is not good that the man should be alone; I will make him an help meet for him.' Will you be that for me, Julie? Will you marry me?"

Julie held up her left hand. "You told me one day I'd come to you wearing this ring and you would have your answer. Well, here I am, and the answer is yes."

Chapter 15

S am was released from the hospital the next day. The first thing he did was to find a minister who could leave the sick and dying long enough to perform a wedding ceremony.

Julie was heading from the hospital to the doctor's office when Sam caught up with her. Protesting all the way, Julie allowed Sam to lead her to the church.

"But Sam," she said as they neared the church building, "I'm still wearing my nurse's uniform."

"It doesn't matter," Sam said with a grin. "You could be wearing long johns and it wouldn't matter to me. Besides, it's white."

Julie sighed and realized the weariness that threatened to overtake her. "I suppose you're right. It's just that, well," she paused as they approached the church steps, "a girl kind of has in mind all of her life the type of wedding she wants. This just doesn't fit my dream."

Sam stopped and pulled Julie into his arms. "Look," he said softly, "if you don't want to get married today, I understand. I won't force this on you."

Julie looked up at Sam, noticing the bandage on his forehead and the discoloration around his eye. He was still handsome to her and with all of her heart she wanted to be his wife. "No one's forcing anything on me," Julie answered as she reached up and pushed a wave of brown hair back off Sam's face. "I want to marry you today."

"Maybe we could have a big church wedding after the epidemic is resolved. I heard that the serum is due in within twenty-four hours—that is, if the weather holds."

"That would be wonderful," Julie said to both thoughts.

"Well then, let's not keep the minister waiting," Sam said and pulled Julie with him up the steps.

It wasn't an ideal wedding, but it was more than enough to serve the purpose for which it was intended. Two people pledged to God and one another that they would love each other forever and never allow anything or anyone to come between them.

———#———

Looking down at the ring on her finger later that day, Julie remembered the hasty ceremony. She tried to imagine how surprised her father and brother would be when they received the short letter she'd sent. With the quarantine in place and no telephone at the Eriksson household, it was difficult to get information to them.

Her father would be pleased; August, too. Of that, Julie was certain. How she wished they could have given her away to Sam. For a fleeting moment, Julie thought of her mother. Agneta would have approved of the hurried wedding.

Julie's reflections were pushed aside, however, in the face of Nome's crisis. Once again she'd been called to the house of yet another victim of diphtheria, and as she felt the forehead of a small Eskimo girl, Julie's happy memories blurred. The child was burning with fever and most likely would die sometime soon. It seemed strange that something as wonderful as her wedding day would also be the day this child's parents would bury their only daughter.

Julie moved from one house to another. Always, she found various stages of diphtheria. Many were frightened at the news that they were showing the early signs of the disease. Julie worked to calm their nerves, reminding each one that the serum was due into Nome any day. Others were too sick to worry, and Julie prayed aloud for them as she nursed their weakened bodies.

As Julie stood beside the cradle of an eight-month-old baby, she thought how unjust it all was. There was help for this disease. She had training and skills that should save lives, but it still wasn't enough.

"God," she whispered, "why must it be this way?" She thought of the verses in Job and of her mother's dying. Surely her father had voiced that question enough times while sitting beside his dying wife. Hadn't Julie herself asked it of God? She remembered how her mother had correlated verses in Job with everyday life.

"Julie, we don't always know why God allows certain things to happen. We can't have all the answers just yet, because God knows they would be too much for our human minds to comprehend," her mother had told her. *"God, in His sovereign wisdom, made all things for a purpose, and how each of those things comes into this world or goes out is entirely up to Him."*

"'Whence then cometh wisdom? and where is the place of understanding?'" Julie's mother had shared from Job 28:20. Julie remembered the moment with fondness. Her mother's greatest desire had been for her family to understand that her illness was neither just nor unjust. It was part of God's overall picture for their lives. That same chapter had answered its questions: *"And unto man he said, Behold, the fear of the Lord, that is wisdom; and to depart from evil is understanding."*

Julie lifted the dying infant into her arms. The baby's lifeless eyes stared up at her as his tiny lungs drew a final breath. She felt the child's body shudder and knew that he was gone. Gone from this earth but at peace in heaven with his Creator. Julie noted the time, returned the infant to his cradle, and recorded facts about the death before breaking the news to the parents.

———*#*———

Several hours later, Dr. Welch found Julie in a near stupor as she sat beside a child while its mother napped.

"You need to get some rest," Dr. Welch said as he checked the child over. "You've been on duty for over twelve hours by my calculations, and that's too much. Go home, Julie. Go home and get some rest."

"I'm fine," Julie said as she stood on the opposite side of the child's bed. "This is Joey. He's only been showing signs of diphtheria for the last eight hours. Temperature is 101 degrees, and his throat is sore but not overwhelmingly so."

"Good," Dr. Welch said as he finished listening to the boy's chest. "The serum should arrive in time to fix you right up, son." The boy smiled weakly but didn't say anything. He'd already told Julie it hurt to talk, and she had encouraged him to remain silent.

Dr. Welch packed his bag and headed for the open bedroom door. "Don't tarry any longer than you have to, Julie. Go home and sleep."

Julie nodded, even though she had no intention of obeying.

When Dr. Welch returned to his office, he picked up the telephone and put a call through to Sam.

"Sam?" he said as a voice sounded through the line.

"Yes, this is Sam Curtiss."

"Sam, this is Dr. Welch. Look, I need you to come get your wife."

"Is she sick?" Panic filled Sam's heart.

"No, but she will be if she doesn't get some rest. She's ready to collapse, and I've tried to send her home to sleep, but she won't go. I was hoping you could come force the issue."

"No problem. I'll be right there," Sam answered. "By the way, where should I look for her?"

"I left her at the Davises' house. I imagine she'll be there for a while."

"I'm on my way," Sam said and hung up the phone. *Stubborn woman,* he thought as he pulled on his coat and hiked out into the darkened streets.

At the Davises' house, Sam knocked, then opened the door and walked in. Mrs. Davis appeared in the hallway just as Sam stepped inside. "Sam Curtiss," she said in a surprised tone. "What are you doing here?"

"I've come to get my wife," Sam said firmly. "I'm sorry to bother you, but Doc says she needs to rest and won't go home."

The woman nodded and led Sam to her son's bedroom. "She's in there," Mrs. Davis said as she opened the door. "I tried to get her to take a break, but she wouldn't hear of it."

Sam looked in to find Julie's dozing form as she sat beside the sleeping boy. Gently, Sam helped her to her feet and led her from the room.

"Sam," Julie protested. "What are you doing here?"

"Doc sent me," Sam said as he took Julie's parka from Mrs. Davis. "He said you were to go home and sleep and that he didn't want to see you back until you were rested."

"But—"

"No buts," Sam said, helping her into her coat. "You're going home if I have to carry you—and you know that's no idle threat—so just be cooperative and we won't cause a scene."

"These people need me," Julie said as the parka fell into place. "I can't leave them."

"You aren't any good to them if you're dead on your feet."

"You don't understand the importance of what I do," Julie said as Sam led her out into the street.

"You're in our prayers, Mrs. Davis," Sam said as he pulled Julie along. The woman waved from her door. "Now listen to me," he continued with Julie, "no job is worth killing yourself over. You have an important duty to these people, but it's certainly not one that anyone expects you to die doing."

Julie tried to jerk away from Sam's grip. Maybe marrying Sam had been a mistake. Maybe he was going to expect her to give up her nursing career. Her mind reeled as Sam forced her along. They hadn't consummated their marriage, Julie reasoned. Perhaps she could dissolve it. But that wasn't what she wanted either. Besides, she loved Sam, and she had made a promise to God to continue loving and obeying him. If Sam told her to quit nursing, she would have to go along.

Just then, George Maynard came rushing down the street.

"It's the serum," he yelled. "The governor's relayed for us to halt the run because of the weather. Gunnar Kaasen will have to lay over in Solomon until the storm clears."

"He can't," Julie said as she felt her strength give way. "He can't!"

"Hush, Julie," Sam said as he pulled her close. "George, are you sure there's no way to get the drivers through?"

"The wind is blowing up to forty knots, and that coupled with the snow is making it impossible for anyone to get through."

"But people are dying," Julie said, nearing hysteria. "They have to get the serum through. They have to."

Sam steadied Julie's trembling body. "Look, keep us posted. I need to get my wife home for some rest."

"Your wife?" George questioned in surprise.

Sam grinned. "Yeah, we were married in between jobs."

"Well congratulations! It's nice that something decent can take place in the middle of this tragedy." George went hurrying off, and Sam helped Julie make it to their house.

By the time they'd reached the house, Julie was sobbing. She'd tried so hard to hold everything inside, but with the fear that the serum wouldn't arrive in time, Julie could no longer control her emotions.

Sam guided her into the house and helped her out of the parka. He could hardly bear the sounds of her sobs, and after pulling his own coat off, he took her into his arms and held her.

"They're going to die without the serum," Julie cried. "I can't bear to watch any more of them die."

"I know. I know," Sam said as he reached up and pulled the pins out of Julie's hair. The ebony mane fell soft across her shoulders, and Sam relished the feel of it.

"I can't help them, Sam," she said looking up with dark, wet eyes. "I'm useless to them."

"Nonsense," Sam said. "Come on. I'm going to take you upstairs and put you to bed. You're tired and distraught with what you've had to deal with today. I wish I could have given you a better wedding day."

Julie allowed Sam to lead her to what was to become their bedroom. Neither she nor Sam were thinking about the romance of their wedding night, however. His only concern was to calm her down and see to it that she got some much-needed sleep.

Julie steadied her nerves and dried her eyes. She was too tired to expend more energy on useless tears. Sam helped her to the edge of the bed, where he knelt down and unlaced her mukluks.

"Now," Sam said as he threw the boots to one side. "You rest, and I'll go get a wet cloth for you to wipe your face with."

"No!" Julie exclaimed. "Please don't leave me, Sam. I can't be alone right now."

Sam smiled and unlaced his own boots. "I'll hold you until you're asleep, and even after that, if you like."

"I like," Julie said and moved over to make room for her husband.

Sam eased his weight onto the bed and pulled Julie into his arms. Neither one of them had ever experienced a closeness like this. It was so intimate, so pure.

"Sam," Julie murmured as she put her head upon his chest. "The serum has to get through. We should pray for a miracle."

"You're right of course. Why didn't we think of that earlier?"

"I don't know. I guess we were just too busy trying to take care of everything ourselves. At least I know I was. I hate myself for always resorting to prayer as a final option," Julie replied.

"Don't hate yourself," Sam stated firmly. "You are a creation of God, and He loves you. I forget the importance of prayer myself. We'll just pray for a miracle and ask God to deliver the serum into Dr. Welch's hands in record time."

"But if the governor has ordered the race stopped," Julie began, "it would be against the law to continue. Wouldn't it?"

"I suppose it might be perceived that way," Sam said with a nod. "However, a guy has to get the message in order to heed it, right? Maybe Gunnar won't get the message."

"I suppose that's always possible," Julie said with renewed hope.

"Thank you for being such an encouragement, Sam."

They prayed together, and Julie fell asleep to the comfort of Sam's powerful, heartfelt words. For the first time in many days, she slept soundly with the assurance that God and Sam were at her side to protect her from the pain of the world.

Sam awoke with a start and, forgetting his wife was nestled in his arms, he woke Julie without meaning to.

"What is it, Sam?" Julie asked as she registered the sound of barking dogs.

"I don't know, but the dogs are going crazy. What time is it, anyway?"

Julie glanced at her watch. "Five thirty," she replied and got to her feet. "Maybe Dr. Welch has come to find me. Maybe things are worse, and he needs my help."

"You aren't going anywhere," Sam said firmly. "You've only had a little over five hours of sleep, and that simply isn't enough. Get back into bed."

Julie felt as though she'd had a week's worth of sleep and stood with her hands planted firmly on her hips. "I will not be treated like a child, Sam Curtiss. I'm your wife, not one of your dogs."

Sam broke into a hearty laugh. "Well, Julie Curtiss," he said trying the name on for size, "my dogs have better sense than you when it comes to taking care of themselves. However, you are right. I'm used to telling, not asking. I'm sorry. Now, would you please get back into bed?"

The dogs had worked themselves into a feverish pitch, and Julie could stand it no longer. "Sam, please find out what's going on. Please."

Sam lost his resolve as he stared into the pleading eyes of his wife. "Oh, all right. But afterwards, you must get some rest."

"Whatever you say, husband."

Sam was gone only a few minutes. When he returned, he tossed Julie her mukluks. "You'd better get these on."

"What is it, Sam?" Julie asked as she hastened to tie her laces.

"Just come with me," Sam said and hurried down the stairs with

Julie close behind him. He brought her parka and waited while Julie pulled it over her head.

"Something's very wrong, isn't it?" Julie asked fearfully.

"On the contrary, Julie. On the contrary," Sam said as he opened the front door. "Hurry."

Sam and Julie raced through the darkened streets and Julie knew instinctively that Sam was leading her to the hospital. They rounded the corner. A dog team stood at the front stairs. Julie's heart skipped a beat as she recognized Balto, a big black-and-white husky who was a favorite of Gunnar's.

"Oh Sam," she breathed against the subzero air. "It's Gunnar's sled! The serum is here!"

"Looks like we got that miracle," Sam said with a grin that spread from ear to ear. "Come on. Let's go see if we can help." Julie nodded and followed her husband up the steps. God was so good!

Chapter 16

Gunnar's arrival had attracted very little attention. It was too early in the morning for most people, and no one thought the serum would come through because of the governor's mandate.

Julie stood by crying tears of joy as Dr. Welch received the cylindrical package and hurried inside to reveal its contents. Sam and Julie joined the party, but their hearts stopped when Dr. Welch announced that the serum was frozen. Everyone waited in pained anticipation, wondering if the trip had been for nothing. Finally word came from Seattle that the serum would be unharmed from the freezing and simply required a slow warming to bring it back to its original state.

Gunnar Kaasen and his huskies had covered the last fifty-three miles in less than seven and a half hours. The entire serum run had covered more than 674 miles in a record 127.5 hours, bringing with it the renewed hope of life.

By February 21, Nome's quarantine was lifted. It had been exactly one month since the outbreak of the epidemic.

With every passing day, life seemed to take on a more normal routine. Schools reopened, much to the disappointment of the children and the relief of the parents. Store owners were happy to have full shops again, and everywhere people were glad to have lived through the crisis. George Nakoota even showed up to reveal a perfectly healed arm to Dr. Welch.

It was no different at the Curtiss house. Julie and Sam had settled into a comfortable life at the edge of town, and although Julie had been extremely busy nursing the sick and helping Dr. Welch, Sam had been patient with her absences. Julie wondered, however, how long it would be before Sam's patience wore thin and he would demand that she stay home more.

Several days after the quarantine had been lifted, Julie contemplated the situation as she prepared breakfast. Her heart belonged to Sam, yet part of her belonged to nursing as well.

"You're mighty deep in thought," Sam said as he came into the room and took a seat at the table. He threw the *Nome Nugget* on the chair beside him and smiled. "I suppose you're thinking about the serum run again."

"Well, as a matter of fact, I heard something quite fascinating yesterday," Julie said as she offered Sam a plate of fried eggs and bacon. She returned to the counter, where she retrieved a stack of freshly baked biscuits. Their tantalizing aroma filled the air, and as soon as Julie placed them on the table, Sam reached for one.

"No doubt another miracle," Sam teased. Julie had been enthralled by the stories of miraculous blessings that enabled the drivers to deliver the diphtheria antitoxin to Nome in only five and a half days.

Julie put her own plate of food on the table and joined Sam. "You know how I love the way God moved in this crisis." She smiled. "I just can't help being fascinated with it."

"I know, Julie, and I feel the same way. Let's have a prayer." Sam took her hands. "Father, we thank You for the bounty of our table and for the healing of our community. We praise You that the deaths were few and that the medicine was provided in a much quicker time than any of us dreamed possible. Amen."

Sam started eating as Julie began to tell what she'd heard. "Leonhard Seppala cut out a lot of distance by taking a shortcut across Norton Sound. The water was frozen solid, but it was difficult for him to see his way, so he had to rely upon the dogs."

"I'd heard that," Sam answered. "It takes a brave man to venture out across an open bay like that. Even if it is frozen solid at the shores, you can't know how it will be once you get out in the middle of the inlet."

"Well, as wondrous as that was, what happened after Leonhard crossed the sound gives even more cause for praise," Julie said, leaning forward. "Not more than three and a half hours after Leonhard crossed Norton Sound, the entire thing broke up, and the ice moved out into the Bering Sea. The crossing would have taken Leonhard's life, no doubt, had he attempted it at a later time. Talk about the hand of God!"

"Incredible," Sam said as he paused between bites. "Our God is truly a God of miracles."

"Leonhard's shortcut saved hours and probably many lives, Sam. I'm amazed that he was able to stay on the sled. After all, he'd driven those dogs for more than 169 miles just to get to the serum at Shaktolik. Then to turn around and travel another ninety-one miles to get the serum closer to Nome, well. . ." Julie shook her head. "It staggers my imagination."

"That lead dog of his is something else," Sam said, sipping his coffee. "His name is Togo, and Leonhard never thought he'd amount to much—that is, until he jumped the fence one day and followed Leonhard across part of the interior. Leonhard finally harnessed him up to keep him out of trouble. Lo and behold, the dog's a born leader!"

"Thanks to Togo and the other dogs, Nome is safe, and the epidemic has been defeated," Julie said. "I simply can't imagine the way God planned this all out. Who can know the mind of God?"

"I know how much you've enjoyed learning about the hazards that the men met on the trail. I have one that I think you will find quite rewarding," Sam said with a smile.

"Oh, tell me, Sam! What did you hear?" Julie asked as she leaned forward, her eyes wide in anticipation.

"You remember we heard that the run was to be halted because of the weather?"

"Sure, I do," Julie said with a nod. "How could I forget? I've never lost control like that in my life."

"Well," Sam continued, "it was just about the time we decided to pray that Gunnar Kaasen made the decision to drive on past Solomon and keep the serum moving. He felt compelled to go on and not waste time with a stop. No one had the opportunity to tell him about the mandate from the governor because he never stopped."

"It's just like you said," Julie remembered. "A man can't be faulted for not doing what he knows nothing about. Good for Gunnar!"

"Well, there's more," Sam said as he finished his breakfast. "The wind came up something fierce, and Gunnar couldn't see a thing in front of him. All of a sudden his lead dog, Balto, stopped dead in his tracks. Gunnar couldn't understand why, but Balto wouldn't budge."

"What happened?" Julie asked, captivated by Sam's story.

"Balto had led the team out across the Topkok River, and it wasn't solidly frozen. Balto was standing in running water when he came to a stop."

"Poor thing," Julie sympathized. "His feet could have frozen to the ice. What did Gunnar do? Balto looked just fine when they got into Nome."

"Gunnar's a good man. He thought fast and unharnessed Balto. There was plenty of powdered snow on the banks, so Gunnar rubbed Balto's feet in it until they were fairly dry."

"How ingenious! I've got to remember that one when I'm out on my route," Julie said, braving a reference to her job. Even though the epidemic was over, Julie hadn't found the nerve to talk with Sam about her nursing career. She started to clear the table to avoid Sam's reaction.

"It never hurts to be prepared, and the more you know about surviving accidents, the better off you are. That's what made me so mad about my own accident," Sam reflected. "I knew better than to take the risks I was taking. I should have slowed down a bit and paid more attention. However," he added with a grin, "there was a certain black-haired nurse on my mind. It seems she had just told me that she loved me." Sam pushed his chair back and pulled Julie onto his lap.

"Oh Sam," Julie whispered against his hair. How she wished she could clear things up and explain how she felt about her work. She was so afraid that if she insisted on continuing her nursing career, Sam would stop loving her.

Sam nuzzled his lips against Julie's neck and began kissing her. Julie found the contact electrifying, yet she knew she needed to finish getting ready for work. As gently as she could, she pushed Sam away.

"I've got to finish up here and get down to the hospital," she said and jumped up abruptly. Sam's surprised face told it all. "I'm sorry," Julie whispered and hurried to wash the breakfast dishes.

Sam's silence worried Julie. She wiped the soap suds from her hands and went back to the table where he was still sitting.

"We should talk," she said and waited for Sam to put down the newspaper.

"What about?" Sam asked hesitantly. Julie hadn't been her normal self the last few days, and he wasn't sure that he was up to dealing with whatever was troubling her.

"Sam, do you know how long I dreamed of becoming a nurse?"

"I know it was a longtime dream. I know too that it was a dream you shared with your mother."

"Yes, that's right," Julie said, searching her mind for the right words. "Being a nurse is very important to me, not just because it's a job I do every day, but because of the need. These people are without many of the comforts available in the States, and I want to be a part of seeing to it that they have what they need in the way of health care."

"It's an admirable position," Sam said as he reached out for Julie. "I've always admired your determination and dedication."

Julie stepped back to avoid Sam's touch. He frowned but said nothing.

"It's my determination and dedication to what I believe God wants me to do," Julie said, stressing the reference to God. She paused to see what Sam's reaction might be. His face was unreadable.

"Go on," he said unemotionally. He was troubled by the way Julie had distanced herself from his touch. She hadn't seemed herself since the critical part of the epidemic had passed. Sam was determined to get to the bottom of whatever was bothering her.

"I love what I do, Sam. I love to help people, and I enjoy my work with the natives."

"I don't see what you're getting at, Julie," Sam said more impatiently than he'd intended. "I know that you love your job. I know you love the people and the land. What I don't know is what this has to do with us and why you're acting so strangely."

Sam got up and took two long strides to where Julie stood. He reached out to hold her, but Julie turned away.

"Please don't touch me. I'm trying to explain this to you, and you aren't making matters any easier," Julie said, close to tears.

"Julie, are you sorry that you married me?"

Julie turned back quickly and shook her head. "No, Sam. I love you, and I hope that you still love me."

"Of course I love you." Sam could no longer stand Julie's coolness. He took her into his arms and crushed her to his chest. "I will always love you," he whispered as his lips pressed a long, passionate kiss upon hers.

Julie melted against Sam. She could never imagine life without him. Maybe giving up her career was the only way she could save her marriage. Tears streamed from her eyes. A sob escaped her throat, causing Sam to pull back.

"What in the world?" he muttered and dropped his hands. "I don't understand what this is all about, but I've had just about enough." He stormed out of the room, barely remembering his parka as he went out into the cold.

Julie jumped at the sound of the front door slamming. Knowing it would be impossible to work, Julie retreated upstairs, locked herself in their bedroom, and had a good long cry.

Chapter 17

Julie lost track of time as she contemplated her misery. How could she explain her heart to Sam without hurting him? She loved him so much, yet she felt torn.

She looked around the room that had been hers for a little over a month. Everything here spoke of Sam; the large walnut dresser, the huge four-poster bed, and even the lamps on the nightstands looked masculine and powerful. The room smelled like the heady cologne Sam liked to wear.

"Father," Julie prayed, "I wanted to serve You." Before she could continue, it came to Julie's mind that if she truly wanted to serve God, she'd open her heart and skills to whatever job He gave her. Perhaps the job God wanted Julie to do now involved being a good wife and homemaker. Maybe she was trained as a nurse simply to help during the epidemic.

"I need to understand, Lord. Please teach me what it is I'm to do," Julie begged. "I can't bear to hurt Sam, and I can't bear the way I'm feeling."

Julie reached to the nightstand and picked up her Bible. She flipped aimlessly through the pages, wondering what God might show her there. When she reached Ephesians, Julie began to read through the verses. "Teach me, Lord," she prayed. "I came home to serve You, and now I have a husband to serve and work with as well."

Just then, Julie's eyes fell upon Ephesians 5:22–24: "Wives, submit yourselves unto your own husbands, as unto the Lord. For the husband is the head of the wife, even as Christ is the head of the church: and he is the saviour of the body. Therefore as the church is subject unto Christ, so let the wives be to their own husbands in every thing." It seemed a clear answer.

"All right, Father," Julie said in earnest, "I trust You to guide me. Sam loves You and seeks Your guidance, and because of this, I believe, without fear, that You will control this situation."

Julie got up and dried her eyes. What should she do? Sam was out there somewhere, and no doubt he was feeling just as confused and troubled as she was. Julie debated trying to find him but chose to wait until he returned. She was determined to make her concerns clear. If Sam insisted she give up nursing, then she'd trust God to give her the grace to do just that.

Julie didn't have long to wait. Within the hour, she heard Sam stomping around through the rooms downstairs. Julie brushed her hair and made her way to the top of the stairs just as Sam was starting up.

"We should talk," Julie said softly.

Sam nodded. The anger was gone and in his eyes shone the love that Julie had come to count on.

Julie made her way down the stairs and took Sam's extended hand. "I'm sorry for the way I've been acting. I know you deserve a lot better, and I feel bad about it."

"If I've done something wrong, you should tell me," Sam said as he led Julie to the couch.

"You haven't done anything wrong, Sam. That's what makes this so frustrating to me. I've always been able to speak my mind, but something about you makes me forget myself. I suppose it has a great deal to do with my love for you," Julie said softly. She looked down at her hands, avoiding Sam's face.

"You make your love for me sound like something oppressive," he replied.

"Not oppressive," Julie answered. "Maybe restrictive."

"Restrictive?" Sam questioned. "How so?"

"I'm not sure that *restrictive* is even the right word. I never expected you to come into my life. I don't know why, but I never considered marrying and having a family. At least not until much later in my life."

"And?"

"And," Julie said with deliberation, "I doubt I would have become a public health nurse if I'd known I would be married so soon into my career."

"I still don't understand," Sam said softly.

Julie looked up at him. "I love my job, but I'm ready to give it up if that's what you tell me to do." There! She'd finally managed to get the words out.

"What in the world are you talking about?" Sam asked, confusion spreading across his face. "Why would I ever ask you to quit nursing?"

"Because it takes me away from you. I have to be on the village routes for most of the year, and those absences would keep us separated for long, long spells. I'm not sure I could bear it myself."

"What makes you think that you'll be separated from me?" Sam asked with a grin. "I know what's required of you on your job. I knew it before I ever married you. I even talked with Dr. Welch at length about it."

"You did?" Julie's surprised voice amused Sam.

"I certainly did. You didn't think I'd walk into something like marriage without knowing exactly what I was doing, did you?"

"I guess I never thought about it," Julie replied. "I was too caught up in the epidemic. What did Dr. Welch tell you?"

"He explained your duties and the schedule you'd be keeping as a public health nurse. He told me you'd go by dogsled in the winter months and horseback in the summer. He also told me that the idea of a woman alone on the trails bothered him. I asked him why someone couldn't accompany you."

"And what did he say?"

"He told me there wasn't funding to support two people on the route. It had been hard enough to get support for one. I told him my idea was to accompany you on the trails without being paid."

"What?" Julie's mouth dropped open. "You'd be willing to go with me?"

"I'd insist. I can't imagine anything more enjoyable than long hours in the wilderness with a beautiful woman who just happens to be my wife. I've had it planned from the beginning."

"I never considered such a thing," Julie said in disbelief. "You'd actually go with me? What a wonderful idea! We wouldn't have to be separated, and you wouldn't want me to quit my job." Julie squealed with delight as she threw herself into Sam's arms.

"Is that what your moodiness has been all about?" Sam asked, holding Julie at arm's length. "Did you think I was going to force you to give up your dream?"

Julie nodded. "I wanted to talk to you about my job before we got married. But then, the epidemic came up, and you nearly got yourself killed, and I just let it go. I was afraid to bring it up after that."

"Never be afraid of me, Julie," Sam said softly. "And please don't ever turn away from me again."

"I'm sorry, Sam, it's just that you being the kind of guy you are, I thought—"

Sam couldn't resist chuckling as he interrupted. "You mean to tell me you honestly thought I'd expect you to give up something as important as your nursing? I can't believe you'd think so little of me. I mean, I know I can be a little demanding and—"

"A little?" Julie interrupted. "A little?"

Sam shook his head and pulled Julie into his arms. "Okay, so I can be very demanding, but I certainly wouldn't make a decision like that for you. I married you knowing you had a job to do. I admired you for it. I think helping the villages is an important task, and I believe strongly in spreading the Word of God to those who have never heard it before. I kind of figured I might help you."

"Honestly?"

"Honestly," Sam said firmly.

"I'm so sorry for misjudging you," Julie said as she reached a hand up to Sam's bearded face. "I love you so much, and I love my nursing. I didn't want to have to choose between the two."

"I would never have asked you to," Sam said as he kissed Julie tenderly.

Julie felt a burden was lifted from her shoulders. She thought of her willingness to accept whatever Sam had instructed her to do and knew that her peace came in being willing to be obedient to God.

As Sam pulled away from her, she nestled her face against his chest and thanked God for the husband He'd given her. Almost as an after-thought, Julie raised one last question.

"Sam, there are bound to be times when you'll be needed here or when you can't go with me. How will you feel about that?"

"Nothing will keep me from your side," Sam declared.

"But what if something happens and it does? I can't stay home and forget the people in the villages. We should be in agreement about what we'll do if that happens," Julie said earnestly.

"If that happens, and I don't believe it will," Sam replied, "then I'll simply wait here with a light in the window until you come home safely to me. Good enough?" Sam's eyes were filled with love.

Julie nodded. She no longer had any doubts about being married to Sam. "I love you, Sam, and I love God for giving me the wisdom to marry you. It will be the light of your love that leads me home and keeps me strong."

"Oh my beautiful Jewel," Sam said as he leaned back and pulled Julie against him. "That's a light that will never burn out. For as long as I live, it will burn only for you."

Destiny's
ROAD

Chapter 1

"T he Royal Canadian Air Force regrets to inform you. . ." Bethany Hogan refused to read any further as the telegram fell from her hand and blew across the yard.

Chubby four-year-old legs ran across the promise of new spring grass to catch up with the papers but were too slow for the job.

Beth watched as two-year-old Phillip followed after his older brother, Gerald. How could she explain to them that their father had been killed? How could she hope that they could understand that a madman named Hitler had made it necessary for their father to give his life in service to his country?

American-born and native to Alaska, Bethany had met her Canadian husband only six years earlier in Fairbanks. He was flying with barnstormers, who for the outrageous price of two dollars would take individuals up into the air to forget the problems and concerns of the Depression.

John Brian Hogan, "JB" to his friends, wasn't exactly what Beth had been looking for. He was a bit too wild and carefree, with a love of life that oozed over into his conversations and chosen profession. Beth thought him reckless but entertaining.

She remembered standing along the sidelines watching as her girlfriends took turns flying with some of the other barnstormers. JB worked for over an hour, missing several paying customers, in order to coax Beth into the air for free.

It all came rushing back to her as the breeze picked up and blew strong across the open field. The roar of the DH-4's twelve-cylinder engine, the seeming frailty of dope and fabric wings, and the rush of the wind as JB eased back on the stick and the biplane became airborne.

Now he was gone. In his passing, two children were left without a father. Bethany squinted against the morning sun and watched as her children came running back across the field. They were laughing, enjoying the moment, the sun, and the excitement of a new day.

"Momma!" Gerald squealed as he wrapped himself around her legs. Phillip mimicked his brother as soon as his little legs could take him to his mother's side.

Beth hugged her children close, refusing to show them her sorrow. *Oh JB*, she cried silently. *Why? Why did you have to leave them now? Why did you have to leave me?*

"Momma, was that a letter from Daddy?" Gerald asked in his boisterous voice.

Beth steadied her nerves, lifted Phillip into her arms, and led Gerald with her to sit beneath their favorite towering pine. Gerald, always the more sensitive of the two, sobered at his mother's expression. He waited quietly while Beth settled herself with Phillip.

"The letter wasn't from Daddy, but it was about Daddy," Beth said and took a deep breath. She breathed a prayer, asking God for just the right words. "Daddy has to go away for a long, long time."

"Did he go to heaven?" Gerald asked, surprising Beth with his bluntness.

"Yes," Beth said softly, uncertain that Gerald could really understand. "What made you ask that?"

"Daddy told me he might have to go to heaven instead of coming home after his job was done."

Good old JB, Beth thought. She should have known he would prepare his child for the possibility of his death. "Do you understand about heaven, Gerald?"

"Daddy said it was a really beautiful place. A place where you got to live if you loved God," the boy answered quite seriously.

"That's right," Beth said as she tried to think of what she might say next.

"Will we see him again?"

"Yes," Beth assured. "We'll see him again in heaven."

Phillip seemed oblivious to the news, but Gerald's little forehead furrowed as he concentrated on his mother's answer. Beth wondered if he would cry or if he'd truly be able to grasp the meaning of his father's death. JB had already been gone from Gerald's daily life for several months.

Gerald began to nod his head and Phillip, ever faithful, did likewise. "Then it's okay," he said as he put his hand on his mother's arm. "If Daddy's in heaven, then it's okay."

Beth looked at her brown-eyed son and smiled. "Yes, it's okay, Gerry. Daddy's in heaven and it's really okay."

Phillip squirmed out of Beth's arms and ran after some birds, while Gerald sat beside his mother and held her hand. He seemed to sense that, while his mother's words were filled with hope and eternity, her heart was empty and hurting.

———※———

Later that night, after Bethany had tucked the boys into the double bed they shared, she made her way to the sitting room. The rolltop desk gave slight resistance as she pushed it open and took a seat.

There was a great deal to be done in order to get everything arranged. Being American, Bethany was determined to return to Alaska and raise her children as Americans, but where should she take them and how would she support them? There was the small nest egg that she and JB had saved, but that wouldn't last long with two growing boys.

JB had always teased her about being so meticulous and organized. Beth would make lists every fall and again in the spring of all the things that needed to be done. JB thought it foolish, but inevitably he relied upon them every bit as much as his wife. So Bethany made another list—in fact, several.

Across the top of the paper she wrote: THINGS TO SELL. THINGS TO TAKE. THINGS TO DO FIRST. Under the final heading, she listed the thing that seemed most important: *Bury JB.*

Beth worked long into the night, going over the contents of the house and JB's shop. She thought of choice items to save as mementos for the boys, things that would give them fond memories of their father. Glancing up, she noticed the framed picture of JB in his uniform.

She put the pencil down and reached for the picture. For the first time, Beth allowed her tears to fall. It was impossible to imagine that the big-hearted man she'd fallen in love with was gone.

"JB," she said aloud, "you told me this might happen, but I never believed you. You were always able to get out of any scrape, no matter how bad." She looked at the photo, tracing JB's outline. He'd obviously been told to look serious for the photograph, but his eyes crinkled with laughter.

"I never ever thought you'd leave me. I trusted God to keep you in His care, which of course He did. I just didn't know He'd choose to care for you in heaven."

Beth got up from the desk and, with the picture still in hand, stretched out across the couch. She intended only to have a good long cry and then go to bed, but instead she fell asleep clutching the picture to her heart.

"Momma." Phillip patted at Beth's face. "Momma, me eat."

Beth roused herself from a dreamless sleep, grateful for a reason to get up. The picture clattered to the floor, momentarily forgotten as Phillip climbed on top of his mother.

"Come here, you sweet boy," Beth said, pulling the two-year-old into her arms. "You don't look like you need food," she teased as she looked underneath Phillip's nightshirt. "But, you look like you could use a good tickling." Phillip's giggles filled the air as Beth ran her fingers lightly across her son's abdomen.

"Tickle me," Gerald called as he climbed on his mother's legs. "I need tickles too."

The three of them rolled around the couch, laughing and giggling until Beth felt her sorrow melt away. JB wasn't really gone. As long as Gerald and Phillip were here, she would have reminders of JB's love for her.

"Come along, you ragamuffins," Beth said as she set the boys aside and got to her feet. "I'll get you some breakfast and then we have some errands to do."

The boys padded after their mother to the kitchen and waited impatiently for her to prepare steaming bowls of oatmeal. After placing the food on the table, Beth went to the refrigerator and brought cream for their cereal.

"Berries too, Momma?" Gerald questioned.

"No, I'm sorry. It's still too early for them. I have a little bit of brown sugar though. I've been saving it just for you two," Beth said as she went to the cupboard and pulled out a small china bowl.

Phillip clapped his hands as Beth spooned the sweetener onto the oatmeal. "Choogar, choogar," he chanted, trying to pick up pieces of the lumpy brown sugar before Beth could blend it in with the cereal.

When breakfast was served, Beth took a seat at the table and she and the boys bowed their heads.

"Father, thank You for the food You've given us," Beth prayed. "We ask for it to nourish our bodies, that we might have the strength and energy to do Your work. Amen."

Gerald and Phillip went to work on their cereal, while Beth pulled a small, worn Bible from the pocket of her apron. Such was their morning routine: breakfast and devotions.

Beth opened to 1 John 2:28 and read to the boys: "'And now, little children, abide in him; that, when he shall appear, we may have confidence, and not be ashamed before him at his coming.'"

She placed the book on the table and turned to Gerald. "Do you understand what that means?"

Gerald got a serious look on his face as his mind struggled to grasp the ancient words. "I know we're little children," he said pointing to himself and then to Phillip.

"That's right," Beth said with a nod. "And abide in Him means to live in God and God in you. Do you understand that?" Gerald nodded his head yes and Phillip mimicked the action before Beth continued.

"We are all God's little children and this verse tells us that we are to remain close to Him. It also tells us why. It says we need to do this so that we won't be ashamed when God comes back for us."

"Like He came back for Daddy?" Gerald asked, surprising Bethany.

"That's right. Daddy loved God very much, and because Daddy lived close to God, he wasn't ashamed when God told him it was time to come to heaven."

"Daddy in heh–hehbeen," Phillip joined in.

Beth held back her tears. "Yes, Daddy is in heaven and he's smiling right now because his two big boys are learning about God and how much God loves them. It makes your daddy happy and it makes God happy when you spend time learning about the Bible."

"Will Daddy forget us while he's in heaven?" Gerald asked with a look of concern. "What if we don't get there very soon? Will Daddy know us when he sees us?"

Beth couldn't hold back the hot tears that filled her eyes. "Daddy will always remember us. He won't forget us and we won't forget him. You wait here for just a minute," Beth said, using the opportunity to wipe her eyes as she went back to the living room for JB's picture.

When she returned to the kitchen, the boys were nearly done with their breakfast. She put the picture in the middle of the table and took her seat. "This picture was taken last year when your daddy went away to fight in the big war."

"He went to fly the airplanes, right, Momma?" Gerald queried.

"Yes," Beth answered. "Your daddy flew the airplanes."

"Did he fly his airplane up to heaven?"

"I'm sure that Daddy was in his airplane when he went to heaven. We never know when God will come to take us home to heaven, so we must always be ready. We must always be good and kind to one another, and we should always live close to God and His Word."

Phillip reached out to the picture. "Daddy?"

Beth grieved that her boys would never remember their father for the person he was. He would only be a character in stories they heard and a friendly face that sat upon their breakfast table.

"Yes, Phillip," she said as she allowed him to hold the picture in his chubby hands, "this is your daddy, and he loved us all very much. Whenever we miss him, we can look at this picture and remember that he doesn't want us to be sad. Can you do that, boys?"

Both boys nodded their heads solemnly. They seemed to sense that the moment was quite important. "How long will it be, Momma? How long before we see Daddy in heaven?" Gerald finally asked.

"I don't know, Gerry. But one day we will see him. Of that you can be sure." It seemed to satisfy his boyish curiosity and Beth dismissed them both to play outside.

After cleaning up the breakfast dishes, Beth went once again to the living room, where she looked over the lists she had made the previous evening. Taking three thumbtacks, Beth posted her lists to the wall, determined to mark each item off as she accomplished the tasks. She was reaching for the telephone to call Pastor McCarthy when a knock sounded at the front door.

Beth opened it to reveal her closest neighbor and friend, Karen Sawin. Karen was always bubbly and happy-go-lucky, but the look on her face told Bethany that she'd already guessed or heard about the newest telegram.

"I thought you might be able to use a friend," Karen said as she extended a freshly baked loaf of bread.

Beth accepted the still-warm bread and ushered Karen into the house. "Thanks. You always seem to know the right thing to do."

"So," Karen started uncomfortably, "I guess you heard something official."

"Yes, JB was killed in action," Beth said matter-of-factly as she put the bread on the coffee table and offered Karen a seat on the couch.

"You'll have to forgive the way I look. I fell asleep out here last night and haven't changed clothes."

"Why don't you go ahead and take a nice hot bath and let me keep an eye on the boys?" Karen suggested.

Beth smiled and reached out to take hold of Karen's hand. "You are such a dear friend. I'd really like that, if you don't mind. Afterward, we can have a long talk."

"Of course," Karen said. "Whatever you need."

An hour later, Beth emerged looking refreshed. She'd washed and dried her pale blond hair and gathered it back at the sides with mother-of-pearl combs.

"I feel like a new woman," Beth said as she joined Karen in the living room. She wore a freshly pressed cotton dress whose bright peach color was trimmed with a white eyelet collar and armbands. The matching belt showed off Beth's tiny waistline.

"You look so skinny, Beth. I'll bet you haven't eaten a decent meal since JB. . ." Karen fell silent.

"It's all right, Karen," Beth said as she leaned over to pat her friend's hand. "What's happened has happened. JB is dead. We can't change it by not talking about it."

"You're taking it awfully well. I doubt I would be as capable as you," Karen said honestly.

"I'm not handling it that well, Karen. I'm just numb and reliant upon the Lord."

Karen nodded at Beth's words.

"No doubt in a week or two, I'll be beside myself," Beth continued, "but then again, maybe not. I do have to be strong for the boys—after all, they can't be expected to lose both of their parents."

"That's true," Karen said as she pushed back her dark hair, "and we both know JB wouldn't want you to be sad. I don't think I ever saw JB with a frown on his face."

"Nor I," Beth agreed. "JB was a terminally happy man. He always joked that St. Peter would meet him at the pearly gates and ask him what was so funny. JB did love to laugh."

"I'll never forget the night before he left," Karen remembered. "He was laughing and dancing with everyone, including old Mr. Thompson." Karen stopped short and looked away. "Here I meant to come over and get your mind off JB, and I'm doing just the opposite."

"I know what you mean. I tell myself I don't have to deal with everything at once. I mean, it's been nearly a year since JB joined the service. Aside from his few brief letters, the void has been something I've dealt with in an ongoing manner. Yet now that I know he isn't coming back, it seems important to put all our affairs in order and to move on." Beth stared intently into Karen's hazel eyes. "Does that make any sense?"

"I think each person must deal with grief in their own manner. I know I'd be inclined to run away from all of it. Please don't think me unfeeling, Bethany, but I pray to God I never have to know. If something happened to my Miles, I just know I'd crumble."

Beth leaned over and hugged Karen tightly. "I don't think badly of you at all. I pray you never have to know either. I pray daily that this war will end and Miles will come home safely to you."

"You are such a dear friend, Beth. Is there anything I can do to help you?"

Beth pulled away and got to her feet. "As a matter of fact, there is. I've made several lists." She paused with a grin. "You know me and my lists."

Karen nodded and returned her friend's smile.

"Anyway," Beth continued, "I plan to leave as soon as I can. I want to return to Alaska with the boys and raise them as Americans. After all, they were born in America, and just because their father is—was—Canadian, that doesn't mean they can't share in my heritage as well."

"But where will you go? You haven't any family still living there. Who will take care of you?" Karen questioned in a concerned tone.

"God will take care of me, Karen. Remember Isaiah 54:4–5: 'Fear not; for thou shalt not be ashamed: neither be thou confounded; for thou shalt not be put to shame: for thou shalt forget the shame of thy youth, and shalt not remember the reproach of thy widowhood any more. For thy Maker is thine husband; the Lord of hosts is his name; and thy Redeemer the Holy One of Israel; The God of the whole earth shall he be called.'"

"You have a strong faith, Bethany. I'll do whatever I can to help you, but I'll miss you sorely," Karen said as she got to her feet. "Just tell me what I can do."

As spring warmed into summer and the nights grew shorter, Bethany finalized her plans for moving her family to Alaska. She left many of her things with Karen, promising to send for them as soon as she and the boys were settled.

Then, despite the fact that an airplane had claimed the life of her husband, Bethany loaded her boys into the plane of JB's best friend and mentor, Pete Calhoon. With a last look at the place she and JB had called home, Beth turned, resolving to put the past behind her and start a new life in Alaska.

Chapter 2

Crash! Bang! Julie Curtiss cringed at the sound of the slamming doors. The clamor could only mean one thing: her brother was home, and he wasn't at all happy.

August Eriksson came stomping into the room. Mindless that his heavy boots were covered in mud, August marched across Julie's clean kitchen floor and threw his body against the back of a chair.

"Bad news?" Julie braved the words. Her dark eyes were sympathetic as she reached out to touch her brother's sleeve.

"They said I was too old," August grumbled the words. "I'm not even forty-two, and they think I'm too old to join the military."

Julie bit back a remark about being glad that August couldn't go off to the war in the Pacific. Ever since Pearl Harbor had been bombed the previous winter, August had been bent on participating in the defense of his country.

"A lot of other people are going off and serving," August said, dejected. Although he was two years Julie's senior, he seemed like a little boy to his sister.

"Maybe God has another plan for you, August," Julie suggested as she went to the huge cast-iron stove and poured two steaming mugs of coffee.

"I don't think He has any plans for me. I mean, just look at me, Jewels," he said, using his sister's nickname. "Pa died a year ago, and you and Sam took over the house."

"But August, you asked us to move in here in order to help with the dog kennel," Julie said defensively. "Sam and I can certainly move back to town if you like."

"No. No. No," August said as he ran his fingers through his dark hair. "I didn't mean for you to think that. I would have gone mad if you and Sam hadn't moved in here. It's just, oh, I don't know."

Julie patted August's hand. "I know you want to help fight the war, but August, maybe there's something special for you here in Nome."

"I used to think that too, but after all these years of being alone except for you, Sam, and Pa, I just want to get out."

"Look, August, it's the middle of the darkest days," Julie said with a glance at the calendar. "It's only the end of March, and with all the darkness we have in the winter, a body is bound to get discouraged."

"It's more than that, Julie. I wanted to have a family. I want to get married and be a father. I want a home of my own, something I can build up with my own hands. I want to have a purpose and be needed by others and to need them in return. I just don't belong here with you and your husband."

"But Sam's your best friend," Julie protested.

"I know, I know, and you're my only living relative. That's my point. I don't want to die without leaving something behind," August answered.

"But if you go off to war and get yourself killed, you won't have a chance to marry and have a family. I can't lie and say I'm not relieved," Julie finally admitted. "When the *Nome Nugget* started reporting the facts of the war, I cringed. I wasn't sure what Sam's response would be, or yours for that matter.

"I cried tears of joy when Sam told me he was too old to go. I'm just as happy to have you stay here, but my heart is broken for your anguish. Please don't hate me for wanting you to stay safe."

"I don't hate you, Julie. I couldn't hate you or anyone else, but right now I'm pretty confused and plenty unhappy," August said and got to his feet. "I'm going for a walk."

"It's awfully cold out there," Julie said and bit her tongue. *No sense in mothering August; he'll only resent it.*

"I know," August said, pulling his parka on. "I shouldn't be too long. Maybe I'll run some of the dogs."

"If you see Sam out there," Julie said, trying to sound disinterested in August's plans, "would you mind sending him my way?"

"Not at all," August replied and started to leave. "Oh, I'm sorry about the mud, Jewels. I can clean it up for you."

"Never mind," Julie said and waved him on. "You just get to feeling better. I'll have some lunch in about an hour."

Julie watched her brother leave in silence. She ached for him and went to the living room determined to pray.

———— *#* ————

August kicked at the snow as he walked. He'd never known a time in his life when he'd felt so completely useless. Nothing in his life seemed right, and he'd lost all faith in the trust he'd once placed in God.

Forty-one didn't seem all that old to August. He felt vital and young. He could run thirty or more miles a day with his dogs, and he was never sick. How could the army tell him he was too old?

Without realizing what he was doing, August hitched a team of dogs to a sled. He hardly gave the process a second thought as he attached his lead dog first, then swing dogs, team dogs, and finally wheel dogs.

Each dog had his own special talent, and those who were weak were quickly weeded out and put to death. The harsh elements of the North didn't allow for anyone, be they man or beast, to exist without purpose. Perhaps that's why August felt so misplaced and out of sorts. He didn't have any real purpose.

August moved the dogs out without any particular destination in mind. He enjoyed watching the muscular frames of the dogs as they ran with a hearty eagerness.

Many Alaskans had traded in their dogs and sleds for gas-powered snow machines, but August found the dogs more dependable. The machines were always breaking down, and often they were incapable of withstanding the subzero temperatures. August reasoned it was impossible to gain warmth from steel and wood if you were stranded in the wilds, but a dog was good to curl up with when the north wind pounded blades of ice into your skin. He'd take his dogs over machines any day.

The dogs worked their way down the roadway to Nome, and when August realized he was nearly at the edge of town, he couldn't decide what to do with himself.

He spoke to no one and didn't offer so much as a wave when people greeted him. He simply anchored his dogs and walked into a nearby café. The look on his face as he pushed back his parka hood was enough to keep people at a distance. Everyone, that is, except his brother-in-law, who entered the restaurant from out of nowhere, on August's heels.

Sam Curtiss ignored August's scowl and motioned the waitress to bring coffee.

"Do you think it will help?" Sam asked, taking a seat opposite August.

"What are you talking about?" August growled.

"Feeling sorry for yourself," Sam said with a grin. "Do you think it will help?"

"If you're here to preach at me, Sam, you can just forget it," August said, refusing to look Sam in the eye.

Sam waited while an older woman poured two cups of thick, black coffee. When she was out of earshot, Sam leaned forward.

"I hadn't planned to preach," he replied. "I just wondered if you were feeling any better."

"No," August answered flatly. "I don't feel any better, and I don't expect talking to you to make any difference."

"Maybe you should give it a try," Sam said, taking a drink. He eyed a questioning look at August.

"Maybe I'd rather be alone," August said firmly. "I don't need you here, Sam. I don't need anybody. The army doesn't want me, women don't seek out my company, and God has apparently deserted me."

"You don't believe that any more than I do."

"I don't know what I believe anymore, Sam." August stared at the steaming cup for a moment before pushing it away. "I trusted God for a full life, and instead I'm left with an emptiness and void that won't be filled. Why should I go on trusting Him when He's left me to stand alone?"

"Think about your words, August. When you accepted Christ as your Savior, was somebody standing there with a list of prizes? Did you think you'd won the All-Alaska Sweepstakes?"

"Don't be snide with me, Sam. I know God didn't offer me a prize package. He did say, however, that I could ask for anything in the name of His Son. He promised to give me the desires of my heart if I put Him first in my life. So where's the fulfillment of that promise?"

"Your life certainly isn't over, August. Why not be patient and let God guide your steps? It isn't a game of 'I'll give you this, Lord, and You give me that.'"

"I never said it was," August protested as he sank back against his chair.

"Besides, you've had a very good life," Sam reasoned. "Be patient, because God will work a miracle when you least expect it. Just look at your sister and me. I wasn't much younger than you are now when she came into my life.

"I'd been praying most all of my adult life for a Christian wife and, although I knew the chances of one coming to me in the wilds of Alaska were slim, God moved. God hasn't left you alone, August. You must have the faith to get beyond this disappointment."

"It's more than the disappointment, Sam. I just don't know that I can trust God with my heart anymore. Things that once seemed clear and inspiring are just rhetoric now."

"Then remember Psalm 37:23–24: 'The steps of a good man are

ordered by the Lord: and he delighteth in his way. Though he fall, he shall not be utterly cast down: for the Lord upholdeth him with his hand.' God hasn't deserted you," Sam stressed. "Have faith that He can get you through this dark time, and you'll soon be walking in light again."

August shook his head. "I don't think I care anymore."

Sam finished his coffee and stood with a smile on his face. "Oh, you care, August. That's what's grieving you so much. You care because you know the truth of the Word. Once you've tasted the truth, Satan's lies can't guide you into any kind of peace. I'm glad you're troubled and in turmoil right now. I'd be more concerned if you weren't."

"I don't get it," August said as he cast a doubtful look at his older friend. "You're glad I feel this way?"

"I'm not glad that you're hurting, but I'm glad that you're struggling against the feelings that are threatening to bury you. You aren't fighting God, August. You're fighting yourself and what you thought God had planned out for your life. Why not go back to Him and seek the answers you're looking for?"

"What if He doesn't listen?" August questioned softly.

Sam nodded knowingly. "What man hasn't asked himself that question? You've got to believe, August. You've just got to step forward and trust God to be there. Now, I'm going home for an overdue lunch. You coming?"

"I guess so," August said as he got to his feet. "There's no reason to sit here."

As August walked out the door of the café, a copy of the local newspaper caught his eyes. MILITARY HIGHWAY TO REQUIRE CIVILIAN HELP, the headline read. August paid the waitress for a copy of the paper and followed Sam into the street.

"Look at this," August said as he scanned the article. "The army is building a road through Canada, the Yukon, and on up to Fairbanks. It says here because of the threat of the Japanese attacking Alaska, the US government feels it's imperative to have access to the territory."

"There's always water routes and air travel. I can't imagine why they're willing to go to the cost of building a road through the wilderness," Sam said, rubbing his chin thoughtfully.

"Well, the paper says that military sources fear the Japanese might have the capability to deny ships passage through the waterways and that their aircraft would be able to shoot down our military planes. It also says they need civilian forces to help the military units with clearing areas for the road and new airstrips."

Sam noticed excitement in August's voice. "I'd imagine an experienced hand at road building would be a tremendous asset," he suggested quietly.

August looked up from the paper with a grin. "I was just thinking that myself. This road will change Alaska's destiny forever. They're bound to make us a state after this."

"It's an awful long ways off," Sam said, wondering if August was seriously considering the job.

"Maybe it's just the right distance to start a new life," August said as he refolded the paper. "I'm going to do it, Sam. I'm going to go build me a road and change my own destiny."

Chapter 3

B eth Hogan worked the dough that would soon be delicious loaves of wheat bread. The kitchen already boasted the aroma of wild berry jelly cooking down, and Beth was grateful for the extra warmth of the stove. The day had turned chilly as a mountain thunderstorm hovered in the distance.

Taking a moment from her task, Beth looked out the window to check on her sons. They were playing happily in the backyard, mindless of the threatening storm. At three and five, the boys were growing up almost faster than Beth liked to see.

Glancing past the boys to the mountains that lined the southern horizon, Beth smiled. There had been so much uncertainty when she'd left Canada the previous year, but when she'd stepped from the plane and viewed the panoramic glory, she had declared this piece of Alaska heaven on earth and arranged for a home for herself and her children.

The land hadn't disappointed her, nor had the people. She had been eagerly welcomed into the caring arms of neighbors and new friends, including an elderly woman who most called Granny Gantry.

Granny had a run-down roadhouse, catering mostly to those who traveled the worn path that residents called a road. While spending the winter of 1941 under Granny's protective wing, Beth had learned a great deal.

Day after day, Beth helped to transform the roadhouse into a prosperous business by adding homey touches. She made rag rugs for the floor and sewed new curtains for the windows. It wasn't long before Beth was even a fair hand at chopping wood and patching walls.

Granny had been pleased with the additional help and company. She seemed to thrive on spoiling the boys by making them special treats. Granny was also a source of Christian fellowship, and Beth relished their times of devotions when the older woman would share her views and knowledge of God.

When Granny passed away suddenly in the spring of '42, Beth again felt the pain of separation. She quickly purchased the property and continued to run the roadhouse, but it wasn't the same without Granny's smiling face.

Shaking off the past, Beth took a deep breath and returned her gaze to the children. They were so little and innocent, but she knew it would only be a heartbeat and they'd be grown. She wondered if they'd be called to war as had so many other mothers' sons. She'd already lost a husband to war; would she lose her children too?

A cold, ominous cloud had settled over the country since the attack on Pearl Harbor, and there wasn't a citizen from Nome to Tok who hadn't felt fear. The entire world was at war, but Alaskans felt the distance between their homeland and the Japanese empire narrow considerably as rumors of impending attacks ran rampant.

Deaths mounted on both sides, each fighting for what they believed to be right. How long would they battle? How many would have to die? No doubt many more would give their lives before the evil that surged throughout Europe and Asia was taken captive and defeated.

Wiping her hands on her apron and seeking to put thoughts of death and war from her, Beth returned to kitchen chores. Business was booming with the arrival of the US Army. They'd come to build a road, a road that everyone said would protect Alaska from the Japanese and one day link the territory to the rest of the world.

Newspapers throughout the nation boasted stories of the undertaking. They likened it to pioneer trailblazing and merited the army with the civilizing of the Alaskan territory. Surveyors were already placing their marks upon the land at Beth's front door.

Now that the national eye was turned upon the rugged wilderness of Alaska, Beth Hogan had little trouble keeping her children fed and clothed. Instead of a roadhouse where people stopped only on their way to somewhere else, Beth found her home becoming a boardinghouse where customers stayed on a more permanent basis.

The onslaught of new business also helped Beth keep her mind occupied. She still thought of JB and the empty place that his absence had created in her life, but the memories didn't cause her as much pain as they had at first. Sometimes she could laugh or smile at a pleasant memory of her husband.

She kept the picture of JB in a prominent place in the living room, and whenever the boys asked her questions about their father, Beth would try to share bits and pieces of his life.

Just then, Gerald came bursting through the door. "Momma! Momma! Guess what!"

"Calm down, Gerald, and lower your voice," Beth said sternly. She kneaded the bread dough into loaves and placed them in greased pans. "Now, take a deep breath and tell me what you're so excited about."

"I saw boats way down the river. Can Phillip and I go to town and see them up close?" Gerald was still panting from the excitement and his run up to the house.

"Absolutely not," Bethany answered. She turned and put the bread in the oven, unaware of the look of disappointment that crossed Gerald's face. "Haven't I told you boys how dangerous the river is? You mustn't go there alone."

"But it looks like fun, Momma. Please let us go see the boats," Gerald begged.

"No, son. You have to obey me on this because it's very important," Beth said as she knelt beside her five-year-old. "Do you understand?"

"Uh-huh," Gerald replied as he nodded his head. "It's important."

"Yes," Beth said as she tousled the child's brown hair. "It's very important. I know you're a big boy and you by yourself might do all right down by the water, but Phillip is too little and he might fall in. As his big brother, it's your job to see to it that he's safe—especially since your father isn't here to watch over him."

"Will Daddy see me watching my brother?"

"I imagine so," Beth said as she straightened up and lifted Gerald into her arms. "I love you both very much. Now, why don't you go outside and keep an eye on Phillip for me?"

"Okay," Gerald said and placed a big kiss on his mother's cheek. "I'll be a big help."

"I'm sure you will be." Beth kissed her son and put him down. As he bounded out the door, her mind filled with worry. Had she said enough to prevent Gerald and Phillip's wanderings? She loved them so much, but then she'd loved JB even more and it hadn't kept him from adversity.

She went back to work with her mind only half on her tasks. She nearly burned the bread and scorched the jam, all the while thinking of how vulnerable her children were. Finally, Beth took herself to her writing desk and pulled out a Bible.

"Lord," she prayed, "I know that worry won't save them, but You can. Father, I can't imagine how You ever sent Your Son, Jesus, to a world You knew would hurt Him. I fear letting my sons from my sight for even a minute. I can't bear the thought that they might get hurt or killed. Please watch over them and care for them. I know JB is in heaven, Lord, and that gives me comfort, but please let me keep my children here with me and let them be safe in my care. Let me be a wise mother, God."

She opened the Bible and scanned Psalm 127:3–5: *"Lo, children are an heritage of the Lord: and the fruit of the womb is his reward. As arrows are in the hand of a mighty man; so are children of the youth. Happy is the man that hath his quiver full of them. . . . "*

Beth smiled, remembering that these verses had been some of JB's favorites. He'd always planned to have a big family, or a "full quiver," as he'd often teased.

"These children are gifts from You, Lord," Beth said with confidence. "I place them in Your hands, Father, and I ask for Your protection of them. Amen."

Glancing at her watch, Beth realized that she was falling behind schedule. Leaving her worries at the feet of her Lord, she returned to her list of duties.

———#———

Late that May, August had arrived in eastern Alaska. He was more than a little anxious about applying for work on the highway. Even though he'd heard they'd take anyone who could work, August still felt the sting of the army's earlier rejection and wondered if the rumors were true.

August gazed across the valley where rows of tents had been erected to house the army. Beyond these were olive drab vehicles and heavy construction equipment. The entire landing buzzed with activity while soldiers and civilians rushed to accomplish the business of the day.

After questioning one of the passing soldiers, August made his way to the tent of the commanding officer.

"You need to speak with the area supervisor of the US Public Roads Administration," the officer told August. "I'm certain, however, that you won't be idle for long. We can use every man we can get."

"Glad to hear it," August said and got up to leave. "I'm anxious to get to work."

"Then you're in the right place," the man said from behind his makeshift desk. "You can find the supervisor at the airfield. While we're clearing this path, we're also laying out new landing strips. Just follow the river to the crossroads and turn right. It's just a half mile or so from there. Like I said, you shouldn't have any trouble getting a job."

"Thanks again for your help," August said and left in search of the airfield.

As August walked the short distance down the river to the crossroads, he noticed how different the land was from his native Nome.

The fertile valley made Nome seem barren. Tall spruce, fir, and pine weaved a rich green pattern across the land. Wildflowers and carefully tended gardens were visible reminders of the sun's power in a land that enjoyed over eighteen hours of light each day.

August had already been told of cabbages weighing nearly forty pounds and of cucumbers that were longer than a man's arm and nearly as wide around. It was a land of many wonders, and August was only beginning to learn of its richness.

The hike to the airfield did him good, and August breathed deeply of the storm-chilled air. All morning, thunder had rumbled in the distance, but the storm seemed to hang in suspended indifference over the snowcapped mountains.

As August approached the airfield, he discovered that it was hardly more than a cleared path. At one end a wind sock had been erected on a pole, and at the other end several tents and wooden buildings stood in sorry contrast to the grandeur of the landscape.

"Excuse me," August said as he approached a mechanic. The man was working on a large tractor, cursing and throwing tools as he did so.

"Whadyawant?" the man asked, garbling the words together.

"I wondered where I might find the supervisor for the Public Roads Administration," August replied.

"Over there," the man said, motioning to the nearest tent.

August thanked the man and walked toward the tent. Suddenly, an older man charged out, nearly colliding with August.

"Sorry, I wasn't paying attention. What can I do for you?"

"I'm looking for work on the road," August explained.

"We can use you," the man said enthusiastically. "Come on inside and we'll talk. Have you any particular job experience that might help us decide where to place you?"

"I can operate most of the machinery," August admitted. "I helped to build roads in Nome."

"So you know the problems we're facing with the permafrost." The man continued without waiting for August to reply. "We have approximately eighty days between frosts and little more. Even at that, a foot beneath the surface the ground is always frozen solid."

"I know the dilemma well," August said.

"The army is in charge of the road, although the Roads Administration has some control because we work in cooperation with one another. Right now, a big part of our civilian effort is aimed at meeting the need for a bigger airfield.

"Our problem is the complications with ground thaw and boggy surface water. Do you think you can render any new thoughts on the matter? With you being an experienced road builder in these conditions, I think you might have a suggestion or two that we haven't considered."

"I'd be happy to offer whatever knowledge and experience I have. I'm too old for the army, or I'd be off defending our country in the war, so I'm open to whatever you have for me," August answered.

"Great. You can start tomorrow. Be here at six and I'll show you around."

"I'll be here," August said as he followed the man outside. "Where can I find sleeping accommodations?"

"That's a good question," the man said as he thoughtfully considered the matter. "I take it you didn't bring a tent with you."

"Nope," August said with a sheepish grin. "I figured you folks were more civilized over here."

"Don't include me in the folks from these parts. I'm from Oklahoma, and this country's a whole sight different from what I'm comfortable with. Your best bet is to ask around town. Some of the folks are bound to have an idea."

"I guess that'll have to do," August said with a nod.

"Wish I could offer you more help, but I've only been here a week myself."

"No problem. By the way, I'm August. August Eriksson."

"Good to meet you," the man said and extended his hand. "I guess we're a little lax on formalities around here. I'm Ralph Greening, the area supervisor for the US Public Roads Administration."

August shook the man's hand, and after renewing his promise to return at six the next morning, he made his way back to town.

———— # ————

At the crossroads, August noticed that the storm had dissipated and moved to the east. The clouds cleared out to make the vibrant colors of the landscape come alive.

August enjoyed the breeze through his dark hair and the scent of pine as it penetrated his senses. He marveled at the blackness of the glacier silt dirt and wondered at the stories he'd heard of a glacier's ability to physically move its location as much as ten feet a day.

Before he turned to head back to town, August paused long enough to glance down the picturesque winding road. *It might be a good place to call home,* he thought.

A child's shrill scream filled the air and caught August's attention. He listened again, thinking it came from the direction of town, but soon realized it came from down the road in the opposite direction. The intensity of the child's cry for help sent August in a full run down the riverbank.

Gerald Hogan stood on the small wooden bridge that crossed the river nearly a quarter of a mile from his home. "Help! Help!" he screamed. "My brother can't swim."

August arrived in time to see a small, brown-haired child slip beneath the churning water. Without thought for his own safety, August rushed into the river and swam with the current to catch up to the flailing form.

The icy water bit into August's skin as he maneuvered himself better to take hold of the little boy. He stretched out his hand as the child came within reach, only to hit a boulder. The impact sent him careening away.

August knew he'd have to fight with all his strength to once again reach the drowning boy. He lunged forward in the water and grabbed hold of the boy's collar, pulling the child back against his chest.

Fighting the current, August moved toward shore, where the water was more shallow. He pulled the sputtering, crying child with him. Once he reached the riverbank, August fell back against it, breathing hard. Every muscle in his body ached from the stress and cold, but the child was crying and that meant he was alive.

"Are you my daddy?" Gerald asked from overhead.

"What?" August asked in surprise. Drenched and freezing, he was certain he'd misunderstood the boy's question.

"You are my daddy!" Gerald yelled with exuberance. "Mommy! Mommy!" He ran off in the direction of home before August could stop him and set him straight.

Getting to his feet and cradling the cold, crying boy to his chest, August followed in the direction Gerald had disappeared.

"Mommy, come quick. It's Daddy!" Gerald yelled as he ran through the roadhouse's front door.

Beth came rushing from the back room. "What are you saying, Gerald?"

"Phillip fell in the river, and Daddy jumped in after him." The excitement in Gerald's voice left Beth little doubt about the truth of his statement.

"Take me to where Phillip is," Beth said without thought of reprimanding the disobedience of her sons. "Hurry, Gerry. Take me to your brother."

"He's all right, Momma," Gerald said as he led the way. "Daddy came back. Daddy saved Phillip!"

Beth shook her head, unable to understand. "Daddy is in heaven," she said as she took hold of Gerald's eager hand.

"I know, but you said this was heaven," Gerald stated. "Remember? You said this was heaven when we moved here. I knew my daddy would come home."

Beth's heart ached. How could she explain the misunderstanding to her excited five-year-old? She was torn. She had to assure herself that Phillip was safe and alive, but she was also concerned that Gerald accept the truth of his father's death.

Taking her eyes from her son, Beth lifted her gaze to see a dark-haired man approaching down the road. Her breath caught in her throat and her heart beat faster. From a distance, she could almost believe that JB was walking toward her.

Beth stopped in her tracks, while Gerald pulled at her arm. "Come on, Mommy. It's Daddy and Phillip," he insisted.

Beth let go of Gerald and held her hand to her throat. She paled at the ghostly image of her husband. The same dark hair and medium build. The same self-confident stride. Pushing aside such thoughts, Beth rushed forward to take Phillip.

"Daddy saved Phillip from the river," Gerald announced.

Phillip had wrapped his arms around August's neck and, as Beth reached out to take him, Phillip resisted.

"No. Want Daddy," he said firmly.

Beth looked into the dark eyes of the man who'd saved her child. She wanted to explain, to say something that would answer the question in the man's eyes, but words wouldn't come.

"You're freezing," Beth finally managed. "Come with me, and I'll get you something dry to wear."

August nodded and followed Beth back to the roadhouse. She paused to open the door with trembling hands, allowing August to pass through with Phillip. "Thank you," she whispered as August moved only inches from her.

He turned his face to meet her pale blue eyes. He saw the concern for her child and something else. August began to realize that he represented an image from her past.

"You're welcome," he whispered.

Chapter 4

P hillip refused to be fussed over, and Beth watched in silent concern for signs of complications. The boy seemed fine, however, and the only real dilemma was how to explain to him that the man to whom he clung so affectionately wasn't his father.

Beth moved uncomfortably around the room as she built up the fire in the stove and retrieved warm towels for August and Phillip. It was hard to allow the stranger such an intimate role in her son's life, but at the moment she didn't know what else she could do.

"I must apologize for my sons' behavior," Beth finally said, noting the confused expression on August's face. "Their father was killed last year in the war. They have a misconception about his coming back, or, well, that's not really where the misunderstanding occurred, but it's a long story."

She reached out and pried Phillip from August's lap. "I can offer you a robe while your clothes dry," Beth said, turning to leave the room. "I'll have Gerald show you where you can change."

August nodded and watched as the petite woman placed a kiss on her son's forehead. He noted the relief in her eyes and the gratitude. He admired the way she handled herself in the midst of the crisis and the tender way she mothered her children. He was so absorbed in watching her as she left the room that he barely heard Gerald's little voice as he instructed August to follow him.

The boy offered August the robe and turned to leave. "I'm glad you came home, Daddy. I missed you."

"Son, I'm not your daddy, but if I were, I'd love having a big strong boy like you," August said with a smile.

"You're not my daddy?" Gerald questioned.

"No," August said offering the boy his hand, "but I'd like to be your friend. I just moved here and I don't have any friends. Would you be my friend?"

Gerald wrinkled his forehead as he often did when considering something important. "I wanted you to be my daddy. You look like my daddy." He paused in thoughtful contemplation before adding, "I guess I can be your friend."

"I'd sure like it," August said as he pulled the wet shirt from his body. "Now why don't you go see if you can give your mommy some help while I change out of these clothes." Gerald nodded and left August to contemplate the situation.

"Momma," Gerald said as he came into his bedroom.

Beth looked up from where she was putting dry clothes on Phillip. She'd already checked his body for injuries that had been missed before, but other than a few scrapes and bruises, Phillip had fared rather well. God had certainly been watching over him, even sending the stranger who so closely resembled JB.

"What is it, honey?"

"That man says he's not my daddy. I thought he was my daddy, but he isn't."

Beth lifted Gerald into her arms and hugged him close. "No, he's not your daddy. Honey, Daddy is never coming back. Not here. Not on earth. Heaven is where he lives now, and he's going to stay there forever.

"Someday, we'll all leave this earth and go to heaven, but when that happens, Gerald, we can't come back here. We won't even want to. Daddy is happy in heaven, and he won't ever come back here, but someday we'll see him again. Do you understand that?"

"I understand," Gerald said with surprising acceptance. "I told that man I'd be his friend. Is that all right?"

"Of course you can. Now, you two play in here while I fix some lunch for everyone. I'm counting on you to behave," Beth said, kissing each of them.

"We be good," Phillip said, causing Beth to smile.

"I'll call you when lunch is ready," she said and turned to go.

"Can my new friend have lunch with us?" Gerald asked innocently.

Beth nodded. "I'll ask him right now."

Beth was already busy with lunch preparations when August came into the kitchen with his wet clothes.

"Here," Beth said as she put down the potato she was washing. "Let me take those and hang them out back."

"I hate to be a bother," August said with a grin. There was something about the small woman that captivated him. She seemed so alive and energetic, and August found it hard to believe that she'd never remarried.

Beth glanced up as she took the clothes, and her heart nearly stopped. August's grin was so like JB's. "I suppose," she murmured, forgetting the lunch invitation, "I should introduce myself. I'm Bethany Hogan."

"I'm August Eriksson. May I call you Bethany?"

"Please, or Beth if you prefer."

"I like the name Beth. I hope you will call me August."

Beth nodded and shifted the dripping clothes. "I'm grateful for what you did. Saving my son's life must have taken an incredible act of bravery. I thank God you were there when he needed you." Before August could reply, Beth quickly moved through the kitchen and out the back door.

She pinned the clothes to the line, cherishing the once-familiar weight of a man's clothing. She ran her hand across the collar of August's shirt.

August stood just inside the doorway, hoping that Beth wouldn't see him. He watched as she seemed lost in the moment and wondered if she would ever put her dead husband to rest.

When she turned back toward the peeled log house, August ducked back and quickly took a seat at the kitchen table. He pretended to be preoccupied with his own thoughts when Beth returned to finish fixing lunch.

"I hope you like fried potatoes and ham," Beth said as she continued with her work. "I've also got canned peaches and fresh bread."

"Sounds wonderful, but I hadn't intended on staying for lunch. I never meant to intrude," August said softly.

"Intrude? You saved my son's life. Your presence here is anything but an intrusion. Lunch is an inadequate payment for such a deed."

"Maybe you could tell me where I might find a place to stay," August requested. "I've just arrived from Nome, and I have a job lined up with the Public Roads Administration. I'm not at all familiar with the area, however, so I need some suggestions."

Beth smiled and allowed a bit of a laugh to escape. "It would seem God threw us together for more than one purpose," she mused. "Northway doesn't offer much in the way of accommodations. I run this as a roadhouse, and I just happen to have lost a boarder this morning. I have a small room with a bed, washstand, and dresser. I don't offer regular meals, what with the rationing and all, but the room rates are reasonable."

"Sounds great," August said enthusiastically. Here was the perfect opportunity to stay close by and learn more about this young widowed mother. He cocked his head toward the stove with a chuckle. "What about lunch?"

"What about it?"

"You said no meals."

Beth laughed in spite of herself. "Well, occasionally I offer a meal or two for especially deserving souls."

"If it's half as good as it's starting to smell, I'll try extra hard to be deserving. Besides, where else am I going to find such pleasant company?"

Beth shook her head with a smile. What kind of man was this August Eriksson? He stormed into their lives, saving her child from certain death, and now he sat as relaxed and easygoing as if they were lifelong friends sharing a passing moment.

"What are you smiling about?" August asked as he leaned forward.

"What?" Beth realized she'd betrayed her amusement with the situation and wasn't quite sure how to explain.

"I saw that smile," August answered. "It's a very nice smile, if I might add."

Beth turned back to her work and changed the subject. "What prompted you to move here from Nome?"

August shrugged his shoulders and leaned back. "I heard about the road project, and I wanted to be part of it. I was too old for the army, and I wanted to do something worthwhile with my life—something that would show after I was gone."

Beth nodded. "That sounds reasonable. Did you leave your family in Nome?"

"I don't have any family," August said, and then corrected himself. "Except for my sister and her husband. My father passed away last year, and I've never married."

"I see," Beth said, stirring the cut potatoes into the hot lard on top of the stove. She turned thick ham steaks in the cast-iron skillet, satisfied with the way they were browning.

"What about you? Any family other than the boys?" August questioned curiously.

"No, there's no one else," Beth answered. She retrieved canned peaches from the cupboard before continuing. "My husband, JB, was a pilot with the Royal Canadian Air Force. He was killed shortly after the Battle of Britain."

"I'm sorry," August whispered. "What happened?"

"His best friend wrote me about it," Beth said and realized it was the first time she'd ever shared the details of JB's death. "JB was one of the best pilots in the service. He always managed to get himself and his

181

plane out of any risky situation, except the last time. JB always had a bad feeling about using anybody else's plane. Sure enough, when he died, he was flying another man's Spitfire in a routine maintenance check."

"Was he shot down?" August asked, intent on the young woman's answer.

"No," Beth said, remembering the words of the letter she'd received. "He took off but didn't have enough power to make the Spitfire climb. He reached the end of the runway with a forest of trees directly in front of him and not enough lift to clear them. He crashed into them and was killed instantly in an explosion."

"How awful," August said, considering the fiery death.

"My comfort is that JB was a devout Christian. He loved the Lord more than anything in this world, and I have confidence that he's in heaven."

August grimaced slightly at Beth's reference to JB's devotion to God. He'd once felt that way about God himself. Now there was only bitter resentment for what he'd lost out on.

"What's wrong?" Beth questioned, noticing August's frown.

"Nothing," August replied as he tried to change the subject. "Your boys must have been very young. No wonder they thought I was their father."

Beth realized she'd hit a nerve with August. "They were very young when JB joined the service and went away. I've tried to keep his memory alive by telling them stories of their father and keeping his picture in the living room, but it isn't the same. I worry about them sometimes, but when I get too concerned, I pray about it and turn them over to their heavenly Father." Beth wondered how August would react to another reference to God.

August didn't have a chance to respond, however, as Gerald called from the other room, "Is it time to eat yet?"

Beth watched August's expression change to one of amusement. "Sounds like I'm not the only one who's hungry," he chuckled.

"I'll be right back," Beth said after giving the potatoes a quick stirring. She disappeared for a moment and returned with the boys right behind her. "You boys take a seat with Mr. Eriksson at the table, and we'll eat."

"Would it be all right if they called me August?"

Beth nodded. "I suppose, if that's your wish."

"It is," August said with a smile. "Would you boys like that?"

"August is a month," Gerald offered as if it were news to the stranger.

"That's right, and you are every bit as smart as you are brave. I imagine your mother is very proud of you."

Gerald beamed from ear to ear, while Phillip leaned over and reached for August's hand. "Daddy," he stated clearly, refusing to have any part of August's first name.

Gerald reached over and pulled his brother back. "No, Phillip, he's not our daddy, but maybe he will be." Gerald looked up at his mother and asked, "Do you think since our real daddy isn't coming back that August could be our new daddy?"

Beth turned crimson at the question, and August fought to keep from revealing his own consideration of such an idea. He was already more than just a little fond of the young mother and her boys. Still, they'd only met, and August knew there was much more to be considered than physical attraction.

"Why don't you just pray about it, Gerry," Beth finally suggested. "God will listen to your prayers, and if He feels that it's important for you to have a new daddy, then He will send one to us."

"I did pray for a daddy," Gerald insisted. "I prayed that God would send Daddy home, but you told me he has to stay in heaven. So maybe God sent this one instead." He pointed at August and smiled. "I think you'd make a good daddy."

"I think you're right," August said with genuine fondness for the boy. "Maybe I could be a pretend daddy," he offered with a glance toward Beth. "If your momma doesn't mind, maybe I could take you boys fishing and teach you how to chop wood and hunt for food. Of course, I have to work at my job with the new highway, but when I'm not working, maybe we could do some things together."

Gerald clapped his hands and bobbed up and down in his seat. At his brother's excitement, Phillip squealed with delight and Beth had no idea how to react. She thought it totally inappropriate for August to even suggest such a thing, while the boys thought it perfectly natural.

Unable to hold back her tears, Beth turned quickly to the food on the stove to avoid worrying the children or causing August to question her reaction. Regaining her composure, she wiped the tears with her apron and joined her family at the table with the steaming food. She started to sit and then remembered the peaches and bread.

"So is that okay, Momma?" Gerald questioned. "Can August be our pretend daddy?"

Beth turned to meet August's dark eyes. He seemed to understand her pain and offered a warm smile that reassured her that his intentions were only those that would benefit her sons.

"It's okay, Gerry. You and Phillip can probably learn a lot from August, but just remember to tell me your plans first." She said the latter for August's sake more than the boys. He nodded a promise and Beth felt calmness wash over her.

She opened the can of peaches and poured them into a bowl, then cut thick slices of her slightly over-browned bread. Bringing these to the table along with the jelly dish, Beth took her seat.

"Would you like to offer grace, August?" Beth questioned, wondering what his response would be.

August shook his head. "I'd like to hear Gerald give grace, if you don't mind."

Beth nodded, thinking how smoothly August had avoided having to pray.

"Dear God," the boy began, "this is Gerald Hogan. You have my daddy in heaven with You, and I want You to tell him that August is going to be our pretend daddy. Tell him we still love him, but we need a daddy on earth."

Gerald's words cut deeply into Beth's heart. She'd tried so hard to be mother and father to her sons and never once thought of the void in their lives.

"And God," Gerald continued as an afterthought, "thanks for the food. Amen."

Beth opened her eyes to find August's gaze fixed upon her. She returned the stare while the boys, mindless of the exchange, helped themselves to bread and jelly.

Beth's expression was almost one of pleading, August decided, but for what? Was she fearful that he'd hurt her young boys, or was she more frightened of how his "pretend fatherhood" might affect her? She looked so young and scared. August wished he could ease her worries.

Without thought, he reached out and placed his hand over hers and gave a squeeze. Then just as quickly, August turned his attention to the food and found himself in an intense conversation with Gerald about the new highway.

A strange sensation crept over Beth. Her heart pounded at the thought of August touching her, yet her mind screamed betrayal. She mindlessly pushed her food around the plate, all the while considering the implication of August's role playing. It seemed such a reasonable arrangement, yet for all she was worth, Bethany couldn't comprehend why.

Chapter 5

Augusts's work with the Alaskan/Canadian Military Highway project took him away from Beth and the boys for long hours each day. Often when he arrived home it was all he could do to clean up before dropping into bed. Gerald and Phillip grew impatient for his company, but Beth faithfully explained why it was necessary for August to spend so much time away from them.

The combined efforts of the United States and Canada resulted in the scheduled creation of a highway that would cover more than 1,486 miles, from Dawson Creek, British Columbia, to Fairbanks, Alaska. Calling it a highway was an optimistic overstatement. The road was clearly nothing more than a bulldozed path through an unyielding wilderness.

Never intended to do more than provide emergency access to the north should the Japanese cut off the water and air routes, this road of mud and ice quickly became a problem of outrageous proportions.

Frozen subsoil, permafrost, muskeg, and long hours of sunlight created problems that made engineers throw up their hands in frustration. Coupled with the fact that there were inadequate supplies and living accommodations for the eleven thousand troops, most of whom were from the southern United States and completely unacquainted with the cold temperatures that seemed to come at will, the highway quickly became a matter of man against nature.

Canada provided access to the lands through British Columbia and the Yukon Territory, as well as much of the needed building materials. All of this was given in exchange for unlimited use of the road following the war.

As engineers and administrators brought their plans together and fine-tuned the design of the project, it was determined that over 130 log and pontoon bridges would be needed to accommodate the hundreds of rivers and lakes that the highway would have to cross.

Added to this were some eight thousand culverts to be dug and reinforced to combat the constant drainage problems created by the swampy soil.

Behind the frustrations of a seemingly endless number of new problems was the threat of Japanese invasion of Alaska. Though few knew of the plan, military experts had found a way to decode Japan's messages in time to learn of Alaska's vulnerability to attack.

Even as far north as the rural villages of Alaska, and perhaps because such vulnerability seemed evident, the mood was one of hushed and guarded silence.

Beth's ten-room boardinghouse was rapidly becoming a common meeting place for the army leadership and the Public Roads Administration. If the weather was cooperative, the group usually assembled outside, where August had placed a number of crudely built tables and chairs. Other times, however, the weather was rainy or cold, and Beth allowed the men to take over her living room while she and the boys holed up in her bedroom.

Glancing outside, Beth could see that the day's weather would allow for an outdoor gathering, and she breathed a sigh of relief. The meetings always made her rather uncomfortable. She never could figure out what disturbed her most: the presence of uniformed men or the worry that military secrets might fall upon the ears of her children, only to be carelessly babbled later.

She finished pulling the last of five wild raspberry pies from the oven as August came striding into the room.

"Ummm, smells wonderful, Beth. Don't suppose you're going to let me buy them for our meeting?"

"What else would I do with five pies?" Beth asked, chuckling. "Are you certain the men will reimburse you? I can't charge you two dollars a pie in good faith if I have to worry that you'll be out the entire amount."

"They stand in line to pay me," August said with a grin and added, "and at thirty cents a slice, they're going out in good shape, and so am I. Helps me pay the rent," he teased.

"I keep meaning to talk to you about that," Beth said as she smoothed back her blond hair and reinserted one of the combs that held it back at the sides.

"Great," August said in a mocking tone of dissatisfaction, "I suppose my rent is about to go up."

"No, not at all," Beth said, mortified that August would tease about such a thing.

"Relax, it was a joke, Beth," August said as he eyed the young woman seriously. "What did you want to talk about?"

"I can't see you having to pay as much as everyone else when you help out so much around here. I mean, you cut most all my wood, you mended the fence and the roof, not to mention that you worked up the dirt for my garden. It's only fair that I offer you some type of compensation."

August smiled and wondered if Beth could begin to imagine the type of compensation he'd like to redeem from her. The fact was he was growing more attracted to the young widow and her sons each day.

"I'm sure we can work something out," August finally said. "But if you're doing it for my sake, then stop worrying. I'm grateful for the time you allow us to meet and disrupt your home in order to coordinate plans for the road."

"I don't feel it's adequate compensation," Beth interjected. "I'd like to at least reduce your rent. If you have something else in mind, I'm open to suggestions."

August grinned and pushed back his black hair. "Well, an occasional hot meal might do the trick," he said, knowing that he couldn't very well come out and say that he'd like to spend more time getting to know her.

"That seems a simple request," Beth said, realizing how pleasant it would be to have August at her table. "But not an occasional meal. I think it's only right that you share all our meals, if you want to. I'll even pack you a lunch if you'd like."

"You'll spoil me," August laughed, "but I'll enjoy it while you do. I'd be quite happy to accept your offer, Bethany."

Beth smiled nervously and made a show of rechecking the oven as if a pie had been inadvertently overlooked. She knew that August was attracted to her, yet she hadn't decided if she liked the idea or not.

It had been over a year since JB had died and longer than that since she'd seen him, but the ghostly image of her husband was never so haunting as when Beth felt the cold, gold band that still adorned her finger. Perhaps when she was ready to put away that last reminder of her marriage, she would be able to deal with the interest of another man.

"Well, I'd best make sure everything is ready for our meeting. The army's bringing the coffee this time, so we shouldn't have any trouble staying awake long enough to resolve any new differences. I'll be back for those pies in about an hour, if that's all right with you."

"They should be cooled by then," Beth said and offered August a smile.

August nodded and left Beth to the task of cleaning up. Beth watched through the window as several army vehicles pulled into her yard, unleashing a throng of uniformed men and a large coffeepot.

A knock on her front door sent Beth to answer it. She opened the door to find two young soldiers looking rather sheepishly at her.

"May I help you?" she questioned softly.

"Ma'am, we're here helping with the road," one of the men began as if Beth wouldn't already be privy to the information.

Beth nodded and the man continued.

"Well, me and Ronnie here, we've been coming to these meetings, and well, ma'am," he stammered for just the right words.

"Go on," Beth encouraged sweetly.

"Well, it's like this. We've been eating your cakes and pies whenever Mr. Eriksson offers them for sale, and we surely do miss our mom's cooking. Army grub just ain't anywhere near as good."

"I'm sure that's true," Beth said, suppressing a laugh.

"We was wondering, hoping really, that we could pay you to make some of our favorite sweet potato pie. We've managed to get our hands on some canned sweet potatoes, and while they won't be near as good as fresh, we'd be mighty happy to pay you to bake us however much it would make. In the way of pies, that is."

Beth felt sorry for the boys. "I'm not sure I have a recipe for sweet potato pie," she said honestly.

"It's pert' near the same as pumpkin," the other boy offered. "But I reckon I can get you a copy of the recipe from somebody."

"Well then, you get me the recipe, and I'll be happy to make your pies. One thing, though, I use mostly honey, due to the shortage of sugar. If you don't think the results will be as good, we'd probably best call off the whole arrangement right now."

"No ma'am," the first soldier offered. "Whatever way you make it will be just fine. We'll be back when we can bring you the recipe and the sweet potatoes. How much you gonna charge us for the pie?"

Beth thought for a moment. "I think a dollar would be a fair amount," she answered. While she charged August two dollars for most of her pies and cakes, she knew he easily made his money back. These boys, however, were not going to be making much profit because Beth was certain they'd be eating most of the pie themselves.

"Sounds just fine by us," the one called Ronnie said as he looked at his friend. "They charge us nearly that much for a single piece at the café in town, and the army could never make anything as good as what you serve, ma'am."

"Well, I appreciate your compliments, boys. Now you'd best get around back, because I've a feeling the meeting will be starting shortly, and tonight we're having raspberry pie."

"Yes ma'am!" they answered in unison and hurried to the backyard.

———— # ————

"So our biggest problem at this point," Ralph Greening was explaining, "is the need for a much larger airfield in order to bring in the bigger planes and more supplies."

"It's not just a problem," an army colonel offered. "It's imperative that we have this runway."

"I understand the need, gentlemen. However, the land around us is most uncooperative. We have a tremendous problem with the permafrost. I've asked August Eriksson to address this problem and to let you know about the progress we've made. August, go ahead."

"As we've cleared land for the runway and grated the sphagnum moss from the topsoil, we've run into the constant problem of ground thaw. The moss has always acted as an insulator that keeps the subsoil frozen and firm. When the moss is removed, we get a swamp."

"But we have to have that runway," the colonel insisted.

"I realize that, Colonel, and if you'll hear me out, I'll explain how we're combatting this situation. By experimenting we've come up with a plan that seems to be working. First, we skim off the topsoil and moss, allowing the ground to thaw. When this next layer of ground has completely warmed up, we grate off another portion and allow this section to thaw as well. We do this over and over until what we have is an excavation several feet deep.

"Next, we fill this area with sand from the river bottom. This sand allows the subsoil waters to rise to the level of the surrounding ground's water table. Then, due to the freezing temperatures of the soil, this water freezes and becomes a rock solid surface, while the sand acts as an insulator. This should then allow us to put the regular asphalt apron on top and leave the surface fixed and sturdy year-round."

"Ingenious," the colonel said, offering his first positive word. "Has it been tested?"

"Yes," August replied, feeling rather proud of himself. "It has, and with the exact results we'd hoped for. Our only holdup is waiting for each process of ground thaw. Other than that, we would have the main runway completed in a very short time."

"Might the usage of steam from a portable boiler speed up this process?" the colonel questioned.

"That is a possibility," August said with a nod toward Ralph Greening. "I'm sure my supervisor would be happy to discuss the matter with you."

"Most assuredly," Ralph answered.

"I believe," the colonel said with thoughtful consideration, "we could offer the use of such army equipment when it's not being used for other purposes. Will you have enough manpower for the job?"

"We've hired many of the locals for additional help," Ralph Greening replied. "We're paying a dollar an hour, so pass the word among the civilians as you're out among them. The more hands we have, the quicker the project will be completed, and we'll be able to get those big transport planes in here."

"The Northwest Transport Command will be grateful for that," the colonel said as he sat back in the chair for the first time.

"I'm sure many of the Tanana people will be happy to help." One of the local men who'd been working with August spoke up. "I know these Indians, and they are good people."

"We'll take them all," Ralph said. "Anybody and everybody. If we're to have this road in place by fall, we can't be picky about who works and who doesn't."

"Well, I'd say the situation is well under control," the colonel remarked. "Now, how about one of those delicious desserts that Mrs. Hogan makes for us?"

August smiled and got to his feet. "It's raspberry pie tonight, and you all know the price. Just take up the collection, and I'll borrow a couple of your men to help me bring out the goods."

Instantly the men began reaching into their pockets. As a hat was passed, the money was eagerly handed over. August grabbed the nearest two men and quickly returned with the five pies. The hat was passed to August, as the men gathered around waiting patiently for their pie. Shortly after the food was gone and the coffee drained, the meeting ended and the satisfied men returned to their tents for some much-needed sleep.

August counted out ten dollars for Beth and pocketed the other two. He was tired, but grateful that it was Saturday. He'd managed to wrangle the following day off and hoped that somehow he'd talk Beth into a picnic with the boys. He was considering just how he might ask her, when Beth appeared to reclaim her pie tins.

"Looks like the meeting was successful," Beth said as she stacked the pans.

"Yes, very," August agreed and added, "Do you have to rush right back?"

The light was fading, and in the twilight that filtered through the tall birch and spruce trees, Beth's face seemed shrouded in the shadows. Still, August could see that she liked the idea of remaining.

"I can stay for a little while, although I hate to keep you up," Beth said, putting the pans down and taking the seat across from August.

"That's one of the reasons I asked you to stay," August replied. "I have tomorrow off and hoped that maybe you would agree to picnicking with the boys and me."

"That sounds like a lot of fun," Beth admitted. "Perhaps you would accompany us to church first." She knew August avoided any reference to such things, but she wanted to find out why he was hesitant when it came to God.

To August's own surprise, he agreed to go. "I suppose that would fall into line."

"Church is at eleven, so you should be able to sleep late. I'll try to keep the boys quiet."

"No, don't," August answered. "I want to get up early and play with them."

"I appreciate the way you look after them. I've never seen them so happy. They care quite deeply for you," Beth said softly. "I hope you realize how much they adore you."

"I do," August said and leaned forward. "Does that worry you?"

"I suppose it does," Beth replied. "They suffered the loss of their father, and then I uprooted them and moved them here. They need to feel secure about their home and the people they care about."

"Do you think I'm incapable of offering them stability in our friendship?" August questioned seriously.

"Not really," Beth said thoughtfully. "I suppose my real concern is that soon the road will be completed and you'll be on your way. I know that would be devastating to them."

"Who says I'll be on my way? If I have something to stick around for, I can't see giving that up," August whispered in a low, husky voice. He wondered if Beth would understand his meaning.

"I think as long as you want a reason to stay, you'll have one. The boys are devoted to you, and I want. . ." Beth grew uncomfortable and got to her feet. "I'd better clean up this mess."

August got up and moved behind Beth. "I'd rather hear you finish that thought."

Beth could feel his warm breath against her neck as August spoke. She wanted very much to get away from the loneliness that threatened to strangle her, but she was also afraid of the feelings that were building in her heart.

"I'm not sure it would be wise," Beth finally whispered.

August very gently turned her to face him. He gazed deep into her eyes just before he lowered his lips to press a gentle kiss upon Beth's mouth. When she didn't protest, he pulled her close and held her for several minutes.

"Now, you were saying?" August asked as he pulled slightly away and lifted Beth's face to meet his stare.

"I don't know what to say," Beth answered.

"Just speak what's on your heart," August urged. He wanted so much to hear Beth say something that would indicate her interest in him.

"That's not always an easy thing to do, August."

"No, maybe not," August said, gently stroking Beth's cheek with his thumb. "But it's always the best."

"I'm afraid." Beth's words were barely audible.

"Of me?" August questioned, hurt showing on his face.

"No," Beth replied. "I'm afraid of myself. Afraid of trusting too much, caring too much, needing too much."

"Don't be," August said, kissing Beth's hand and holding it close to his heart. "Just tell me what you started to say. Tell me what you want."

"Stay," Beth murmured. "I want you to stay."

Chapter 6

D ays later, Beth sat considering her situation. There was, of course, the constant threat of war hanging over like an ever-present storm cloud. Added to this was the continual demands of the roadhouse and the responsibility of raising two boys without a father.

Her sons concerned her most, along with the fact that Beth was finally admitting how much she missed the companionship of a husband.

She hadn't realized how lonely she was until the night August had held her and kissed her. It was hard to admit to loneliness with hundreds of uniformed men and civilians milling up and down the path that ran in front of her roadhouse, but Beth was lonely. August only made that fact more evident.

True to his promise, August had accompanied her and the boys to Sunday school and church. He had appeared aloof and uncomfortable during the worship service, but he said nothing and acted as though he were simply preoccupied. Afterward, they'd enjoyed a wonderful summer afternoon, picnicking, fishing, and simply enjoying each other's company.

It was hard not to think about those moments with August, as well as their first kiss. Beth had made it very clear to August that she wanted him to stay. What she hadn't said was that she needed him to stay; she needed his company and his friendship in a way she couldn't begin to explain.

August had wanted Beth to talk about her feelings, but how could she when she scarcely understood them herself? And what about the issue of why August was avoiding God? There was a great deal about August Eriksson that Beth didn't understand, and those issues were important enough to her so that she wanted to go slow.

Beth pulled out her ledger books and tried to concentrate on the numbers. She made it through one or two lines before her thoughts drifted off. Suddenly, she was a million miles away from balancing the roadhouse books.

August's appearance in her life had brought so many benefits. The relationship he shared with her sons was a precious friendship that filled some of the void their father's death had created.

Phillip and Gerald accepted August as if he'd been JB returning from the war. It didn't matter to them, even after countless explanations, that August wasn't their daddy. Phillip refused to call him anything else, and often Gerald slipped up and referred to him that way. Beth found it increasingly acceptable for her boys to use the title, and when Gerald put JB's picture in the china cupboard, she realized he was symbolizing an end to his need for JB's memory.

Beth couldn't explain why she didn't fight the action or why it seemed perfectly natural to share her meals and spare time with a man she barely knew. But for the first time in months, her boys were happy, and neither one had bad dreams or moped around looking for a man who would never come home.

Looking down at her hand, Beth suddenly realized that she'd nearly twisted her wedding ring off her finger. She stared at the band for a moment, then pulled it off quickly and put it in the desk drawer. JB was gone, and August was here. Perhaps it was time to deal with the matter head-on.

Giving up on the ledgers, Beth made her way through the house picking up toys and misplaced items. What a difference one year made! Where once baby rattles and teething rings had dotted the counters, now blocks and trucks sprouted up. Her babies had grown up so fast that it left Beth aching for the feel of holding them close. Perhaps she'd have more children one day.

The thought stunned her. She hadn't considered remarrying until August came into her life, and now she was contemplating a larger family. Maybe August wouldn't want more children.

"Stop it!" Beth said aloud. "I can't think this way. I've got myself married off and having more children, and all to a man I scarcely know!" The empty house absorbed her words, perfectly content to keep her secrets.

Outside, a summer storm was brewing. Beth could hear thunder rumble in the distance. She fought the urge to cry. Things weren't going badly at all, so why did she feel so blue?

The boys were spending the day in town with the woman who led their Sunday school class at the small interdenominational church. Mrs. Miller was a pleasant woman with graying hair and a grand-motherly shape. Being a widow of several years as well as childless, Mrs. Miller had aligned herself with Beth.

She was particularly fond of Phillip and Gerald, and when the older widow had invited the boys for lunch at her house, Beth had agreed, understanding Mrs. Miller's need. Now, however, Beth reconsidered. The house seemed empty and far too quiet.

Beth sighed. What was wrong with her? She had but to look out her front window and see more activity than most small towns could boast.

The path was being widened to meet road specifications, and Beth could count on no less than twenty different men pounding on her front door daily, seeking everything from water to food to permission to use the privy. She caught on, only after August informed her, that most of the men were doing it to have a chance to talk to the handsome widow of Gantry Roadhouse.

Beth blushed crimson as she remembered August's laughing eyes and boyish grin. He was amused that she had been too naive to figure it out for herself.

"You're a beautiful woman, Beth Hogan," he had said, "and most of these men haven't had the opportunity to see, much less visit with, a woman of any kind since leaving the States and being assigned to this wilderness. Women are mighty scarce up here, so you might as well get used to being popular."

Beth had feared August would think she'd done something to encourage the attention, but he never spoke of it and never seemed to mind when the boys told stories of visiting strangers.

The highway had been excellent for business, and because of this and the workers' avid interest, Beth could boast a lengthy list of men who were waiting their turn to take residence in her boardinghouse. Many of these made the excuse of checking on the availability of rooms and stayed on talking of the weather, the highway, or anything else that would delay their return to work.

Yet Beth was still lonely, and she couldn't understand why.

The clock in the hall chimed two, and Beth realized that her cakes were ready to come out of the oven. She had doubled up on baking, knowing that the next day would be devoted to washing clothes and linens, a job that always took an entire day. Often she was still hanging laundry after August arrived home.

Hurrying to the kitchen, Beth pulled out two cake pans along with an experimental recipe she was trying. The sourdough coffee cake, complete with berries and honey, looked every bit as good as it smelled, and Beth was hopeful that its flavor would match its appearance.

Silently, Beth thanked God for the endless supply of honey that one of her bachelor neighbors provided in exchange for mending and sewing. The older man seemed more than happy to give Beth all the honey she could use and even happier to spend time visiting and telling the boys tales of the old days when he'd lived off the land and searched for gold.

Beth realized that, because of such generosity and bartering for goods, she and the boys scarcely felt the effects of rationing that the war had made necessary. God had been truly good to them.

When her baking was completed, Beth was amazed to realize she still had almost two hours to pass before the boys and August would be home. August had agreed to pick the boys up at Mrs. Miller's house in order to spare either of the ladies from making the trip. At the time, Beth couldn't find any reason not to accept his offer. Now she wished she had a reason to take the long stroll into town.

Heaving a sigh, Beth decided to stop feeling sorry for herself. Instead, she would cook a special meal for her family's return. Putting her hands to work usually occupied her mind as well. Hopefully, working on dinner would make the afternoon pass more quickly.

She thoughtfully chose foods that she knew everyone was fond of. Smoked salmon would be their meat, and for a side dish, Beth blended new potatoes, fresh green beans, and pieces of side meat. For dessert, they'd try her new berry coffee cake, a sure way, Beth decided, to know whether or not it was acceptable.

She was just finishing the table setting, using her finest tablecloth and wedding china, when she heard the boys' nonstop chatter as they drew near home. *What a beautiful sound,* Beth thought. She was so used to the constant noise of the road construction that when the men had stopped for supper, Beth hadn't noticed.

She was grateful that the army was taking time away from the project to have their own evening meal. No doubt with the added hours of light there'd soon be another shift at work, but for now Beth was going to thoroughly enjoy the noise that her sons raised and the words that August Eriksson would share at her dinner table.

"Mommy!" Gerald hollered as he came through the door. August followed with Phillip on his shoulders.

Beth smiled and welcomed Gerald into her arms. "Did you have a good time at Mrs. Miller's house?"

"Uh-huh," Gerald said and held up a small sack. "We made cookies, and Mrs. Miller said we could bring them home."

"How nice of her," Beth said, and turned her attention from Gerald to Phillip. "And how about you, buster? Did you have a good time?"

"Had fun," Phillip answered. "Got to ride on Daddy."

"And I believe this child is eating too much," August said as he lifted Phillip over his head and placed him on the ground. "Well, well. What's all this?" he said as he noticed the table.

"I just thought something special might be nice," Beth answered. "I had so much time on my hands with the boys gone. I never knew a body could get so lonely."

August offered a tender smile, and Beth quickly turned her face away to avoid feeling the impact of his clear eyes. "You boys go wash your hands and we'll sit down to dinner."

Handing his mother the cookies, Gerald scurried off to the washroom with Phillip close behind. Both boys were giggling and chattering all the way, leaving Beth with a much lighter heart.

"I'm sorry if I made you uncomfortable," August said as he paused before following the boys. "I just don't like to think of you lonely. Seems like such a waste, especially when so many enjoy your company."

Beth wondered if it was her imagination or August's feelings that caused her to read more into his statement.

When August and the boys returned from washing up, Beth allowed August to seat her while the boys scampered into their assigned places.

"Who wants to say grace?" Beth questioned.

"I will!" Gerald said enthusiastically.

"All right, Gerald." Beth nodded in agreement. "You go right ahead."

"God, this is Gerald again," the boy began. "I sure do like living in Alaska 'cause You sent us a lot of great people and we're having fun here. God, Mommy told me to pray about a daddy for Phillip and me, so I'm praying about it. I like August, God, and I really want him to be my daddy. So if it's okay with You, me and Phillip will take him. Amen."

"What about the food, son?" August questioned softly, noticing that Beth's head was still bowed.

"Oh yeah," Gerald said and quickly bowed his head again. "Thanks for the food, God. I really like fish. Amen."

August was grinning when Beth raised her gaze to meet his. She grew more beautiful with each passing day, and August heartily agreed with Gerald's prayers that they become a family.

Beth handed Phillip's plate to August. "If you would serve the salmon"—she motioned—"I would appreciate it."

August nodded and filled the plates as they were passed to him. He liked acting as the head of the family, and he enjoyed the warmth and comfort of the company he kept.

Supper passed much too quickly. "I suppose I should be going," August said, getting up. Beth's roadhouse was set up so that the ten boarding rooms all faced north or west and had individual entrances facing the outside.

"Can't he read us a story?" Gerald asked with pleading eyes.

"Please?" Phillip questioned.

"That's up to August," Beth said as she began to gather the dishes. "It's all right with me, August, if you want to read to them."

"I'd be happy to," August said, grateful for the excuse to remain close at hand. He followed the boys down the hall to their bedroom, giving Beth a quick smile over his shoulder.

Beth felt her pulse quicken. What would it be like to have August join her for the evening every night after putting their children to bed? It had been so long since she'd known the warmth and comfort of a man's company. Was it wrong for her to think of such things?

"Well, that didn't take long," August said as he came into the kitchen. "They're nearly asleep."

"Thank you for everything," Beth said, and tried to think of how she could express her gratitude for August's indulgence of their fatherly references. "I appreciate your patience with them. I've asked them not to call you Daddy. . ." She paused, embarrassed as she remembered Gerald's prayer. "But they love you so much."

"I'm sure that they loved their father a great deal. They're just show-ing me what they can't show him."

"It's more than that. JB was a soldier first. He was so bent on serv-ing his country and being a hero," Beth said as she finished drying the dishes. She didn't see August bite his lip at her words.

"Don't get me wrong," she said, turning to face him. "JB was a good man and a fine father. He loved children and we were planning to have a half a dozen or more, but his need to serve someone else or something else took him away from us. I don't blame him or resent him for his decision, but I don't think I'll ever understand the feelings that drive a man to leave his family and die a world away from those who love him."

"It's a powerful drive indeed," August said softly. "I'm sure JB felt proud, and in his heart he knew that he was offering his children the best he had. He gave his life that others might live free."

"Much like Christ gave His life for us," Beth said, startling August.

"I suppose that's true," he agreed. "If Christ felt it necessary to come on our behalf and give His life, then maybe you can understand JB's desire to offer what he could for those he loved."

"Maybe you're right," Beth said as she considered August's words. "Jesus certainly loves us more than we can comprehend."

August looked uncomfortable, so Beth decided to say no more. "I'd better go," August finally said. "I'll have to be up pretty early, so don't worry about breakfast. I'll get something in town."

"All right," Beth said and watched as August walked quietly from the house. She whispered a prayer that August would find a way through whatever problem was causing him to feel alienated from God's peace.

———*H*———

August made his way to his room. Even though it was still light outside and would be for many hours, August closed the heavy shutters and prepared for bed. It was warm enough that he wouldn't need to light the stove.

He lay awake for a long time, thinking about the things Beth had said and how she constantly tried to steer him back to God. His conscience bothered him as he thought of the truth that he continued to deny.

God clearly wanted his attention, but August wasn't inclined to let go of his bitterness. God still hadn't listened to the desires of August's heart, and because of that, August questioned what purpose faith served.

As he drifted into a fitful sleep, August remembered how his inability to get into the army brought him to both his important job with the highway and Beth Hogan. One door had closed while another had opened and shown him a new way of life. But where did God fit in?

Chapter 7

With the boys busy playing in the backyard tree house, Beth took a moment out of her morning chores to enjoy a hot cup of coffee and a letter from her friend, Karen Sawin.

Karen shared bits of information, including the news that her husband had suffered an injury and was being sent home. Beth wished she could be there to help her friend but travel was nearly impossible because of the war.

Reading on, Beth was glad to learn that the family who'd purchased her home was being blessed with yet another child and had plans to build onto the house in order to accommodate the addition.

Finishing the letter, Beth noted the fear and apprehension that Karen expressed as she awaited her husband's return. Beth whispered a prayer for her friend as she refolded the paper.

Setting the letter aside, Beth picked up a pad and pencil and scratched out a reminder to write to Karen at the first possible moment. She knew Karen would need all the encouragement she could get.

Beth glanced out the window to make certain the boys hadn't fallen out of the tree. She had faced the tree house with fear, but August had convinced her that boys needed such things. Who was she to argue with his wisdom? Giggles filtered down, assuring Beth that nothing was amiss.

Back at the table, Beth sipped weak coffee and tried to plan out the rest of the day. She jotted notes about lunch and supper, but inevitably her mind returned to thoughts of August. She could picture him standing in the yard playing with her children or chopping wood. He was an appealing man with a handsome face and a gentleness that she'd rarely seen in others. Her feelings for him were growing, but she knew he was troubled about God.

What was it that had hurt August so much that he couldn't deal with God? Beth contemplated that question as she continued to enjoy the quiet.

"Beth?" August called from the front room.

Beth glanced at her watch and then at the clock on the wall. It was only nine o'clock. What was August doing back at this hour?

"In here," Beth called and got to her feet. August came through the kitchen door with a worried look on his face. "What is it?" Beth questioned, knowing that August had something to tell her.

"You'd better sit down," August said and pulled the chair out for Beth.

"What is it?" Beth repeated the question.

"What I'm going to tell you has to be kept secret, at least until you read about it in the newspapers."

"I don't understand," Beth said, and felt her stomach knot.

"You know why the highway was planned, don't you?"

"Sure," Beth replied. "The government felt it was important to have an emergency road in order to get supplies through."

"That's right," August said. "Well, now we may very well need the road."

"Why?" Beth questioned. "What's happened?"

"This is the part you mustn't tell anyone. The army took us into their confidence this morning. The Japanese have attacked the Aleutian Islands," August announced.

"The Aleutians? But that's less than six hundred miles away," Beth said as the color drained from her face. "Dear Lord, preserve us."

"Look, Beth, the Aleutians are a long ways off. We're safe here, but the road project has been stepped up. We've got work to do and not much time to do it in. The troops are holding the Japanese back, but it's critical we get this road through."

Tears filled Beth's eyes. "Are we really safe? I mean, are you sure?"

August saw the tears and heard Beth's voice tremble. He got up and put his hands on her shoulders just as she broke down.

"I can't bear it, August. I can't stand the fear, the worry. I have children whose safety depends on me. I just can't bear the thought of the enemy storming in here and, and. . ." Beth's sobs filled the air.

"Don't torture yourself, Beth. We really are safe. After all, there are more than ten thousand soldiers in Alaska and Canada. There's more than enough manpower here to keep us safe."

Beth pushed away from August and got to her feet. "We probably had thousands of men in the Pacific as well. If men are so capable, why are we at war?"

"We're at war because we have to fight to keep free of dictators like Hitler and Mussolini, as well as military monsters like Tojo. Beth, please don't cry. Everything will work out. You'll see. Just have a little faith."

Beth managed to compose herself. "Yes, of course you're right, August. Faith is the key. Faith in God, though, not in the American military. God will give them strength and wisdom. Prayer is going to be the key to this victory, and I'm sorry that I let go of that wisdom."

August stepped forward and put his hand on Beth's arm. "I just wanted you to know what was going on before you heard about it from someone else. No doubt the newspaper will have enough about it in the days to come, but I never wanted to upset you. I know news like this can be frightening."

"I'm all right now," Beth said as she lifted her apron and dried her eyes. She wanted so much to prove her faith to August. Perhaps he'd once had faith too, a faith that he'd lost because of tragedy. Maybe this was the reason God had sent August Eriksson into her life—not for love or marriage, but for him to see the truth of God's love.

August studied her for a moment. He wanted to hold her, to make her believe that everything would be all right, but in spite of the feelings that continued to grow, August held himself back.

There was something in Beth's eyes that signaled aloofness. She was content to put the entire matter in God's hands, and it seemed to August that she didn't need or desire his comfort. Shrugging his shoulders, he left the roadhouse with an ache in his heart for something he couldn't explain.

———— # ————

The hot June sun caused sweat to pour down August's back as he maneuvered the Caterpillar into position. He was frustrated by Beth's attitude and wondered how he could combat it. She never came out and talked with him about her true feelings. She always managed to hide behind God or biblical principles, almost as if she knew it would distance August from her.

Wiping his forehead with the back of his hand, August acknowledged that his biggest problem wasn't Beth. God was pricking his conscience.

It was the little things that got to him. Things like the way Beth would ask him to say grace or the way Gerald would talk about something from Sunday school. Sometimes it was the simple, quiet moments when August was alone in his room and the silence came over him as if roaring out God's name.

He'd not known a single moment's peace since turning away from his heavenly Father, and the turmoil within his heart only grew. August wanted to shout out for God to leave him alone, but the pressure continued, mounting day by day.

The roadwork took August away from Beth and the boys for longer periods of time. Sometimes he never made it home because the midnight sun allowed them to work nearly around the clock. Often, August would drop exhausted into a sleeping bag inside one of the administration's tents. The cots weren't nearly as comfortable as the bed back at the roadhouse, but as tired as he was, it wouldn't have mattered if he'd been sleeping on the ground.

Day after day the work continued. They called it "bulldozer surveying," and it was little more than plowing a path through a place where a road had never been intended. Trees, brush, and rocks ended up in messy piles along the road, constant reminders of the haste in which the design was completed.

August would often stare for a long time at the tall spruce and birch trees, trees so thick and full that they were impossible to penetrate with the human eye. It seemed a pity to destroy them.

Dense forests were relieved by brilliant, crystal lakes so blue and inviting that August could almost forget his purpose. Glacier-fed rivers flowed in milky wonder, leaving reminders of the ice mountains that had carved the valleys.

In the distant south, snowcapped peaks rose majestically above green and blue valleys, and everywhere wildflowers carpeted the earth in colors so dazzling and radiant that words could not describe them.

"Eriksson!" a voice called above the roar of the Cat's engine. August shut the motor off and climbed down.

"What's up, Bill?" August questioned, recognizing the man beneath layers of dirt and sweat.

"I'm supposed to take over your shift. Supervisor wants to see you."

"Oh?" He wondered about the request as he went in search of Ralph Greening.

Ralph was waiting for August in his tent. "Come on in." Ralph waved him in as he finished up a radio call. "Sorry for the interruption, but I have some good news for you."

"Well, I'm always in the mood for good news interruptions," August said with a smile.

"You've done a tremendous job for us, August, and I'd like to offer you a permanent position with the Public Roads Administration.

You'd actually be left in charge of the Northway area after we pull out. They are going to want to establish a permanent road next year, and I can't think of a better man to leave behind."

"I'm flattered," August said.

"Well, you've certainly earned it," Ralph replied as he shuffled through a stack of papers. "I'll be happy to return to the States and get away from these monstrous bugs and all this light. A body needs regular nights and days. I can't figure out how you folks put up with constant light and then endless darkness."

"I guess when you're born here you don't give it a lot of thought. We do suffer in the winter though. It's hard to wake up in the dark, spend the day in the dark, and then go to sleep in the dark. Coupled with the cold—and I mean bitter, subzero cold—it is a problem," August replied. "But there are winter compensations."

"I don't intend to be here long enough to find out. We plan to have the road completed before then, and after that you can put up with it."

———— # ————

Hours later, August contemplated his promotion and the full responsibility that would be his when Ralph returned to the States. Did he want to head up such a task?

As he settled down for bed, August wondered at the turn of events. Not long ago he'd thought God had deserted him. How did he feel now? Hadn't he proved to himself that he could live life without God?

He missed Beth and the boys. It had been over a week since he'd seen them. They were so important to him, and thoughts of them were never far from his mind. Did they ever think of him? Did they miss him like he missed them?

August closed his eyes, envisioning Bethany as she moved around her roadhouse. She was so gentle and pure, and her heart was devoted to God.

His heart had once belonged to God too. August shifted uncomfortably as he thought of his efforts to put God away from him. *"But whosoever shall deny me before men, him will I also deny before my Father which is in heaven.*" August remembered the words of Matthew 10:33 almost against his will.

"But You took away all my dreams, God," August argued, realizing that, for the first time in months, he was speaking to God. "You took it all: my dreams, my hopes, my family. Am I to be forsaken because I dared to think for myself, dared to make goals and dream dreams? I thought You wanted Your children to be happy. Am I to give up my dreams, even my very life, in order to be at peace with You?"

"He that findeth his life shall lose it: and he that loseth his life for my sake shall find it." August pulled the pillow over his head as if he could block out the haunting words of Matthew 10:39. The words, however, would not be put aside. God's Word had made its home in August's heart for many years, and it would not leave just because August wished to escape its power.

Chapter 8

After spending two weeks without August in their home, Beth, Gerald, and Phillip were excited to see his weary frame coming up the path late one afternoon.

"Daddy!" Phillip announced when he spotted August. "Momma, Daddy's here!"

Beth glanced out the window, and her hands automatically smoothed back her blond hair. August was home!

Gerald went dancing out the door, rushing into August's arms. "I missed you," he said as August whirled him around.

"And I missed you! Have you been a good boy?"

"I've been very helpful, just like you told me to be," Gerald said as August put him down.

Phillip hurried to be next in August's arms, while Beth stood to the side of the door, wishing she had the freedom her children enjoyed.

August's eyes met hers over Phillip's back. He noticed the softness and grinned at her, causing Beth's heart to pound harder.

"And what about you?" Beth heard August ask Phillip. "Have you been a good boy?"

"Uh-huh. I been helping in the garden," Phillip said, holding up his dirty hands. "See!"

His enthusiasm was contagious. "Yes, I see." August said, inspecting Phillip's hands. "Since you've both been so good, I'll take you fishing tomorrow. That is, if your mother doesn't mind."

"Can we go, Momma?" Phillip and Gerald asked in unison.

"I suppose so," Beth replied softly. "Now, why don't you go inside and get cleaned up? It's almost suppertime."

The boys hesitated as they looked from August to their mother and back again. "You go ahead, boys. I'll be here for a day or two." At August's reassurance the boys disappeared into the house.

"I've missed you," August said warmly. "I never knew how good I had it until I had to live out on the road. I've missed everything about this place."

"Even the bugs?" Beth asked with a smile.

"The bugs are even bigger down the road. Out there we have to shoot them down rather than swat them." August laughed and Beth joined him. When the amusement passed, silence bound them together.

"You look beautiful." August braved the words and allowed his eyes to travel Beth's form. The dusty-rose dress she wore brought out the flush in her cheeks.

Beth didn't know what to say. She was excited by August's appreciation of her appearance, yet she was troubled by the warning her mind kept flashing.

"Are you hungry?" she finally questioned, growing uncomfortable in the silence.

"Yes," August replied. "I suppose I'm keeping you from something."

"Only dinner," Beth answered and opened the screen door. "Come on inside. I'll work while you tell me about the road's progress."

"It's a deal," August said, following Beth into the house and on to the kitchen.

"I took a moose roast out of the freezer several days ago, and we've been eating it ever since," Beth said as she opened the oven door. "We're having moose pie tonight."

"Moose pie?"

Beth smiled as she took the casserole from the oven. "That's right. It's moose roast cut up with eggplant, onions, egg, cheese, and seasoning. It's baked with a piecrust topping, and that's why we call it moose pie."

"Sounds good," August said, sitting down.

"I can fix up a mess of goose tongue greens, if you've a mind for a salad, and I have fresh sourdough bread."

"Don't go to any more trouble than you already have," August said.

Before Beth could answer, a knock sounded at the front door. "I'll be right back," Beth said as she excused herself.

"What a surprise," Beth said as she opened the door to Mrs. Miller. Ushering the woman inside, she asked, "What brings you here?"

"I know it's last-minute and totally out of line, but I was wondering if I could borrow the boys to help me gather blackberries. I've promised the army a great deal of jam, and there's a huge field of berries ready to pick."

"Well, I'm not sure," Beth said as she led the way back to the kitchen. "Mr. Eriksson is back, and the boys are very fond of him. I don't know if we could separate them just now."

"I understand, but I could sure use the help. I'd be happy to pay the boys," the older woman added as she struggled to keep up with Beth.

"Oh no, you needn't pay them," Beth said as they entered the kitchen. In her absence, the boys had been taking turns playing with August and asking him questions.

"Boys, Mrs. Miller wants to know if you can help her pick blackberries."

"But August just got here," Gerald protested from August's lap.

"And I'll be here for a while," August said and gave Gerald a reassuring pat. "Don't worry about it. You go ahead and help Mrs. Miller. We can certainly catch up on our talking tomorrow while we're fishing."

"Well, I guess we can help," Gerald said once he felt certain of August's presence.

"I'm afraid the boys haven't eaten yet, Mrs. Miller. Would you like to join us for supper?" Beth asked, proud that Gerald had put his own wants aside to help someone else.

"No thanks, and if you don't mind, I'd like to treat the boys to a picnic. I have sandwiches and cold drinks, as well as some special cookies that they are very fond of," Mrs. Miller answered.

"Well, what do you say, boys? You want to have a picnic with Mrs. Miller?" August questioned before Beth could ask. "I'll bet it'll be a load of fun."

"Really, Daddy?" Phillip asked with wide eyes.

"Why, sure. It's a beautiful evening, and Mrs. Miller makes mighty good cookies. I know 'cause she brought us some while we were working on the airstrip."

"Okay," Gerald said as he hopped down from August's lap. "We'll go."

"I'm really grateful, boys," Mrs. Miller said, motioning toward the door. "Let's hurry so we can eat before we pick the berries."

The boys went along with Mrs. Miller, and Beth was left to face August alone.

"I guess we'll have more than enough supper," Beth said as she finished putting the food on the table. She took a seat across from August and realized it was the first time they'd shared dinner alone. Always before they'd had the comfort of the boys to dispel any tension, but now they sat face-to-face, both seeming to know they were going to deal with more than supper.

"I'll say grace," Beth said, avoiding August's eyes. She bowed her head without waiting to see if August would and began, "Dear Father, we thank You for this meal and the fellowship we share. Bless us now and guard us in our steps. Amen."

August held out his hand for Beth's plate, dished out a generous portion of the steaming casserole, and handed it back to her.

"Thank you," Beth said. She wanted to say so much more, yet she felt a sense of quiet come over her, as if it were more important that August begin the conversation.

"This is real good," August said with a nod of approval. "I've had moose steak, moose roast, moose stew, but I don't think I've ever had moose pie. I'll have to send my sister the recipe."

"I'm glad you like it," Beth replied between bites. Food stuck in her throat, and she remembered she hadn't set out any beverage. "I'll get us something to drink. What would you like?"

"It doesn't much matter to me. Whatever you had planned is fine," August answered.

"I have some powdered lemonade that one of the soldiers traded me for pies. I fixed a batch this morning, and it ought to be good and cold by now."

"That sounds good."

Beth smiled and went to fix the glasses and juice. Once this was accomplished, she sat back down to face the unnerving silence.

"I think the boys have grown a foot taller," August said as he ate.

"Yes," Beth replied. "I'm going to have to get them new mukluks this fall."

"Say, I saw some dandy native-made ones just down the road. There's a small village not far from where the highway is going through, and a bunch of us went over to check out the situation and found a wealth of handmade goods."

"It would certainly be great to buy something without worrying about ration stamps. Is it too far to walk?" Beth questioned.

"I wouldn't think so," August said, trying to remember the exact distance. "But maybe you could get someone to run you over, just to be on the safe side. I'll talk to Ralph and see if I can borrow one of the vehicles and drive you there myself."

"Oh, I wouldn't want to take you away from your work," Beth replied.

"It wouldn't take me away from anything," August insisted. "I've been given a couple days off due to the long hours I've been putting in. I'll see what I can do and let you know."

"All right," she reluctantly agreed.

The silence returned to hang between them like an impenetrable veil. Even August shifted uncomfortably and nervously picked at his food. Finally, he put his fork down, folded his hands, and eased back against his chair.

"I have something to say," he began.

"I thought you might," Beth answered and put her own fork down.

August gazed across the table, allowing himself several moments to take in the vision of Beth's beauty. Beth's pale blond hair was pulled back from her face, revealing high cheekbones and soft white skin. Her blue eyes seemed to grow larger under August's stare.

"I don't know all the sweet words or wily ways that men work with women, but what I have to say comes from the heart. While I've been gone I've done a lot of thinking."

"I see," Beth murmured.

"No, I don't think you do," August said softly. "I mostly thought of you. And, of course, the boys." August waited for Beth to make some reply, but she only lowered her eyes.

"I guess I came to realize how important you were to me. I found myself thinking of you and how wonderful you felt in my arms. I thought of the boys and how they always treat me like their father—how Phillip even calls me 'Daddy.' And I had to explain to you."

"Explain what?" Beth asked.

"I love you, Beth. I think I've loved you for a long time, but since I've never been in love, I just didn't recognize it. I knew you were special to me and the boys were always great, but it wasn't until I had to spend a long time away from you, from all of you, that I realized how important you were to me."

"What exactly do you mean?"

"I want to marry you, Beth. I know you're still mourning JB's passing, but I can wait for you. I want to help you make a new life, and I want to be a father to your children and to have more children, together."

Beth wasn't surprised at August's declaration, but neither was she prepared for the proposal. Shadows fell across the room as the sun continued its journey west, and Beth got up to turn on the lights.

August waited impatiently for her to say something, anything that might let him know how she felt. He watched Beth come back to the table and stand behind her chair.

"When I learned that JB was joining the air force, something inside me came undone. Phillip was just a baby, and Gerald wasn't much out of diapers. I cried when JB told me that he would have to go away and that once his training was completed, he'd be sent to Europe immediately. He told me it might be years before we saw each other again, and a part of me died." Beth drew a deep breath before continuing.

"JB had such a love of life and of God, and I knew that I couldn't make him stay. Truly, I didn't want to impose my will upon him, but in my heart I knew he'd never come home again. Of course, I never told JB that. I prayed about it, pouring out my heart before God, and I sought the scriptures, hoping and praying to find something sensible to ease my worries.

"'Trust in the Lord with all thine heart; and lean not unto thine own understanding.' That's Proverbs 3:5," Beth said.

"Yes, I know," August replied with a nod. "Go on."

"Well, that was the verse God led me to. I kept wanting to trust my own understanding about things. I reasoned that I had it all figured out. After all, God had sent me a wonderful Christian husband and two beautiful sons. I didn't have any reason to believe that all wouldn't be well, but in my heart I had a gnawing fear that wouldn't pass. When I received notice that JB was dead and knew that my fears were fulfilled, I almost felt relieved. Does that sound strange?"

"Not really," August said and added, "everyone deals with things the best way they can. You were anticipating the worst and the waiting is always the hardest part. When the worst that could happen finally happened, you were able to relax, knowing that things were as bad as they were going to get."

"I suppose that's true," Beth said as she gripped the chair back. "I turned my heart and soul to God for comfort. There was nothing else to do and no one else to pull me through. Do you understand?" August nodded. "I hold my relationship with Him quite dear. He pulled me through losing JB and kept me sane so that my children didn't suffer from the loss."

"Why are you telling me all this? I already know that you still mourn JB. I wouldn't intrude on that. I only ask to remain close at hand until those feelings pass."

"That's what I'm trying to say," Beth said softly. "I've already buried the past and JB. He was an important part of my life, but he's in heaven now. I don't have to worry about JB anymore. I miss him occasionally, but those times come rarely now. I've been able to get on with my life, and JB's death is no longer an issue with me. But my love of God and His Word are."

"I don't understand."

"You have an obvious problem when it comes to fellowship with the Lord. Forgive me if that sounds judgmental, but even Gerald knows that you are alienated from God. He's come to me before and asked me why you never pray and why you never talk of God the way I do or the way JB did. He was so tiny when JB went away, but he remembers his father telling him about heaven and God. Proverbs 20:11 says, 'Even a child is known by his doings, whether his work be pure, and whether it be right.' It's obvious to those around you that things are not right." Beth saw a shadow of denial pass through August's eyes.

"I'd love for you to talk to me about what has hurt you and turned you from God. I'd love to be able to help you through your anger and frustration, but you won't let me. You turn away at every possible opportunity."

"Talking won't resolve anything," August stated firmly.

"And marriage will?"

"I love you, Beth!" August said as he pounded his fist against the table.

"And I love you, August," Beth whispered, ignoring the outburst. "But I can't marry you when your heart isn't right with God. It would always stand between us and eventually divide us. I can't serve two masters, and I won't give up God."

"The verse about two masters referred to money," August said stiffly, remembering Luke 16:13.

"The verse says, 'No servant can serve two masters: for either he will hate the one, and love the other; or else he will hold to the one, and despise the other. Ye cannot serve God and mammon.' I think it works in this situation as well," Beth said with a gentle tone.

"I can't hold fast to raising my sons as Christians who will respect the Word and fellowship with believers when their father denies the need. I can't love you and serve you properly as your wife, and hold onto my faith and serve God as well. Sooner or later, the two will clash, and the battleground will be our home. Would you really have the lives claimed be those of your adopted sons and wife?"

August stared in silence. Beth had forced him to face the one thing he'd refused to admit for so long. How could he explain to her that he'd faced such disappointment that he was no longer certain that he wanted God's will?

"Look," Beth continued, feeling suddenly strengthened, "God has a purpose in all of this, and I believe He has sent us to one another for a special reason. Maybe it's to help each of us deal with the past and the sorrows we've faced. Maybe not. But I know that this problem must be dealt with before we can marry. Do you understand?"

"I don't know," August said as he folded his arms against his chest. "I just don't know. It's all well and fine to use this as a reason to turn me away, but are you sure there isn't something more? You said you love me; was that true?"

"Yes," Beth nodded. "I love you very much."

"Then why not trust God to work everything out after we're married?"

"Because we're both old enough to know it doesn't work that way. August, I would love to marry you. Believe me, I don't like being alone, and I hate the fact that my boys have you only as a friend and not their father. I want us to be a family as much as you do, but I want us to be a family under the hand of God. If we married now, that wouldn't be the case, would it?"

August's dark eyes narrowed, and he clenched his jaw tightly. "If that's the way you want it, then I'll leave. I'm sorry I'm not good enough for you and your children."

August turned on his heel and stormed through the house. Beth followed after him, wishing she could say something that would stop him from leaving her in anger. "I love you, August," she whispered as he opened the screen door.

"But not enough," August replied. He slammed the door behind him and stalked down the drive.

Tears streamed down Beth's face as she watched the man she loved walk out of her life. "It's not enough without God, August," she whispered. "It would never be enough without Him."

Chapter 9

August faced each new day with bitterness and trepidation. The highway project kept his hands busy, but his mind continued to be haunted by images of the woman he'd left behind.

He was angry with Beth and with God, but mostly with himself. He knew he'd disappointed Gerald and Phillip by leaving without a word, especially after promising them such a grand day of fishing and storytelling. It grieved him that he was causing them pain. Why did life have to be so difficult?

From time to time, as news trickled in about the progress of the war, August felt his anger rekindled. He should have been one of the troops. If only God would have worked things out for him and heard his prayers. If only God cared.

Every day, August operated machinery, issued orders, and helped to assess progress. While he knew the job demanded his undivided attention, his mind incessantly wandered.

Log bridges were built to cross the multiple rivers and creeks, but the problem of boggy, wet ground made progress slow and uncertain. Riverbanks had to be reinforced to hold the bridges, and while gravel was readily available, the waterlogged land seemed to have an insatiable appetite. Load after load of rock was brought in to stabilize that which refused to be stable.

Danger lurked behind every tree, and each new and unexplored position placed the highway crew in jeopardy. Despite difficulty and hardship, the highway was steadily becoming reality. August wondered what he would do when the roadwork was completed.

Ralph Greening expected him to stay on and work for the Public Roads Administration. There were plans to make continued road improvements and to see to it that eventually the Alaskan/Canadian Military Highway would be more than a mud trail through the wilderness. But even for the promise of a secure job, August didn't know if he could live close to Beth and the boys and not be part of their lives. August tried to put such thoughts from his mind as he joined his crew. Rains had slowed progress, and after a two-day dry spell, every man available was out on the road making up time. Testing the ground, August grimaced. It remained spongy from the deluge, and such conditions only added to the danger of the situation.

August climbed aboard a Caterpillar tractor and started his shift with great reluctance. His duties seemed meaningless, and his life once again held no purpose. But there were tree stumps to be removed and the road to be graded.

Paying little attention to the twenty-ton machine he maneuvered, August wasn't aware of how precariously close he had come to the edge of a sheer drop. His mind was too preoccupied to notice the ledge giving way, and by the time he recognized the danger, it was too late. In a mass of rubble and a cloud of diesel smoke, the machine slid down the embankment. All August could do was hold on.

It seemed an eternity of bouncing, pitching, and turning. Then the tractor came to rest on its side, pinning August beneath.

August felt the warmth of his own blood as it gushed from a cut above his left eye. He tried to assess the situation, but his mind was clouded and dull, and his eyes refused to stay open. He struggled to move his arms, but any movement was impossible.

I have to get out of this, August thought. He strained against the weight that pinned him firmly against the ground. He could feel cold, boggy dampness against his back, and he tried to remember if a lake or pond sat near where he'd been grading. His mind offered only hazy memories.

He heard voices overhead and knew his men would come to his aid. It was hard to figure out just where they were and how soon he could expect relief, but just hearing them gave him comfort.

"Why is this happening, God?" August wondered aloud. "Why must I suffer these torments and pains?" As it became a monumental effort just to breathe, August fell silent.

Minutes or maybe hours passed as August faded in and out of consciousness. He thought he heard people working overhead, but the roar in his head made it impossible to know for certain.

"August. August," a voice called out, and though he couldn't see the face, August answered.

"I'm here! I'm under here!"

"I know where you are. August, do you trust Me to get you out?"

What a strange question, August thought. *Why would anyone ask me that?*

"I don't know who you are," August replied, "but if you can help to get me out of here, I'd be much obliged."

"August, do you believe in Me?" the voice whispered.

August shook his head. "What are you talking about? Just get me out of this. I'll believe you, shake your hand, dance a jig, whatever you want. Just get me out from under this thing!"

August knew his words sounded harsh and ungrateful, but this man was beginning to bother him.

"August, you called upon Me. Dost thou believe on the Son of God?"

A tingle ran down August's spine. Those words were scripture. He remembered them very well. Jesus had asked that question of a blind man.

August's breath quickened. What was it that the man answered in the Bible? August thought for a moment before quoting John 9:36 in a hesitant voice. "'Who is he, Lord, that I might believe on him?'"

"Thou hast both seen him, and it is he that talketh with thee." The words paralleled Christ's reply in the Bible.

August felt a trembling that started in his toes and worked all the way up through his body. The love of a Savior whom he'd so long denied penetrated the darkness and cold that engulfed his body.

Suddenly all the bitterness melted away from August's heart. In an instant, the blindness of his anger lifted, and he could once again see. He remembered the closeness and comfort that came from being right with God.

"I've really made a mess of things, Lord. Forgive me," August cried out. "Please forgive me."

August wept tears of repentance as he thought of God's love. Even though he'd rejected that love, Jesus had reached through the wall of August's disappointment and denial to be at his side when August needed Him most. What a precious friend!

The presence of Christ at his side never subsided, even as the tractor was lifted from overhead. August struggled to open his eyes, but they felt heavy and weighted down.

"August, August, old buddy, wake up. Wake up!" one of the men called.

August opened his eyes to see the hazy image of several men. Above them the spruce trees parted to reveal a brilliant sky of cobalt blue. August tried to sit up, but firm hands held him down.

"Don't move, August. You're hurt pretty bad. We're going to get you some help. Just hang on."

August tried to remain conscious, but his mind flooded with blackness, and his body went limp.

"Maybe it's better this way," one worker said to another. "I wouldn't want to be awake when they moved me. Not with the way his body must be broken up inside." The men agreed as they waited for a stretcher.

———#———

Coming out of the darkness was much like surfacing after diving deep into a lake. Fighting against the urge to remain in the dark stillness, August awoke to strange voices and blinding pain. Feeling as though every part of his body was broken, August moaned in agony.

"He's awake, Doctor," a young woman's voice called.

A man peered down at August with a look of concern. "Mr. Eriksson, I'm Dr. Butler. Can you understand me?"

"Yes," August answered slowly. Even speaking seemed painful.

"Mr. Eriksson, you've sustained some injuries. We won't know the extent of those injuries until our examination is complete. You have a concussion and a deep laceration on your forehead. Other than that, it's hard to tell. We'll do what we can to make you comfortable."

"Where am I?" August asked, knowing that there hadn't been any hospitals in the area where he had been working.

"Anchorage. They flew you in yesterday."

"I've been unconscious that long?"

"I'm afraid so, but don't worry. It isn't at all unusual after sustaining a severe head injury. For now, I'd just like you to rest and let us do our job."

August gave a slight nod before drifting into a deep, peaceful sleep.

—— *#* ——

Three days later, August was propped up in bed, trying to absorb a full assessment of his condition.

"You are most fortunate, Mr. Eriksson," the doctor explained. "Had you landed on a hard surface, you'd most likely be dead. Instead, you landed in wet muskeg, which caused your body to sink beneath the weight of the tractor. When they were able to pull the machinery from you, they discovered that you were beneath the ground's surface. No one can explain why the tractor didn't sink right along with you, but perhaps the weight was better distributed. There's really no way of knowing," the doctor said as he glanced back and forth from August's face to the chart he held.

"Some might, in fact, call it a miracle. It took over four hours to free you, and you were unconscious the entire time. Fortunately, you didn't lose much blood," Dr. Butler added.

"But I remember being awake. I remember talking to. . ." August's voice fell silent.

"I can only go by what the pilot passed on to me from the road crew. However, it would fit with the nature of your injuries. Besides the concussion, you have a broken collarbone on the left side and some relatively minor lacerations elsewhere. We were fearful that you might have sustained several fractured lumbar vertebrae."

"Several what?" August questioned. Although his sister was a registered nurse, he had never taken the time to learn much more than the basics that kept him alive.

"We thought your back might be broken, but it appears that all is well. I'd say several weeks will right what's wrong, and you'll be able to return to your home. I strongly caution against any strenuous labor, however, for at least two or three months."

"That long?" August asked in a weary voice.

"I'm sorry, Mr. Eriksson," the doctor sympathized, "but as I've already stated, you're lucky to be alive."

"Not lucky," August said with a weak grin. "God saved me from death, and believe me, I'm grateful."

"Well then, I expect a good patient who's obedient to orders," Dr. Butler answered and turned to leave. "And I happen to agree with you, Mr. Eriksson. You were very blessed."

August nodded and relaxed as the doctor left. No sooner had he walked through the door than a gray-haired nurse entered the room.

"Good day, Mr. Eriksson," the pleasant-voiced woman said. "I'm Nurse Roberts. How are you feeling?"

"Well enough, I suppose."

"Good, good. I'll need to take your temperature and pulse now," the woman said as she automatically popped a thermometer in August's mouth and took his wrist.

The woman reminded August of his mother. She was firm, yet gentle in her touch, and her voice was like a spoken lullaby.

"I'll bet you'd enjoy some breakfast," she chattered after marking down his pulse rate. "Well, I have just the thing for you. Eggs, toast, juice, and maybe even some bacon. How about it?" she questioned, removing the thermometer from August's mouth.

"It sounds wonderful," August agreed.

"Then I'll fetch you a tray and be back in a jiffy," Nurse Roberts announced and hurried from the room.

August contemplated the tight bandaging that held his left arm firmly against his body. He was grateful that it was his left collarbone rather than his right that bore the break. At least he could still use his right hand.

Nurse Roberts came into the room with a steaming tray of food. "Here we are. This ought to make you feel considerably better. You'll notice that I've brought you some coffee as well. Now, can I get you anything else?"

"I appreciate all that you've done. If it wouldn't be too much trouble, I'd be most grateful if you'd get me a Bible," August said, struggling to sit up. "I have some catching up to do."

"Here, let me help you," Nurse Roberts said as she put the tray down. She lifted August with ease and even managed to keep from causing him greater pain.

August looked into the soft brown eyes and sighed. He missed his mother.

"Thank you," August whispered.

"Not at all," the woman said, and brought the tray to his bed. "Now, you eat everything here, and I'll be happy to search out a Bible for you."

August reached out and placed his hand to cover the older woman's hand. "Would it offend you if I told you that you remind me of my mother?"

The woman broke into a big smile. "Certainly not. Is she nearby? Can I call her for you?"

"She's dead," August said thoughtfully. "No, she's gone, but she's in heaven. She loved God more than anything or anyone, and I know I'll see her again."

"That always makes it easier, doesn't it," the woman observed. "Knowing that your loved ones are safe in the arms of Jesus and that you'll one day see them in heaven—it's all that gets me through each day when I think of those who have gone before me."

"You talk as one who knows," August replied softly.

"I do, son. I do. I lost my husband and children in the influenza epidemic. I decided to train and become a nurse after that. But even after all these years, it hurts to remember them and know that I must wait." The woman's voice was barely audible.

August squeezed her hand. "Someone is always left behind. I guess that's our job."

The woman smiled and patted August's hand. "Of course, you're right. Now, you eat, and I'll go find you a Bible."

———— # ————

It wasn't until the next day that August came to realize the doctor had given him a great deal of painkiller. As the medication wore off, deep, penetrating pain filled August's body. He struggled to forget it, forcing his mind away from the hospital and to the small rural village where Beth and the boys lived. He tried to imagine Beth at work and the boys at play.

He was grateful when Nurse Roberts brought him more pain medication. While August waited for the drugs to take effect, he leaned back against the pillows and prayed.

"Dear God, I need to be free from this pain. Such pain and misery takes my mind from the hope that I should have in You." August shifted uncomfortably. "I know I could just as easily be dead or dying—perhaps I really am—but Lord, I want to live. I want to see Beth and the boys, and I want to set things right with them.

"Father, I love Bethany Hogan, and I believe You sent me to her and her children to be a husband and father. I know I've doubted Your blessings, but I don't doubt them any longer. Deliver me, Lord. Deliver me and let me live. Amen."

Chapter 10

Beth discarded her mending and sat wringing her hands. She was miserable, her boys were heartbroken, and August was nowhere to be found. She blamed herself for driving him out. The image of August's angry face would forever burn in her memory.

She'd only said the things that needed to be said. She'd never meant to hurt August, but she couldn't be married to a man who was obviously fighting God.

The month had been miserable and rainy, leaving Gerald and Phillip bored and stuck inside. Mrs. Miller had graciously shown up to take the boys to her house, but Beth knew they were pining for August, and it was an impossible void to fill.

Then there was the constant worry of war. The Japanese still held strongholds in the Aleutians, and every day rumors fed fear and anxiety.

The army insisted there wasn't any immediate danger, yet there were practice drills from time to time, reminding everyone that the danger was close enough. Civil Defense officials spoke of blackout drills, insisting everyone have heavy curtains to place at their windows. Bethany wondered at this order, given that they were enjoying close to twenty hours of sunshine a day.

Rationing was tightened, and people were encouraged to do without and buy war bonds. Beth thought of the soldiers who labored long and hard to build the highway through Alaska. She thought them fortunate that no one was shooting at them while they worked. At least not yet.

People seemed more neighborly than ever, offering food, oil, and whatever help they could spare. In Alaska, life depended upon such generosity, but the war made their dependency upon one another more significant than ever.

The summer had been busier than Beth had expected, and it seemed there was never a moment to call her own. She had taken in laundry for highway workers, prepared baked goods for the army, and always had more requests for rooms at her roadhouse than she had rooms to offer. It kept her mind occupied for the most part, but not her heart.

Every day she passed by August's room, wanting to check whether his things were gone, and every day as she reached for the door handle, she stopped. She'd refused to rent August's room, hoping and praying that he'd return, but deep inside, Beth had lost any confidence in that possibility. Opening the door might prove once and for all that her fears were well founded.

Persistent knocking brought Beth hurrying to the front door, hoping that August had returned. The door opened to reveal Mrs. Miller, and Bethany couldn't hide a frown.

"I'm sorry, dear. Have I caught you at a bad time?" Mrs. Miller asked hesitantly.

Beth immediately felt bad for having given Mrs. Miller the wrong impression. "No, please forgive me. I'm just a bit preoccupied. Won't you come in?"

"Are you sure I'm not causing you a problem?" the older woman questioned as she followed Beth into the house.

"I'm sure. I must apologize for my demeanor these days," Beth said as she motioned Mrs. Miller to a chair. "Would you like some refreshments? I have lemonade and gingersnaps."

"No, I'm fine. I just wanted to visit with you. I know you haven't been yourself, and I wondered if I might help. I know how tedious widowhood can be."

Beth smiled and swept her blond hair back over her shoulder. "You are such a dear to me, Mrs. Miller. I seriously doubt I would have made it had it not been for Granny Gantry and now you."

"You mustn't let the past get you down."

"It isn't that," Beth said and bit her lower lip.

"Then what?" Mrs. Miller asked and reached across to pat Beth's hand. "I know I'm being a nosy old woman, but believe me, there are times when talking to someone who understands helps much more than keeping it bottled inside."

Beth smoothed imaginary lines in her olive-green skirt. "It isn't the widowhood that grieves me, Mrs. Miller. The problem does relate to a man, however."

"What widow doesn't have man problems?" Mrs. Miller laughed softly. "What seems to be the trouble?"

"I've fallen in love," Beth said matter-of-factly. "But you mustn't tell anyone."

"Your secret is safe with me," Mrs. Miller insisted. "Now, why don't you tell me about it? Perhaps you'll feel better afterwards."

Beth poured out all the details of August's appearance in her life and how her feelings had quickly developed into love. "I care far more than I ever thought possible. When JB died, I feared I could never love another, but God has graciously allowed me to love again."

"Then what's the problem?"

"I'm afraid I sent him packing," Beth said sadly.

"Why? What happened?" Mrs. Miller asked in surprise.

"August has something troubling him. Something that won't allow him to feel the closeness to God that I suspect he once felt. I tried to get him to talk about it, but he grew angry and stormed off."

"That was the day the boys helped me pick berries," Mrs. Miller stated.

"That's right," Beth agreed. "I felt so bad after convincing the boys that August would be here when they returned and then he wasn't.

Gerald didn't even talk for two days, and when he finally opened up, all this hurt came pouring out. He felt betrayed, and I had to explain that I was responsible."

"But you weren't," Mrs. Miller said gently. "God is working in August's life. You were simply weeding a garden that God planted long ago. If God is striving to bring August back to the fold, you aren't responsible for anything more than living out God's goodness and standing on His Word. If that drove August away, then it is still part of God's plan."

Beth nodded. "Yes, I'm sure you're right. But—" She paused and lowered her face. "I love him, and I'm so afraid of losing him. What if he won't ever deal with his problems?"

"If it's meant to be, it will be," Mrs. Miller said firmly. "You must stand strong in your faith. God understands your grief and frustration. Trust Him."

Beth studied the older woman for a moment. Her gray hair had been pinned on top of her head without a single wisp escaping its bounds. It gave Mrs. Miller an extremely well-organized look.

The plump woman was wearing a cream-colored dress with pastel flowers splotching it from neck to knee. She carried an air of respectability and solitude, yet Beth was surprised that Mrs. Miller had never remarried.

"Mrs. Miller, may I ask you something personal?"

The widow nodded. "Certainly. I can probably guess what your question will be. But I have one condition upon which I will insist."

"And what is that?" Beth questioned.

"You must stop with the Mrs. Miller title and call me Hazel."

Beth smiled. "I would love to, Hazel."

"Much better. Now ask your question."

"I just wondered why you've never remarried. After all, you live in an area where women are scarce and the companionship of a wife is highly prized and sought after."

Hazel laughed. "That's true enough, and God knows there have been offers. Mostly men who needed a nursemaid or housekeeper though. I guess the right man never came along."

"How do you bear the loneliness? I mean. . ." Beth paused trying to think of a tactful way to speak her mind. "I have the boys as well as the roadhouse, and they keep me busy, but you're down there in town all alone."

The older woman sobered noticeably. "It does get hard, especially at night or in the winter. I've been widowed for over five years, and I don't think I'll ever get used to the winters. They're so cold, dark, and endless. The first year I would cry every time the sun set." Her eyes took on a distant look as she remembered those haunting days.

"You don't have to go on," Beth said sympathetically. "Unless of course you want to."

"That's all right," Hazel said and continued. "I know you understand. Those first months, I just wandered around trying to figure out what was what. I kept hearing my Zeke calling me, and when I'd realize it was just my imagination, my heart was heavier than ever. At night, I'd wake and reach out for him, but he was gone. When I'd come fully awake, it hurt so much that I wished I'd never wake up again."

"Oh Hazel," Beth murmured, "I'm so sorry."

"Sometimes I still find myself waiting for him to come home from working his trap lines, but of course he never does," Hazel concluded.

Beth nodded. "I know. I think it would have been harder on me, if JB hadn't already been gone for so long. When he left for duty in the air force, I probably felt his absence worse. When I knew he wasn't coming back, I comforted myself in God and my children, but I still couldn't bear living in the house we'd built together."

"I thought about leaving," the older woman agreed, "but I wanted to stay for the very reasons that you wanted to leave. I needed to feel Zeke close at hand. I needed to know his presence at least until the pain was less. The house was a strong reminder of our love. Every scratch or nick reminded me of something Zeke and I had gone through. I needed the comfort of memories."

"The boys are constant reminders for me," Beth said softly. "And though both bitter and sweet, they have been my lifeline. God was so merciful to give them to me. I don't know how I could have gotten through those first days without their love. They truly sustained me."

"Zeke and I wanted to have children," Hazel said honestly, "but God never blessed us with any. I guess that's why I take such pleasure in your boys. They are such joys to have around and so well behaved. They are a credit to you, Beth."

"Thank you for saying so, but teaching them manners has been the easy part. The hard part is playing both mother and father. I feel that my abilities always fall short of what they need, and now the only man they've truly known as father is gone. How can I possibly help them understand?"

"Trust God and wait, Beth. Trust God and wait," Hazel said firmly.

Beth nodded, but her mind was ever on her sons and their broken hearts.

―――#―――

That night, the silence hung heavy between Beth and her boys. Dinner was eaten with little interest, and when Beth suggested a game of dominoes, the boys only gave it a half-hearted effort. When the clock in the hall chimed nine, Beth ushered her sons to their bedroom.

"Momma, when will August come back?" Gerald questioned as he got ready for bed.

"I don't know, Gerry. He has to work on the road, and that takes him far from us. I don't know if he'll be able to come back any time soon."

"Is he mad at us?" Gerald asked in earnest.

Beth wanted to assure her son that August would never hold malice toward him or Phillip, but the words stuck in her throat. No doubt he was mad at her. He'd been so angry the night he'd left, and Beth was afraid he'd never want to see her again.

"I miss him," Phillip piped up from his bed.

"I know. We all miss August and want him to come back." Beth turned and made a pretense of picking up Gerald's discarded clothes to keep the boys from seeing the tears in her eyes.

"I'm going to ask God to send him back to us," Gerald said as he knelt to say his prayers. "I love him, and I still want him to be my daddy."

"I pray too," Phillip said, scooting out from under his covers. "I want Daddy."

Beth opened the door and turned off the bedroom light. The boys' kneeling figures were illuminated by the shadowy light from the hallway.

She watched in silence as the boys prayed. Their little-boy voices lifted up pleas of love to their God, a God they trusted without doubt. Could Beth somehow do the same? Was it possible to regain the trust she'd once felt when life was more simple?

Seeing the boys safely tucked in, Beth made her way down the hall and to her desk. She'd long ago given August over to God, and there was nothing to be gained by taking him back.

Resting her head in her arms on the desk, Beth prayed for strength to endure the loneliness and for guidance for August. Wherever he was, God could reach him.

Chapter 11

When Saturday came, Bethany awoke to a strange silence. Straining her ears for the sound of her children, she was more than a little surprised to realize they were quiet.

Enjoying the warmth of her bed, Beth reasoned that the children were simply extra tired. They had, after all, spent most of the previous evening helping Mrs. Miller pick berries again.

She was just fading back into dreams of August when something caught her ear. Bolting upright in bed, Beth waited and listened. Moaning sounds came from the boys' bedroom, and Beth knew instinctively that it was Gerald.

As Beth hastily threw on a robe and tore down the hall, a feeling of dread settled over her. By the time she reached the boys' room, her hands were trembling.

"Why am I so afraid?" she whispered to the air. "Surely he's only had a bad dream." She fought desperately to reassure herself. There was no reason for her uneasiness, yet a mother's heart told her something wasn't right.

She opened the door and found a bleary-eyed Phillip sitting beside his brother's sleeping form. All looked well, at least on the surface.

"Good morning, sweetie. How's Momma's boy?" Beth asked, fluffing her younger son's hair. Phillip scurried off the bed and into his mother's arms.

"Gerry's hot," Phillip said, planting a kiss on his mother's cheek.

"I'm sure he's fine. Let's go see," Beth whispered and shifted Phillip from one hip to the other. His legs draped down the side of her body, reminding Beth that he was quickly passing out of babyhood.

"Gerry," Beth said as she put Phillip on the floor beside the bed and took a seat by her sleeping son. She reached out and brushed back the sandy brown hair that had fallen across Gerald's forehead.

His skin was hot and dry, a sure sign of fever. "Gerry, wake up, honey." Beth shook her son gently.

"Mommy," Gerald moaned and opened fever-glazed eyes. "I hurt, Mommy. My head hurts real bad."

"You have a fever," Beth soothed, checking her son for any other symptoms. There weren't any spots to indicate measles or smallpox, and his body seemed free from any swelling or rashes.

"I'll get you an aspirin and a cool towel. You just rest, Gerry. Phillip and I will take care of you." Beth's calm voice masked the dread in her heart.

Beth carried Phillip from the room, speaking as she made her way to the kitchen. "We'll get Gerry some medicine and then he'll feel better." Phillip nodded as Beth hurried to get the aspirin.

Beth put Phillip down and rummaged through the cupboards until she found a small bottle of aspirins. Putting the medicine in her pocket, Beth then poured a glass of water.

"Me thirsty," Phillip declared as Beth picked up the glass.

"I'm sorry, sweetie. Here, have a drink and then we'll take a drink for your brother." Beth waited impatiently as Phillip satisfied his thirst. Then, after refilling the glass, she returned to Gerald's bed and gently lifted his head to swallow the tablet.

"Ouchy, ouchy, Mommy. It hurts," Gerald cried, recoiling from her touch.

Phillip had padded down the hall to find his mother bent over Gerald. "He sick, Momma?"

"Yes," Beth whispered. "Your brother is very sick."

"The light hurts my head, Mommy. Please turn off the light," Gerald cried softly.

Beth shook her head. Fever usually caused some pain, but never this much. Something was very wrong. She pulled the heavy curtains across the windows and turned back to face the situation.

"Phillip, I need you to stay here with Gerry while I go get the doctor. Can you do that for me?" she asked the tiny boy.

"I take care of Gerry," Phillip said as he planted himself firmly beside his brother.

"Good boy," Beth said. "Now, it's really important that you stay right here and that you don't get off the bed. Do you understand?"

"I be good, Mommy," Phillip said gravely. "I pray for brother."

"That would be good," Beth agreed. "I'm going to go change my clothes, and I'll check in before I go. I'll be right back."

Beth hurried around her bedroom, mindlessly choosing her gardening slacks and one of JB's old shirts. She quickly tied her blond hair back into a ponytail and made her way down the hall to the boys' room.

A light touch to Gerald's forehead confirmed her fears. The fever was rising. "Phillip, I have to go now. When I come back, I'll fix you a special, big-boy breakfast. Would you like that?"

"Can I have applesauce?" Phillip asked, requesting his favorite food.

"You be a good boy, and you can have whatever you like," Beth replied. "I'll be back in a jiffy."

She hurried down the hall, dreading the desertion of her children. She pulled on socks and boots to wade through the muddy roads of the rain-drenched community, and after one final peek at the boys, she rushed from the roadhouse and ran all the way into town.

Beth marveled at the transformation of her small town. The landscape literally became a sea of tents as the army continued to bring in men and supplies. She picked her way through the mud while soldiers whistled or waved in appreciation of a feminine form. The attention made Beth nervous, but she ignored it. Gerald's restless form filled her mind.

She breathed a sigh of relief upon finally reaching the doctor's office.

Pushing open the door and mindless of the mud she tracked into the office, Beth made her way to where a nurse sat writing in a ledger.

"I need to see the doctor," Beth said breathlessly.

"What seems to be your ailment, Miss. . . ?" The nurse fell silent waiting for Beth to fill in her name.

"Mrs. Beth Hogan," she offered impatiently, "and it's not for me; it's my son. He has a high fever."

"The doctor isn't here right now, but I can send him over as soon as he returns," the nurse replied.

Beth's brow furrowed as she bit her lower lip. "I suppose I'll have to wait then. Do you have any idea how long it might be?"

"Don't worry," the nurse answered sympathetically, "the doctor is setting an arm on the other side of town. He won't be much longer, and I'll send him right on to you. Now, why don't you tell me everything about your son's illness, and I'll pass the information to the doctor."

"He just woke up with a fever. I didn't bother to take his temperature, but I'm certain it's already very high, and it's climbing."

"Anything else?" the nurse questioned as she jotted the information down.

"He says his head hurts and his eyes are very sensitive to light," Beth replied and added in a near sob, "He's only five."

"Try not to worry, Mrs. Hogan. Tell me where I can send the doctor when he returns."

"I run the Gantry Roadhouse east of town. Just follow the road, and our place is a quarter mile past the crossroads," Beth directed in a trembling voice.

"All right, Mrs. Hogan. You go on back home and I'll do what I can. And, Mrs. Hogan"—the nurse paused—"please try not to worry. Give your son some aspirin and wash him with a cool cloth."

Beth nodded and made her way back toward home. She'd never run as much as she had this day, and by the time she reached the roadhouse, she was winded and every muscle in her legs ached.

Kicking off her muddy boots and slamming the door behind her,

Beth raced to Gerald's bedside. Phillip sat faithfully beside his older brother, wiping the cloth over his forehead.

"What a good boy you are, Phillip," Beth said as she reached down and felt Gerald's brow. He felt as hot as ever, and Beth noticed that he didn't even stir at her touch.

"Come along, Phillip. I'll get you dressed and fix you applesauce pancakes."

"Yummy," Phillip said as he jumped down from the bed. "I took care of brother," he stated simply.

"Yes, you certainly did," Beth replied and helped Phillip off with his nightshirt. She replaced the gown with a shirt and pants and led him to the kitchen.

Beth hastily prepared breakfast between trips to the boys' bedroom. She alternated swabbing Gerald's fiery body and flipping pancakes. She had just placed a plate of pancakes and applesauce in front of Phillip when a knock sounded at the door.

"You stay here and eat. I'm certain that will be the doctor, and I'll have to talk to him about Gerry," Beth said as she left the room.

The doctor stood at the door, and Beth breathed a sigh of relief as she took his coat and showed him to Gerald's room.

"My name is Dr. Stevens," the man said as he began to examine Gerald. "My nurse tells me the boy's symptoms just started."

"Yes," Beth affirmed. "He was fine yesterday, although I do recall he seemed a little tired."

The doctor forced Gerald to sit, causing the boy to cry out in pain. Beth knelt by his side.

"It's all right, Gerry. Momma's here."

"It hurts real bad, Mommy," Gerald managed between his cries.

"Son, can you bend your neck as if you were going to look down your nightshirt?" the doctor questioned.

Gerald made a valiant effort, but it only caused more pain. "No, no. It hurts," he whimpered. Tears formed in Beth's eyes as she watched her child suffer.

"It's all right, son. I'm a doctor, and I'm going to help you."

Gerald said nothing as the doctor eased him back on the bed. The boy reached out for his mother, and Beth immediately took hold of his hand. She waited in silence while the doctor finished his examination and took Gerald's temperature.

"You just rest now, son. I'm going into the hall with your mother so we can figure out how to make you feel better." The doctor finished putting his instruments into his black bag and motioned Beth to follow him.

Beth knew by the look on the doctor's face that the news would not be good. She felt her knees weaken as she pulled the bedroom door closed behind them.

"I'm afraid your son has all the signs of spinal meningitis," Dr. Stevens began. "I can't be certain without running a number of tests, including a complicated procedure called a spinal tap. I don't have the facilities in town to help your boy."

"What is spinal meningitis?" Beth asked anxiously.

"It's an infection that attacks the membrane surrounding the brain and spine. I'm afraid it's often fatal."

"What am I to do?" Beth questioned frantically. "He has to have help. I don't care what it costs or where we have to go."

"I know. I know," the doctor said as he put his arm around Beth. "What we have to do is get your son to a good hospital."

"But how and where?" Beth asked.

"My suggestion would be Fairbanks. I happen to know there's a supply plane headed there in two hours. I believe we should have your son on that plane."

"Then he'll be there," Beth said, regaining a bit of her composure. "I'll get him ready. Just tell me what to do."

"We'll need to keep him from getting chilled, so bring his blankets. I'll get my nurse to accompany you on the trip. She'll know what to do."

"What about Phillip?" Beth questioned. "He's my younger, and he shares a room with his brother." Fear reverberated in every word.

"He should be fine," the doctor replied, placing a hand on Beth's arm. "We don't quarantine for meningitis because there is no conclusive information about the risk of contagion."

Beth felt only minor relief at the doctor's words. "I'll need to get word to Mrs. Hazel Miller on Second Street. She'll need to come and stay with Phillip. I'm afraid I don't have a telephone. Could you send word to her when you get back into town?" Beth asked hopefully.

"I'd be happy to. I'll also get a couple of soldiers to drive you and your son to the airport. Just wait here until they arrive," the doctor instructed.

"I'll be ready."

An hour later, Beth waved a hesitant good-bye to Phillip and Mrs. Miller. The soldiers showed up as promised, and with them came the nurse who'd assisted Beth at the doctor's office. The woman literally took over and left Beth with nothing to do but look on in helpless frustration.

The drive to the airstrip was a short one, but to Beth, every minute smothered her in apprehension. The soldiers pulled up next to the transport plane and within moments had moved Gerald and the nurse to the stripped-out fuselage of a Lockheed Vega.

Beth's worried look caught the attention of the pilot. "Don't worry, ma'am. We'll have your boy to Fairbanks in less than two hours."

Beth offered the man a fleeting smile. "Thank you. I know you'll do your best." She allowed him to help her up into the plane, her mind filled with only one thought.

"Dear God," Beth breathed against the drone of the airplane's radial engine, "please help my son. Please heal my baby."

Chapter 12

August rotated his shoulder gingerly and waited for any indication of pain. When none came, he smiled. Finally, he was able to move with nearly the same mobility he'd had before the accident.

He offered a wave to the pilot who'd just landed him at the Northway airstrip, then went in search of the Public Roads office and his boss.

Several minutes later, August was sitting beside the cluttered desk that Ralph Greening continued to work from whenever in Northway.

"Catching up on paperwork is worse than dealing with the dirt, rain, and mosquitoes," Ralph griped. "I just got back from our old camp. You certainly gave us a scare," he added, offering August a cup of coffee. "This stuff's getting mighty hard to come by up here, so don't ever say no when somebody offers you a free cup," he teased.

August took the coffee and lifted the mug slightly. "To your health!"

Ralph laughed and joined him in the salute. "And to yours!"

The coffee tasted stale and was only lukewarm, but August didn't care. He was finally going to see Beth again, and he was anxious to complete his work with Ralph.

"Doc says I can go back to work, but nothing too strenuous," August said with a grin. "Whatever that means."

"It might mean that you're not to be dumping Caterpillars over the edge of muddy embankments again." At this both men laughed.

"Yeah, I suppose that's what he meant," August agreed and continued. "Anyhow, the way I see it, it's all up to you. You just tell me where to report, and I'll take care of getting there."

Ralph nodded, but then the thought of Bethany Hogan's hasty retreat from Northway came to mind. He'd only learned of her troubles that morning. His frown and knitted brows caused August to put his coffee mug down.

"What is it? What's wrong?" August asked.

"I went to see Mrs. Hogan today. You know, I wanted to tell her about your accident. I already felt bad that so much time had passed since you were flown to Anchorage, but I had no way of getting back here to tell her," Ralph said apologetically.

"I understand, Ralph, and I'm sure that Beth did," August offered.

"No, she wasn't there," Ralph said with a shake of his head. "Mrs. Hogan had one of her boys take sick. He was pretty bad, and they had to get him to a hospital. They flew out a couple days ago. I think they took him to Fairbanks."

August turned ashen. "Which boy?"

Ralph leaned back and closed his eyes. "I think it was the older one, but I can't be sure. Can't picture him in my mind. You'd best go on down to the roadhouse and ask Mrs. Miller. She's been taking care of the place and the other boy."

August was already on his feet. "I'll do that. I guess it might be a spell longer before I'll be ready to work after all," August said as he made his way out.

"I kind of figured that," Ralph called after him.

August took off at a full run for the roadhouse. He came up the path panting and out of breath, with an aching in his shoulder that hadn't been there that morning. He pounded on the front door and waited impatiently for someone to open up.

"Why, Mr. Eriksson," Mrs. Miller stated in disbelief. "We thought you'd left for good."

"I was injured in an accident and flown to Anchorage. I just returned not more than a half hour ago, and Mr. Greening tells me that Gerald is sick."

Mrs. Miller nodded, and her eyes turned misty. "Poor little boy," she said in a hushed tone. "The doctor doesn't expect him to make it."

"What?" August nearly yelled the word. "What in the world are you talking about? What's wrong with him?"

"Spinal meningitis," Mrs. Miller said ominously. "Beth flew with him to the hospital in Fairbanks, but the doctor said he might already be too far gone. With meningitis, there's just no way of knowing."

"What about Phillip?" August asked with dread.

"Oh, he's fine," Mrs. Miller answered with a smile. "We've been baking since before light. He's asleep right now, but I could wake him if you like."

August barely heard the words. He felt sick at the thought of Gerald dying and knew that it would be hard to see Phillip just then. He thought of Beth in Fairbanks, bearing alone the burden of her desperately ill child. "No, don't wake him. I've got to get to Beth," he muttered.

"I know it'd mean the world to her," Mrs. Miller said with a bit more composure. "She talked so often about you, wondering where you'd gone and if she'd ever see you again."

August nodded. "I've thought a great deal about her too. Being in a sickbed does that for you—gives you plenty of time to think about the things you wished you'd done differently."

"I know she'll be needing you now," Hazel replied, touching August at the elbow. "She cares a great deal about you."

"I know," August said, turning to leave.

Hazel called out after him, "Please let us know how Gerald is."

"I'll do that. I only hope I'm not too late," August called over his shoulder as he bid the older woman a hasty good-bye. "Tell Phillip that Daddy was here and that I'll see him real soon."

"I will, Mr. Eriksson. I will," Mrs. Miller called out and waved. She whispered a silent prayer for the man as he rounded the bend and disappeared from view.

———⚔———

God was with August as he hurried back to the airstrip. He managed to secure passage on a plane going to Fairbanks, and after their scenic flight and bumpy landing, August went in search of the hospital.

The Fairbanks hospital wasn't a stately affair, but it was efficient. August hastened to find a nurse who could direct him and then made his way to the room where she said he'd find Gerald and Bethany.

At least he's still alive, August thought as he made his way down the corridor. Through the doorway of Gerald's room, August saw Beth.

She looked frighteningly small and helpless as she prayed at the bedside of her dying child. He could nearly hear her pleading words as she begged for the life of her son.

Hesitating on the threshold, August wondered how she'd react to his arrival. He glanced at Gerald's pale, nearly lifeless form and back again to the boy's mother. "Dear God," August breathed, "please hear her prayers."

August stepped forward. The noise caught Beth's attention. Her mouth dropped open at the sight of August.

"August," she breathed the word.

Beth looked gaunt and drawn, but August thought her beautiful. He opened his arms, praying that she'd come to him.

Without hesitation, Beth got to her feet, crossed the room, and wearily fell into August's arms. "Oh August, I prayed you'd come. I prayed that God would find you and deliver you to me. Does that sound hopelessly selfish?" she questioned in a sob.

"He heard your prayers about that and then some," August stated. "I've come back to you, but only because I came back to God first."

Beth pulled back with tears streaming down her face. "Really? Oh August, that's the best possible news. Now if only. . ."

August cupped Beth's quivering chin in his hand. "If only Gerald would get well," he answered for her.

"Yes," Beth replied. "August, he's so sick, and Dr. Matthews doesn't know whether he can get well or not."

"Is it meningitis as they feared?" August asked softly. He glanced over Beth's shoulders at Gerald.

"Yes," Beth answered and reached up to take hold of the hand that held her. "They sent for an experimental drug from the States, but it hasn't seemed to help."

"Well, we will have to pray together for him," August said tenderly.

Beth closed her eyes and nodded. "I've prayed alone enough for both of us, but I know there's strength in numbers. I'm afraid this time we need all the help we can get."

"Don't worry, Beth. You never have to be alone again. I've done a great deal of thinking and growing up as well. While I had nothing to do but lay in that hospital bed—"

"What?" Beth said pulling away from August. "You were in the hospital? But why? Are you all right?"

"Relax," August said, pulling Beth back against him. "I was in an accident awhile back. It happened while I was grading the highway. The tractor fell over an embankment that had been weakened by rain. I'm fine now—just a little stiffness in my shoulder and a scar on my head."

Beth's eyes searched for the red welt. She reached up a hand and pushed back August's hair to reveal the scar. "Oh August!" she exclaimed. "Does it hurt you still?"

"Not much. My collarbone was broken, and it still smarts a bit if I overdo, but really I'm fine. I just didn't want to send a letter to explain all that had happened. I wanted to wait until I could see you in person."

"I thought you hated me and had left for good," Beth blurted out honestly. "I felt so bad for sending you away." She glanced back at Gerald. "The boys were just heartbroken."

August nodded. "I knew they would be, and I hated myself for walking away. I knew I needed to listen, but I couldn't make myself turn around. What you said was exactly what I needed to hear. Of course, I couldn't see that until I was half-dead. Then, it was as if God had seen that simple methods wouldn't work with me, and He reached down with something I couldn't ignore."

"He usually does," Beth said with the slightest beginnings of a smile.

August acknowledged hers with a smile of his own. "God knew He was dealing with a particularly stubborn case. I'd run as far as I could, and when God couldn't pin me down any other way, I guess He used a tractor." August's words were lighthearted in spite of his ordeal.

"I confessed my sins, knowing that the only thing real in my life was my relationship with God. I remembered when my mother had put me on her knee and explained that each of us needed a Savior. Some people seek one in a lifestyle or a job, she said. Others try to force people into that role, but what we need is Jesus.

"I remember even now how amazed I was that Jesus had come to earth to save my soul. It only took remembering that simple wonderment to make me take a more realistic look at what I'd done to myself. You were a brave woman to stand your ground with me, Beth."

Moaning from the bed brought Beth and August to Gerald's side. "I'm not so brave," Beth murmured, looking fearfully into August's eyes. August placed his hand against the boy's fiery brow, while Beth took his hand.

"I'm here, Gerry. Momma's here," Beth whispered softly. Gerald calmed, opened his eyes, then closed them again. Beth began to cry softly. Exhausted by her vigil at Gerald's sickbed, she collapsed across the edge of the bed.

August came and lifted her to her feet. "Beth, come on. You have to rest."

"No! I must stay with him," she protested as August led her from the room. "He might wake up, and I don't want him to be afraid."

"We'll just be down the hall. I'll tell the nurse to watch over him. She'll let us know if he wakes up," August said firmly as he pulled Beth along.

Beth's protests only further weakened her. Finally, she gave up and allowed August to take her to the waiting room. August's strong arms offered her the strength that she'd prayed for. She breathed a prayer of thanks while August helped her to a chair.

"You wait right here, and I'll see if I can't get us a cup of coffee or something," August said.

Beth nodded and watched as he walked to the nurses' station. How grateful she was for his direction and strength. She had been so afraid of never seeing him again, and now, just when God knew she needed August the most, he was at her side.

The aching in her heart refused to abate, however. The doctor had told her there was no hope for her son. No hope whatsoever.

Beth knew better than to give up hope. While there was life, God could work. But it was hard to maintain hope in the face of such devastation. How could she explain to a doctor she'd only met that this child had to live, that without him a part of her heart would be forever broken? He was a man of medicine, and his cold, scientific attitude left Bethany empty.

Her eyes misted at the thought of Gerald's suffering. He was so little and defenseless. He didn't deserve this sickness. Beth felt weak to the point of being sick. How much more could either of them take?

God had heard her prayers, Beth reminded herself. After all, August was here, and he'd renewed his faith in God. God had surely sent August to help her through Gerald's illness. Leaning back against the chair, Beth closed her eyes and tried to pray. She was so tired, so weary of fighting alone.

Within moments, sleep washed over her. August returned to find Beth eased back against the chair sound asleep, but she still wore the worried concern he'd noted when he first saw her at Gerald's bed.

"Give her peace, Father," August prayed as he sat down beside her. "She's remained faithful and true, Lord. Please renew her strength."

Chapter 13

Throughout the long evening, August maintained his watchful guard over Bethany's sleeping form. He managed to find a blanket to cover her with and continued praying for both Beth and Gerry as she slept.

August watched the seemingly motionless hands on the clock. Nine, then ten o'clock dragged by, and still what sky he could see through the window showed streaks of light. The long summer night made it impossible to judge time.

Eleven, twelve, and finally one o'clock passed without word of Gerald's condition. August hesitated to ask for fear of waking Beth. She needed sleep more than anything else. He'd nearly decided to risk the disturbance when the nurse appeared with Gerald's doctor.

"I'm afraid I have bad news," Dr. Matthews said as he stood before August.

Beth stirred at the sound of voices and sat up. "What is it?" she questioned.

"Your son is failing rapidly. I suggest you and your husband come say your good-byes," the doctor replied. Neither Beth nor August sought to correct the mistaken reference to their relationship.

Beth began to cry, and August could only hold her close and stroke her head. He turned weary eyes to the doctor before asking, "Are you certain there is nothing else we can do?"

"I'm sorry," Dr. Matthews answered. "It is never easy to tell parents that their child won't make it. Gerald has fought hard to get this far, but he's too weak and the disease is taking too great a toll. He won't make it through the night."

"No, no," Beth sobbed. "He must live. He mustn't die!"

"Mrs. Hogan, please don't do this to yourself. It is of no help to your son. He's beyond our care now, and nothing can be gained by making yourself sick over his passing." The doctor's words seemed callous to Beth.

"You talk as though he were already dead," Beth replied as she pushed August away and got to her feet.

"For all intents and purposes, Mrs. Hogan," Dr. Matthews said without emotion, "he is. I can't do anything more for him. He's not responding to medicine, and his body is too spent to continue fighting. Let him go. You're a young, healthy woman, Mrs. Hogan. I'm certain you and your husband will have other children."

"I want other children, Doctor," Beth said with an undercurrent of anger to her voice. "But not to replace a dead child. I refuse to give up hope that God can deliver my baby from this illness. I have faith that He can work beyond your abilities."

The doctor shrugged his shoulders. "I cannot deny your tenacity, Mrs. Hogan. I only hope that your faith is not misplaced."

"It isn't," Beth stated firmly as she pushed past the doctor and his nurse. "If you can't give me any reason to hope, I know who can."

August watched as Beth moved down the hall with renewed determination. He turned to the doctor and spoke. "I can understand a portion of your unemotional response to her, Dr. Matthews. You must see dying every day and find it as grotesque and unbearable as I do. However, I will take it as a personal insult should you feel the need to ever resort to crushing her hopes again."

"I assure you, sir," the doctor interjected, "that stripping that young mother of hope was never my intention. She has labored long and hard at the bedside of your child. She has demonstrated a strength beyond human capabilities. I admire all that she has done, but I also want her to understand that there comes a time when nothing more can be done. We have reached that point with your son."

August felt a tug at his heart with every reference to Gerald as his own child. "I cannot accept that the situation is without hope," he stated firmly. "I refuse to believe it."

"Most people do," the doctor agreed. "But people get sick, and people die. We doctors can only do so much. I have done everything in my power, and now I must stand aside and say it is out of my hands."

"You're absolutely right, Doctor. It is out of your hands, but not out of God's." August moved with determined strides to Gerald's room.

When he entered, Beth was stretched out over Gerald's tiny frame. He could hear her praying in a hushed whisper. She was a determined woman, August admitted. She had been determined for him to come back to God, just as she was intent on seeing her son healed of meningitis.

August thought back to those long moments spent beneath the tractor. His accident had opened his eyes to God's love and forgiveness, but it had also given him a glimpse into the power of prayer. Beth had been praying for him. His sister, Julie, and her husband, Sam, had both written letters of encouragement and mentioned their prayers for his well-being. Other people had prayed for August without him being aware of their concern.

That was it! August turned quickly from the room and went in search of a telephone. He would call Julie and ask her to pray for Gerald. He would ask her to gather as many people as possible and get all of them to pray. Then he would call and leave word for Mrs. Miller and the flock that attended church in Northway. There was power in prayer, of this he was certain, and August would leave nothing to chance where Gerald was concerned.

Locating a telephone, August quickly gave the operator all the needed information and waited impatiently while she connected him to his sister.

"Hello," a sleepy Julie sounded on the other end of the phone.

"Julie, it's August. I need you to pray about something!" August knew Julie would have received his letter explaining his return to God and the love he held for Beth and her sons.

"August!" Julie exclaimed. "What's wrong that would have you calling me at this hour?"

"It's Gerald. He's one of the little boys I wrote you about. He's the older boy, and he's terribly ill," August explained.

"What's wrong with him?" Julie asked in an authoritative voice. Her years as a nurse would require August to give her all the details.

"Spinal meningitis," August spoke the dreaded words.

"How long has he been sick? What have they done for him?"

"I guess he's been sick about three, maybe four days. I just got here myself and don't know what all they've done for him. I heard something about an experimental drug from the States, but the doctor says Gerald isn't responding and that there's no hope. He told us to say our good-byes."

"How awful," Julie whispered. "I'll be praying for you."

"That's why I called. I want you to pray for a miracle. Beth can't bear losing him, and neither can I. In my heart, he's already my son, and I want God to heal him so I can be a real father to him."

"A miracle is exactly what it will take," Julie said hesitantly. "I know God can do anything, but—"

"No buts," August interrupted. "God can do anything. The doctor may have given up on Gerald, but Beth and I haven't. I want as many people praying and pleading for his life as I can get."

"Then you'll have Sam and me," Julie assured. "I'll even wake up our friends and get them to pray."

"Thanks, Jewels," he replied, using his sister's nickname. "I knew I could count on you. Now, if you don't mind, I'm going to make another call and get back to Beth and Gerald."

"I don't mind at all," Julie replied. "And August," she added, "welcome back to the family. I missed you and your encouraging faith. I knew God would work in a mighty way in your life, just as I know He will work in Gerald's. Good night, brother."

"Good night, Jewels."

The warmth of his sister's love bolstered his courage, and August quickly made the call to Northway. Ralph Greening readily agreed to trek out into the night and rally the town to pray for Gerald.

Making his way back to Gerald's room, August found Beth sitting beside her son, holding his hand. Her eyes were closed, and August wondered if she'd fallen asleep or if she still prayed. He touched her lightly on the shoulder, and Beth opened her eyes.

"I was worried," she said. "Where were you?"

"I was rounding up support for our efforts," August said with a sheepish grin. "I've rallied the troops, so to speak."

"You've what?" Beth questioned, wondering at August's smile.

"I called my sister in Nome and Ralph Greening in Northway. They're in turn going to rally their friends and ask for prayer for Gerald. We'll have so many requests for healing going before God's throne, we won't be able to count them," August said with contagious excitement in his voice.

"How wonderful," Beth said and dropped Gerald's hand to take August's. "You truly amaze me, Mr. Eriksson. Not long ago you would have scoffed at God's power. Now you call upon it, knowing that even though the doctors have thrown up their hands, God can turn things around."

"I have you to thank for this," August said, pulling Beth into his arms. "You never lost faith that God could turn me around. I simply took that principle and put it into practice."

Beth allowed August to engulf her with his sturdy arms. Her blond hair fell across his arm, glittering like gold in the pale hospital light. She looked up into dark eyes that bathed her in love. Silently, she thanked God for answering her prayers for August's change of heart and then thanked God for hearing her prayers for Gerald. She felt hesitant at the latter, but it seemed important to trust God for those answers.

August felt his heart nearly burst with love for the woman he held. He longed to convey those feelings and ask Beth to marry him, but he knew the moment wasn't right. He didn't want her to say yes out of gratitude for his presence. Nor did he want her to refuse him because of the strain of Gerald's ordeal.

"I hate waiting," August murmured. Beth assumed his words were about Gerald's condition.

"I know. God has things under His watchful eye, but it doesn't always seem that way as we wait and wonder," Beth replied.

"Waiting all these years for someone or some purpose to come into my life has been difficult too," August said cautiously.

"But now that you've waited, God has been faithful to send you people who care for you and love you," Beth whispered as she hugged herself close to August. "That little boy loves you nearly as much as I do. You mean the world to him, and I can't imagine God allowing Gerald to die without knowing that you're back here with him."

"All of this is a testing time," August stated firmly. "A time of trial such as Jesus said we'd experience in this world. But Jesus also said we could be of good cheer for He'd already overcome this world."

Beth nodded. "I believe that," she said, pulling away. "I believe that we will overcome this situation and that God will bless our boy." Beth thought fleetingly of JB and knew in her heart that he would approve of August as father to his son.

"Come on," August said and pulled Beth with him to Gerald's bedside. "Let's join our friends and pray for Gerald."

Chapter 14

It was close to three o'clock in the morning when Dr. Matthews reappeared to check Gerald's condition. The nurse ushered Beth and August into the hall while he conducted his examination. Within moments, the nurse brought them back. The doctor was writing notes on Gerald's chart.

Beth immediately went to Gerald's side, while August followed the doctor into the hall.

Dr. Matthews opened his mouth to speak, but August held up his hand. "There's nothing you can say. I know the odds are against that child. I know all of your medical expertise and skills have been tested and tried. Furthermore, I realize that even faithful servants of God lose loved ones in death. It's part of life."

August paused, pushing his hands deep into his jean pockets. His face took on a thoughtful look. "However, I also know the power of prayer."

Then with a smile of sudden peace on his face, August added, "Gerald's going to make it, and of that, I'm certain. He's going to get well because God will heal him."

Without waiting for a reply from the doctor, August turned back into the room, passing the nurse as she was leaving. August wanted to share his new feelings of peace with Beth. He entered the room and paused as Beth lovingly wiped her son's forehead.

"Gerry," August could hear her saying. "It's Momma, Gerry. I need you to get well. I'm asking God to make you well because He said I could ask for anything in Jesus' name and He would hear me. I'm doing that, Gerry. I'm asking in Jesus' name that your life be spared."

August could bear no more. "Beth, I know God will make Gerald well. I feel a calm and peace about it."

Beth stopped praying and looked up at August. "Honestly? You aren't just telling me that to give me hope?"

"I am telling you that to give you hope, but only because it's true. I feel such confidence that I want to sing it out. I even told the doctor that God would make Gerald well."

Beth crossed the room to where August stood. "I want to believe that, August. I know God is capable, but is He willing?"

"I believe He is," August replied. He looked into Beth's eyes and prayed she'd see the confidence in his own.

"Then I'm no longer worried," she said slowly. "If God has given you that certainty, then I shall praise Him for it and await my son's healing. I will believe!"

"Thatta girl!" August said, pulling Beth into his arms. "You're something special, Bethany Hogan."

Together they prayed and kept vigil at Gerald's bedside. Pulling chairs alongside the bed, August and Beth sat together, holding each other's hands and Gerald's as well.

Shortly before dawn, August and Beth awoke. Gerry seemed to be in a deep, natural sleep. Beth reached out and touched the brow of her son.

"Oh August!" she exclaimed. "He's not at all feverish. And look—" she pointed to his chest—"he's not straining to breathe."

August stared at the rhythmic rise and fall of the tiny chest and nodded. "He's getting well, Beth. God is healing him even as we watch."

"Thank You, God," Beth said as tears ran down her cheeks. "Thank You for the life of my baby."

"Amen," August said in agreement.

Taking Beth with him to the window, August pulled back the heavy drapes to reveal a glorious sunrise bursting from the horizon. He reached out and wiped away Beth's tears. "Joy has truly come in the morning, just as the psalmist said. No more tears, Bethany. Now we will rejoice."

Beth nodded and threw her arms around August's neck. "I will spend the rest of my life rejoicing for the miracles of God," she whispered.

Just then another voice joined in. "Mommy!" Gerald called out. His voice sounded hoarse but strong.

Beth and August rushed to Gerry's side and found him not only awake but also free of the glassy-eyed, feverish look. Staring in amazement, August and Beth could only smile.

"How do you feel, son?" August asked as he bent over the boy.

"Daddy," Gerald said, forgetting himself. "You came back. I thought maybe you didn't like me anymore."

"That could never happen, Gerald," August replied. "I was very far away in a hospital, much like this one."

"A hospital?" Gerald questioned. "What's a hospital?"

"Oh Gerry," Beth said as she sat down beside him. "A hospital is a place for sick people to get well. You've been very sick, but God has made you well."

"I had nice dreams," Gerald said, surprising them both. "I dreamed about lots of pretty flowers and a big river. Bigger than the one Phillip fell into."

Beth glanced in amazement at August and then back to her son's shining face. "I'll bet it was wonderful," she replied. "I'm so glad you're feeling better," she added, placing a kiss on his forehead.

"Me too. I'm hungry, Mommy. Can I have some breakfast?" Gerald asked.

August laughed loudly. "Spoken like a true boy."

"Always hungry," Beth admitted. "We'll see if we can't manage to find something for you to fill that empty tummy of yours."

"I'll go right now and speak with the doctor," August said. But before August had made it to the door, Dr. Matthews entered the room and stared in shocked surprise at the sight of Gerald sitting up in bed.

"What's going on?" the doctor asked as he crossed the room.

"I told you God would make him well," August said with a hearty slap on the doctor's back.

"It's impossible," the doctor whispered in amazement. "That child should be dead by now." His words were spoken so softly that only August could hear them.

"Well, he isn't. In fact, he's very much alive and very hungry," August informed the man. Gerald agreed with an enthusiastic nod of his head.

"I simply don't believe it," Dr. Matthews said, walking over to Gerald's bed.

"Many people never do," Beth said firmly, refusing to take her eyes from her son's face. "And because of that, they never know the fullness of God's powerful love."

The doctor shook his head as he examined Gerald. He took a thermometer from his medical bag and put it into Gerald's mouth. While he waited for the results, the doctor felt for a pulse. His eyes registered surprise when he found a strong, steady beat.

Taking the thermometer from Gerald's mouth, Dr. Matthews again shook his head. "It's normal, and his pulse is strong and steady," he said, looking to Beth and August as if for an explanation.

"God has worked a miracle, Doctor," Beth said as she tousled Gerald's hair. "He has given me back my son."

The doctor nodded. "I suppose you're right." He had Gerald bend his head back and forth and from side to side. When he was satisfied that no symptom of the meningitis remained, he declared the boy could eat some breakfast.

Beth and August joined Dr. Matthews at the door of Gerald's room. "I'll need to run some more tests, but I must say, I am completely amazed," the doctor said humbly. "I have never seen God work a miracle such as this in the life of anyone, let alone one of my patients. Makes me feel rather useless."

"We want to thank you for all you did to help Gerald," Beth said as she extended her hand. "We know you did what you could, and we don't believe it useless for one moment. You simply operated under human limitations. We took it beyond that and expected divine results." Beth's words were gentle and supportive.

August nodded as his arm encircled Beth's waist. "If we could do everything ourselves, there'd be no need for God. Since we can't, we must turn to Him on a daily basis and pray for guidance, strength, and direction. I hope you feel inspired by this miracle."

"I certainly feel a wonderment about it," the doctor admitted. "It's like nothing I've ever seen, and it certainly bears consideration. Now, if you'll excuse me, I'll send a nurse in with a breakfast tray."

Beth smiled. "I know that'll make Gerry a very happy boy." The doctor nodded and turned down the hall, a baffled look covering his face.

"I guess that'll teach him to question a woman of faith," August said with a laugh as they turned back to Gerry.

"Where's my brother?" the boy asked eagerly. He was already trying out the bounce in the hospital mattress.

"He's back at the roadhouse with Mrs. Miller," Beth explained. "This hospital is in Fairbanks."

"That's far, far away from home," Gerald said, amusing both August and Beth. "How did I get here?"

"We took the airplane," Beth answered. "The soldiers helped us get here. Do you remember anything at all?"

"Nope," Gerald replied. "I just remember sleeping and sleeping. I'm glad you came back, August. You aren't going to leave again, are you?"

"No," August said, reassuring the child. "I don't plan on being far from you ever again."

"Good," Gerald said with a grin. "It made my mommy sad when you went away."

"Gerald!" Beth said with a finger to her lips. "You mustn't tell August about all that."

"Of course he must," August said with a grin to match Gerald's. He lowered his head to Gerald's and added, "I want to know everything that happened while I was away."

Beth shook her head at the grinning faces. "It isn't the past that matters," she chided with a smile. "It's the future that counts, and I intend that we should have a glorious one."

"I agree," August said, holding his hand out to Beth. "You can tell me all about it later," he added with a wink to Gerald.

"You are quite impossible, Mr. Eriksson," Beth said in mock exasperation.

"Not at all, Mrs. Hogan," August said as he lifted Beth's hand to his lips. "Just determined."

The touch of his lips on Beth's hand caused her to tremble. She could feel her pulse race and her breathing quicken. For the first time, nothing stood between her and August.

As if reading her thoughts, August smiled. He could feel her quiver at his touch. His eyes met hers, and in their reflection he saw all of his long-held dreams coming true.

"When's the food going to get here?" Gerald interrupted. "I want to eat, and then I want to go home."

August and Beth laughed and pulled Gerald into their arms. "I think that sounds wonderful," Beth agreed.

Chapter 15

S everal bowls later, Gerald gobbled down oatmeal with raisins while Bethany told him about his days spent in the hospital. Meanwhile, August made arrangements for their trip home. He felt a lightheartedness he'd never known.

"Julie?" August spoke into the receiver of the phone. "It's August."

"August, how's the little boy?" Julie questioned through a static filled line.

"He's fine. We got our miracle, Julie. Gerald rallied in a remarkable way," August replied.

"Praise God," Julie replied. "I knew He'd hear our prayers. How is Beth?"

"She's exhausted, but otherwise great. You would like her, Jewels. She has a strong faith just like you. She never doubted that God could make a difference," August said with pride.

"She sounds like the perfect woman for you," Julie remarked. The static played havoc with the line. "I'm sorry about the connection. I don't know if it has anything to do with it or not, but we're in the middle of a fierce storm. High winds and snow. You know the type."

"I do indeed. The temperatures dropped considerably here, but good weather is holding, which is another blessing. They're still trying to finish up the highway. I think they'll be done within a matter of a week or so," August replied.

"Will you be coming home after that?" Julie asked hopefully.

"I'd just begun thinking about that," August answered. "I want to come back, at least to get my things. I miss my dogs, and I want to teach the boys how to drive a sled."

"We'll look forward to seeing you," Julie said enthusiastically. "Sam has missed you a great deal," she added.

August thought of how much Sam would have enjoyed working on the highway. "I've missed him too. Tell him hello and that I'll see you both soon. I'll talk to you again before I actually come back. Thanks again, Jewels."

"I'm glad we could be a part of your miracle," Julie replied. "It was good to hear your voice. Please take care of yourself."

"I will. I love you, sis."

"I love you too. Good-bye." Julie's voice was barely audible through the static.

After another quick call to Ralph Greening, August was free to return to Beth and Gerald.

"It's all set," August said as he entered the room. "As soon as the doctor gives his approval, we'll be on the first transport plane for Northway."

Gerald had finished his breakfast and waited eagerly for his mother's permission to get out of bed.

"Dr. Matthews said we could leave as soon as he has one of the other doctors take a look at Gerald," Beth said with a smile.

August looked at her with appreciation. Now that his own bitterness toward God and Gerald's serious illness no longer filled his mind, August was beginning to recognize the perfection of the woman before him. She was everything he'd ever needed or wanted.

"Did you hear what I said?" Beth questioned.

"Huh? No, sorry. What did you say?" August asked as he crossed the room.

Beth laughed. "It wasn't important. I have you and Gerald, and soon we'll go home to Phillip. That's what matters."

Dr. Matthews came into the room unannounced just then. With him was an elderly man Beth didn't recognize.

"This is Dr. Barnes," Gerald's doctor announced. "I've asked him to evaluate our patient and give his opinion."

"How nice to meet you, Dr. Barnes," Beth said as she extended her hand. "So you've come to see our miracle boy."

"Yes, Mrs. Hogan," the man said, shaking her hand. "I must say, I was quite enthralled by the boy's recovery. I understand your son was only two days on the experimental medicine from the States."

"Yes, that's true," Beth said and added, "but I don't believe that's what cured him. After all, you folks had given him up for dead."

Dr. Barnes picked up Gerald's chart and studied it for a moment. Gerald finally broke the silence. "Are they going to let me go home, Momma?"

"I think so, Gerry, but you must be quiet and let the doctors do their job," Beth replied, giving her son a hug.

Dr. Barnes continued his examination of Gerald and finally turned back to Beth with a smile. "I see no reason to keep this child here any longer. Your son is completely healed to the best of my knowledge."

"Thank you," Beth replied. She threw a knowing smile at August, who had held back in silence while the men examined Gerald.

August stepped forward and put an arm around Beth. "How soon can we leave?" he asked.

"As soon as you're ready," Dr. Barnes replied. "I release the boy as of now."

Gerry let out an excited scream at the verdict, and August and Beth thanked the doctors once more for their help as the medical men turned to leave.

When the doctors had left, August turned to Beth. "Ready to go home, Mrs. Hogan?"

"Definitely," she replied, taking his offered hand.

August and Beth hugged Gerald close. August silently thanked God for the loving family He'd provided.

"You know," August began, "I think we should have a word of prayer and thank God for all He's done for us. Then I think we should get out of this hospital and head home to Phillip and Mrs. Miller."

"I agree," Beth said, lifting her eyes to August. In that moment she wanted nothing more than to spend the rest of her days loving this man and her children.

"Father, we come to You with thankful hearts," August began. "We praise You for the healing of Gerald's body and for the mercies You showed me in bringing me back to the truth."

Beth listened intently as August prayed, agreeing with his words and enjoying the blessings of God's love. Silently, she added her own requests.

I love him, Lord, she prayed. *I love him so very much, and if it is Your will, I pray You'll see us married quickly so that we can be a whole and complete family.*

August ended his prayer and Gerald joined in with a hearty "Amen." Beth lifted her face to reveal tears that she'd not realized she had cried.

"Why are you crying, Mommy?" Gerald asked with a worried look on his face. "Is something wrong?"

August turned, seeing the tears for the first time. "I think your mommy is happy, Gerald. Sometimes folks have a hard time expressing the wonder of how happy they are."

Beth dabbed her eyes with the corner of a handkerchief that August offered her. "I am happy, Gerry. I'm so very glad that God has made you well and that He brought August back to us."

She turned to August, feeling confident for the first time that she could speak what was on her heart. "Please don't leave us again. We need you. I need you."

Beth's blue eyes pierced deep into August's heart. Years later he would remember the moment as one of the most precious in his life. She was so needy, yet so strong. Somehow, the two qualities balanced perfectly, creating one incredible woman.

"And I need you," August whispered, his dark eyes shining with love. "I'll always need you."

Gerald refused to be left out of the conversation. He was bored with the adult seriousness. "Can we go home?" he asked, breaking the spell of the moment. "I want to play in my tree house."

Beth laughed, and August lifted Gerald into his strong arms.

"Yes," August said enthusiastically. "Let's go home!"

Chapter 16

From Fairbanks to Northway, Gerald chattered about the plane and the view. August pointed out the highway below and explained to the boy about the work involved in building such a road.

Gerald listened in awe as August spoke of the powerful machinery that helped clear the way. "I'd like to do that too," Gerald said in animated excitement. "I want to do work just like you."

"I thought you wanted to be a pilot," August replied, shifting Gerald so he could get a better view.

"That was what my old daddy did. Now I want to do work like my new daddy. You are going to be my new daddy, aren't you?" Gerald questioned sincerely.

"Would you like that?" August asked with a grin.

"I sure would," Gerald answered. "Phillip would too. He told me so."

"Well, then," August said with a glance at Beth, "we'll just have to see what the good Lord works out."

Beth felt a twinge of disappointment at August's words. She'd held her breath, waiting for his reply, and then she'd only heard a "wait and see" answer. Hiding her frustration, Beth was relieved that Gerald seemed satisfied with August's answer.

Folding her hands in her lap, Beth thought about the situation and glanced up to find August watching her. She offered the briefest smile, and when August winked and grinned back, Beth felt relieved. There was no way of knowing exactly what August had in mind, but Beth was certain he loved her and the boys. Wait and see wasn't an easy thing to accept, but it did offer the possibility of more, and Beth clung to that for reassurance.

———— # ————

The plane touched down shortly before dinnertime with Gerald already complaining that his stomach was growling. Stepping off the plane, August offered a hand to Beth.

"It's good to be home," Beth declared and breathed deeply of the crisp air. "I've missed it so much and Phillip too."

August easily lifted Gerald into his arms and swung in step behind Beth. "I suggest we get your things, and I'll see about securing us a ride home. After all, this little boy is about to starve to death."

"I'll square getting the suitcase," Beth offered with a laugh. She watched as August hoisted Gerald over his head and onto his shoulders. What a great father he would be for her sons!

August waited until Beth was deep in conversation with the pilot before going off in search of a ride to the roadhouse. It was hard to believe that autumn had come in their absence. The fireweed was snowy with its cotton plumes floating through the air, and aspen shimmered with their hues of gold and orange.

In the distance, August could see that the Wrangell Mountains were already glistening with thick layers of snow. It wouldn't be long before snow would hug the ground in a white, insulating blanket. Thoughts of cold weather made August think of his dogs and sled travel. He'd have to find a way to bring them here from Nome and teach the boys to drive a team.

It wasn't hard to find a ride to Gantry Roadhouse; most everyone had heard of Gerald's illness and were anxious, even pleased, to lend a hand to the little boy.

The driver of the jeep turned out to be Private Ronnie Jacobs, one of the soldiers Beth had baked sweet potato pies for.

"It's mighty good to see that your boy is healthy and strong again," Ronnie said as he helped Beth into the seat.

"Thank you, Private," Beth returned. "Have they kept you well fed in my absence?"

The young man laughed. "Not on this army's food. I missed coming down to the roadhouse to buy the extras. I guess pretty soon we'll be out of here altogether. It'll sure be good to go back where it's warm. I miss Georgia."

"Who's she?" Gerald asked as August handed him to Beth.

Ronnie laughed. "That's not a girl. It's the state I live in."

"Is it as pretty as Alaska?" Gerald asked.

"I think so," the private responded, taking the driver's seat while August jumped in the back. "Now, if everybody's set, I'll get y'all home."

―――― *H* ――――

The drive to the roadhouse was over quickly. August had barely put a foot out of the jeep when Phillip came bursting out the doorway.

"Mommy! Daddy!" he called out. Running down the dirt pathway, he held out open arms for August's embrace. August tossed him high in the air. Phillip's giggles sounded like music to Beth's and August's ears.

"Phillip, you must have grown six inches since I last saw you. Come give Mommy some love," Beth said, reaching out to take her son from August.

"I missed you, Mommy. I missed you whole bunches." Phillip's muffled voice fell in kisses against his mother's neck.

"Oh, and I missed you, pumpkin. I missed you so much," Beth replied. "And look here," she said as she put Phillip down. "Gerry's back, and he's all better."

"I helped take care of him, didn't I, Mommy?" Phillip questioned, catching sight of his brother. "Gerry!" he squealed as he rushed to hug his sibling. The boys were great friends and had missed each other terribly. Soon they were laughing and talking at once as they shared their adventures with each other.

Mrs. Miller came outside to join the reunion. "Gerald!" she called out and waved. As the foursome approached the older woman, Beth could see there were tears in Hazel Miller's eyes.

"Praise be to God!" she exclaimed, embracing Gerald.

"I was real sick," Gerald explained seriously.

"You sure were," the older woman agreed. "But God made you well, and I've made a celebration dinner to thank Him."

"Hazel, how nice!" Beth remarked. She was weary to the bone and anxious to drop into bed, but she wouldn't have spoiled Hazel's celebration for all the world.

"I could eat a moose," August declared with a grin.

"Well, I just might have some of that too," Mrs. Miller said, laughing. "You'll just have to wash up and set yourself down to see."

The boys and August hurried in the direction of the washroom while Beth lingered a moment with Hazel.

"Hazel, I'm indebted to you for life," Beth said as she hugged her friend. "Without you I would have worried constantly about Phillip and the property."

"I'm happy to have helped. I finally felt useful, and I think it taught me something else," Hazel said, taking a step back.

"And what's that, Hazel?" Beth questioned.

"I've just been wasting myself and the talents the good Lord gave me. I've been hiding myself away, picking and choosing what I'll be a part of and what I won't. I hadn't realized how cloistered away I'd become."

"Don't be too hard on yourself, Hazel," Beth interjected. "You have done much to live for God. You teach Sunday school at the church and sing in the choir. Everyone who knows you or has had an opportunity to speak with you knows your heart."

"That may be, but I know I can do more and I intend to," Hazel replied. "But enough about me. What about you and Mr. Eriksson?"

"Oh Hazel," Beth said, smiling broadly. "God has renewed August's heart. He's found his way back to the truth, and he loves me."

"How wonderful!" Hazel exclaimed. "God truly has answered our prayers. Has the man asked you to marry him?"

"Not in those words, but I am certain it's his intention. I can hardly wait until we're a family," Beth said happily.

"I believe you already are," Hazel stated and pulled open the door. "Now come along. My fine supper is getting cold, and those men of yours looked mighty hungry." Beth nodded with a smile and followed Hazel to the kitchen.

Dinner was as fine an affair as any Beth or August had ever known. Hazel had prepared so many specialties that Beth lost track of what she'd sampled.

Smoked reindeer sausages lay in long, steaming strips atop a bed of seasoned rice, while another pot held sliced moose in a tantalizing barbecue sauce.

Sourdough bread from a starter Mrs. Miller claimed was over seventy years old was quickly devoured with huge spoonfuls of home-made blueberry jelly.

Accompanying all this richness was an array of vegetables and fruit that bowed the table under its weight. On top of the stove sat strawberry-rhubarb pies and a fresh pot of coffee. There was decidedly more food than five people could eat, but no one seemed to mind.

"I know you'll want to put those boys to bed," Hazel said as she began to clear the table. "Why don't you run on ahead and take care of them? I'll clean up this mess."

"I can't let you go on taking care of us," Beth said, stacking the boys' dishes together and reaching for August's.

"Now, I'll be gone in an hour or two and you'll have yourself and your family to take care of. Let me do this for you while you enjoy getting back to your routine," Hazel insisted.

"I think that's mighty fine of you, Mrs. Miller," August said. He got to his feet and patted his stuffed stomach. "I can't remember the last time I had anything quite that good. After they get done with rationing, you ought to open up a restaurant."

"I think that would be a grand idea, Hazel. Maybe that's the purpose you've been looking to fill," Beth remarked. "Better yet, maybe we could add it to the roadhouse. I know my boarders would be a lot happier if I offered meals with their rooms."

"And if you were careful with the things you served, you could probably get started before the war is over," August said, contemplating the possibilities. "We could build on to the kitchen, maybe over here." August walked to the south wall of the kitchen where the stove stood. "I don't think it would be all that difficult."

"I don't expect you to alter your roadhouse for me," Hazel replied evenly, but in her heart was born the first ray of excitement.

"It would be beneficial to both of us," Beth replied. "Besides, I don't expect to run a roadhouse all of my life. Maybe you could eventually buy me out."

Beth's revelation was news to August. He wondered what her plans were for the future.

"Well, you've certainly given an old woman a great deal to think about," Hazel murmured, moving the hot food back to the stove. "But right now, you have two boys who are nearly asleep as they stand," she said and motioned to where Gerald and Phillip were swaying on their feet.

"Come on, boys," August said, scooping a child into each arm. "I think it's time to tuck you in."

The boys needed little in the way of tucking in. They were both asleep almost before their heads hit the pillows. Beth stood for a moment at the door of their bedroom. She took a deep breath and sighed. The boys slept healthy and comfortable in their beds, and in the kitchen, August waited for her to join him. What more could she possibly want?

Gently, she pulled the door closed and went to August. "Seeing my children at rest has to be the most precious moment of the day. I never fail to be amazed at the comfort and joy it gives me," Beth said, taking August's hand in her own.

Thinking they would be helping to clean up the dishes, Beth

registered surprise as August maneuvered her past Hazel with a wink and out the back door into the chilly night air.

They walked hand in hand for several yards, enjoying the solitude of the moment. Beth felt a peace she hadn't dared hope for after JB's death.

Pausing, she turned to face August. "I want to thank you for all you've done—especially coming to me in Fairbanks. I think I would have fallen apart if you hadn't been there."

August's dark eyes stared down at her for a long time before he spoke. He was eager to make Beth his wife, yet there seemed so much that had gone unsaid between them. "I needed to be there," he finally whispered, "as much as you needed me to be there."

Beth silently hoped that August would take this opportunity to propose to her. She felt light and airy, and her heart was fairly flying on wings of its own. Surely August felt the same.

Leading Beth to the long bench he had made for evenings such as this one, August searched for the right words to speak what was on his heart. "I brought you out here for a purpose," he began. "I needed to tell you something and explain."

Beth's brow furrowed. This didn't sound like the beginning of a marriage proposal. "What is it, August?"

"I'm going back to Nome," he replied.

Beth felt her chest tighten. Her mind whirled in a thousand directions as she wondered what August meant by his words. She gripped the arm of the bench and forced herself to be silent. Had she misunderstood his words in Fairbanks? Didn't he intend to marry her after all?

"I have an entire life back in Nome that you know nothing about," August explained. "I have a sister and a lifetime of mementos, not to mention a dogsled team to rival any in the territory."

August's words held such longing that Beth couldn't maintain her silence. "You're leaving us?" She dreaded hearing the answer.

"Only to get my things," August said with a grin. "You can't get rid of me that easily. I don't intend to be gone a moment longer than is necessary to pack my sled and mush my team back here." August noticed Beth's look of concern. "You didn't really think I'd leave you for good, did you?"

Beth shrugged her shoulders. "I didn't know what to think. I mean, I knew how I felt, and I thought I understood how you felt, but—"

"But then I told you I was going to Nome," August interrupted, "and you started to worry?"

"Nome is hundreds of miles away," Beth said, feeling little relief that August intended to return. "So much could happen to you on the way back. There's so much open, empty space between here and there. What if you have an accident or a storm comes up?"

"I've traveled those trails hundreds, even thousands of times. I know every inch of land between Nome and Nenana. Nothing is going to happen to me," August insisted.

"I wish you didn't have to go," Beth replied honestly. "I've said too many good-byes."

"Then we won't say good-bye," August stated firmly. "You could come with me. Mrs. Miller could watch over the roadhouse. We could fly to Nome and drive the dogs back together."

Beth shook her head. "I couldn't leave the boys that long. They need me to be a constant in their lives. They've said good-byes too, remember? And their father never came home again. I couldn't put them through that, and taking them on the trail would be much too difficult, especially with Gerald just recovered from meningitis."

"I guess I wasn't thinking," August offered by way of apology.

"It's all right. I understand you have to go back, and you understand I have to stay. I guess the thing for me to do is give you over to God once again," Beth said, fighting tears that threatened to spill from her eyes.

"Who better to place me with?" August said, putting his arm around Beth's shoulders. He lifted her face to meet his and spoke with such tenderness that Beth thought her heart would burst. "I love you, Bethany Hogan. I've loved you for so long now, I don't remember a time when I didn't love you. And I love your children as if they were flesh of my flesh. I want to be a father to those boys, and I want to live my life in the warmth of your love."

Without waiting for her reply, August lowered his lips to kiss her long and deeply. He felt her tears fall against his cheek as she clung to him.

When he lifted his face, August was surprised to find Beth smiling. "Tears and smiles?" he questioned. Gently he brushed away a glistening drop from her face.

"I love you, August," she whispered in a voice more composed than August thought possible, given her reaction to his news. "I know your trip is necessary, but I wish you didn't have to leave me for so long."

"I'll be back before you know it, and when I return, I'll bring my mother's wedding ring and marry you. That is, if you'll have me," he added with a broad smile.

Beth reached out to push back his dark hair. The light from the moon illuminated his face as if it were day. "I'll marry you, August Eriksson. I'll be your wife, and bear your children, and all of my days I will love you as I have loved no other."

Chapter 17

August spent the final days of the highway project behind a desk. After eight months of tedious work and precarious conditions, the Alaskan/Canadian Highway was completed. Nicknamed "the Alcan" by those who worked it, the roadway was a miracle of cooperative countries and their people.

Destiny's road stretched over nearly fifteen hundred miles and constituted the efforts of more than eleven thousand individuals.

It wasn't much to look at, August decided as he flew from one isolated airstrip to the next, surveying the wonder from the air. Little more than a dingy brown ribbon, it wove its way through the country-side. Occasionally, strips of gray or blue indicated a lake or river, while either side of the narrow highway was lined with dark spruce forests and snow-filled permafrost meadows.

The army was pleased with the accomplishment. The road provided a way to transport oil and other goods to far north bases, should the shipping lanes become too dangerous. But an unanticipated benefit was what a morale booster the road had become. It proved to two nations and millions of their citizens that they could combine their energies on the home front to aid their loved ones serving in battles so far away. It made the people feel important, useful, and necessary for the war effort.

August smiled as the plane touched down in Northway. This was his final official duty for the project. After great consideration and prayer, August had decided against taking the permanent job offered by Ralph Greening.

Instead, August had shared with Beth his desire to raise sled dogs and help her with the roadhouse. She had enthusiastically agreed to having him around the house on a daily basis and had even begun to make a list of jobs August could be responsible for. August had laughed when he learned of the list.

"Good to know I'll be needed," he'd ruefully observed.

The weather had turned cold. Excitement gripped the town of Northway as it bustled with activities commemorating the new highway. But the dropping temperatures and significant snows signaled to August that it was time to go to Nome and retrieve his property. Once done with this, he would settle down to a new life with Beth and the boys.

August shook his head in amazement, remembering his first day in Northway when he was seeking a job on the highway. The road had given destiny to more than the countries through which it passed. God had used it to bring August his own destiny and a new life.

Snow blanketed the ground around the airstrip, leaving August to tramp out his own way to the crossroads. He didn't mind; it reminded him of days out on the trail hunting or checking traplines. Remembering his father and the home he'd known as a boy, August was filled with longing to return to that life.

Nearing the roadhouse, August paused in order to take the sight in. Nestled among the tall spruce and leafless aspen and birch was the place he now called home. Black smoke rose from the chimney, contrasting against the gray, snow-heavy sky. The sight warmed August and prompted him to hasten his steps to the family he'd soon call his own.

Kicking off his snowy boots, August entered the roadhouse through the back door and pulled off his parka to hang it beside Beth's at the entrance to the kitchen. He was surprised to find Beth and the boys sitting at the table, smiling up at him as if they knew a secret.

"What?" August asked with a grin. "What are you up to?"

Phillip and Gerald giggled, while Beth lowered her eyes to keep from laughing out loud. August joined them cautiously at the table and looked on his chair for any sign of a pinecone or other such souvenir of the boys' mischievous behavior. Finding none, he sat opposite Beth, between the boys.

"Is somebody going to tell me what's going on here?" he asked, reaching for Phillip. "Or am I going to have to tickle it out of you?"

"Don't tell him, Phillip," Gerald squealed.

Phillip laughed in glee as August's fingers found his ribs. "You're going to be our daddy," Phillip laughingly gave up the secret.

"Mommy said you had to go to your old house and get your stuff, but that you were coming back to live here with us," Gerald added.

Beth looked at August with a shrug. "I couldn't help telling them," she replied. "And since you never said I couldn't, I gave in to my joy and let them be part of it."

August laughed as he reached out and pulled Gerald to his lap. Holding each boy on a knee, August gave them a squeeze. "And what do you boys think of that?" he asked.

"We like it!" Gerald exclaimed and Phillip echoed.

"Well, that's certainly a good thing for me," August proclaimed. "I guess I would have had a lot of trouble on my hands if you had said you didn't want me."

"I don't want you to go, Daddy," Phillip said with a pout.

"Me neither," Gerald agreed. Beth's expression confirmed that she felt the same way.

"Look, boys," August began, "I'm not going to be gone very long, and when I get back I'm going to be bringing my dog team. I'm going to teach you the old-fashioned way of getting around in the snow."

"We've never had a dog. How many dogs will you bring?" Gerald asked, suddenly interested.

"I'll probably bring twenty or so," August replied. "And twenty dogs are going to be a lot of work. I'll need extra help from you boys."

"Will we play with the doggies?" Phillip asked.

"Of course," August answered. "We'll give them lots of love and care every day. And we'll play with them and work with them. You'll see. It's going to be a great deal of fun."

"What about Momma?" Gerald questioned.

"Your momma is going to have fun with the dogs too," August said with a wink at Beth.

"And it won't be long, boys," Beth added, "before you'll be ready to start learning to read and write."

"That's true," August agreed. "This roadhouse is going to need a lot of care too. Your mother has already made long, long lists, so every day will hold plenty of things to keep us busy. And"—August paused, looking purposefully into Beth's eyes,—"I promise I'll never be away from here for any longer than I have to be, because I love you all so very much."

"We love you too, Daddy," Gerald said, glancing at his mother. "Momma said we could call you that, if you didn't mind."

August choked up from the emotion surging through his heart. "I would love it if you would call me Daddy," he replied. "I want very much to be the best daddy in the world to both of you."

The boys hugged him tightly around the neck, while August and Beth exchanged a look of love that bound them forever to one another. *God is so good,* August thought. In His perfect way, God had saved the best in life for the last, and August could not imagine a sweeter future.

"Why don't you boys go play for a little while? I need to talk with August—your dad—for a moment."

"But he just got home," Gerald protested.

"Can't we stay?" Phillip moaned.

"Now, boys," August said, putting them from his knee. "You must always mind your mother and me. Sometimes your safety or lives might depend upon it. Right now, your mom simply wants to talk to me, but obeying her is always important. Do you understand?"

The boys sobered at August's serious tone. "Yes, Daddy."

With a smile, August broke the somber moment. "Good. Now, you run and play, and when I'm done talking to your mother, I'll come help you build something with your blocks."

The boys scampered off to their room, discussing at great length their plans for the toy building project.

"You have such a loving way with them," Beth remarked. "I'm amazed that you've never spent much time with children."

"There were never any around to spend time with. There was Julie of course," he said, "but I was a child as well. I've always known, though, that I wanted to be a father. I've always wanted a house full of children and a home full of love."

"I feel like I've got so much to learn about you," Beth said wistfully. "You've never told me much about Nome or your sister. It's another part of you that I know nothing about."

August nodded. "Just remember, there's a great deal I don't know about you either. But we have all the time in the world."

Beth frowned for a moment, remembering the war that engulfed the world. "It's a rather frightening time. The world is in such conflict. So many young men are dying to give us freedom and a future. It cuts my heart to imagine waving my sons off to war. I pray I never have to know that feeling."

"Yes," August said, remembering that he once wanted to be one of those marching away to war. "I've never looked at it quite that way. I was angry at God because He wouldn't let me be one of those going off to serve. I never thought of how it affected anyone but me. Now that two little boys I love could well face that responsibility, I feel the same way you do. I want to protect them and keep them far from the reaches of such a monster as war."

"Do you suppose the world will change so very much in the years to come? I mean after the fighting is over and the men have come home," Beth questioned.

"War always changes things," August said thoughtfully. "I remember reading about World War I. It seemed so far away and unimportant. Somebody else's war, I thought. Somebody else's land and people. But it wasn't that way, and neither is this. We're every bit as much a part of those who are fighting as they are of us. We give them a reason to fight, a reason to win. They need us, just as we need them."

"Is it selfish to want a good life with you and the boys, in the face of the adversity our soldiers are living with?" Beth inquired.

"I don't think so. I believe it's just as they would expect. Life goes on, and just as one war is over, another begins. Whether it's on a battlefield or in a hospital bed, it's a never-ending cycle, and God's hand is upon all," August replied.

"Then our destiny is in His hands, and nothing the world does or doesn't do will change that," Beth said with new certainty.

"That it is," August agreed and added, "A future with God's loving protection doesn't seem at all frightening."

Beth nodded and reached across the table for August's hand. His warm fingers wrapped around her own, and Beth knew there truly was nothing to fear. With God and a good man at her side, the challenges of the world seemed to shrink under a shroud of faith.

Destiny's road would be God's road, and though the way might hold pitfalls and obstacles, Beth and August would travel it together, always guided by the Creator of it all.

Iditarod

DREAM

Chapter 1

Rita Eriksson shifted into overdrive and watched the highway miles pass by in disinterested silence. Although she'd been away from her childhood home for over five years, the idea of returning held little interest for her.

Born Rita Anne Eriksson, she was the last of ten children and the least cut out for rural life. At least that's what she told herself when she left for college and a degree in nursing.

She'd spent the better part of a lifetime living forty minutes outside the small town of Tok, Alaska. A town seemingly misplaced in the middle of nowhere, between Fairbanks and the Canadian border. Its claim to fame was dogsledding and touristy native art, but to Rita, its only appeal was the fact that the Alcan Highway ran through it. It was on that highway, shortly after she'd finished school, that Rita took off for Anchorage and never looked back.

Ignoring the speed of her car, Rita gave anxious thought to her return home. Most of her brothers and sisters had moved away from Tok, although an older brother and his family had settled in town. Her family was seemingly scattered to the four winds, and for Rita, it was just as well. She'd never fit in with any of them and had come along too late for most of them to even bother being interested in her. Her closest sibling, Edgar, was nearly nine years her senior and, being a boy, he had little interest in the surprise arrival of another sister.

Rita had been only too happy to escape the mundane lifestyle of a home that, until recently, hadn't even afforded them the luxury of electricity or an indoor bathroom. It might not have been so bad had they lived in town. In comparison to the desolation of the Eriksson homestead, there were many things to do in Tok. But Rita had decided to put it all behind her and be done with that way of life.

Yet, even though that had been her choice, here she was driving back home at her parents' urging. Well, not really her parents' urging, more like her father's. She'd always felt closer to her father. For reasons that were beyond Rita's understanding, she and her mother had never gotten along. It seemed that no matter how hard Rita tried, her relationship with her mother only deteriorated to the point that neither of them put much effort into mending the emotional cavern.

Her father, however, loved her, and of that Rita was certain. He never failed to call her on Monday nights to find out how her weekend had gone and how the week to come was shaping up. During the entire five years in Anchorage, Rita could remember her mother calling only twice and both those times were on Christmas.

With a shake of her head, Rita tried to ignore the pain she still felt whenever she thought of her mother. There was no sense in letting the past get a stronghold, Rita determined. Nothing was going to change between them. Hadn't time already proved that?

She didn't know how long the flashing red lights of the patrol car had followed her, but when the officer behind the wheel hit the blaring sirens, Rita nearly jumped out of her skin.

"Oh no," she muttered and pulled the car to the side of the road. "I wonder how fast I was going."

She rolled down the window and ran a hand through her newly cropped black hair. This trip was turning sour rather soon, she thought to herself.

"May I see your driver's license?" a voice called out from overhead.

Rita didn't even bother to look up. She reached over for her red clutch purse and produced her license. Without a word, she handed the license over and then sat tapping her fingers against the steering wheel.

"You were doing eighty-five miles an hour, Ms. Eriksson. Say, you wouldn't be related to August and Beth Eriksson?" the officer questioned.

Rita perked up. Maybe she could beat the ticket if she turned on a little hometown charm.

"Why, yes. They're my parents," she said with a honey-smooth voice. Glancing up behind thick black lashes, Rita offered a smile to the stout-looking patrolman whose name tag read "Williams."

The officer took off his sunglasses and returned Rita's smile. "Good friends of mine, your folks. I doubt they'd enjoy burying one of their own," he stated evenly. "Being a native, you know better than to drive that fast on this highway. If the road doesn't tear up your vehicle, wrapping it around a moose or grizzly sure could do the job."

"Sorry," Rita said, trying hard to maintain her temper. She didn't appreciate being told what she should and shouldn't do.

"I would hope for at least that much," the officer said as he returned Rita's license with a ticket attached. "I'd let you off with a warning, but being you're a native and not all that sorry, I'd just as soon you learn a lesson."

Rita's temper got the best of her as she snatched the ticket and license from his hand. She thought to say something but instead stuffed the items inside her purse and turned to roll up her window.

"It was a pleasure meeting you, Ms. Eriksson. I'm sure we'll be seeing more of each other. By the way, I'm Mark Williams."

"It wasn't a pleasure meeting you, Officer Williams, and I hope we don't meet again," Rita said curtly and rolled up the car window. She barely waited for the man to walk past her car before hitting the gas and spraying gravel behind her as she pulled back up on the highway.

Rita watched uncomfortably for any sign that the patrol car intended to follow her. When it remained in place at the side of the highway, she breathed a sigh of relief and glanced at her watch.

She'd already been driving for four hours without stopping to get out and stretch, and her legs and some other body parts were beginning to ache.

She calculated that her destination was still another hour away. Making mental note of the scenery and the mile markers, Rita realized there wouldn't be much in the way of places to take a break, and when the first available turn off the highway presented itself, she took it.

Bouncing down the dusty gravel road, Rita found herself coming to a stop when the road dead-ended. Grimacing, Rita walked several yards into the trees and decided to walk a little farther and stretch her legs.

Tall, black spruce rose up in contrast against the long, white trunks of birch trees, while the lavender petals of fireweed waved welcomes from their red stems.

Rita pushed on through the trees and underbrush, enjoying the walk in spite of herself. Something about the area seemed more than just vaguely familiar, and when the trees gave way to a small lake, Rita recognized the place as one she and her father had dogsledded to on many occasions.

The very thought of dogsledding caused Rita to smile. If the truth were known, it was the main reason she'd allowed her father to talk her into coming back home for a visit. He was trying to help her dream of racing in the Iditarod come true.

The Iditarod! A dogsled race to equal no other and Rita was determined to one day be a part of it. She still remembered stories her father had told her about the old dogsled mail trails. Moonlit nights on the trail, the icy winds, and the solitude of having nothing and no one but yourself and the dogs against the elements. It thrilled Rita like nothing else and she wouldn't be complete until she'd experienced "The Last Great Race."

"Ooof!"

The sound caused the hair to prickle on the back of Rita's neck. Snapping her head up, she searched the area for the unmistakable sound of a disturbed bear.

No more than twenty feet away, a mother grizzly woofed a command to her cub before striking a protective stance between Rita and her young.

Rita knew better than to run or cry. Bears seemed more inclined to attack humans when they made noises similar to animals in distress. August had told his daughter on more than one occasion to stand her ground silently and only as a last resort should she curl up into a ball and play dead.

Rita shoved her hands into the pockets of her fleece-lined sweat top and made eye contact with the grizzly. The bear took a step forward and made a grunting woof.

Rita could feel her legs trembling beneath her jeans. She knew she was in grave danger, but there was nothing to do but wait out the situation. Somewhere to her left, Rita heard a rustling in the brush. Would it be another bear? Perhaps the cub had somehow gotten behind her.

The bear advanced another two steps at the same time Mark Williams emerged from the trees. Rita's relief was short-lived, however, as the mother bear let out a roar.

"Don't move," Mark said in a hushed tone.

"Don't worry," Rita breathed, "I won't."

Rita struggled to keep from going back on her word. Her fear told her to run, and yet her mind rationalized that it would be exactly the wrong thing to do.

"Give her your jacket," Mark suggested.

"What?" Rita questioned in a whisper.

"Take off your jacket and toss it on the ground. Move real slow and don't throw it at her, just over in that direction," Mark said, while slowly pulling his revolver from its holster.

Rita slowly pulled her hands from her pockets. "But it's not a jacket," Rita argued under her breath.

"I don't care if it's a ball gown. Just give it to her and maybe she'll be satisfied enough to let you back away. If not"—Mark leveled the .44 magnum in the direction of the bear—"I'll shoot and you back away."

Rita contemplated his words for only a moment before reaching up to undo the zipper. Making deliberate, slow moves, Rita eased out of her top and tossed it to the side of the grizzly.

"Now, move away," Mark said as he put himself between Rita and the bear.

The bear grunted and stomped at her shirt while Rita and Mark backed away. The bear clamped mighty jaws around the fabric of Rita's top and trotted off in the direction the cub had disappeared. When she was out of sight, Mark stopped and put a hand on Rita's arm.

"Are you all right?" he questioned.

Rita suddenly became conscious of being cold, wearing a thin, form-fitting tank top.

Mark tried to hide a grin while he eased out of his jacket. "Here, I wouldn't want you to catch a chill."

Rita couldn't bear the humiliation and grabbed the jacket without a word. She pulled it on while walking back to her car.

"I have more clothes in the car," she called over her shoulder. "I'll give this back to you in a minute."

"What, no thanks?" Mark questioned in a teasing tone.

Rita refused to give in to his bantering. "I was doing okay," she said, fumbling in her jeans for her car keys.

"Oh, yeah, I could see that," Mark replied sarcastically.

Rita opened the trunk and pulled out a suitcase. Grabbing the first thing she could find, Rita produced an ecru-colored sweater, which she put on.

"There," Rita said as she threw the jacket against Mark's back. "Now that you've done your good deed for the day you can go."

Mark turned around and picked up his patrol jacket. "Is there some reason you can't be civil?" His tone of voice told Rita he wasn't kidding.

She stared for a moment at the brown-haired man. His dark eyes seemed to pierce her conscience. "Sorry," she offered by way of an apology.

"Well, that's at least civil," Mark said as he pulled his jacket back on. "Look, I'm mighty fond of your father and mother, and I know it'd pretty much break their hearts if you were to get yourself killed."

"Don't worry about it," Rita said, reverting to her anger. "*I* don't."

"What's with you?" Mark questioned the angry, petite woman.

"I don't see that my private life is any of your business. This whole situation has been more than a little embarrassing, and now, if you'll excuse me, I'm expected at home," Rita stormed the words and climbed into her car.

"Don't speed," Mark said with a grin.

Rita felt more frustration than she was willing to put into words. She flashed her dark eyes at Mark. "Like I said, don't worry about it. I'm a big girl."

"I'm well aware of that, Ms. Eriksson," Mark offered with a chuckle. "I'm very well aware of that."

Chapter 2

"We're mighty glad to see you home safe," August Eriksson said, embracing Rita.

Rita nearly fell into her father's arms. How she longed for a human touch, although she would have never admitted it. "It's good to see you, Dad," Rita whispered against his ear. She pulled back and scrutinized the man before her. He seemed so much older than she remembered. His hair was snowy white and his face much more wrinkled and worn.

Beth Eriksson emerged from the kitchen to appraise the scene. "Hello, Rita," she offered with a smile. "Good to have you back."

"Thanks, Mom," Rita replied and went to where her mother stood. The embrace they shared wasn't the same as the one Rita had just given her father. It was curt, almost a polite symbolic gesture.

"Are you hungry?" Beth asked her daughter.

"Starved and then some," Rita answered with a laugh. "I didn't plan on taking so long to get here."

"Well, I have some sandwich makings in the kitchen. Why don't you just leave your things until after you eat. Then you can get settled in your old room," her mother said in an unemotional way. From the tone set between mother and daughter, it would have been impossible to tell that they were anything more than acquaintances. And, in Rita's mind, they were merely that and little more.

Rita followed her mother and father into the kitchen. They seemed as happy with one another as they had when she was a child. Her father still looked at her mother with a glow of admiration in his eyes. What was it that he saw in her that merited such praise?

Rita sat politely listening as her parents filled her in on the community and all that had happened in five years. She hung on her father's every word, while barely commenting on her mother's information regarding the family.

"And so, have you considered what I suggested?" August asked.

"And what was that, dear?" Beth asked with a note of surprise in her voice.

"I suggested that our daughter take time off before joining the workforce grind and race the Iditarod next year," August answered his wife.

Beth's face masked any reaction she had to August's words and instead she simply replied, "How interesting."

Rita wondered how her mother really felt about the matter. Would she resent her youngest daughter's presence in the big, rambling log home?

"I have been thinking about it," Rita admitted. "I know the opportunity is one that will probably never come again."

"That's why you should jump at the chance," her father remarked.

"I'm so out of shape though. What with all my studies and work at the hospital, I haven't been outdoors long enough to walk around the block. I can only imagine what it would be like to run with a dogsled team," Rita replied, taking the plate her mother offered. Despite their differences, Rita noted that her mother had made her favorite, roast beef sandwiches.

"Thanks, Mom," Rita added and offered her mother a hint of a smile.

"But all of that will come back to you. You can start this summer and run with the dogs. You can spend all fall and winter on the trails around here, maybe even run in another race or two just to get primed for the big one," August said in a way that almost sounded as though he were begging.

"And you really think I'd be able to do it?" Rita asked, hopefully. "You think I could manage it all? All the training and getting into shape?"

"You're no Eriksson if you can't!" August exclaimed good-naturedly. "Besides, you'll have nine months to do it in. I've got plenty of good dogs and there's a friend or two in the area that would be happy to have you along on practice runs."

"What do you mean? You'd be handling my training, wouldn't you?" Rita inquired.

"Now, Rita, I'm not the young man I used to be. I can't handle the trails like before. I'll take care of things around here, but when you start practicing on the rougher trails, you'll have to do it without me," August answered.

"But being with you was the biggest reason I was considering it," Rita said in a pouting tone.

"Rita," Beth said a little harsher than she'd intended, "your father is entitled to take care of himself. I need him as much as you do."

Rita turned to face her mother for a moment. There was no need for sharing their differences only twenty minutes into their visit. "I understand that, Mother. I guess if I do it, I'll just run alone."

"There's really no need to do that. Like I said, I have a couple of trusted friends in the area and you could learn a lot from them. Especially where the newer techniques come into play. Both of them even raced in the Iditarod last year. They know a whole heap more about what to expect than I do. You know very well that my only attempt was several years ago and I didn't even finish the race."

"Yes, but you won the silver ingots for being the first to reach the halfway point," Rita offered as consolation.

"I know, but I dropped out shortly after that and these men have both completed the race. Besides, I trust them completely and I know you'd like them. They'd make interesting company and maybe you'd even find yourself fancying one of them. They're both single."

"Oh Dad," Rita moaned and rolled her eyes. "I'm certainly not up here to husband hunt."

"Then what are you up here for? You haven't seen us in over five years and yet I know that it wasn't for the joy of seeing us that you came home. You want that race. You've always wanted it. Are you going to throw away the only chance you may ever have to race the Iditarod? Are you going to give up your dream?" August asked seriously.

Rita contemplated her father's words for a moment. She was grateful that her mother remained silent. Her father was perfectly right about the conditions being too hard for him. He wasn't young anymore, and yet Rita really needed him to be.

"All right," Rita finally spoke. "I'll go for it. I'll do it your way and I'll finish the race for both of us!"

"Good girl," August said, slamming his hands down on the table. "By next March you'll be able to run with the pros and I'll expect a healthy finish."

"What? You don't demand that I win?" Rita said with a laugh.

"No, it'll be enough just to see you run it and do your best," August replied with pride beaming in his eyes. None of his other children had taken the interest in dogsledding that Rita had, and he was excited about her decision.

Rita turned to her mother. Beth sat quietly eating her sandwich, her face void of anything that would signal to Rita what she thought of the plan.

"Will it be all right with you, Mom?" Rita dared the question.

Beth looked surprised that Rita would consult her about her feelings on the matter. "I support whatever your father wants, Rita. I too hope to see you accomplish your dream. It won't be an easy task, but then good things seldom come free of strife."

Rita nodded. "I guess when I'm done here, I'll unpack my things. Then you can tell me where we go from there, Dad."

"Oh, I nearly forgot," August remarked with a quick glance at his wife, "we've planned a bit of a homecoming party for you."

"I wish you hadn't," Rita said, with noted frustration in her voice. "You know how I hate parties."

"That's what I told him, but he insisted," Beth offered.

"Well," August continued, "it's just a small get-together. Old friends, new friends, maybe even some family. Tonight at seven, and I promise not to throw another one without consulting you first." His eyes betrayed the anticipation of showing his youngest daughter off, and so Rita agreed without fuss.

I only have to get through this evening, Rita thought as she ate her sandwich. *After that everything else will be simple.*

———— *#* ————

Rita tried on three outfits before finally settling on a calf-length denim skirt and light blue cashmere sweater. She was finishing dressing by pulling on high, black boots when a knock sounded at the door.

"It's open," Rita called out as she finished with her boots.

"Are you nearly ready?" Beth asked her daughter. She noted how graceful Rita looked as she crossed the room and ran a brush through her short, dark hair. She was so much like her father.

"Just finishing up," Rita replied over her shoulder. "I couldn't decide what to wear."

"You look fine," Beth offered, hoping that it wouldn't offend Rita. Sometimes the strangest things seemed to set her daughter off.

"You really think so?" Rita asked, running a hand down her skirt. "Everything seemed wrinkled."

"It looks nice, Rita. Your father is really anxious to show you off, and since most everyone is already here, I thought I'd escort you. That is, if you don't mind," Beth stated hopefully.

Rita was surprised at her mother's gesture but refused to show it. "It sounds fine, Mom," she said, following her mother into the hall.

Descending the stairs, Rita could hear the soft, classical music her mother had put on the stereo. Mozart. No, Chopin, Rita decided. It sounded nice, and Rita turned to tell Beth so but found her mother's attention already directed to the crowd as they stepped into the vestibule.

"Beth, don't you look pretty," an older man said as he stepped forward and kissed Rita's mother on the cheek.

"You're kind to say so, Ernie, but I think you'd best have the eye doctor check out your vision," Beth replied, and Ernie laughed. "Rita, you remember Ernie, don't you?"

"Of course," Rita said and smiled sweetly.

"Well, don't be telling me this is the baby of the family," Ernie replied, giving Rita a hearty squeeze. "It don't seem possible."

"I know what you mean," August said as he came up from behind Beth. "Rita's become a nurse just like her aunt Julie. I can't believe a person could change so much in just five years."

"I grew up, Daddy," Rita offered. "That's all. Are you still in the kennel business, Ernie?" Rita hoped her question would take the focus off of herself. She remembered Ernie loved to talk about his dogs.

"Naw, gave it up about a year ago. Got to be too much work for just me," Ernie replied.

"Boy, that's the truth," August said, sounding tired. "That's why I got a partner. None of the kids seemed interested in joining me, so it seemed the logical thing to do."

"A partner?" Rita questioned her father in surprise. "When did you get a partner?"

August chuckled at Rita's reaction. "I guess I forgot to tell you about that. I'll introduce you to him tonight. He's a real nice guy, and one of those fellows I was telling you about earlier."

Rita bit back a response as her mother pulled her along and into a sea of people. "I thought you said this was a *small* get-together," Rita commented.

"To your father, this *is* a small get-together," Beth reminded her daughter.

Rita nodded, knowing how her father loved to keep friends and family close at hand. He was always inviting someone over for some reason.

"Rita!" a woman's voice exclaimed.

Rita looked up to find an old high school friend. "Janice?"

She barely resembled the girl Rita had known. Her once-long blond hair was cut short, and her figure was generously rounded in the expectation of a new child.

"It's really me," the woman replied. "I can't believe you're finally here. You will come over to spend some time with me and Dave, won't you?"

"Of course," Rita said, still stunned by her friend's appearance.

"We're living in Tok, same old place, so just make your way on over whenever you can. But I warn you, the place is a mess, what with the kids and all," Janice said with a laugh.

"Kids? I thought maybe this was your first one," Rita said, indicating Janice's condition.

"Oh no. This is number five," Janice replied.

"Five?" Rita questioned. She could see that Janice was radiant and happy and knew there wasn't any sense in spoiling it with lectures of world conditions and such. "How nice," Rita added instead and left the woman with promises to visit.

She made the rounds bidding hellos to all the neighbors and church friends that she'd known. That life seemed a million years ago, however, and Rita felt rather out of place. So many of these people had drifted out of her thoughts and heart, and now she felt hesitant to allow them back in.

Independence had made Rita hard. She knew it and she actually found herself supporting the role. Being aloof and indifferent left her more time to herself and with more control in her life.

She was just trying to figure a way out of the room when August called from the doorway. "Rita, come meet my partner."

Rita made her way through the crowd of well-wishers and glanced up in time to come face-to-face with Mark Williams.

"Rita, this is Mark Williams, my partner," August stated. "Mark, my youngest daughter, Rita."

Mark grinned from ear to ear and extended his hand. "Rita, it's a pleasure."

"I don't believe this," Rita said, refusing Mark's hand and turning to her father. "*He's* your partner?"

"Do you two know each other?" August asked, looking curiously from Mark to Rita.

"You'll have to excuse me," Rita said and hurried from the room.

She hated herself for the way she'd responded to Mark's presence, but she couldn't imagine anything more embarrassing than having to face Mark Williams again. Making her way through the kitchen and out the back door, Rita didn't stop moving until she was well behind the house and halfway to the creek that ran the full length of the property.

"I don't believe it," she sighed aloud. "It's bad enough Dad's taken on a partner, but why did it have to be him?"

The breeze picked up, chilling Rita momentarily. She hugged her arms to her chest and gazed up into the sky.

"You really should learn to layer your clothes," Mark teased.

Rita snapped around to find him not two feet from where she stood. "Haven't you put me through enough? First you give me a speeding ticket, then you make me give up my clothes to a bear, and now I learn that I must endure your company for the months to come if I'm to get the training I need for the Iditarod."

"In the first place, you deserved the speeding ticket," Mark said with a shrug. "Now, are you going to dispute that?"

"No, I suppose not," Rita muttered.

"And secondly, as embarrassing as it was, giving your top to that grizzly got her attention on something other than you, and finally, I told you that your folks and I were good friends," Mark stated firmly.

"Good friends are one thing. Partners are entirely something else. I had no idea my father had even taken on a partner, much less that it was you," Rita said and turned to walk away.

"I wish for the sake of your father and mother, you'd just drop what's gone behind us. I'd like to start over," Mark said, following Rita back to the house.

Rita stopped and turned to face the man who'd caused her nothing but embarrassment and grief. "Look, for my father's sake I will act civilly and cooperate. But, and this is most important," Rita said with determination, "I don't need you or anyone else telling me how to live my life. I can take care of myself, just as I have for the last five years. I came here to train for the Iditarod, not to make friends or hunt for a husband, as my father would like me to do."

"I can't imagine wanting to be either one," Mark replied sarcastically and left Rita to stare open-mouthed after him.

Chapter 3

At breakfast the following morning, Rita was still thinking about Mark's words. She wasn't sure why it should bother her so much, but it did.

He had no right to talk to me that way, Rita thought. She shoveled scrambled eggs and toast into her mouth without even tasting the food.

"You're kind of preoccupied this morning, aren't you?" August asked his daughter and took a seat beside her.

"Sorry," Rita offered, wiping toast crumbs from her T-shirt. "I just keep thinking about all the work I need to do." It wasn't a lie, Rita decided. She really had been thinking of a variety of things. It was just that Mark Williams seemed to take up most of her attention.

"Well, I think the first thing we do should be to reacquaint you with the dogs. There's a few of the older ones we use for breeding who'll remember you, but the dogs you'll need to use for the race will be the three- and four-year-old ones."

"I thought of that," Rita said, sipping hot coffee. "I can do the feeding and care for the ones you pick out."

"We'll work together to pick out twenty or thirty that look like good possibilities for the race. You can work with those dogs on a daily basis," August stated. "We can choose them after breakfast, if that's all right with you."

"Sounds good to me," Rita replied. She looked forward to working with her father, and in spite of her worries about his health and age, Rita knew the kennel was his domain.

Half an hour later, Rita followed her father from dog to dog. The Eriksson kennel had over one hundred dogs, far more animals than had been there before Rita had gone to Anchorage. It was easy to see why August needed a partner.

After only ten minutes of listening to her father point out the virtues of one dog after the other, Rita was annoyed to find herself having to deal with Mark again.

"Good morning," Mark said as he passed by with a bag of feed hoisted over his shoulder.

"It was," Rita muttered and turned to her father. "What's he doing here?"

"I told you. He's my partner. One hundred and ten dogs need a lot of attention. We work at this thing on a constant basis," August replied.

"But I thought he was a cop," Rita said without thinking her father might wonder how she knew that detail of Mark's life.

"Oh, that," August said with a shrug. "He just fills in on the weekends. Most of the time he's here with me."

"Great," Rita stated sarcastically and walked away to look at the dogs on her own.

"There's a lot of anger in that woman," Mark stated, putting the feed on the ground beside him. He pulled out a ball cap from his back pocket and secured it on his head.

"I know," August replied. He watched as Rita moved from dog to dog. She'd always gotten along better with animals than people, August reminded himself. It wouldn't have been all that surprising had she handled Mark with cool indifference, but her hateful attitude seemed out of place, even for Rita.

August turned to Mark. "What happened between you two? She has a real mean streak for you."

Mark chuckled and relayed his first and second meeting with Rita.

He finished up by telling August about their conversation the night of the party.

"I guess she thought she was losing control of the situation. Control has always been a big issue with Rita." August's words caused Mark to sober considerably.

"She won't have as much control out there on the trails. The weather, the wildlife, all of it has a mind of its own," Mark stated as if August didn't already know it.

"Rita's always cherished independence," August replied. He was still watching Rita and knew she was trying not to notice Mark and August as they talked. "Since she was a little girl, Rita has alienated herself from just about everything for fear it might require she give up some form of control in her life. Didn't matter what or who it was. She put up a wall between herself and her mother, God, teachers, friends, and sometimes even me."

"I wonder why she feels so insecure?" Mark questioned.

"Insecure? I've thought of Rita as a lot of things but never insecure. Why, she trekked out of here on her own as fast as her car could take her. Of course you know how she is behind the wheel," August added with a laugh.

Mark smiled, but he challenged August's words. "Rita strikes me as the type of person who's never found her niche. She seems out of place, and I think she purposefully makes it that way in order that no one and nothing get too close. I think she's insecure about forming relationships. Maybe she's afraid that the feelings she puts out won't be reciprocated."

"I suppose that's a possibility. I just never thought about it. Now that I do, it seems to make some sense. I just always thought she was spoiled and headstrong."

"Oh she is that, August," Mark agreed. "But I don't think it's the reason she distances herself. No, I think Rita's been hurt by someone, and she's not about to let anyone have the chance to let her down again."

August grimaced at Mark's words. He knew only too well of the soured relationship between Rita and Beth. Rita had turned away from her mother at a very early age, but for what reason, August was never sure. Beth had never wanted to discuss it, and Rita claimed to never understand it. August had been forced to stand by helplessly while the relationship deteriorated at a rapid pace.

"Dad!" Rita called from the dogs. "Is this dog one of Blueberry's pups?"

August smiled. Blueberry had been Rita's favorite pet before she'd left for Anchorage. "You've got a good eye, Rita. That's Dandelion, so named because he used to chew on them all the time. He's a good runner and one of the very dogs I thought you could use."

Rita ran her hand over the husky's backside. "He feels real firm," she replied.

"And he's a great leader," Mark added. He and August walked to where Rita continued to check him out. "I've run him in lead just about every time I've had him out. He seems to get out of sorts if you do otherwise."

"I know the feeling," Rita muttered under her breath. Mark caught the words but said nothing.

"Look, Rita," August began, "I want you and Mark to work well together. Do you suppose you could put whatever is bothering you aside and just try to make the relationship work?"

Rita's head snapped up. She bit off a rhetorical reply when she saw the pleading in her father's eyes. He was the only man for which she'd even consider backing away from a fight.

Mark noticed the change in Rita's facial expression as she caught sight of her father. She truly loved the man, which gave Mark hope. At least she was capable of love. Now, why did that matter? Mark tossed the thought from his mind and waited for Rita to make some formal statement of peace.

Rita struggled for the right words. She didn't like giving in or letting Mark win, but for some reason it was important to her father and that made it important to her. "I'm sorry, Mark," Rita finally said, turning to face her adversary. "I guess I got carried away with my anger. Truce?"

"Truce," Mark said and offered his hand.

Rita reached out and took Mark's hand. She was instantly aware of the way his big hand engulfed her smaller one. It was difficult to allow the contact and yet almost pleasant the way he squeezed her hand and smiled.

Rita quickly dropped his hand, confused by the feelings Mark had stirred. "So what dogs do you recommend, Mark?" she quickly asked to cover up her feelings.

By late in the afternoon, Mark, Rita, and August had picked twenty-two dogs that seemed to fit the description of what Rita needed. These dogs had endurance and youth, experience and grace. They were a sturdy breed of husky, with crystal-blue eyes and stout, firm bodies.

Rita worked with the men to relocate the dogs. They moved dog houses, straw, stake-out chains, and dogs, until Beth called them for supper.

"Have dinner with us, Mark," August said, walking with Rita to the outdoor pump.

"Naw," Mark said, pulling off the ball cap and stuffing it into his back pocket again. "I've got things to take care of at home. Besides, I threw a roast in the crockpot before I left this morning."

Rita was relieved at Mark's reply but said nothing. She pushed and pulled at the pump handle until icy water flowed in a steady stream. Washing her hands and face with the strong, disinfectant soap that was left on a metal stand beside the pump, Rita felt refreshed and famished.

The days that followed found Rita in a constant state of retraining. Things she'd learned as a child had to be reviewed, while new ideas and techniques were introduced.

Rita had taken to jogging with Dandelion, whom she immediately dubbed "Dandy." She wanted to establish a strong relationship with the dog before working with the others. If the leader and driver were to work as one, they had to know each other intimately.

Rita enjoyed the playful dog. He was easy to love and filled a void in Rita's heart. No wonder she'd always found the dogs such pleasant company. They didn't ask about your feelings but simply accepted whatever you were capable of giving.

One crisp morning as she finished her run with Dandy, Rita was surprised when Mark appeared on the gravel road astride a motorcycle.

"Morning," he called out as he came up alongside Rita and Dandy.

"Hi," Rita said and slowed to a rapid walk.

"Want a ride back?" Mark offered.

"No, I'm fine," Rita replied, trying to soften the severity of her tone. "I need to walk. I still have flappy legs and no muscle tone."

"You look pretty good to me," Mark said with a grin.

Rita blushed and tried to ignore the fact that Mark noticed her discomfort with a broader smile.

"Dad tells me that you're going to race in the Iditarod," Rita said, hoping to steer the conversation away from herself.

"That's right," Mark replied, keeping even pace with Rita. "I wouldn't miss it. Last year I came in high enough to make money on it. I intend to win it this year."

"Oh, really?" Rita said as her eyes met Mark's.

"Do I detect a bit of challenge in that question?" Mark asked.

"You might," Rita said, enjoying the banter.

"You realize the odds are against you. Few women even race the Iditarod, much less win it. Besides, I'm more experienced than you and you have flappy legs. Remember?" Mark's amusement was contagious.

Rita smiled in spite of her resolve to be serious. "I thought you said they looked pretty good," Rita answered.

"They do, but not for dogsledding. I think they'd look great beneath the hem of a skirt while accompanying me to dinner." Mark's statement was a clear invitation.

Rita shook her head. "I'm not about to fraternize with the

competition," she replied. "You might learn all my strategies, and then I'd lose the race to you."

"You will anyway," Mark said with a laugh. "And I already know all your strategies. I'm the teacher, remember?"

Rita tossed her head and ignored the laughing man at her side. She didn't like the way he made her feel. She was afraid of feeling too much for him and determined within herself to avoid a deeper relationship than that of student and teacher.

———※———

Later that night, Rita took a quiet moment for herself and walked down to see her dogs. They were a good bunch. Dandy was white and tawny brown with streaks of black. Muffin was black and white, while Raven was so named for her coal-black coat. Toby and Teddy were matched with white blazes against silver and black fur, and the others were a hodgepodge of black, brown, and white.

"There isn't a bad one in the lot," August stated, breaking Rita's solitude.

"I was just thinking that myself," Rita responded. "I want very much to know them all at once, and yet I know there's plenty of time."

"It might be a good idea to start hitching them up to the four-wheeler. You could run them up and down the road like Mark does with the others," August suggested.

"All right, but I doubt I'll be any good at it. It's been so long since I've even hitched a team. I've probably forgotten all about it," Rita answered.

"Don't worry about it, Rita. You'll do just fine, and if you need anything, Mark and I will be here to help."

Rita nodded and braved the question she'd been wanting to ask. "Why Mark? For a partner, I mean. Where's he from and why did you pick him?"

"I met him at church the summer you left home. He seemed like a good man. He had a great love of animals and from the start all he ever talked about was raising a sled team. I offered to help him. We've been working together ever since," August replied.

"I didn't realize you'd had a partner that long."

"I haven't. I just made him a partner last fall. He's a good, Christian man, Rita. I hope you'll give him a chance. I believe he was an answer to my prayers and your mother's," August stated, even knowing that Rita thought very little about the power of prayer.

"I didn't even know you were looking for a partner," Rita said, trying not to sound too disappointed that her father hadn't confided in her.

"I guess I just started showing my age. The mornings got to be such a chore that all I wanted to do was stay in bed. I gave serious thought to getting rid of the dogs altogether, but I kept hoping you'd come home and fulfill your dream. So I hung on," August replied and added, "I suppose after you're gone, I'll sell out to Mark and let him take it all."

Rita fought back a sadness that threatened to materialize into tears. If her father was getting rid of the dogs, he must feel that his life was coming to an end. The dogs were everything to him, and Rita knew that August wouldn't part with them otherwise.

"Look," August said, noting Rita's sudden quietness, "God will take care of me, just as He always has. You'd do well to remember that and give it a little thought for yourself. You know I don't like to preach at you, but things haven't changed. I still worry about you, and I worry about your soul."

Rita hurried to embrace her father. "Don't worry about me, Daddy. I'm strong and quite capable of taking care of myself. You do what you have to, but don't worry about me."

Rita couldn't bring herself to admonish him for his reminder that she was still walking outside of God's truth. She was informed more often than not, by her mother, that she was the only one of the Eriksson children not to have made a decision for the Lord. It seemed to hang on Beth like a grievous weight.

Maybe that was why Rita clung stubbornly to her own nature. She refused to allow herself to think on the matter any further. God was only a tiny part of her worries. Mark Williams was quite another matter.

Chapter 4

Rita couldn't believe how quickly the summer passed. Before she knew it, the first heavy frost was upon the land, leaving an icy signature on the once-green valleys. The air was noticeably colder, and every morning Rita saw subtle changes that pointed clearly to the inevitability of winter.

The idea of snow and ice excited Rita. There was a quickening in her step and an energy unleashed that she'd not known existed. Daily, she ran the dogs and watched each one with careful interest, trying as she did to remember the things Mark and her father had told her to look for.

"Some dogs are just along for the ride," August had said, and Rita could see that this was true by watching the tuglines that connected the dogs to the gangline. She weeded out three dogs from the twenty-two simply because they refused to pull their own weight.

Others seemed prone to problems, sporting everything from simple injuries to the inability to keep up. They were hard workers but just not cut out for long distances. Rita had no choice but to eliminate them.

Rita spent much of her time in Mark's company, listening while he told her things that could well make a difference out on the trail. She remembered her father's caution to always carry dry kindling for long runs, as well as extra food and boots.

Days were long and arduous, usually starting by five in the morning and not ending until nine and sometimes ten at night. There was always the necessity of seeing to the dogs. Feeding, grooming, doctoring, running—all of these activities took precedence over nearly everything else. Then there was the work with the race sleds, harnesses, and assorted items that Rita would need to take with her when she raced the Iditarod. The work seemed never-ending and, as the student, Rita was frequently overwhelmed.

As autumn moved toward winter, Rita found herself actually enjoying the work and the company. It worried her, because often she found herself concentrating too much on what Mark was doing, whether it had anything to do with her training or not.

It was on one particular Saturday when Rita learned that Mark wouldn't be joining them that she actually found herself asking her father why.

"Mark has to fill in for one of the patrolmen," August replied to his daughter's question. He had come to notice that Rita was far more accepting of Mark's participation in her training. Maybe Rita was changing.

"So then," Rita said with a smile, "it'll be just you and me today?"

"You, me, and your mother," August replied without a thought.

"But Mom's not out here with us," Rita commented. Her mother had never been one to take a great deal of interest in the kennel.

"I'm sure she's got enough to keep her busy in the house," August said, untangling a long length of rope. "She always has run a tight ship. Even when she owned that roadhouse near Northway. Her boarders never lacked for anything. I can vouch for that."

"I'm sure that's true," Rita answered and sought to change the subject. "When do you think we'll get our first snow?"

"I'm not sure," August said, glancing up at the gray sky. "It doesn't feel like it just yet, but soon. Probably in another couple of weeks."

"I can hardly wait," Rita said wistfully. She longed to run the dogs on snow again and get the feel of handling the team behind a basket.

"You're doing good work," August said, offering the praise Rita craved. "I just know you'll be more than ready when March gets here."

"Dad, do you think I should run any of the shorter races first?" Rita took the rope from her father and hung it on a nearby nail.

"Rules say you have to have written proof of at least one sanctioned race of two hundred miles or more," August replied.

"Which races should I participate in?" Rita asked.

"You could warm up with some of the shorter sprint races. As far as a race of some distance, Mark thinks the Copper Basin 300 is your best bet. It's run in January and it's close to home. The terrain will be similar to that which the dogs are already used to and yet offer them the feeling of competition and crowds," August answered thoughtfully.

Rita remained silent while considering her father's words.

"It would give you a good chance to get to know some of the other racers and dogs," August continued. "And you might even make a name for yourself before the Iditarod."

"That could be bad though," Rita replied. "It could put a lot of pressure on me to perform. Say I did really well in one race or another, then I'd be expected to achieve an even better performance in the Iditarod."

"That is a possibility," August said. "But, it could also be a challenge, and I know how competitive you can be."

"You sound like that's a fault and not an asset," Rita said with a frown. "There's nothing wrong with healthy competition."

"Healthy competition, no," August agreed. "However, competition can often lead to dangerous rivalry. Many mistakes are made by the person who thinks nothing of the rules and only of the achievement."

Rita shrugged off her father's concerns as she always had done in the past. It was impossible for him to understand her sense of competition. After all, he'd been an only son with a single sister to round out the family. He knew nothing of being the youngest of ten. When you were the baby of a huge family, you always found yourself striving to make a place for yourself, Rita reasoned. Her father simply misunderstood her need.

"You know," August began, "I may sound a little old-fashioned, but I'd like for you to make your own sled."

Rita shook her head adamantly. "I wouldn't be any good at that. You know I've never had the touch for creating things that you have."

"But it's the only way to get a real feel for your equipment. Once you've been a part of creating the sled, it truly becomes a part of you. When it starts to run rough, you know instinctively what's wrong. When a piece breaks, you know from having created it just what's required to repair it," August answered.

"I guess that makes sense," Rita admitted. "But I don't know anything about it. You'll have a great deal to teach me."

"You're a quick student," August said with a laugh. "I tell you what, Monday we'll get started with the details."

"August," Beth called from the back door. "Gerald's on the telephone. He wants to talk to you."

"I'm coming," August answered and turned to Rita. "You keep on sorting out these ropes and harnesses." Rita nodded and watched as her father headed toward the house.

She felt a twinge of disappointment in having to share her father with her oldest brother. She scarcely knew Gerald, even though he settled in Tok. Gerald and Phillip were her mother's sons from her first marriage. Rita had heard many times the story of how her mother and father met.

Her mother was a war widow, having lost her Canadian husband in World War II. Beth Hogan was running a roadhouse and trying to raise her children all alone when August had appeared to work on the Alcan Highway. Gerald and Phillip had appealed to August's heart, as had their mother, and, in no time at all, they became a family.

After that, many children came to bless the home of August and Beth Eriksson, but Rita saw it more as a curse. She hated being the youngest and felt completely insignificant to her family.

Plopping down on the ground, Rita tried to ignore the anger she felt. Many people presumed that because she was the baby of the family, she surely would have enjoyed the most attention. However, nothing could have been farther from the truth.

"I've scarcely seen you," Beth commented, causing Rita to jump.

"I've been busy," Rita offered, refusing to look her mother in the eye.

"Yes, your father has told me," Beth replied. "He also tells me that you still seem very unhappy."

Rita's dark eyes flashed a warning as her head snapped up to meet her mother's face. "I'm just busy," she stated firmly. "This is hard work, you know." Rita knew the words sounded sarcastic, but she didn't care.

"You needn't take that tone with me, Rita," Beth said, standing her ground. "I won't cower beneath your anger and you can't wile your way around the issues with me. That's why you avoid me."

"I don't avoid you," Rita answered, tossing the harness aside and getting to her feet. "I avoid your preaching. You can't have a regular conversation with me. You never just want to know how I am or what I've been doing. You just want to pass judgment on me because I ruined your track record at church!"

Beth was noticeably hurt by the harsh words Rita hurled. "I'm sorry you feel that way, Rita. I do care about the things you're doing. I care very much."

"Yes, yes, I know. You care only because no matter what I do, it'll be wrong in your eyes," Rita said, trying to show nothing but the anger she felt inside. "I can't live up to your standards, Mother, so why not just give up?"

"I can't give up," Beth replied and pulled her sweater closer to ward off the cold. "It isn't my standards I want you to live up to. God's standards are the only ones that count."

"Yes, and you and God are like this," Rita said and intertwined her first two fingers.

"Don't take that tone with me," Beth snapped. Her anger was piqued—a typical reaction whenever she spoke with her youngest daughter about God. Why, out of ten children, was this one the most difficult? "I cherish my relationship with God," Beth continued. "He is the only constant in our lives. He is the only one that can offer us hope and eternal salvation. I only want you to come to understand His love for you."

"I've heard it all before, Mom," Rita answered impatiently. "I don't need your religion. I grew up all my life listening to preaching—yours, the pastor's, even Dad's. I've had enough preaching to last me a lifetime. Why can't you understand that I don't need a crutch like you do? I make my own way, and when I know what I want...I go after it."

"And what do you want, Rita?" Beth asked her daughter honestly.

"I want to live my life without restraints. I want to experience everything and anything. I don't want to be hemmed in by a list of dos and don'ts. Besides," Rita continued, "I don't see where your relationship with God has helped you in your relationship with me."

Beth swallowed hard to keep from snapping a retort. It was true. She struggled to have a decent relationship with her youngest daughter. There was always so much hostility to get through that Beth usually gave up long before Rita wore down.

"You are absolutely right. Our relationship lacks for much," Beth answered softly. "But, I'm always hopeful. You may have grown up and left home, but I will continue to endeavor to help you see the truth and God's love for you."

"It's always God's love, isn't it?" Rita questioned. "Never your love or our relationship. You use God like a shelter you can hide in whenever things get too tough. Learn to deal with me, one on one, Mom. I don't need this constant triangle. Then again," Rita said, turning to leave, "don't bother to deal with me at all."

Beth stood fixed to her spot as Rita walked off toward the creek. She was no longer shocked by her daughter's attitude and words. After all the years she'd sought to find a way to reach Rita, Beth had nearly given up trying. How could one child hold so much anger and hate inside and never give a clue as to where it came from or how it could be dealt with?

Walking slowly back to the house, Beth found herself whispering a prayer for Rita. It was really her only recourse, Beth decided. Rita had made it quite clear that she didn't want to talk about it, so Beth would leave her to God.

"Where's Rita?" August asked as he met Beth at the door.

"We had words," Beth admitted. "She stormed off to the creek and I'm here licking my wounds."

August enfolded Beth in his arms. "Don't lose hope, Bethany," he encouraged. "God has had worse cases to deal with."

Beth smiled. "She takes after her father where stubbornness is concerned."

"Ah, so you do remember," August replied with a grin. It had been Beth's honest determination that had led him back to God so many years earlier. "I guess I was just about as tough a nut as God ever had to crack. I remember feeling so angry that I couldn't join the army and fight in World War II. I blamed God for my misfortune of having no wife and no children. Now, I have ten beautiful children and a gorgeous wife, but only after I came back to Him first. Rita will come to understand the truth one day. We just have to hold on to that."

"I know you're right, August. But it hurts so much. Why does she hate me the way she does?" Beth questioned in a trembling voice.

"I don't believe she hates you, sweetie. I think she's just so miserable in herself and you are the closest reminder of what she could be if she turned her life over to God. I think that causes her more grief than she can own up to," August stated, giving Beth a squeeze. "You just keep praying, Mrs. Eriksson. Even the prodigal son in the Bible came home."

Beth tried to smile, but her heart was much too heavy. "Will you talk to her?" she questioned.

"For what it's worth," August said, dropping his hold on Beth. Beth nodded and watched for several minutes as August made his way past the pile of harnesses and ropes that Rita had left in disarray. She whispered a prayer for her husband and then another one for her daughter. Surely God could work a miracle in the heart of her hurting child.

———#———

"I thought I might find you here." August came upon Rita where she stood beside the icy creek. "I understand you and your mother had a fight."

"What else do we ever have? Certainly not a relationship." Rita's sarcasm hung thickly in the air.

August kicked at the dirt thoughtfully. "Your mother cares a great deal about you, Rita."

"Oh, I can certainly see that," Rita said sardonically and turned her back to her father. No sense in letting him see the tears that had formed in her eyes.

"I felt just like you did when I was younger," August remembered. "When I met your mom, I was a hard man with a grudge against God. I felt like God had disappointed me one time too many and therefore I didn't want anything more to do with Him."

"I've heard this story before," Rita muttered.

"I know," the aging August answered. "But, it seemed important to share it with you one more time. Your mom confronted me with my hard heart and, even though she loved me, she watched me walk away because she had the guts to stand up to me."

Rita said nothing. She stuffed her hands deep into her jeans pockets to ward off the chill. If only there was someplace to warm her frozen heart.

"Well, anyway," August said, running a hand through his salt-and-pepper hair, "I kept thinking about the things she'd shared with me and the way she assured me God was still there for me. I ran as far and as fast as I could and finally God pinned me down in a place I couldn't fight Him anymore."

"I know," Rita replied. "He buried you under a construction tractor after you fell over the embankment." Rita remembered the story from its many tellings. Her father's tractor had plummeted over a soft shoulder as he graded the roadway. He had been pinned beneath the equipment, broken and bleeding, and God had spoken to his spirit.

"I know it sounds silly," August admitted with a grin. "But sometimes God has to get your attention. He'd done everything else He could, but my stubbornness required drastic measures."

"Look, Dad," Rita began, turning to face her father. "Couldn't we just drop the subject? Isn't it enough that I know how you feel and you know how I feel?"

"You mean agree to disagree?" August questioned.

"Yes." Rita came to her father and put both hands on his shoulders. "I love you, Dad, and I need for you not to harp at me. Mother has preaching down to a fine art form, and I'd just as soon not have you hassling me as well."

"All right, Rita." August embraced his daughter. "I'll leave it be. At least for now."

"Thanks, Dad," Rita whispered. She couldn't help but wonder how she'd deal with her mother, but maybe if she put it off long enough, she wouldn't have to do anything about it. Maybe Beth would just leave well enough alone and realize that Rita was a grown woman with a mind of her own.

Chapter 5

The first snows fell and autumn quickly became winter. Rita was in better physical shape than she'd ever been, and her heart was eager for the challenge of the Iditarod.

After spending six months working with her dogs, Rita had chosen a team of fourteen, twice as many as the minimum requirement for the race. They were a hearty, well-bred group of dogs, and Rita felt a genuine pride whenever she worked with them.

Week after week, Rita found herself engulfed in conversations that dealt with the business of dogsled racing, conversations that made her eager to feel the icy winds upon her face and the solitude of the long trail.

"You have to remember," Mark told Rita as she worked to attach the brush bow to the front of her handmade sled, "it's not always best to be out in front. If you head out early in the race and find the trail blown over, you may break trail through hip-high snow. . .maybe even higher. That's tedious, exhausting work, and the dogs pay a toll for it as well as the musher."

"So it's better to pace yourself behind?" Rita questioned. She sat up and adjusted the hood of her insulated sweatshirt.

"Sometimes, but not always. It's a matter of attitude and decision. You have to keep your mind cleared of other clutter and totally devoted to the trail. Then the choices are easier to make. You have to have a feel for the course. When you're out there all alone and faced with decisions like where to make your camp and whether your dogs are up to another twenty miles without a rest, you realize that this is where experience, training, and attitude all make the difference between life and death."

"But how do you decide when it's right to take the risks when you've never run the Iditarod before?" Rita asked.

"Every Iditarod is different. No matter how many times you run it, you can't predict what the elements will be or how the terrain will have changed. Then, too, the route changes from year to year. From Anchorage to Ophir, it's the same trail for all years. After that, however, the northern route, during the even years, goes up to Ruby from Ophir and down the Yukon River to Nulato and Kaltag, to name a few. The odd year, the southern route leaves Ophir and goes down to Iditarod and across to Anvk. From there you follow the Yukon up to Kaltag, and then the race resumes identical trails again. And while I'm the first one to say that repeated experience on the trail is an important issue, it isn't everything."

Rita listened intently while Mark shared his secrets. She was still uncomfortable in his company, but she didn't feel the anger she once had. With so much else to concentrate on, Rita had less and less time to consider her lifelong struggle to find her niche.

"How's it going?" August asked as he joined Rita and Mark.

Rita gave her father a smile. "It's going slow," she replied honestly. "I told you this sled building thing wasn't my forte."

"But you've done very well," August encouraged. "Your first sled turned out great, and this lightweight racer will be even better. I think you're going to be pleased with the results."

"I think so too," Mark agreed.

"I hope so," Rita said, thoughtfully checking her work for any errors.

"Are you two still planning on going out tomorrow?" August questioned, referring to the week-long sledding and camping trip that Rita and Mark had arranged.

"Yep," Mark answered before Rita could comment. "We're all set and the dogs are more than anxious. I figure we'll set out around dawn and be back in a week, maybe ten days."

"Just like we used to do when we were younger, eh, Rita?" August teased.

"Something like that," Rita replied. She was still uncertain about spending time away from her father and out on the desolate trail with Mark.

"Look, I'm going to finish up here and go home. I still have some gear to take care of and dog food to pack. I'll come over in the morning, and you be ready to leave by sunrise," Mark said, getting to his feet. "I hate being kept waiting," he added in a joking voice.

"Don't worry about me." Rita glanced upward. Her heart did a jump as she noticed Mark's warm brown eyes. She tried to steady her nerves and sound more severe than she felt. "I told you I could take care of myself," she added.

Mark laughed and gave a little bow. "Then I shall await the pleasure of your company on the trail tomorrow, ma'am." With that he was gone, and Rita stared after him, shaking her head.

"He's a good man, Rita," August said as if reading the question on his daughter's mind. "I trust him, and I know he'll take good care of you on the trail. Trust him, Rita. He might very well teach you something you don't know."

Rita nodded slowly and gave her father a brief smile. Trust him? She didn't even know him outside the realm of the Eriksson dog kennel. Why should she believe him to be so trustworthy?

"Dad?" Rita questioned with a sudden thought. "I'd like to have a pistol. May I borrow one of yours?"

August nodded. "That's a good idea. I'll make sure you have one for the Iditarod too. Sometimes it's necessary to put down an animal. You can never tell when a moose is going to jump in the middle of your dog team. It's happened before, and they almost always have to be shot."

"I remember a moose wreaking havoc with one of the teams several years back," Rita agreed.

"I do too," August replied. "I'll make sure you have what you need."

"I have you, Daddy." Rita jumped up to hug her father. "And you are all I'll ever need."

August embraced his daughter but said nothing. He certainly couldn't tell her what was in his heart. He couldn't explain that she needed the Savior and that without Him she would be hopelessly lost. Breathing a silent prayer, August gave his youngest daughter over to God, knowing that there was really little else he could do.

———*H*———

The wind had picked up and the sky threatened snow, but nevertheless, Rita and Mark, with lamps secured on their heads, mushed out into the darkness with their dog teams. They had decided to explore the area to the south and maybe even check out the trail for the Copper Basin 300.

The snow wasn't all that deep, but it had glazed over with ice from a recent warming and refreezing. It made a good trail, and Rita was surprised to learn that Mark had already spent many hours in the area, choosing the path they would take.

When they stopped for lunch, several hours later, Mark explained.

"I wanted this first day to be rather simple. You know, that way you could get used to the trail and being out away from civilization. And, it wouldn't be all that taxing for the dogs. We'll make camp about twelve miles down the way. There's a nice place by the river where we can set up camp under the trees. We'll have all the water we need and plenty of shelter," Mark told Rita.

"I didn't realize you had this all mapped out," Rita replied. She enjoyed some warmed-up tuna casserole her mother had sent along.

Mark stirred up the fire, enjoying himself and the freedom of the vast wilderness before him. "I am the teacher, remember?" His words were spoken in a gentle reminder, and for once Rita knew, in order to object, she'd have to work hard to conjure up her anger.

"I just meant that I didn't realize you'd spent so much time and preparation on this trip. I figured we were just kind of heading out into the great unknown," Rita answered.

"After today," Mark replied, "we will be. I haven't planned every detail out. Rest assured there will be many elements of surprise on our adventure." He lost himself for a moment looking into Rita's eyes. She quickly captured his heart. Turning away before Rita could perceive his thoughts, Mark called over his shoulder, "You ready to press on?"

"More than ready," Rita responded, unaware of Mark's emotions.

They broke camp and pressed to the south. The valley floor soon gave way to foothills and dense forests of black and white spruce, as well as aspen and birch. From time to time, stunted black spruce and the absence of hardwood trees betrayed the sure signs of permafrost ground. This was ground that never thawed, and nothing rooted well in its frozen subsoil.

It reminded Rita of the parable of the sower. The seeds that fell upon the rocky soil couldn't take deep root. She shook off the image, wondering why she'd even thought of it. No doubt eighteen years of Bible stories and Sunday school had to exist in memory somewhere. Sending the reminder of her mother and father's faith deeper within the dark recesses of her memories, Rita pressed on to keep pace with Mark.

Without warning, a snowshoe hare darted out across the trail, causing Rita's team to take off in a free-for-all chase. Rita struggled to keep her grip on the sled's handlebars. She wouldn't forgive herself if she lost her team, especially in front of Mark.

"Gee, Dandy!" she yelled above the barking huskies, trying to tell her dogs to go back around to the right. By now, they were nearly heading in the opposite direction from which Rita and Mark had been making their way. "Come gee! Dandy, come gee!" Rita called out. When Dandy finally heard his mistress's instructions, he managed to direct the team back to the trail, much to the disappointment of the other ten dogs behind him.

Rita tried not to look flustered, but she was keenly aware that Mark watched and evaluated her every move from where he'd brought his own dogs to a stop back on the trail. Expecting some sarcastic comment regarding the incident, Rita was surprised when Mark turned back around and called out the command that sent his dogs forward. Breathing a sigh of relief, Rita tried to be more prepared for any more interferences with her team.

Shortly before the last bits of muted sunlight faded from the sky, Mark brought them, without further mishap, to the place he'd planned for their first night on the trail.

Rita put up her small domed tent only after seeing to the needs of her dogs. August had explained to her on many occasions that the dogs were her lifeblood on the trail. Taking care of them first insured that they'd be in prime condition to take care of her later.

Rita found spruce boughs and made beds for each of her dogs, while a roaring fire heated up August's personal choice of dog food. It was a hearty combination of commercial dog food blended with beef liver, vegetable oil, and eggs. All were chosen to give the highest degree of benefit to the active sled dogs.

With the dogs now fed and sleeping in fuzzy balls to ward off the minus-twenty-degree winds, Rita found herself able to settle down to preparing her own supper.

"I've already got the stew on the fire," Mark offered when he spied Rita digging into the food packs.

"I'm glad," Rita replied, plopping down beside the fire. "I'm absolutely starved." It felt good to sit and rest, even in frosty air that stung her eyes.

"I'd kind of like some coffee," Mark said, pulling out a zippered bag of instant coffee.

"That does sound good," Rita agreed. While Mark found cups, Rita studied the surroundings. She realized how perfect their camp was. They were sheltered from the wind by a rocky ridge that followed the river for a short way. This was coupled with the canopy of spruce trees that lined the river.

They also had water—even if they did have to break the surface ice with an ax. With a little more effort, they soon had enough firewood to enjoy the evening, allowing both of them to sit back and bask in the warmth. Mark had been very wise to choose this place, Rita decided. A part of her wanted to tell him so; another part warned her not to make any kind of comment that betrayed her emotions.

Supper passed in relative silence. Mark seemed content to enjoy the quiet and the meal, while Rita nervously wondered how to relate to her traveling companion. Before, their talk had always revolved around sledding, dogs, and the Iditarod. What if she were required to talk of something more?

As if reading her mind, Mark began to speak. "You know it's hard to sit out here in the middle of nowhere with all of this monumental beauty around you and not be in awe of it."

"It is impressive," Rita agreed in a guarded tone. "It makes it hard to consider leaving."

"Leaving?" Mark questioned. "Where would you go?"

Rita shrugged. "I don't know. I've thought about moving to Texas."

Mark chuckled. "Cowboys and oil wells instead of dogsleds and snow?"

"I don't know. It was just a thought," Rita replied. "I've always liked the things I've read about it. Lots of sunshine and wide open spaces. You can have it rustic and rural or live it up in the glamorous city night life. I guess Texas has a little bit of everything."

"Maybe I could call you 'Texas Rita,'" Mark joked, but Rita just lifted her chin defiantly.

"Maybe you wouldn't need to call me anything."

Mark hid his smile and turned away from Rita. There was no sense in irritating her further. "Look," Mark said and pointed to a glowing green light that loomed up from the horizon and grew in size until it seemed to fill the sky.

Rita watched as it changed in shape and size. The green soon gave way to a more prominent outline of pink, and then, as the color intensified and darkened to a reddish hue, yellow fiery flickers sent fingers upward through the image to paint the sky.

"The northern lights," Rita commented as she watched the night show. "I've always loved them."

"I just don't know how anyone could watch them and doubt the existence of God," Mark said in a low, husky whisper.

"What's God have to do with it?" Rita said rather flippantly. "It's a natural phenomenon. I read all about it and it has something to do with the sun."

Mark turned from the light show to study Rita a moment before replying. "I don't understand how you could have spent years in church and fellowship with other Christians and say such a shallow thing."

Rita instantly felt defensive. Obviously, Mark was yet another devout Christian. Why hadn't she considered that before? There wouldn't have been any way at all that her father would have taken on a less than fully devoted man of God as his partner. Oh, she knew her father had told her Mark was a good man and a Christian, but since Mark had never bothered to make it an issue with her, Rita had felt safe to let things lie undisturbed.

"Look," Rita said with only the slightest hint of irritation in her voice, "I've tried to look at things like my folks, and apparently you do. I've joined all the groups, read all the Bible handouts, prayed all the prayers, and held my head just so when the minister preached his sermons. I've spent a lifetime being preached at, prayed at, and talked at and, as shallow as it might seem to you, I just don't feel the same way you do."

"I think that's the most honesty you've given me since we met," Mark remarked in a way Rita hadn't expected. It so flabbergasted Rita that she said nothing as Mark continued. "I know how hard it is to feel like God is real. I went through a bad time of that myself. People kept saying, 'Well, if you just believed the way you should, you'd understand.' Then they'd all kind of stand around with this knowing look, all nodding at each other like I'd missed the joke. I hated it."

"Exactly," Rita said, totally amazed that Mark actually had put her feelings into words. "Or they give you that little shake of their head, where you can practically hear the 'Tsk, tsk' under their breath, and they talk about turning you over to God to be dealt with. Like you were a sack of potatoes that needed to be washed up for dinner."

Mark chuckled out loud, momentarily breaking the tension. "My favorite one was when they'd tell me that my faith wasn't strong enough. Just have faith, they'd say. Faith is the key. Faith is the answer. Faith is your foundation. And then they'd never tell me how it was I was supposed to get it, keep it, or understand it."

"I can't believe we're having this conversation," Rita said suddenly. "My parents would never understand. Especially my mother."

"You and your mom have a difficult relationship, don't you?" Mark spoke the words hesitantly. He worried that if he prodded Rita to reveal too much, too soon, she'd bolt and run like a frightened deer.

"That's the understatement of the century. Negotiating peace among warring nations would be a simpler project than dealing with our relationship," Rita retorted.

"I would imagine that makes it quite difficult for you." Mark's words pulled Rita out of her defensive mode for once in her life.

"That's really the first time anyone has ever mentioned that our relationship might be hard on me. Usually, there's all this sympathy for my mother," Rita stated with a sadness to her voice. "She has a prayer group. . .you know the type. It's made up of the local church women and they all pray for the issues of the day. My mother never hesitates to tell me that they've been praying for me for roughly the last twenty-some years. It's no wonder that people see things her way. She probably goes to the meetings and pours out her heart and cries her miseries of life with a difficult child. It drove me from home and now that I'm back, nothing has changed."

"And exactly what is it that hasn't changed?" Mark asked, throwing another log on the fire.

Rita grew quiet for a moment, and Mark thought for certain he'd pushed her too far. When she finally spoke, he realized he'd been holding his breath and exhaled rather loudly.

"My mother can't deal with me as a daughter. I'm nothing more to her than a challenge. A soul to win to God so that her tally sheet is complete when she stands before her King. She's never cared for me as a mother would a child, and I resent the only concern she bears for me is that which is on the behalf of another."

"And this is also why you resist a relationship with God?" Mark asked without thinking.

"I picked up the Bible as a young girl," Rita said, turning. Mark's expression was gentle. "I was thinking about giving my life over to Him. I really was. But I opened the Bible to Isaiah and a verse that put me off in a way that even now causes me grief."

"What was it?"

"It said something like, 'As a mother comforts her child, so will I comfort you.' I'd never known anything but pain and frustration from my mother. Certainly not comfort. And if God was as comforting as my mother, then that meant nothing to me. I slammed the Bible shut and sulked for weeks. I had never felt more betrayed." Rita got to her feet and walked a few steps from the fire before turning around briefly. Her eyes narrowed slightly, blinking back tears. "I'm sorry. I should never have told you these things."

Mark watched Rita walk to the river's edge. She just stood there for several minutes, looking out as if seeking peace for her soul. He allowed her the time to compose herself before he joined her.

"I'm glad you talked to me," he whispered at her back. "I think it helps friends to understand one another when they know each other's pain."

"Friends?" Rita questioned, whirling around to find herself only inches from Mark. "I thought you didn't want to be my friend."

Mark smiled through the shadowy light. Rita noted the change in his eyes. "I'd like to be much more," Mark said before pulling Rita into his arms and kissing her.

Rita was shocked into silence and passive acceptance. She found herself enjoying the kiss, while she fought in her mind to resist the pleasure of Mark's touch. Warnings went off in her brain. *Don't get too close! Don't care too much! Don't reciprocate!*

When Mark released her, Rita shook her head and took a step backward. Mark reached out to steady her as she found her foot give way on the unstable riverbank.

"Let me go," she whispered without malice. She sidestepped Mark and felt his grip give way when her feet were fixed on firm ground. Without looking behind her, Rita hurried breathlessly to her tent and the solitude it afforded her.

Chapter 6

Rita returned from her sled trip more withdrawn and quiet than before. She purposefully went out of her way to avoid Mark, and very little was offered in the way of explanation.

August and Beth watched helplessly. How were they to help this child who so obviously didn't want their help? They sat alone in their kitchen one evening, long after Rita had retired for the night. Holding each other's hands as they shared a prayer, August and Beth found comfort in the Lord and each other.

"I'm really afraid for her," Beth said after August ended the prayer. "She's so miserable and unhappy with her life. She wants to blame everyone else for her problems. Do you know that she told me she would never have bothered to come home except for the fact that her college roommate had decided to move to the lower forty-eight. Never mind the Iditarod. It was as if she couldn't accept that she'd made the choice to come home all by herself."

"I'd hoped things would be different," August admitted, pouring himself another cup of coffee. When he offered to pour Beth a cup, she shook her head.

"Did Mark say anything about their trip?" Beth questioned curiously.

"He mentioned that he kissed her," August said with a half-smile. "But she made it clear that he was to keep his distance and, well, you know Mark. He's a good man and he put it behind him."

"Does she still plan to race?" Beth asked.

"As far as I know," August answered with a shrug of his shoulders. "But with Rita, who can ever be sure? It wouldn't surprise me at all if she came downstairs tomorrow with her bags in hand." Beth nodded and said nothing. What else could be said?

———— ⁂ ————

Rita didn't show up the following morning with bags in hand, nor was her disposition as sour as it had been upon her return. She had just answered her mother's inquiry about what she'd like for breakfast when a knock sounded at the front door.

"I wonder who that is." August put down his newspaper.

"I'll get it, Dad," Rita offered and took off for the front room.

"Aunt Julie!" August heard his daughter squeal in excitement.

"Julie?" August said and exchanged a look of surprise with Beth. "Julie said nothing about visiting." He got to his feet and met his sister and daughter halfway.

"Jewels," he said, using her nickname, "why didn't you tell us you were coming?"

"Sam and I wanted to surprise you," the white-haired Julie replied. She hugged August through her bulky knee-length coat.

"Where is your husband?" August questioned. He and Sam had been best friends long before Sam had married Julie. It must have been a lifetime ago when they'd all lived in Nome. "It's been years since I've seen him."

"You know Sam," Julie answered. "He's out there getting our things."

"I'll give him a hand," Rita said, but Julie waved her off.

"Don't bother," Julie replied. "There's already a nice young man out there helping him."

"That would be Mark," August offered. "He's the partner I wrote you about."

"Seems like a great guy," Julie said as Beth came into the room. "Bethany, you look great. Eastern Alaska must not take the toll on a body that western Alaska does. You look a hundred years younger than I feel."

Beth laughed and reached out to embrace Julie. "It's just the traveling that makes you feel that way. I know you. After a good rest, you'll be down here teaching me some new recipe or sewing shortcut."

"I told her this was a vacation," Sam called from the doorway. "She'd better take it easy. After all, that is what the doctor told her to do."

"Are you sick, Jewels?" August asked in a serious tone.

"I had pneumonia," Julie admitted. "But I'm much better now."

"Well, you will take it easy while you're here," Beth said, ushering Julie down the hall. "I have the perfect room for you. Remember the way the girls used to have the greenhouse bedroom all fixed up? Well, I have taken the project back on."

The group followed Beth to the bedroom. On one wall were huge double doors that Beth opened to reveal a greenhouse filled with potted plants.

"It's beautiful!" Julie exclaimed. "Imagine all that green in the dead of winter."

"It's well insulated too," August said, moving aside for Mark to bring in the luggage he'd wrangled away from Sam.

"By the way," Mark said and placed the bags on the highly polished, wooden floor, "I'm Mark Williams."

Sam took his hand and shook it vigorously. "You know who I am already, but this here is my wife, Julie. She's August's sister."

"Yes, I know," Mark replied as he took Julie's hand and held it. "August has spoken most fondly of you."

Julie exchanged a look of love with her brother. They had always been close, and even when August had moved so far from Nome, he'd managed to keep Julie and Sam as important parts of his life.

Rita took the opportunity to slip from the room. She hated herself for leaving without getting an opportunity to talk with her aunt, but there would be time for that later.

She quickly made her way to the back porch, where she retrieved her insulated coveralls and boots. She had finished dressing to tend the dogs, when Mark appeared.

"Are you going to keep avoiding me?" he asked in a gentle voice.

Rita made the mistake of meeting his eyes. "I, uh. . ." Her words trailed into silence. She wanted to say more, but the words were stuck in her throat.

"Well?" he pushed.

"I don't want to talk about it," Rita stated firmly and started past him.

"Rita," Mark called and took hold of her arm.

"I don't want to talk to you right now," Rita repeated. "Don't you understand? You are annoying me with this pressure."

"What are you afraid of?" Mark asked her. He dropped his hand and waited for her reply.

Rita's eyes flashed the warning that her anger had been piqued. "I'm not afraid of anything, and I don't owe you any explanations. You've trained me now, and I can make the Iditarod a reality without any more interference from you."

"Where is all this fury coming from?" Mark asked. "Is this because I kissed you or because you opened up to me?"

Rita quickly lowered her head to avoid Mark's reading her eyes. She knew that saying nothing was like surrendering, but in truth, she was afraid to say anything. Pushing past him, Rita made her way to the dogs.

Mark stood on the steps watching her walk away. When had he come to care so much about this hurting woman-child? He was almost afraid to search himself for the depth of his concern. What if he learned more than he was willing to deal with?

———※———

Rita's opportunity to speak in private with her aunt Julie presented itself the following morning. Beth and August had volunteered to take

Sam and Julie shopping in Tok, and when Julie chose instead to stay home, Rita offered to keep her company.

Preparing them both some hot tea, Rita took two steaming mugs with her to Julie's greenhouse sitting room.

"I'm so glad you came here," Rita stated bluntly, handing Julie the tea. "I've always been able to talk to you, even when I couldn't talk to Mom or Dad. You never seemed to judge me or make me feel inadequate."

"I knew you needed me," Julie replied. "I felt the most overwhelming need to keep you in my prayers and not for the reasons you think, so stop frowning. I'm not going to start preaching at you; I just knew you needed some extra care."

"Thanks," Rita managed, a bit uncomfortably.

"Now, why don't you tell me what's bothering you?" Julie smiled.

For the next two hours, Rita shared her heart with her aunt. She mentioned her mother's attitude and her worries about her father's advanced years, at which Julie only laughed.

"We aren't that many years apart you know," Julie remarked. "And I feel fit as a fiddle. Of course, Sam and I know we aren't young kids anymore. In fact, it wouldn't surprise me at all if one of us were to die in the near future."

Rita frowned at her aunt's words. "I don't like to think about that. I don't know how you can talk so unemotionally about it either."

"Rita, you don't like to talk about it because you're young and because you don't know what the future holds for you after death. That's all. Sam and I aren't afraid to die. Oh, we don't like the idea of the separation here on earth, but we know that it won't be for long, and then we can share eternity in heaven."

"You make it sound so wonderful," Rita replied with a weak smile. "I know that Dad feels the same way. I guess it's just my selfishness that keeps me worried."

"Rita, I think it's fear, not selfishness that keeps you bothered. For all of your life, I've never seen you a single time without fear in your eyes. What is it that you're so afraid of?"

The words rang in her ears. Mark had asked her the same question. What was she afraid of?

"I don't know," Rita answered with a heavy sigh. "I try not to believe that I'm afraid of anything. It makes you vulnerable to be afraid."

"And vulnerability is probably what you fear the most," Julie replied. "Vulnerability means that you aren't 100 percent in control. Vulnerability means that someone might see something more than the facade of independence you wear. Vulnerability might mean that someone will get too close to you."

"Yes," Rita admitted.

"Why do you fear getting close to others?" Julie asked softly.

Rita put her cup down and paced the room. "I don't know. I guess because it hurts so much when they reject you."

"And who rejected you, Rita?" Julie pressed on.

"Lots of people," Rita answered. "My brothers and sisters never had much to do with me. Even my own mother. . ." Her thoughts fell short of words. "I don't really want to talk about them. I'm having a problem, however, with Mark Williams."

"He seems nice enough," Julie replied.

"He is," Rita said and stopped. "That's the problem. I've managed to put off every guy who's ever shown the slightest bit of interest in me. I knew I wanted to go to college and become a nurse like you, and I knew that someday I wanted to race in the Iditarod. A man would interfere with that."

"I once worried about the same thing," Julie laughed. "It's so like God to put you through something so that you can be a help to someone else later down the road."

"What are you talking about?" Rita questioned.

"When I married Sam, I did so without ever really understanding how he felt about my career as a nurse. Remember, my job was with the Public Health Department and I was often dogsledding out to the villages for many weeks at a time. I didn't know how to talk about my fears to Sam. I just knew that he would never approve."

"But he did, didn't he?"

"Yes, he did," Julie remembered. "He had it all planned out ahead of time to be with me on the trail. So for the most part, Sam joined me whenever I had to be gone for long periods of time. Eventually, I learned we were to have a baby, and so I quit my job and planned to stay home for a spell. Of course, you know that our son died when he was very small."

Rita nodded. "Why didn't you have other children?"

"I wanted to. I learned that I was to have another baby only three months after little Sam's death. But, I miscarried and nearly bled to death. They had to perform a hysterectomy and that meant no more children."

"I'm sorry, Aunt Julie," Rita said sadly. "I never knew."

"It's all right, Rita. God had other plans for Sam and me. We learned a great deal just being together, and we worked well as a team among the Eskimos and Indians. I have no regrets and have thoroughly enjoyed my life. But in order to do so, I became very vulnerable."

"I can well imagine," Rita said in a barely audible voice. "I'm just not sure that I could deal with it as well."

"A body never knows what it can endure until it goes through it. You're planning on putting yourself to a test of the elements when you race from Anchorage to Nome. You will be vulnerable because of the position you place yourself in. Do you want to back away from the responsibility of the Iditarod just because of that challenge?" Julie asked her niece.

"Well, no." Rita shook her head.

"You like this Mark, don't you?" Julie questioned again. "That's why this situation has become so disturbing to you. It's why your mother's words about God are so frightening to you. You know the truth about God. How could you not? You were raised in an atmosphere of Christian love. You attended church on your first outing after birth. Yet, even with all of this knowledge and wisdom at your fingertips, you chose instead to turn away from God's love. Why is that, Rita?"

"I don't know," Rita answered, forgetting to be angry that Julie had referenced salvation.

"I think you do," Julie replied. "You don't trust yourself enough to love God or Mark."

"What?" Rita questioned as her head snapped up to meet her aunt's eyes. "What in the world has trusting myself got to do with loving God or Mark?"

Julie shifted uncomfortably in the wicker chair. Rita jumped up to retrieve a pillow while she waited for her aunt's insight.

"Thank you, dear," Julie said as she eased against the cushioning bulk. "Now, what I was trying to help you see is the huge mistrust you have in yourself. I think you're the only one who can say why it's there, but its effects are clear. God stands with open arms, offering a free gift of love and salvation. Mark apparently offers at least friendship, possibly more. In both cases, I don't believe it's God or Mark who frightens you the most. It's Rita. For whatever reason you have contrived, you don't believe yourself trustworthy and deserving of love."

Rita frowned and bit at her lower lip. Was her aunt Julie right? Was this the demon from which she had so long run? Sitting back down, Rita seemed to withdraw into her thoughts to find the answers.

Julie reached out and covered Rita's hand with her own. "I know this is hard for you, but may I suggest something?"

Rita nodded.

"Good. I want to outline some scripture for you. Maybe you can better understand what I'm saying and what God's plan is, if you read His Word. Now, don't get defensive with me; just trust me. I want you to read the verses I mark and just think about them. Then, if you want to talk to me about them, I'll be happy to share whatever I know. Deal?"

Rita hesitated for a moment. She looked into Julie's dark eyes. Eyes that held so much love and concern for Rita that she wanted to cry for the very need of it.

"All right, Aunt Julie," she finally answered. "It's a deal."

"And Rita," Julie added with a smile, "try not to be so hard on that young man. I think your father is an excellent judge of character. After all, he led me to my Sam. Mark may very well be a special gift for you. Maybe he'll only be a friend, maybe more. But you'll never know if you aren't decent to him. Just open your heart a bit. You might be surprised at the results."

Rita nodded slowly. "I'll try. But it's those results that I'm worried about."

Chapter 7

R ita sat in the quiet solitude of her room. For the first time since she'd stopped going to church, she found a Bible spread out before her. Her aunt Julie had given her several scriptures to look up, and most of them were in the first book of Corinthians.

Rita knew the Bible forward and backward, and as she turned in her New International Version Bible to the thirteenth chapter of Corinthians, she already knew what the verses would say.

"If I speak in the tongues of men and of angels, but have not love, I am only a resounding gong or a clanging cymbal," the first verse began. Rita scanned the verses, remembering them well. She once had to quote the verses from memory in order to win a new Bible. It hadn't meant that much to her, but it seemed terribly important to her mother and father.

Then Rita quoted the fourth, fifth, and sixth verses aloud. "'Love is patient, love is kind. It does not envy, it does not boast, it is not proud. It is not rude, it is not self-seeking, it is not easily angered, it keeps no record of wrongs. Love does not delight in evil but rejoices with the truth.'"

Rita stopped and thought immediately of her mother. *Love keeps no record of wrongs,* she thought. So much had passed between them. So many angry words, so much ugliness and hurt. If love truly kept no record of wrongs, then maybe Rita didn't love her mother.

It was as though she'd had the wind knocked out of her. Rita had realized the anger and distance she felt toward her mother, but never once had she considered that she might not love her.

Glancing down at the Bible, Rita read on about how love does not delight in evil but rejoices with the truth and that it always protects, always trusts, always hopes, always perseveres. She didn't feel that way at all toward her mother. She didn't trust her mother or understand her. How could she love her?

The realization bothered Rita more than she could bear. Where had they gone wrong? From where had the pain come? Rita stretched out across her bed and closed her eyes. In her mind she saw herself as a child, long black pigtails trailing down her back. Her mother had always insisted that Rita wear her hair long and Rita, in turn, hated it. But why?

Rita saw herself playing alone in her room. There were no other siblings her own age and nobody seemed to notice that she was lonely.

"Go play, Rita," she could hear her mother saying. She was fitting one of Rita's older sisters for her wedding dress.

"There's nobody to play with," answered a five-year-old Rita.

"Then just find something to do, Rita. I'm busy!" her mother had exclaimed in complete frustration.

Rita had walked away from the room, head hanging down like one of the dogs after being told "no" to some forbidden activity. She had almost made it to her room before hearing her mother tell her sibling how hard it was to live with Rita. There were other words too. It was more pain than Rita wanted to deal with. Opening her eyes, she thought instead of Mark Williams.

She couldn't deny that she enjoyed his kiss. Nor could she ignore the way her heart had jumped at his touch. She saw his face in her mind and the soft gentleness of his eyes. Rita buried her face in her pillow. Why were these things happening just when she should be clearheaded and single-minded. The race was in such a short time, and Rita knew she needed to devote her thoughts to it.

"If I hadn't read the Bible," Rita thought aloud, "this wouldn't be happening. This is why I don't like all this soul-searching. It brings up things I'd rather not think of."

Rita thought of her aunt Julie's words about trust. Rita didn't trust people and she didn't trust herself. Trusting meant opening yourself up to more hurt. It meant being vulnerable, and Rita believed when a person was vulnerable, others took advantage of you.

Rita was just starting to doze off when a knock sounded at the door. Getting wearily to her feet, Rita opened the door to find her father.

"Am I interrupting anything?" August asked.

"No, come on in, Dad. I was just about to go to bed." Rita stepped back.

August walked into the room and pulled Rita's desk chair up beside her bed. He noticed the Bible, and although he wanted to ask about it, August decided to let Rita bring it up.

"It's kind of early for you to be going to bed, isn't it?" August questioned. "You aren't sick, are you?"

"No, Daddy," Rita said with a smile. "I'm just tired. It's been an exhausting day with the dogs, and then, of course, I've been doing a great deal of thinking about the race and all the complications and problems we still have to overcome."

"There is a lot to consider," August agreed. "We need to finish buying your supplies for one thing. Then we have to arrange for transporting dog food and whatever else you'll need to the various checkpoints on the trail. I thought I'd send you and Mark over to Fairbanks tomorrow."

"Fairbanks? But that'll take a whole day coming and going," Rita protested. "Can't we get everything we need in Tok?" What she really wanted to say was that she couldn't imagine having to bear Mark's company for a whole day without revealing her feelings. Then again, what were her feelings?

"We'll get some of the stuff in Tok, but there are several things I want you to pick up in Fairbanks," August replied.

"I could go alone," Rita offered.

"No," August answered. "Mark has things to pick up as well. You'll need his help, and I know he'll enjoy your company."

"Why do you say that?" Rita asked, suddenly interested in what Mark might have said to her father.

August grinned. "It isn't hard to see that he cares for you."

"Has he said that?"

"Well, I suppose it wouldn't be fair to share our conversations with you. But, suffice it to say, his opinion of you is quite high." August reached out to take Rita's hand. "I get the feeling you're kind of fond of him as well."

Rita couldn't contain her surprise. "I don't know what you're talking about."

"Rita, this is me you're talking to," August said softly. "I've seen the way you watch Mark, and I've seen the way he watches you. I know there's a chemistry there, but I also know there are a lot of problems to overcome. Please believe me, I'm not trying to push a romance between you two. I just realize that you share an interest. Mark's a good man, Rita. You could do a lot worse."

"I know," Rita said, finally giving in. "He is nice, and I do enjoy his company. I'm just not ready for any relationships. I hope you understand. I mean, I know you worry about me being alone, but don't. I'll be fine, Daddy."

"I don't think you're as tough as you'd like any of us to believe, Rita. But nonetheless, I'll bide my time," August stated. "Now, are you up to the trip tomorrow?"

"Sure, but I really need to be careful. I'm running out of money fast," Rita answered.

"I've sold a couple of dogs," August said. "We have to have enough set aside to ship the supplies to the checkpoints, as well as the one thousand two hundred forty-nine dollars that it takes to register in the Iditarod. Your mother is making your dog booties and some of your insulated gear."

"She is?" Rita questioned in amazement.

"That's right. She's also freezing snacks for your dogs. She's making honeyballs right now," August said, referring to a popular treat that many sledders used. The treats were made of lean beef, honey, powdered eggs, brewer's yeast, and vegetable oil. To this, vitamins and bonemeal were added and rolled into pieces the size of baseballs. It gave the dogs a tasty, high-protein snack that helped to meet the 10,000 calories a day that each dog needed to sustain energy on the trail.

Rita said nothing. She'd had no idea her mother was involved in making her Iditarod dream come true. It made Rita uncomfortable. Somehow it made her feel vulnerable.

"Now, have you kept track of the mandatory requirements?" August continued. "You know about the maximum ratings on the sleeping bag and the minimum weight requirements?"

"Sure, Daddy," Rita said, and recited the requirements for both. "I also need an ax with a head weighing at least one and three-quarters pounds, and the handle has to be at least twenty-two inches long. Then I need a pair of snowshoes thirty-three inches by eight inches, eight booties for each dog, one cooker, one pot capable of holding three gallons of water, two pounds of food for each dog, and one day's rations for myself. Oh, and it all has to fit on the sled. Did I leave out anything?"

August laughed. "Not as far as the mandatories go. You've done your homework, and I'm very proud of you. When you and Mark get back from Fairbanks, we'll start going over the critical points of the route itself." August got to his feet and studied his youngest daughter for a moment. She was willowy and graceful, but there was still a hardness to her that he didn't understand. "I love you, Rita," he said, turning to leave.

"I love you too, Daddy," Rita called out. She noted the look of concern on her father's face and hoped silently that he wasn't feeling ill. She couldn't help but notice the way he seemed to slow down more and more each day.

Long after their conversation, Rita still lay awake in bed thinking of her father's interminable aging. She wished she could have known him as a young man, wished he could have parented her as a young man. With thoughts interwoven with images of Mark Williams, Rita finally fell into a restless sleep. Tomorrow she would spend a great deal of time alone with Mark, and the thought weighed as heavy on her mind as that of her father's strength and health.

For most of the trip into Fairbanks, Rita allowed Mark to set the conversation. She answered only when the situation required her to do so and refrained from offering her opinion when it did not. She stared out the window watching the endless spruce forest, now heavy with snow. The trees seemed to weave an impenetrable labyrinth across the landscape and Rita wished silently that she could lose herself out among them rather than travel in confinement with Mark.

Mark sensed Rita's reluctance to open up to him even before they'd climbed into his truck for the long trip. He wondered if her silence was due to her efforts to concentrate on the upcoming race or something more personal.

Their business in Fairbanks passed swiftly and satisfactorily, and Rita was grateful that Mark had to see to many of his own needs. Before Rita slipped away to take care of a personal matter for her father, they agreed to meet back at the truck by three o'clock.

The jeweler's shop for which August had written the address was only a block away from where Rita had parted company with Mark. She walked into the building, jingling the bells on the front door as she did. A gray-haired man in a dark blue business suit met her before she reached the counter.

"May I help you?" he asked in a rich baritone voice.

"I'm here to see Mr. Simons," Rita related. "My father sent me with this package and instructions that I am to pick up a gift he ordered for my mother."

"You must be Rita Eriksson," the man replied. "I'm Jim Simons." He extended a friendly hand forward that Rita took with less enthusiasm.

"I'm glad to meet you. This is the package my father sent me with," Rita stated, quickly dropping the man's hand. She handed the heavy box to Mr. Simons, halfway expecting him to open it. When he didn't, Rita couldn't contain her surprise. "If you need to look it over," she said, "I have time to wait."

"That isn't necessary at all," Mr. Simons replied. "Your father and I have already arranged the matter. I have your mother's gift already wrapped." Mr. Simons moved to the back side of the counter, where he placed the package Rita had brought and retrieved a smaller, gift-wrapped box. "He'll find everything in order."

Rita nodded and took the gift.

"May I show you anything?" the man questioned. "I have some lovely necklaces just in and also there's a sale on some of my finest rings."

"I don't think so, thank you," Rita said with a glance at her watch. "I have to meet Mark, I mean my ride, at three o'clock and I still have a few more stops to make."

"Would your companion be Mark Williams?" Mr. Simons asked, surprising Rita.

"Why, yes," Rita answered. "How did you know?"

Mr. Simons laughed. "I guess that does seem a bit strange, doesn't it. I seemed to recall your father mentioning that you and Mr. Williams would be riding into town together. I have the wedding ring Mr. Williams picked out when he was here last weekend, and I presumed he would stop by today and pick it up. I wasn't certain, however, that it would be ready so I didn't call him ahead of time. If you would be so kind as to tell him that it's finished, I would sincerely appreciate it."

Rita felt as though she'd been delivered a blow. A wedding ring! Mark had never mentioned having a girlfriend, much less someone he planned to marry. Trying hard to keep her astonishment to herself, Rita agreed to pass Mr. Simons's message on to his client.

Walking from the store, Rita tried not to let the news bother her. Of course Mark was free to see whomever he chose and marry whenever he decided to, but Rita was amazed that her father hadn't even alluded to the fact that Mark was dating someone. In fact, Rita thought, her father had pushed her toward a relationship with Mark. Maybe he didn't know that Mark planned to marry someone else.

Unless. . . Surely Mark hadn't bought the ring for Rita! No, Mark wouldn't do things that way. He was too straightforward and honest. *Honest to a fault*, she thought.

Rita hadn't realized the apprehension and disappointment that was creeping into her heart. Had she really become more interested in her father's rugged business partner than she'd allowed herself to see?

"He's getting married," Rita muttered under her breath. "I would never have guessed it in a million years."

She made her other stops, barely able to concentrate on what she was doing, and made her way back to where Mark sat waiting in the pickup.

"Well, Texas Rita, get everything you were after?" he asked with a good-natured smile.

"I guess so," she answered, not even acknowledging the nickname. Rita looked up at him as if really seeing him for the first time. She felt saddened to realize they would never be more than friends. How could she have been so blind to the fact that she was falling in love with Mark Williams?

"Well then, we'd best head home. We can stop and pick up something to eat on the way out of town. That is, if you don't mind fast food," Mark said, reaching down to start the truck.

"I don't mind," Rita replied. She suddenly remembered Mr. Simons's request and reached out to prevent Mark from starting the engine. "I almost forgot. I had to pick up something for Dad at Simons's Jewelry Store. Mr. Simons said to tell you that your package is ready."

Rita watched purposefully to catch Mark's reaction. He smiled broadly and patted his coat pocket. "I've already taken care of it," he answered.

Rita thought he seemed quite pleased with himself. She fastened her seat belt and nodded. "Then I'm ready to go," she said and turned to stare out the passenger window.

Aside from giving Mark her order for a hamburger, french fries, and iced tea, Rita was silent in her brooding.

"How could I have been so stupid as to let my guard down and get interested in him?" she whispered to herself. She sighed and accepted the food that Mark had generously paid for.

Wasn't this exactly why she didn't allow herself to be vulnerable? The pain she was feeling brought it all back to her. She had to build the wall up higher to protect herself from ever feeling this way again. How could she have been so stupid?

Of course, she reasoned with herself, *I never gave Mark the slightest bit of encouragement. He had no reason to believe I was interested.* Rita made a pact with her heart that from that moment forward, she would care about nothing else but the Iditarod. She wouldn't allow herself to care about anyone else in a way that would distract her from accomplishing her dream of racing and completing the Iditarod.

From now on, Rita vowed silently, Mark was nothing more than the rival she'd originally seen him as and, despite her aunt Julie's encouragement to be less severe with him, she wouldn't allow him even an inch into her life.

Mark was baffled by Rita's silent treatment. Just when he thought she was thawing a bit and starting to open up to him—bang! She always slammed the door in his face.

When they got back to Rita's house, Mark started to say something about it, but Rita darted quickly from the truck and nearly ran into the house. What was with her, anyway?

Mark started unloading the supplies, and August soon came out to join him. August immediately noticed the furrows that lined Mark's forehead and knew the cause was most likely Rita.

"You want to talk about it?" August asked, following Mark into the shed where they stored dog supplies.

"I suppose that would be the logical thing," Mark said, slamming a fifty-pound bag of commercial dog food to the ground. "However, I'm not feeling very logical. I'm confused and frustrated, but that's nothing unusual after spending the day with your daughter."

August grinned; he knew how infuriating Rita could be. "What happened?"

"I don't even know," Mark began. "She was reserved as always when we headed out, but by the time we got to Fairbanks, I thought she was starting to relax a bit. I figured on having a really nice trip home. You know, maybe talk through some of our feelings, but she was quieter than ever and never offered me so much as a single word."

August frowned and followed Mark to the truck. "She never said a word? She didn't even fight with you?"

"Nope," Mark replied and hoisted another bag of dog food on his shoulder.

"That's not like her," August said. "She must have it bad for you."

Mark nearly dropped the feed. "What? I just told you she wasn't even speaking to me. How can you say she has it bad for me?"

"Because Rita fights with people she doesn't care about. If the relationship isn't that important to her, she won't be put down, cast aside, or trod on in any manner. However, if she has feelings for you and the relationship is important to her, she handles it totally differently. Look at her and her mother. They scarcely share two words. Now, on occasion they will argue, but Rita hardly ever handles it in the same flippant manner she does when dealing with strangers," August stated. "Rita cares for you, Mark, of this I'm certain. Her silence speaks more clearly than any words could."

"Then what do I do?" Mark asked seriously.

"Pray for her, Mark. Pray good and hard for her. I found the Bible open on her bed the other night. I think the Lord is really working her over and she needs to come to terms with Him first."

Mark nodded. "I'll pray."

Inside the house, Rita found herself face-to-face with another mountain of emotion—her mother. Beth had purposefully sought out her daughter in order to take some measurements for Rita's insulated pants.

"Did you enjoy your time with Mark?" Beth asked innocently.

"Why?" Rita snapped, rather irritably. "Why do you ask that?"

"I just thought maybe you and he—"

"Well, don't think about him and me," Rita interrupted. "There is nothing to think about. He's my trainer along with Dad, nothing more."

"You sound awfully firm on the matter," Beth said, taking the final measurement.

"I am," Rita replied. "Getting close to people only hurts you when they don't return your feelings."

Chapter 8

I can't believe you sold them!" Rita nearly yelled the words. "How could you give up your Iditarod ingots, just to finance me in this race?"

"They weren't that important to me," August said with a shrug. "And I didn't think they were that important to anyone else."

Rita stomped her snowy boots against the straw-covered floor of her father's supply shed. "Well, they were to me," she finally said. She tried to ignore the fact that Mark was sitting not three feet away.

"Look, Rita," August began, "Mr. Simons wanted to make them into tourist necklaces. He paid me more than I deserved to be paid because he's a fair man and knows that by adding a simple silver chain to each, he'll net a small fortune. Added to that I sold four more dogs. Now we have enough money to travel in style and keep everyone fed and healthy. Don't begrudge me doing things my way, Rita. It's important for me to see you accomplish this. It may be your only chance to ever compete. Don't spoil it now."

Rita bit back a retort and nodded her head. "If that's what you want, Dad," she murmured.

"Good," August said with a smile. "We've got a lot of work to do and a great deal of information to go over. Mark, did you bring your notes on the trail?"

"Yup." Mark got to his feet, patting the pocket of his insulated overalls. "They're right here."

"Well, why don't we get started then. Let's go into the office where it's warm," August suggested, and the other two followed his lead.

Mark set aside his gloves and pulled a thick packet of papers from his pocket. Rita and her father joined him at the small table. "It's important to keep checking your list of supplies. You never know when you'll leave something out," Mark began the conversation.

Rita nodded and tried to quell the rapid beat of her heart when Mark gave her a quick wink.

"You know the mandatory items, but you've got important decisions to make about the rest of your gear. Most mushers on the Iditarod don't bother with the weight of a tent; they usually sleep on the sled or at one of the offered shelters—"

"If they sleep," August interrupted. "I don't imagine I got more than seven hours that first week."

Mark nodded and added with a laugh, "I think that's why they insist on the mandatory layovers. There's the twenty-four-hour one that you must take at one time or another and a six-hour stop in White Mountain before the final push to Nome."

"Where do you take the twenty-four-hour stop?" Rita asked.

"A lot of folks take it at Rohn," answered Mark. "You've just come through the mountains, and you're physically and emotionally drained. There's good shelter, food, and water there, and the people are great too, but we're getting a little ahead of ourselves. First, you have to get that far."

"I'll get there," Rita said in a determined way that left both men little doubt that she would.

"There are other things to consider," Mark continued. "We'll head down to Anchorage in plenty of time to have the race-appointed veterinarians check out the dogs. You have to have all the shots up to date for parvovirus, rabies, and distemper."

"I have the records for all of that," August assured them. "You'll be given the Official Iditarod Cachet to carry with you. This is promotional material from the racing committee. It usually weighs about five pounds and has envelopes to be postmarked in Anchorage as well as Nome. It kind of celebrates the fact that the Iditarod trail is the old mail trail. The top finisher's envelopes are usually auctioned off to raise money for the race."

"Sounds like I'll have a crowded sled basket," muttered Rita.

"That's why what you choose to take along is so critical," Mark said, meeting Rita's dark eyes. He wished silently that he could find some sign of closeness in them, but Rita was expert at masking her feelings, and he saw nothing. "You can always dump stuff off as you go, but you can't get what you need in the middle of the Alaskan interior when you realize you've neglected to bring something."

"That's true," August stated. "I ran low on headlamp batteries early on and then I forgot to pack an extra pair of boots as well. When I got my only pair soaking wet and the windchill made the temperature seventy below zero, I knew I'd just cashed in the race."

Rita nodded, remembering how her father always reminded her to take extra boots whenever she and Mark trekked out into the wilds.

"Boots, extra clothes, batteries, lightbulbs, gloves, ropes, harnesses, even sled runners are all things you'll have to choose carefully. You must also be able to transport any injured or ill dog on that sled and, in a pinch, sleep in it instead of on top of it. You have to be careful, and you have to be smart," Mark added.

Rita tried to absorb it all. She wanted very much to show both Mark and her father that she was fully capable of caring for herself. It was a dangerous position to put herself in, because with her prideful attitude, she purposefully avoided asking important questions, questions that could very well mean the difference between life and death.

"There are also rules of the road," Mark continued. "You'll get most of these on paper, but some are just givens. There's the Good Samaritan Rule that says no racer can be penalized for helping another in an emergency. You have to explain the incidents to the race official at the next checkpoint, but there shouldn't be any problems."

"Also, there are regulations related to the wildlife. If you have an incident arise where wildlife has attacked you, there are rules that relate to the situation. If the game is killed in defense of life or property, you are responsible to get that animal gutted and cared for," August remarked.

"But that could take a long time and by then you'd lose your place in the race," Rita said irritably. "That doesn't seem fair."

"No other racer can proceed ahead of you," Mark said, setting the record straight. "You don't lose your place." Was it Rita's imagination, or did Mark sound rather disgusted with her?

"If it's impossible to take care of the animal, for whatever reason," August continued, "you need to report the incident to the racing committee."

Rita nodded, still disturbed by Mark's intonation.

"Of course, we don't have to worry about cruelty to the animals," Mark began, "but rule number thirty of the Dog Procedures states that racers aren't allowed to commit any action or inaction that causes preventable pain or suffering."

"And they are quite severe on this rule," August added. "Violation of this rule results in disqualification. The whole world watches the Iditarod with extreme concern for the health and safety of the animals. It's almost as if it doesn't matter what happens to the drivers as long as the dogs are pampered and cared for. Now, don't get me wrong," August continued, "I believe the dogs should always be cared for first. It's what I've taught you since you first started working with them. Your dogs are your life's blood out there. You feed them first, bed them down first, go over their bodies for injuries or problems, all before you take any form of personal comfort."

"I know all of that, Dad," Rita articulated.

"We're just trying to help you remember," Mark joined in. "There's so much that you must keep in mind." Mark noted the frown on Rita's face. "Look, Rita, no one is trying to make you feel stupid. We know that much of what you need to be aware of will come second nature to you. But, there will be those things that don't, and they'll probably be the very things that will not only make or break the race for you, but may result in a great many problems for you if you aren't on top of them."

"Okay. Okay," Rita retorted. "I'm all ears."

"Well, let's get on with the race itself," August suggested.

"That sounds good," Mark agreed. "Now first of all is Anchorage to Eagle River. This is mostly urban, and as much as the dogs love to race, they hate the crowds and noise. There are hundreds of thousands of people, cars, helicopters, and, above all else, noise. It makes the dogs jittery and the drivers tense. Fourth Street is where it all starts. At a banquet a couple of evenings before the race, you'll draw your starting position. Nine o'clock marks the ceremonial start of the race with the honorary number one racer send-off. After that, the race officially begins at nine-o-two. Racers will take off every two minutes after that, and during the ride to Eagle River you'll carry a passenger."

"That's you, Daddy," Rita said, offering August a smile. August couldn't help but return his daughter's gesture.

"Who's riding with you, Mark?" August questioned.

"I have a friend in Anchorage and I've asked him to ride with me. It's kind of a pre-wedding present," Mark replied. "In fact, after the race, I'm going to be his best man."

"You never mentioned this, Mark," August commented with a quick glance at Rita. He noted the flash in her eyes that bespoke of sudden interest.

"I meant to. When I was arranging help for the kennel so that you and Beth could spend time in Anchorage, I arranged to cover the extra day I'd be away for the wedding. I was going to mention it to you the other day because I needed to pick up the wedding ring in Fairbanks, but you made it easy on me with that trip to town, and I just forgot."

Rita nearly fell off her chair. So the ring wasn't Mark's. This changed everything. But did she want it to? When she'd thought that Mark had someone else in his life, it was easier for Rita to separate her feelings from her thoughts.

Rita's reaction wasn't lost on August or Mark, but both men kept their thoughts to themselves, while Rita struggled just to hear what was being said about the trail.

—— # ——

February came quickly to an end and Rita found herself on the way to Anchorage with her father. Her mother was coming down with Gerald and his wife in order to join in the festivities. After the Iditarod started, they would drive the dog vehicles to Eagle River, where they would meet Rita and her team after the first leg of the race. At Eagle River, the dogs and sleds would be loaded into trucks and driven to Wasilla, where the entire race would start again. The trail in earlier years passed over the mudflats of upper Cook Inlet to Knik. Due to the hazards of this area, when unseasonable warmth left the ground and water unfrozen, the race was officially changed to restart in Wasilla.

"It only gets better," August said with a smile.

"I love the anticipation. Just knowing that something glorious like the Iditarod awaits is enough to keep me on the edge of my seat. I keep thinking of how it's going to be, and even though I've never been there, you and Mark have made me feel as if I know how it will be," Rita chattered.

August nodded. "I'm glad you're excited. I knew you would be. You're finally realizing your dream and that's something quite special. I'm grateful to be a part of it before I die."

"Don't talk about dying, Daddy." Rita's voice betrayed her fear.

"Rita, you don't need to worry about me. I'm not afraid to die; and when my time comes, I'll be ready. I guess my only real concern is whether or not you will be."

Rita swallowed hard. She thought of the verses her aunt Julie had shared and all of her mother's speeches. Somehow those things were easier to deal with than her father's worries.

August tried not to notice the way Rita paled. Death, particularly the possibility of his death, caused Rita a great deal of fear. "Rita," he began gently, "you must let go of the fear you feel inside. Trust isn't an easy thing, but trust in God is something that will never let you down, because God will never let you down."

"How can you be so sure?" Rita barely whispered the question.

"It's a matter of believing in the promises that God has given in the Bible, Rita. He said He'd never leave us and He never will."

"It's so hard," Rita replied. "The whole concept is difficult to believe. I mean, I see that God is real to you and Mom. I guess even Mark sees Him in a real way; but it just doesn't feel that way to me. I've prayed before, but I never felt as though my prayers went any farther than the room I was in. God just never made Himself very evident to me."

August nodded. "I can understand your predicament. I went through a time like that too. Of course, you know all about that, and it isn't what's important right now. What is important is that you can have God in your life in a very real way. If you want Him, Rita, God will be there for you and He will help you to see Him."

"I'm afraid of trying." Rita's honest words hung in the air. "I mean, it seems like everyone I've ever cared about has deserted me. Everyone but you, that is."

"Do you really believe that?" August questioned.

"I don't know, Daddy. All I know is that ever since I was a little girl, I tried to understand why Mom felt so angry with me all the time and why none of my brothers or sisters seemed to have the time of day for me."

"Your brothers and sisters were all so much older than you. You turned out to be a surprise gift from the Lord. You have to remember that you came nearly nine years after we presumed we were finished with diapers and bottles. Nevertheless, we loved you as much as any of the rest," August replied.

Rita shook her head. "No, I don't think so. You may have felt that way, but Mother didn't. I overheard her tell Sarah that she'd never wanted me."

August looked stunned. "I find that hard to believe, Rita. I mean, I know the pregnancy was a shock to your mother and that we had to change a lot of plans, but I remember when she gave birth to you. I watched her nurse you. Your mother loved you as much as any of the others."

Rita winced and fell silent.

"Look, Rita," August said, dividing his concentration between the road and his daughter, "the issue here isn't the past, but the future. I'm going to pray that God will reveal Himself to you in a very real way, and I'm going to pray that you can somehow get over your hurtful relationship with your mother and start over."

Rita looked out the window to avoid her father's face. She didn't want to appear vulnerable to his words, but the truth was she felt compelled to listen.

"I mean it, Rita," August said in an authoritative voice. "I want you to figure out what the problem is between you and your mom and deal with it. I don't want to leave this world with the concern that either one of you is alone. I want you to be there for each other. I want you to love each other."

August's words hung on the air, stifling Rita into silent submission. "*I want you to love each other*" resounded in her mind as the forested miles of highway ticked by.

Chapter 9

The noise at the starting line on Fourth Street was intense and nerve-racking. Rita stood beside her dogs, soothing, quieting, and rechecking every harness and line. She could feel the adrenaline surging through her veins, making her heart pound hard against her temples.

Mentally, she made a list of the items she'd packed, and one by one she went over them. With each crunch of snow beneath her heavy boots, Rita felt the urge to be off building inside.

Dandy gave a whimpered howl that was quickly followed by howls from the other dogs. Rita saw her father lean over and give the lead dog a quick pat on the head. She thought he whispered something to the dog, but a tap on her shoulder distracted her from finding out what it was that August had said.

"Yes?" She whirled around to find Mark's intense eyes. His cheeks were red from the wind, but his expression of excitement matched her own.

"Are you ready, Texas Rita?" Mark asked in puffs of icy air.

Rita couldn't help but grin. "I feel like I've worked a lifetime to get here."

"You have worked hard," Mark agreed. "I'm proud of the way you put aside our differences."

Rita prickled at Mark's words. "I don't know what you're talking about."

Mark laughed. "You weren't the most cooperative student, as I recall."

Rita started to answer but found her reply interrupted by one of the race officials.

"I'm here to mark your dogs," he told her as he moved with paint to dab on each dog's fur for purposes of identification. This would prevent the switching of dogs while out on the trail. Rita anticipated this from things her father and Mark had told her; still she didn't like anyone else handling her dogs.

She followed the man in silence, however, her mind still on Mark's words. *Forget about him,* she chided her heart and mind. *You don't need him or anyone else.* Yet even as she tried to convince herself of this, her father's words of salvation and heavenly security kept pounding at her.

By the time the official moved on, Rita found Mark gone as well. August came up with a grin a mile wide.

"Okay, Number Nineteen," he said, referring to the number Rita had drawn for her position in the start of the Iditarod, "it won't be long now."

"I know," Rita mumbled.

"What's wrong?" August asked, suddenly concerned.

"Umm? Oh, nothing," Rita said, noting her father's worried look. She wanted to assure him, but in order to keep her guard up, she also needed to distance herself. "It's just jitters, Dad."

"I understand. Look, we're going to be taking off shortly. Do you have everything?" August asked.

"I think so," Rita answered. "Where's Mom and Gerald?"

"Oh, they're out there somewhere. Don't you worry about them. They'll be there at Eagle River waiting with the dog trucks."

"Well, I guess that's all I can ask," Rita said with a hesitant smile.

"Don't worry," August said as he patted his daughter's hand. "Everything will be fine once the race starts."

Rita wanted to believe that, but in her heart she knew the turmoil was about much more than the race. "One more, Rita," August called from the sled basket. "One more racer and then we're off."

Rita said nothing. Her mind was a blur of fanatical fans waving and yelling their support. Where in the world had all those people come from? There were television cameras and reporters everywhere, not to mention five blocks of colorful, screaming people and extremely bright lights.

The next thing Rita knew was the numbing grip of her hand on the sled handle and the pounding of her heart in her ears.

"Nineteen—go!" the announcer called.

"Dandy, hike!" Rita yelled above the crowd's roar. Dandy led the pack of dogs without need of encouragement. The team was in a near frenzy as they shot down the street.

Rita knew nothing but the feel of the dogs and the frosty air against her cheeks. The sounds were all muted in her head while the faces blended into one.

I'm really doing it! Rita thought. *I'm finally racing the Iditarod!*

The race trail headed down Cordova Hill, with a spectacular view of downtown Anchorage. Rita worked to slow the team as they plunged down the slope, but the dogs were as excited as she was. It was exhilarating and no one wanted to slow down for any reason.

The next miles followed inner-city trails where people still cheered the mushers on. It wasn't until the trail finally began to parallel the Glenn Highway that the people thinned to sporadic gatherings.

"Isn't this great!" August yelled over his shoulder.

"Yes," Rita replied. "It's everything I knew it would be."

August laughed heartily. "You ain't seen nothin' yet, kid. Hang on for Act Two. It's a doozy!"

Amid the noise of people and crowds, Rita worked hard to keep the team under control. Each time they approached an intersection, traffic was stopped from all directions while her team moved through, but the honking of zealous fans and general pandemonium made driving the team a tiresome task.

Rita had hoped to think through her anger and frustration on the trail, but if the run from Anchorage to Eagle River was any indication of how her time would be spent, there wouldn't be much time for thinking.

———⸸———

Two hours and eighteen minutes later, without a single mishap, Rita and August passed under the banner welcoming them to Eagle River.

"Good time, Rita," August said as they checked in.

Rita nodded and looked around for Mark. He'd left a good ten places behind her, but that didn't mean a great deal. She'd no sooner cast a squinted stare at the horizon when she caught sight of him. He was making incredible time.

August spotted him about the same time. "I bet he'll be under two hours!" The excitement in August's voice left a jealous mark on Rita's heart.

Mark came flying across the trail and clocked in at one hour and fifty-eight minutes. While August stomped off through the snow to congratulate his partner, Rita cooled her heels and unharnessed her dogs.

"You did well, Rita," her brother said as he came to help her with loading the animals.

"Thanks, Gerald. It's good to see you again," she answered rather mechanically, not really meaning a word she said. Rita knew it wasn't fair to take out her fury on Gerald, but she ignored her pang of conscience and kept her distance.

"Rita!" Beth called as she got out of the pickup. "What was your time?"

"Two-eighteen," Rita replied, surprised at her mother's enthusiasm.

"Fantastic!" Beth stepped forward and hugged her daughter. She laughed as she pulled away from Rita. "There's so much padding to you, I'm not at all convinced that you're really under all of that," she said, pointing to Rita's insulated coveralls.

Rita laughed in spite of herself. She'd never seen her mother so happy, especially when it involved Rita. Surprisingly enough, it was her father who spoiled Rita's moment of happiness.

"Mark did it in an hour and fifty-eight minutes!" said August. "Can you believe it, Beth?"

"That's great," Beth agreed. "I'm so proud of Rita and Mark. They've done really well, haven't they?" It was more a statement than a question.

"They certainly have," August said. "Now we need to get these animals loaded up and move up to Wasilla."

Rita felt disappointed in the lack of fanfare from her father. Somehow she'd presumed he'd been her biggest fan, not her mother. Putting it behind her, Rita knew she'd have plenty of time to contemplate it on the way to Wasilla.

———#———

The next day the whole thing started all over. This time Rita waited behind while Mark disappeared down the trail. In her mind was the overwhelming drive to beat his time and win the race.

For all the truly important reasons, Wasilla was where the Iditarod really began. The race restarted with the biggest difference being that this time the racers went out alone. Rita refused to even look back when her time came. When the signal was given, she steadied herself behind the sled and ran for all she was worth.

The first one hundred miles out of Wasilla was called "Moose Alley" and for a good reason. It was here that the race trail passed through an area where large numbers of moose spent the winter. When the snow became too deep for the moose to find food, they often took to the roadways, railroad tracks, and any place else that had been cleared of the blanket of white.

Rita kept alert for any interference and, in the process, passed two other teams who were already experiencing problems. She was out less than four hours when the snow began to fall. At first the flakes came down in gentle flurries, but within a matter of several miles, the conditions had built into a full-fledged blizzard. Rita came upon four teams who had backtracked their way in order to relocate the trail, and rather than lose her place and assure everyone they were headed in the right direction, Rita took a gamble and headed on.

The gamble paid off and Rita soon found one of the trail markers. "Good," she said aloud, adrenaline racing through her system. "I've moved out ahead of six teams already. If I'm just willing to take a few chances, I can win this race!"

When the snow let up a bit, Rita knew it would be a good time to rest the dogs. She pulled off the trail and dug out dried fish for each of the team. She felt hot inside her multiple layers of clothing, and it was then that she realized the temperatures were warming.

Glancing around her, Rita could see a clearing in the skies up ahead and bright sunlight filtering through the sporadic cloud coverage. The snow had stopped falling altogether, but the trail had been partially obliterated by the storm. In the far distance, Rita thought she heard dogs barking. Her pulse began to race. "I can't lose ground, now."

Rita resecured the sled cargo, shed her heavy parka, and pulled on a beaver fur hat that her mother had made for her as a Christmas gift. She pulled sunglasses from a pouch near the handle bar, stuffed them in her insulated coveralls, and pressed the dogs forward.

Rita believed luck was with her as the skies cleared and the trail markers appeared faithfully. She urged the dogs to go faster and faster, but they slowed as the trail grew mushy from the sun's warmth.

Rethinking her strategy, Rita reasoned that waiting for sunset might be better for her time and the dogs' health. She drove them another couple of hours and finally located a place near a stream. Her mind whirled as she rationalized her decision.

"Everyone will be slowed down by the thawing trail," she spoke to herself. "No one will make good time, and if I stop now, rest and feed the dogs and take a nap myself, we'll be able to push through all night." It was sensible, but with each team that passed her, Rita felt the urge to get back behind the sled and join them.

Instead, Rita built a fire and heated food for the dogs. After seeing each of them fed and bedded down, she pulled out her heavy snow parka and lay down on top of her sled. Setting the alarm on her watch for four o'clock, Rita placed the timepiece in her fur hat so that it was right up against her ear. Then, pulling the parka over her body and face, Rita slept. Again the gamble paid off. When Rita awoke, the sunlight was fading and the trail was already growing firm again. After making sure to water the dogs one more time to keep them from trying to eat snow on the trail, Rita moved out for her next checkpoint—Skwenta, Alaska.

When she arrived at the checkpoint, most of the teams had been there far ahead of her. Some of the drivers were giving their dogs extra rest; but as soon as Rita checked in, she felt like hitting the trail again. The Delia House, long known for its hospitality, held a welcome aroma of chili, stews, and freshly brewed coffee.

Rita sat down nervously to a bowl of beef stew and bread while she mentally calculated who was who and what kind of time they must have maintained. She gulped the food down. While most of the other drivers went to sleep, Rita donned her parka again and went back to her dogs.

The one thing she hadn't counted on was a deluge of reporters. Flashbulbs went off, making the dogs nervous and blinding Rita.

"You're not pushing out again, are you?" one reporter asked and thrust a tape recorder in front of Rita.

"Y—yes," Rita stammered and tried to shield her eyes from the television camera lights that were added to the flashing lights.

"The other drivers are giving their dogs a longer rest. Aren't you concerned that your dogs will be overworked?" a woman interviewer questioned. "I thought there were strict rules about the dogs."

"I rested early in the day when the trails were mushy. My dogs are fine," Rita replied in clipped tones that betrayed her agitation. "Now, if you'll excuse me."

Rita hurried to leave the checkpoint, and after meeting all her obligations, she quickly found her way down the trail and headed for Finger Lake.

In the bright moonlight, the trail was easy enough. The stars filled the skies overhead, and Rita thought she'd never known anything as beautiful. Following the Skwenta River, Rita calculated that Finger Lake was some forty-five miles away. She knew she'd have to rest the dogs for short spells before then, but Finger Lake would represent her next major stop.

Silently, she watched the miles pass by. She saw the heavy cloud bank that edged its way across the western skies, while over her right shoulder northern lights danced in the March sky. What a land of contrast!

Lowlands gave way to foothills and foothills passed into the mighty Alaskan Range. Even though each passing mile offered more difficult obstacles, one thought haunted Rita's mind—*Where was Mark and what kind of time was he keeping?*

Chapter 10

The following day wasn't quite as warm, but Rita repeated her system between intermittent snows. She knew that other drivers were following the same plan, and she kept moving as quickly as possible to gain distance.

True to what her father and Mark had told her, she couldn't count more than a few hours of sleep in total. The lack of sleep didn't discourage her, however. Rita kept reminding herself of how easy the trail had been so far, and despite her desperate need for sleep, she kept to her self-appointed schedule.

"I've taken chances," she said aloud, "but they've paid off and I know they were the right things to do."

Rita smiled to herself as the dogs moved at a steady lope. At Finger Lake she'd moved up nine places, and after an uneventful roller coaster ride through Happy River Gorge, Rita was beginning to feel smug in her self-confidence. "I knew I didn't need anybody," she reminded herself. The cold wind made her cheekbones numb, but she didn't care. She knew she could win the race.

In the back of her mind, August's words mingled with her self-assured thoughts. Her father said she needed God, and no matter how she tried to deny Him, Rita knew it was true. That was the biggest problem about all the miles of solitude on the trail—it gave a person too much time to think.

Rita thought about stopping the dogs in order to get her headphones. Maybe listening to some of her favorite music would help her to keep her conscience in check. She glanced at her watch and decided against it. She could just as well block out the thoughts by forcing her interests elsewhere. At least, she hoped she could.

The dogs were holding up well, and each checkpoint had shown them to be in excellent shape despite the way Rita pushed them. It was Rita who suffered. At times she thought she imagined teams just ahead of her, but when she rubbed her eyes with the back of her mittens, the images faded. It wasn't until Rita thought the dogsled was floating up into the air that she decided to rest. Rohn was only a few hours ahead of her, and both Mark and her father had suggested she spend her twenty-four-hour layover there. All she had to do was hold on until Rohn.

While Rohn and a good night's sleep waited just down the trail, Rita knew she would still have to face the challenge of Dalzell Gorge. Her father had described this stretch of the Iditarod as a nightmare.

First, there was the climb from Puntilla Lake to 3,200-foot Rainy Pass. The dogs had managed this with relative ease, and Rita was beginning to think they were living a charmed life. Maybe her father had just been overly tired by the time he'd come this far, she surmised. Maybe it was just that he was so much older when he'd run the race.

As the team crossed over the divide, Rita had to turn her full attention to the trail at hand. The path ahead plunged into a steep, winding trail that moved rapidly downhill at a rate of about one thousand feet in little more than five miles.

Rita clung to the bar and rode the brake constantly to counter the dogs' continued slipping. At one point she saw Dandy go down and slide several feet. Over and over the dogs recovered their falls while Rita found herself near to prayer for the safety of the team.

Things went better for several minutes and Rita breathed a sigh of relief. She tried to get her bearings on the situation, feeling her pulse racing wildly. Ahead of her, the narrow canyon was lined with boulders and crossed several ice bridges that spanned partially frozen creeks. If the dogs lost their footing while traveling over the bridges, they could send the entire team, sled and all, into the water below. Rita couldn't afford to lose the time, nor would she endanger the dogs.

"Dandy, whoa!" she called and held the brake tight to bring the dogs to a near stop. Easing them forward, Rita held her breath with each crossing and didn't let it out until they'd safely reached the opposite side.

"Just get us to Rohn," Rita murmured, uncertain to whom she was speaking. "We'll be fine if we can just get to Rohn."

The shelter cabin at Rohn waited as official Iditarod Checkpoint Number Eight. Rita dragged into the clearing running behind the sled on nothing but sheer determination. She was now two hundred seventy-five miles from Anchorage, and while the halfway mark was still to be reached, Rita was simply grateful for having made it this far.

Coming to a halt, Rita was quickly surrounded by people. One by one she answered questions and even signed an autograph book, before the crowd dispersed and left her to work.

"I see you're still in one piece." It was Mark.

Rita cast a weary glance upward from where she had bent down to check over her dogs. "You too" was all that squeaked out.

"You gonna lay over here?" Mark asked sympathetically.

"Yes." Rita straightened out and nearly fell over.

"Easy," Mark said, reaching out to steady her.

"I'm fine, really," Rita answered and tried to push away. "I have to log in and let them know I'm staying." She started to walk away but turned back around. "What about you?"

"I'll be leaving in a few hours," Mark replied. The concern he held for Rita was evident in his expression.

"You're that far ahead of me?"

"Is that all that concerns you?" Mark asked a bit sarcastically.

Rita rolled her neck to relieve the strain. "It isn't everything, but it's important."

Mark shook his head as Rita moved off to speak to the officials. He knew it was difficult to truly enjoy the race while you were running it, but in Rita's case it was even worse. She was all driving competition and no pleasure. The fire of that drive was clear in her eyes, in spite of her exhaustion.

Rita tried to ignore the way Mark stared after her. She met her race responsibilities, picked up supplies, and moved away from the shelter area to bed down with the dogs.

"The wind's due to pick up tonight," Mark said from somewhere behind her.

Rita turned wearily to find him toting a bale of straw. "What are you doing?"

"Just bringing the dogs some bedding." His casual reply left Rita no room to protest.

"What's the temperature?" she asked instead and reached into her pocket for a knife to cut the baling wire.

"Thirty below and dropping. When that wind comes down the pass, it's going to feel like a hundred below. I'd climb in that sled and in my sleeping bag if I were you," Mark answered.

"Just put the bale here." She motioned. "I'm going to stake out the dogs and then I'll distribute the straw." Mark dropped the bale and stood back wishing he could do more to ease Rita's exhaustion. He knew she needed to do everything for herself, but he also knew her pride wouldn't allow her to think rationally.

"May I keep you company while you get the dogs fed and watered?" he questioned.

"I guess so," Rita said and moved painfully slowly to position her dogs.

No other conversation passed between them until after Rita

had a hearty fire roaring. She thawed rich mixtures of commercial dog food, liver, chicken, and salmon to feed the dogs, then melted snow and poured water for each one until she was certain they'd had their fill. Mark made conversation that was solely responsible for keeping Rita on her feet, but she never would have admitted his help.

"You gonna eat?" Mark asked when he saw that Rita was finished with the dogs.

"No," she sighed. A gust of wind blew through the trees just then. "It's getting colder and I'm going to sleep. Will I see you when I wake up?"

"I doubt it. You won't surface dreamland for ten or twelve hours if my guess is right. I'll be gone in two."

Rita nodded. She wanted to ask him about his time, but her mind begged for sleep. "I'll see you when you cross the finish line in Nome, then." Her reply amused Mark.

"Not likely, Eriksson. Not likely."

Rita watched Mark walk away. She hadn't realized how comforting his presence was until he stood in the lighted doorway of the Bureau of Land Management cabin and turned to offer her a wave before going inside.

Stripping off her parka and wet coveralls, Rita quickly pulled the sleeping bag around her and nuzzled down into the sled basket. She wiggled around to work the sled cover up over her before burying her head inside the sleeping bag. The warmth eased her aching muscles and sleep was immediate. For the first time in days, Rita gave in to the demands of her body. When Rita awoke nine hours later, she could hear the wind howling from outside her sled bag. She pulled her wristwatch to her face and hit the light button to reveal the date and time. Seeing that she was still early into her twenty-four hours, Rita allowed herself to linger in the warmth.

Licking her lips slowly, Rita realized for the first time how cracked and dried they were. Water sounded even better than food, and her

stomach was protesting quite loudly for that substance. It was a difficult choice. Food and water or restful warmth?

Finally choosing the food, Rita pushed back the basket cover and
peered out. During the night, the winds had brought snow and buried
the dogs and the basket in an insulation of white. Rita pulled her frozen coveralls on and secured her parka, while Dandy lazily peeked blue
eyes out from where his bushy tail covered his muzzle.

"Well, boy," Rita called out. "What do you think? Are we going to
win this race?" Dandy whimpered, then yipped. "I'll take that as a yes,"
Rita answered and went to work melting snow.

By the time Rita's layover was completed, the wind had picked
up to forty miles an hour and the temperature registered at forty-five
below. Thick, heavy snow clouds hung in a gray lifeless form over the
entire area. There would be little, if any, light today, Rita surmised.

She quickly harnessed the dogs and stood ready to leave when her
official twenty-four hours was up. It was almost like starting the race
again. The dogs were refreshed, well fed and watered, and eager for the
trail. They lived to do this work and they loved it. Rita smiled as she
stroked Dandy one last time, remembering a woman in Anchorage
who thought it cruel that Rita raced her dogs. The woman couldn't
understand. She saw the harnesses of confinement and the weight of
the load. What she didn't see was the animation in the dogs, their yips
of enthusiasm, their jumps of excitement. Nor did this woman know
of the dogs left behind to howl and mourn their misfortune. It was all
a matter of how one looked at the situation.

Something in Rita's heart took notice at that thought. Her mother's
indifference came to mind. Rita frowned at the memory and quickly
brushed it aside. A matter of perspective or not, Rita had a race to run
and now wasn't the time for soul-searching. Or was it?

The trail was firm beneath her feet as Rita ran behind her sled.
The dogs, ever faithful to their job, kept a steady lope as they moved
out of the Rohn area and past the Kuskokwim River's south fork. Rita
had been thoroughly warned about the trail to come. She would soon

be passing into the Farewell Burn. This 360,000-acre area of tundra and spruce forests had been destroyed many years prior in a forest fire. It left behind an obstacle course of fallen trees and regrowth of sedge-tussock tundra. The tussock, clumps of grass that mushroomed out two feet high or more, froze solid in the winter and presented rock-solid opposition to the racers of the Iditarod. Many a driver had been injured, some even seriously, when their sleds and teams had run up against the tussock.

Rita calculated the checkpoints to come. There would be Nikolai first, then McGrath, Takotna, and finally Ophir. Ophir was where the trail would separate and take the southerly route and pass through Iditarod, and it was Iditarod that represented the halfway mark. It seemed like a whole world away. The hours rushed by and the distance passed too. Rita had found the "Burn" painfully tedious and slow. Snow made visibility difficult, but, one by one, Rita located the trail markers and pressed on. The checkpoints passed quickly, and with them came the cultural change from areas that had been heavily influenced by the whites to lands primarily settled with native Athapaskan Indians.

She was greeted enthusiastically at Nikolai, finding herself in fifth position, but still behind Mark. The villagers had greeted each arriving team with shouts of praise and welcome. A huge bonfire had been built for the purpose of heating water for the dogs, and the school had been dismissed to allow the children to run from team to team seeking autographs.

Rita was given a hot meat sandwich that she quickly wolfed down before pushing on. Leaving a single sled team behind while the driver changed runners, Rita pushed ahead for McGrath.

———#———

By nightfall she'd made Takotna. This river town had served as a landing and supply center during the gold rush days in Alaska. Although Takotna now only numbered around fifty in population, Rita was welcomed every bit as heartily as she had been in Nikolai. She'd never seen so much food in all her life and graciously ate her fill after seeing to it that her team ate first.

The snow fell heavier still as she mushed out to reach Ophir. More than one native encouraged her to stay on in Takotna until the storm abated, but Rita was feverish with the thought of passing Mark.

It was the endless miles of darkness that gave Rita too much time to think. "If I can only make it to Iditarod first," she whispered to the night skies, "I could win the silver ingots and give them to Dad." *There are only five teams in front of me and one of them is Mark,* she thought to herself and disregarded the beliefs that being the first one to reach the halfway point jinxed you from winning the race. She knew that only once had the midway winner gone on to win the Iditarod, but she simply didn't care. She wished there were some way to slow down the other teams.

When she finally arrived in Ophir, amidst near-blizzard conditions, Rita felt as though she'd been granted her wish. All five of the teams ahead of her, including Mark's, were still there.

Mark met her and noted the frenzied excitement in her eye. "The weather's too bad to push ahead," Mark commented as Rita's team approached him. "We've decided to hold up a spell."

"Have they put a freeze on the race?" Rita questioned, feeling her fervor fade.

"No," Mark replied. "We just know what these storms are like. It'll blow over in a short time and we can be off then. There's no use in risking life and limb."

"I can't believe you're all afraid to go out in this," Rita said, waving her hand. "I've come the last twenty miles in this storm and, while cold and extremely frustrating, it's not worth stopping for."

"You don't mean that you plan to move on out in it?" Mark's question fanned the flame of Rita's pride.

"I certainly do. As soon as I get the team cared for, we're out of here." She hurried off before Mark could say anything to stop her. There was a chance to win the ingots. There was a chance to win the race!

Chapter 11

"I don't want you to go, Rita," Mark stated. He put his hand out to take hold of Dandy's harness. "I owe it to your father to keep you from risking your life out there."

Rita's eyes blazed holes in Mark's heart. "Let go of my dogs. It's my choice to run, just as it was your choice to stay. My father isn't out here running this race; I am. Now let me go."

Mark dropped the harness and took hold of Rita with both hands. "It's suicide to go any farther," Mark tried to reason. "If you don't care about your family, I do. I don't want to have to explain to them how I allowed you to go out and become the first human life lost in the entire history of the Iditarod."

"I never asked you to babysit me," Rita said in a surprisingly calm tone.

"I just care about you, Rita. Think about it. I think I've proven it enough times. It's not just August and Beth. I care about what happens to you."

Rita felt her resolve giving way; her eyes softened for a moment before she shrugged away from Mark's hold. "I don't want you to care," she whispered and walked back to the sled. She gave a soft whistle barely heard through the wind, but it was enough that Dandy's sensitive ears picked it up and then they were gone.

Mark kicked at the snow and muttered all the way back to where his team was contentedly curled up beneath the snow. He began to ready his sled without real thought to what he was doing, but in his heart he knew that he'd have to follow Rita. He'd never forgive himself if something happened to her.

"Williams!" a voice sounded above the wind. "Where are you going?" It was one of the checkpoint officials.

"I'm heading out for Iditarod," Mark replied.

"I can't let you go," the man returned. "They've put a freeze on the race. Can't get supplies flown up to the next checkpoints because of the blizzard. Until they can, the race stops."

"But Rita Eriksson just left a few minutes ago. She'll be out there all alone if I don't follow her," Mark protested, even knowing how foolish his argument sounded.

"Sorry, Williams. She took off before the word came down, but if you head out, you'll be breaking the rules." The man saw the look of concern on Mark's face. "It shouldn't be a long wait. Try not to worry." But it was a long wait, and team after team arrived in Ophir only to be told they had to stay put until supplies could be sent on ahead. Most took the opportunity to sleep or repair their sleds, but Mark paced and fretted until he was nearly sick from the thought of Rita meeting with an accident.

"Lord," Mark found himself praying, "I don't understand what gets into that woman, but I care for her in a way I wasn't sure I could ever care for another human being. Lord, I don't want her to die and yet. . ." His words trailed into silence as he remembered a sermon he'd once heard about people thwarting God's efforts to work in the lives of rebellious souls. "God, I don't want to interfere in Your plans for Rita. Go with her and help me to leave it in Your hands. Amen."

The prayer made Mark feel marginally better, but when one day passed into two and the checkpoint official gave him the news that Rita had never made it to Iditarod, Mark could stand it no longer.

"I have to go after her!" he said as he readied his dogs.

"You'll just get yourself killed," the official told him. "Or, you'll be disqualified from the race."

"I don't care. I'm a certified search and rescue team member. I can't just sit here knowing that she's out there somewhere in this storm. I have to try to find her, or I'm afraid she's not going to come out of this alive. Do you really want to be the one remembered for keeping a racer from being saved?"

"I'll send out other people," the man replied. "I assure you, Miss Eriksson will be located as soon as possible, but I can't risk the lives of ten other people because of the foolish gamble of one racer."

"I'm not asking you to," Mark said, taking hold of the sled bar. "I'll gladly give my own life for hers."

The man's face changed from angry frustration to confusion. Mark took the man's silence as a form of understanding and pushed the dogs out into the storm.

———— # ————

Rita knew she was hopelessly lost. She hadn't been able to locate a marker or tag of any kind and the trail was long since obliterated.

The blizzard raged on around her, making it impossible to care for the dogs or even set up a proper camp. The few times she'd tried, she'd failed miserably and struggled to push on. When the wind let up a bit, she strained to hear the sounds of civilization. Nothing came back to her ears but the deathlike silence. Exhaustion hung round her like a mantle of fur.

"I've got to make camp. I've got to rest," she said aloud. The dogs were wearing out fast, and Rita knew she was pushing them dangerously close to dehydration and death.

Feeling her way along the team, Rita checked the dogs' feet. She needed to change the booties on two of the dogs' paws. She hated this job that, even under good circumstances, was difficult to do. Each dog represented four booties and four dancing paws, and Rita would have to discard her mittens and gloves because it was impossible to put the tiny socks on and get the closures secured through padded fingers.

The exposure to windchills of minus one hundred degrees could freeze flesh in a matter of seconds, and Rita knew the only way to combat the cold would be to pull her gloves off and on for each bootie.

"This isn't fair," she screamed to the howling wind. "I deserve to win this race. I've taken the chances. I've sacrificed my comfort. Why are You against me, God?"

A blast of wind slammed into Rita, knocking her into the team. The dogs yipped and tangled, while she fought the harnesses and lines to recover from the fall. She felt tears form and just as quickly they froze to her lashes and burned her eyes.

"What is it You want of me, Lord? I can't go back. I can't go forward. If You won't help me," Rita moaned, "why must You hurt me?"

Rita crawled on her hands and knees to get back to the sled basket. Each inch covered was filled with pain, but Rita was determined to make it. She managed to open the covering even though she couldn't see it through the snow and her painful eyes.

Now the worst was upon her. Rita knew she would have to shed her wet clothes if she was to ever gain warmth in her sleeping bag. With nearly frozen fingers, Rita placed her mittens inside the basket and worked her way out of the layers of clothes. At the first possible moment, she scurried into the sleeping bag and snuggled down into the basket.

Mark knew his plan was foolish, yet he also knew he maintained an edge of experience that Rita didn't have. He and his team had been in situations like this before and would no doubt be in them again.

Wind and snow pelted them as Mark led the team forward at a steady walk. Moving slowly and working his way diligently, Mark managed to find the first marker without too much difficulty. He reassured the dogs with praise and pressed on. All the while he looked for anything that would indicate that Rita had passed through the same area.

Pausing in the storm, Mark lifted up a prayer. "Please, Lord, help me in this search. You know where Rita is and You can guide me to her. Please abate this storm, in the name of Jesus, amen."

Mark kept moving. Through the blowing snow he constantly had to break trail for the dogs. He felt the exhaustion of hours spent in snowshoes rapidly draining his strength. Just when he thought he'd have to turn back, a miracle happened—the snow stopped.

"Thanks, God," Mark whispered under his breath.

———#———

Rita finally felt her body begin to thaw and, with the warmth, she was able to think more clearly. Her first order of business had to be caring for the dogs. She could hear the wind howling outside the sled basket; in fact, it rocked the sled as she lay inside. No doubt the dogs had curled up to sleep and were now buried beneath a layer of snow, oblivious to the perils at hand. Rita wished silently that she could be as incognizant.

Shifting her weight, Rita pushed back her fur hat and moaned. A painful knot had formed on her forehead where she'd hit it when the wind knocked her to the ground. Rita knew she wasn't seriously wounded, but her head was pounding as her body warmed.

"I guess my charmed portion of the trip is over," Rita mused. She tried to encourage her weary heart, but it was difficult at best. Were she in the habit of praying, she might consider talking things over with God, but that wasn't her style. In the back of her mind, however, Rita couldn't help but think of a hundred different Bible stories where people found themselves facing problems and hardships. Memory verses from childhood reminded her of their commitment to God and how they cried out to Him when they were in trouble.

"Mother would like this," Rita laughed. "She's always pushing God at me. Now here I am in the middle of Alaska, in a blizzard, without a clue as to where I am, and all I can focus on is how God helped people in the Bible."

Rita felt the sled still and the wind grow calm. The storm was finally abating, and Rita knew it was time to get to work.

Pushing out of her cocoon, she crawled from the basket and surveyed the damage.

Dry, drifting snow still swirled in tiny whirlwinds around the sled while Rita pulled on her insulated clothes and went into action to get a fire going. The exhausted dogs barely stirred, although Dandy raised his head to give Rita an appraising look before going back to sleep.

Within an hour she had food and water for both the dogs and herself. The skies overhead had cleared to a pale, powder blue. Even with the sun hanging above the southern horizon, there was little warmth. At least Rita could get her bearings now and hopefully relocate the trail. Her optimism returned and her heart grew lighter. The dogs, sensing the change in their mistress, grew excited again. They were pacing and yipping, and Rita knew they were ready to be back on the trail. But where was the trail?

Rita pulled on her snowshoes and led the dogs out. There was no clear direction that beckoned Rita more than another. She looked for anything that might indicate civilization or symbolize a connection with the Iditarod race, but there wasn't anything. She pulled out her compass and depended on it alone to guide her in a direction that would lead them to safety.

Hours later, the biggest mistake Rita had made was, once again, ignoring the weather. The snow moved in from the west and with it came the wind.

Old snow blew with the new, and soon Rita found it again impossible to see. The dogs whined and slowed, and Rita felt her courage slipping away. She halted the team and tied a rope to the sled and to herself. Using her headlamp, Rita left the dogs behind and ventured ahead to find some sign of shelter.

"I can't give up," she said, even though she knew she was now several days behind the other teams. She had no way of knowing that the other racers had just been allowed to leave Ophir.

Finding nothing to aid her on her way, Rita turned around and headed back to the dogs. She retraced her steps following the rope, and then she felt her heart skip a beat. The rope had come untied; the sled was nowhere in sight!

Chapter 12

Cold permeated the insulation of Rita's coveralls. She stomped aimlessly through the blowing snow, watching, calling, and hoping.

"Dandy!" she yelled at the top of her lungs, but the wind muted the sound even as the word left her lips.

The dogs were nowhere to be found and visibility was impossible. Rita knew the seriousness of the circumstances. Without the dogs, she would most likely die!

"I have to keep moving," she reasoned. "I'll freeze to death if I stand here and wait." She thought of building a shelter with the snow. Her aunt Julie told her that once such a shelter had saved her life. Rita remembered that her aunt Julie had survived two days just off the Bering Sea in a haven she'd built with her own hands out of snow and ice.

"No!" Rita spoke aloud. "I'll find the dogs. Dandy would never have left without me." But, even as she said the words, Rita knew it was improbable that the team was awaiting her return.

Step after step, Rita forced herself forward. Her feet were beginning to ache and her legs were cramping from the strain. It was fast becoming a hopeless situation.

After what seemed hours, Rita was ready to face the facts. "I'm not going to make it," she whispered. "I'm going to die out here doing the one thing I dreamed a lifetime of doing. All I wanted was to race the Iditarod and now it's going to kill me."

But running the race wasn't all, Rita's conscience quickly reminded her. *Winning the race was what you planned on. Winning was so important that you ignored the advice of seasoned racers, people who knew the trail and have more experience than you could ever hope to have.*

"I've been extremely foolish," Rita said and stumbled forward another step. Her thick boot caught the edge of a fallen tree and sent her sprawling, face down, onto the snowy ground.

Why get up? She challenged herself to find a reason to go on. There was none. "This is God's punishment for ignoring Him and turning away from my mother," she announced. She had never felt so alone.

The thought of her mother made Rita's heart ache. All her life she'd wanted to feel close to Beth, and in spite of the times Rita had determined to put her hurts aside, inevitably, she added another brick to the wall between them.

"When times are difficult and you are most alone," her mother had told her, *"God is no farther away than a whispered prayer."*

The wind lessened and with it the snow, but Rita couldn't see anything but white. A whispered prayer came to Rita's mind, but not of her own making. The prayer she remembered was one from her childhood memories. It was her mother's prayer at Rita's bedside that came to mind. *"Father, this child was given to me from You and by Your love. I give her back. Watch over her, Father, as only You can, and help her to know Your voice when You call her."*

Such a sweet yet simple prayer, Rita thought, and the memory warmed her. Nothing to offend or harm, only a mother's desire for her child to know God. The memory wasn't painful; it was pleasant, and Rita wondered silently how she could have allowed such hatred to grow against others, especially her mother.

Rita struggled to sit up and pulled her knees tightly to her chest. "I'm afraid to die," she whispered. "I know the truth, just like Mother said. I know what God did for me by sending His Son, Jesus, to die for me. I've always wanted God to somehow make Himself real to me. Yet, even sitting here waiting to die, He still doesn't seem real and I'm not convinced He'd listen to me even if I whispered that prayer." Absent-mindedly, Rita began packing snow around herself to form a shelter.

Mark saw the reprieve in the storm as a godsend, but he also noticed the heavy clouds that pushed in from the west. The air was strangely still around him, and Mark found the silence almost hypnotic.

He urged his team forward but knew he'd lost track of the trail markers some time back. "God, give me the wisdom to find my way through this. Guide me to find Rita and safety. Amen."

Just then a blurred image in the distance came into focus. It was a dog team. No, Mark realized as he squinted his eyes, it was Rita's dog team!

Having worked with those dogs since they were pups, Mark gave Dandy a whistle that the dog instantly recognized. "Here Dandy, come," Mark's authoritative voice called.

Dandy perked his ears and heeded the command. Mark anchored his own team and stomped across the frozen ground to retrieve Rita's team. He searched the horizon for Rita but found no one following the team, not even at a distance. Maybe she was in the basket, injured or sick, he reasoned. But when he finally brought the team up even with his own, Mark could see that Rita was not with them.

"Where is she, Dandy?" Mark questioned, giving the dog a rub on the muzzle. Dandy gave a yip, as if trying to answer the question.

"I wish you could talk." Mark sighed. "I'd best feed you all instead and then we'll push on to find Rita." The delay cost Mark precious time, but he knew that the dogs had to be cared for. He piggybacked the sleds and harnessed Rita's dogs to run with his own. All the while, Mark kept eyeing the skies and the ominous clouds that threatened his success.

When Mark finally put out once again to look for Rita, light was fading quickly. He scrutinized the trees for any sign that Rita might be nearby. There was nothing.

Mark was losing hope when flakes of snow began to fall. "God, please help me!" he called out. Just then Dandy yipped and followed it with a deep throaty howl. Mark halted the dogs and watched Dandy's actions. The dog strained in his harness and pulled to the right as if he planned to pull the entire team with him if necessary.

Mark turned the team and brought Dandy to the lead. "Take us to Rita, boy," he urged. "Find her for me."

Dandy began barking in urgency then. He knew what Mark expected of him and was more than willing to respond to the call. Mark moved the dogs out and allowed Dandy to choose the course. Within moments, Mark spotted something red in the distance. Rita had worn red coveralls. It had to be her.

When he got closer, Mark began to panic. She wasn't moving or acknowledging his calls. "Please, God, don't let her die," Mark whispered.

Mark anchored the team and hurried forward to where Rita sat in a tight ball. She'd obviously tried to pack a wall of snow around her. "Rita!" he called and knelt down to push back her parka hood.

"Cold," Rita whimpered. "So cold."

Mark pulled her close and Rita moaned in agony. "Don't you go dying on me, Texas Rita." Mark tried to drawl good-naturedly. "Otherwise, you'll never see Texas, where the sun shines all the time and it's never cold."

Mark knew he was babbling, but his mind couldn't accept the possibility of Rita being anything other than healthy and strong. Hurrying back to the sled, Mark pulled out Rita's sleeping bag and his own as well. He brought both to where Rita had still not moved and began to work to get her wet parka off.

"Listen to me, Rita," he said as he unzipped her coveralls. "I've got to get these wet things off of you. Hopefully, the clothes beneath your coveralls are dry. When we finish with this, I'll put you inside the sleeping bags. Do you understand?"

"I understand," Rita whispered.

Mark wasn't convinced. "What do you understand, Rita? Tell me what I said."

"You're going to put me in the sleeping bag," she said in an irritable tone, "and you didn't call me Texas Rita."

Mark grinned. She still had fight left in her. He wasn't too late!

"What about my dogs? I lost my team," Rita mumbled.

"Dandy found me," Mark answered. "They're safe and in good shape. I only hope we can say the same thing about you."

Mark knew that once he had Rita inside the bags, he'd have more time to set up a proper camp. He was one of those few racers who liked to have a tent along in case of an emergency, and this time, it served its purpose well. He put Dandy with Rita before going to work.

Camp was set up in record time. Mark soon had the tent up, with a hearty fire glowing in the cookstove. The time would have been even shorter had he not run back and forth to check on Rita.

"The tent's ready," Mark said as he lifted Rita in his arms. "I'm going to put you inside and then I'll get you something hot to drink."

Rita said nothing until Mark had deposited her inside the tent; then, with teeth chattering, she thanked him. "Mark, I don't know how you managed to find me, but I'm glad you did."

"Me too," Mark said and reached out to touch Rita's frostbitten cheek. "You have no idea."

Then Mark went to get the hot coffee. When he returned with it, Rita wasn't sure she could even handle the cup. She felt as though her hands were on fire as they thawed, and her mind still seemed blurred.

"Drink it down and I'll make you some soup. I've got packages of dried chicken noodle," he said with a grin. "Isn't that supposed to be a cure-all?"

Rita smiled even though it hurt to do so. The skin on her face felt tight, as though it might pull apart at the slightest movement. "I think it'll take more than chicken soup to cure what ails me."

Mark nodded. "I told you not to go out. I wish for once in your life you would have swallowed your pride and realized that sometimes others know best."

"I know I was wrong," Rita admitted. "I know it only too well."

"Well, this is a different side of you," Mark commented in surprise.

"Some people have to make their own foolish mistakes before they realize what fools they are. I guess I was one of those." Gone from Rita's voice was the severity and aloof reserve. "I just wanted to win the race. I wanted to show everyone that I could do it...that I didn't need anyone looking out for me."

"And now?" Mark questioned.

"Now, I know better," Rita replied. "I was scared to die, Mark. Not because I would never again see Mom or Dad, or even you...." She fell silent for a moment. "I didn't know what would happen. I didn't know where I would go or what death would really mean. I kept thinking about the Bible and the stories I'd learned as a child and a teenager. I thought of my mother's lectures on needing to be saved from my sins, and I thought of what my father told me on the way to Anchorage."

"What was that?" Mark asked with a feeling he knew what Rita would say.

"Dad said, 'Rita, you must let go of the fear you feel inside.' He told me, 'Trust isn't an easy thing, but trust in God is something that will never let you down, because God will never let you down.'"

"Did you believe him?" Mark's face was stern, but his eyes were soft and warm.

"Not then," answered Rita.

"But what about now?"

"Now I realize I've been living on fear most all of my life. It's become such a part of my nature to distrust that I never saw the way it controlled me." Rita paused and looked thoughtfully at the cup in her hand before setting it aside.

"It's easy for other things to control us," Mark assured. "Things creep in that way, and before we realize it, we've become their victims.

God's control isn't that way. He wants us to recognize Him as the controller. He wants us to see that He's in charge and find comfort in that fact."

Rita nodded. "I suppose I can see that now, but I've always been so independent." Outside, the wind picked up and moaned through the trees. "Even now, I'm skeptical. Not of God," she added at the look of bewilderment on Mark's face. "I'm skeptical that I can hand over the reins to my life and trust God to lead me."

"Do you want that, Rita?" Mark's question pierced Rita's heart.

From somewhere in Rita's memory, she began to quote Philippians 3:10–11. "I want to know Christ and the power of his resurrection and the fellowship of sharing in his sufferings, becoming like him in his death, and so, somehow, to attain to the resurrection from the dead.'"

"Truly, Rita? Do you want to accept Christ as your Savior?"

Rita hesitated only a moment. She didn't want to commit to God out of a sense of fear, yet wasn't she supposed to fear hell and eternal damnation? "I want to know about the love," she whispered, with tears falling freely from her eyes. "I know about the fear and the pain of rejection, but I want to know about the love."

Mark's heart nearly broke for her. She was so vulnerable and child-like that he moved from his spot and put his arms around her. "God is love, Rita. I know you're familiar with that verse if you can quote Philippians."

Rita nodded and tried to wipe away her tears. "I think it's the first verse I memorized as a small girl."

"It's true," Mark continued. "God is love and He demonstrated His love for us in sending Christ to take our punishment. He doesn't want you to come only out of fear; after all, the Israelites feared Him long before He sent Christ to them. He wanted to draw His people to Him, to show them His merciful love and eternal devotion. God loves His children, Rita. He loves you, and He wants you to love Him."

"I do," Rita sobbed. "I always have, but my pride made me fear it. I just didn't want to get hurt again." She cried freely, unashamed of the tears.

Mark held her in silence until she was spent. When Rita finally lifted her face, her eyes were gentler than Mark had ever known them.

"Are you and God at peace now, Rita?"

"Yes," Rita replied. "I know Jesus says that He's the only way to come to God. I know the Bible well; I've just never lived by it. I've asked God to forgive me, Mark, but I don't believe for one minute that life will all of a sudden be wonderful and perfect. I've a great deal of my past to put right."

"What past?" Mark asked with a grin. "You're a new creation in Christ, right? You've sought forgiveness for all those sins and the Bible says God remembers them no more."

"Yes, but people aren't God and people remember them," Rita countered.

"People aren't responsible for your salvation, Rita." Mark drove his point home. "God is the one you answer to. God is the one who will clear the way for you to mend fences with others. Trust Him, Rita. He can handle the job."

Rita put her head upon Mark's shoulder, enjoying the comfort of another. "I know you're right, but I'm still afraid."

"There's a verse in Psalm 56 just for you. It says, 'When I am afraid, I will trust in you.' Trust doesn't come easy for you, Rita. I know that. But you can believe in this. You can trust God."

Rita lifted her head, remaining silent. Her dark eyes looked up into Mark's. She basked in the hope that Mark's encouragement would prove true. Trust was not an easy thing for Rita Eriksson. But trust in God was a start, and Rita was eager to take that first wobbly step forward.

Chapter 13

T he next day dawned bright and clear with frosty, cold temperatures
that left a filigree of ice upon the tent walls. Rita found herself no
worse for her experience and began the day by going outside and joining Mark in a hesitant prayer. After that, when the silence threatened
to unnerve her, Rita fell back to her defensive nature.

"Shouldn't we be pushing on for Iditarod?" she questioned as she
began to repack her sled.

"Definitely. We've lost a lot of time, and since the weather has
cleared, the others will no doubt have already passed us," Mark replied,
acting as though it wasn't a big deal.

Rita's face fell. "I wanted to be the first to Iditarod. I wanted to
give Dad the ingots."

"They wouldn't mean much to him," Mark replied. "He'd rather
know that you enjoyed yourself and that you managed to stay alive
and well."

"How would you know?" Rita retorted. "I know it meant a great
deal to Dad to have won those ingots."

"Then you really don't know him very well at all," Mark said behind
steamy breath.

"What's that supposed to mean? He is *my* father," Rita said.

"The money, prizes, and laurels were never what drove your father
to race the Iditarod," Mark began. "As a young man he traveled these

trails in order to deliver the mail. He raced because he needed to prove to himself that he could do it one last time. He needed to taste the ice with each breath, to hear the silence of the interior, and feel the dogs working beneath his hands. The ingots never meant to him what they obviously mean to you."

Rita felt a rage building inside her. How dare Mark tell her what her father felt or who he was. She opened her mouth to speak and then shut it again. What could she say that would make any sense? It wasn't easy to refute the truth. Mark was right, and that's what bothered her most. She walked away to consider his words, still feeling his eyes burning holes through her facade.

Retracing their way back to the trail proved easier than either one had imagined. Rita was surprised to learn that she'd been only a matter of miles from Iditarod. Somehow, through the blizzard and all of the trials that had plagued her way, Rita had still managed to keep the team going in the right direction.

"That's some nose," Mark teased as they made their way to the checkpoint officials. "You wandered around, blind in a snowstorm for three days, and still managed to put yourself in a decent position to regain the lost time."

Rita said nothing as people pressed in around her.

"We'd just about given up hope of finding you," one man remarked behind a fur-trimmed parka. "Are you injured?"

"No," Rita answered. "A little frostbite on my face, but nothing serious."

"I guess that's pretty typical." The man laughed. "I've heard more than one racer talk about his or her new Iditarod skin. Losing frostbitten skin off your face is pretty routine, and the skin beneath is baby soft."

Rita smiled and waited for the officials to check her dogs over. She'd lost track of Mark, and it wasn't until she overheard a comment by the man who'd first spoken to her that Rita realized something was wrong.

"I'm sorry," she said, placing a hand on the man's parka, "I couldn't help overhear your comment that Mark Williams is in some kind of trouble."

The man turned and pushed back his parka enough to reveal a weather-lined face with a graying beard. "He disqualified himself coming out after you. He disobeyed the official's direct order to stay in Ophir after a freeze was put on the race."

"But he only left to come after me. What about the Good Samaritan Rule? It wasn't that he was trying to get ahead in the race. No doubt there are plenty of racers who've moved out ahead of us. Mark isn't a threat to anyone's victory," Rita protested.

"I'm just working here," the man said and threw up his hands. "But as I understand it, the problem isn't that he helped you so much as he disregarded a direct order. The real decision has to come from a three-member panel of the race officials. They're appointed by the Iditarod Race Marshall and they have to reach a unanimous decision."

"Then I need to get word to them," Rita said, suddenly fearing that Mark would have come all this way, only to be disqualified by an unselfish act of concern for her.

"I'm not sure what to tell you," the man replied. "You'd probably better talk to the man in charge. He's over there in the blue coveralls."

"Thank you." Rita saw to her dogs, then went in search of the race official.

Although Rita had fully intended to push right out of Iditarod and head for Shageluk on the Innoko River, she found herself unable to continue until she learned of Mark's fate.

She'd explained everything she could to the official and pleaded Mark's case in every way she could conceive. The man had been sympathetic and considerate of her testimony and promised that the officials would take everything into consideration. The answer would be radioed to them within a matter of minutes.

"I'm sorry for the trouble I've caused you, Mark." Rita's sincerity was evident as she took a seat beside her father's partner.

"I would do it all again," Mark said in a peaceful way that eluded Rita.

"Aren't you angry?"

"No," Mark said with a shake of his head. "Why should I be?" He looked up from where he'd been mending a harness. Mark was never one for wasting a single minute. "Anger wouldn't change a thing and would only ruin this beautiful day."

"I've possibly cost you the race. They may not let you finish the Iditarod. Doesn't that mean anything? After all, that's why we're here," Rita argued.

"I would debate that," Mark said matter-of-factly. "God has many purposes for us in life. I believe it's entirely possible that the only reason I raced this year was in order to be there for you. God knew you'd need help, both physically and spiritually. If He used me for that purpose, then I'm content."

"You mean to tell me," Rita began, "that you wouldn't be the least bit disappointed if they disqualified you here and now?"

"Of course I'd be disappointed," Mark replied. "I planned for this race all year, just like you did. I'm just saying that the race isn't everything. I made the decision, knowing full well what the possible consequences could be. You nearly lost your life out there, Rita. Is life so unimportant to you that you wouldn't risk being disqualified from the Iditarod if it meant that you could save someone from dying?"

Rita swallowed hard. She'd always put herself first, and now she couldn't honestly say whether she would have given up her lead, even the race, to help someone else out of their own foolishness. Suddenly, Rita felt repulsed at the image she had of herself. Would she really have let someone die?

Mark sensed the inner struggle in Rita. His sympathy for her was evident. "You've had a hard time of it, Rita. Nevertheless, I don't doubt for one minute that you would not only risk disqualification of the race, but that you'd risk your very life in order to save another. You aren't the vicious, heartless person you believe yourself to be."

"I don't know about that," Rita admitted. "You may know my father well, but you don't know me."

Mark smiled in a way that caused Rita's heart to race. "I think I know you better than you imagine."

"Just because you rescued me doesn't mean you know everything about me." Rita's words were strangely soft-spoken.

"I wouldn't pretend to know everything about you, Miss Eriksson," Mark said with a chuckle. "I just propose to have more insight than you give me credit for."

"Williams!" the race official's voice rang out. He crossed the distance with long, quick strides. "The panel has cleared you to continue. You haven't been disqualified!"

The small crowd that had waited to hear the announcement gave up a cheer, while Mark and Rita embraced without thinking.

"I'm so glad!" Rita nearly squealed. Mark wrapped his arms around her, lifting her into the air and twirling her around.

"Me too!" he replied then placed a kiss firmly upon Rita's lips.

Rita found herself returning Mark's kiss before her mind could offer up any protest. She lingered in his arms while the people around them offered congratulatory praises and encouraging words. When the revelry died down, Rita's senses seemed to return. She became very aware of Mark's firm hold and dropped her arms.

Raising her eyes slowly, she found Mark's laughing eyes and smug expression. "I told you I knew you better than you think."

Rita felt her face turn hot in spite of the subzero temperatures. She pushed away from Mark, stammering for something to say, but words escaped her.

"You'd best get a move on it," someone said, and Rita nodded.

"Yes, I'm going," she said and backed away from Mark. He was still standing there, looking quite satisfied with himself, when Rita finished securing her team.

Moving out of Iditarod, Rita's mind moved in a hundred different directions. She'd become a Christian, but what did that really mean in the way that she'd now live her life? Could she somehow find a way to reach out to her mother and overcome the past?

She smiled to herself as she imagined her father's pleasure in her decision to accept Christ. He could rest easy now, and that gave Rita peace. Maybe it wasn't too late to make up for the past.

She tried to ignore the images of Mark in her mind, but when his voice called out behind her in the traditional "Trail!" requesting that she yield the right-of-way to his passing team, Rita couldn't help but think of him.

She glanced up behind dark glasses as Mark gave her a brief salute and was gone. Watching his team disappear in the distance, Rita found that she had no desire to pursue him. She needed distance between them. Distance to think and to understand why she'd so shamelessly reacted to Mark's kiss.

———#———

After eight days on the Iditarod, the Yukon River presented itself to Rita. She was tired of the ice, cold, and wind, but that was what this race was all about—that and inner strength, guts, and sheer willpower.

Now over six hundred fifty miles from the starting line of the race with a little over five hundred yet to go, sleep was quickly becoming a thing of the past.

Rita found the breaks shorter in length and farther apart. She craved sleep like a starving man craved food. Pushing north on the frozen river, Rita found it necessary to strap herself to the sled to prevent falling off of it when she dozed. She struggled to stay awake, hearing voices that weren't there, seeing sights that had never known creation in the real world.

She made her checkpoints at Grayling, Eagle Island, and finally Kaltag before moving west toward the Bering Sea and Unalakleet. Following trails that were centuries old, Rita pressed her team along the

Kaltag Portage for nearly one hundred miles. The routine of fighting fierce winds and death-defying cold with brief naps and feeding periods took an even greater toll. Rita was nearing exhaustion and wouldn't feel free to sleep for any long period of time until she reached White Mountain, where she'd have to take a mandatory six-hour stopover. Until then, she'd have to catch just bits and pieces of rest on the way.

———#———

Unalakleet, "place where the east wind blows," was an Inupiat Eskimo village of nearly eight hundred people. Positioned on the Bering Sea, this small town represented the place where camaraderie gave way to competition. It was here that racers would dump off all but their most necessary equipment and often pick up sleek, lightweight racing sleds for the final push into Nome.

After a welcome of sirens and bells from the town's natives, Rita fed the dogs and left them to rest while she changed over her sled and made decisions about her supplies. Every time a new team came into sight, the revelry would sound again, reminding Rita of her competition. In all the time since she'd last seen Mark, Rita hadn't even thought to check on his progress. Now Rita's only competition was herself. It wasn't that she didn't want to win the race; it was just that everything had changed on the way to Iditarod. Now, it was enough to push herself to the limit and do her best without causing harm to the team or risking them in any way.

Each team was appointed to a Unalakleet family and cared for during their stopover. Rita was grateful for her host family and made her way to an offered meal and bed, after finishing with her sled. It was a tradition Rita totally approved of and found herself thanking God for as she set her alarm and fell instantly into deep sleep. Hours later, Rita awoke to a rosy dawn and steaming coffee. She ate and chatted with her hosts before seeing to her duties. With the final stretches of the race ahead of her, Rita would do as most of the other team drivers did and reduce the number of dogs on her team. She had mentally calculated each choice after watching her dogs on the trail.

She walked quickly among the dogs, surveying and deciding before finally reducing the team to ten. The other dogs were then taken to the holding pens to be flown back to Anchorage. It was hard to part with any of them, and Rita felt almost as though she were betraying them, even knowing that it was for their benefit.

Reluctantly, Rita departed Unalakleet following two other teams as the trail rose into the coastal Blueberry Hills. Their next checkpoint would be Shaktoolik.

Rita found herself surprisingly invigorated after her rest in Unalakleet. Maybe it was changing the sled and dropping the dogs, but whatever it was, Rita suddenly found herself revitalized and eager to race.

She pushed out against the twenty-mile-an-hour gusts that bore down from the northwest to pass two teams. With each gained position she felt the race spirit alive and well within her heart. She wanted to do well and make her father proud!

Shaktoolik was only forty miles from Unalakleet, and the time passed so quickly that Rita could scarcely believe her good fortune. She had gained a total of three positions and learned that another four teams ahead of her were still resting at the checkpoint. Deciding to push on, Rita's enthusiasm was picked up by the dogs, who yipped and strained to be down the trail at a run.

Land soon gave way to frozen Norton Bay. This was the part of the race that Rita had feared most. It unnerved her to realize, as her team moved out across the ice, that beneath her was nothing but water. Sure, there was a thick frozen surface, but an early warming or sudden storm could quickly create a life-and-death situation.

The skies were still clear, however, and in spite of the strong winds, Rita found the trail markers easily. She settled her nerves by reminding herself that all was in God's hands and pulled her parka hood tight against the wind.

She stopped once on the icy surface to change booties on her dogs and offer them a quick snack of honeyballs. Her fingers numbed as she whipped off her gloves and mittens to pull off worn, tattered booties and replace them with new ones.

Soon they were back on their way, and Rita looked forward to the next checkpoint. For the first time she found herself wanting to know what Mark's ranking was and how he was doing. With a fondness that startled her, she remembered his embrace. She wanted to let go of her fears and reach out to Mark, but should she?

"What should I do, God?" Rita found herself praying. "For so many years I've put people away from me. I've fought to keep my distance and never let people get too close. I can't ignore how Mark made me feel, Lord, but what do I do?"

Conditions started to deteriorate as Rita's team approached the checkpoint at Kouk on the opposite shore of Norton Bay. The winds had picked up to a fierce forty miles per hour with a heavy blizzard to present near-whiteout conditions. Rita pulled into the checkpoint riding on sheer nerves and adrenaline.

"You're doing a fine job, Ms. Eriksson," the official told her. "How are your dogs doing?"

"Great." Rita gasped for air; she had run the last mile to lighten the load for her dogs.

"You've moved into nineteenth place," the man added as he walked away.

"Wait a minute," Rita called out. "What about Mark Williams?"

"Let me see," the man replied and paused to check his list. "He was here eight hours ago."

Rita smiled to herself. "Thanks. Has anyone crossed the finish line yet?"

"Not yet, but it's getting close. Several of the front runners will soon be within reach of it. My guess on a finish time will be thirteen days and some odd hours."

"Fantastic!" Rita exclaimed. She couldn't imagine the speed that the others would have to maintain to pull off a thirteen-day race completion. Her own pace had been grueling enough.

"Let him do well, Lord," Rita whispered as she went about heating food and water for the dogs. "I want Mark to do well," she added, knowing that she meant it with all her heart.

Chapter 14

Rita crossed the finish line in Nome amid the cheers of well-wishers and residents. Television cameras still worked to capture the race; the healthy finish of Rita in seventeenth place merited special attention. It would also earn her the sum of six thousand dollars. Rita found herself calculating expenses for the race; they might just break even.

Rita answered questions for the press, giving them her outlook and feel for the final miles of the trail. They also quizzed her about her lost days near Iditarod, and Rita was quick to give Mark credit for her rescue.

"I probably wouldn't be here now if it weren't for Mark Williams," Rita told a newspaper reporter. "He risked not only disqualification from the race, but his life in order to go out and search for me."

"Mark Williams is your father's partner in the Eriksson Dog Kennel, is he not?" the man questioned her.

"That's true," Rita admitted. "He's also a good friend of the family."

"Any chance that you and he are more than good friends?" the man asked with a grin.

Rita was surprised at the question and noticed that the other reporters awaited her answer with an almost anxious look.

"I'd say that's between Rita and me," Mark's voice rang out from somewhere behind the crowd. "Now, if you don't mind, we need to care for the dogs." Then in a whisper for only Rita's ears, Mark added,

"Good to see you, Texas Rita."

There was a bustle of activity and several other questions posed, but Mark waved them off and managed to pull Rita away from the press.

"Why did you bait them like that?" Rita asked, forgetting how happy she was to see him.

Mark laughed. "I thought it sounded good." Mark thrust his gloved hands deep into his pockets and shrugged his shoulders. Rita thought he looked rather like a little boy who'd been caught red-handed with the cookie jar.

"But you saw the way they reacted to your reply. You might as well have told them something far-fetched, like we were planning our wedding," retorted Rita.

Mark grinned and reached out to take hold of her arm. "And what would be so bad about that?"

Rita stared up in shocked surprise. She opened her mouth to answer but never got the chance, for just then her aunt Julie appeared in the path before them.

"Aunt Julie!" Rita cried and fell into the older woman's arms. "I'm so glad you're here. I wasn't sure I'd make it, but I knew you'd be waiting here for me and that helped me to push on."

"I knew you could do it," Julie remarked beneath layers of mufflers and fur. "You've got that tenacious Swedish blood from your grandfather Eriksson. You put your mind to complete the race and the rest just followed naturally."

Rita laughed at her aunt's words. She turned to say something to Mark, only to realize he'd slipped away from her. She looked around her, hoping to catch a glimpse of him, but to no avail. People filled in every inch of the street, and the noise was incredible.

"Are you looking for that young man of yours?" Julie questioned loudly.

Rita put her hands on her hips and with a raised eyebrow asked, "Why do you call him 'that young man of yours'?"

Julie smiled. "Never mind. We can talk about it at home. I've got a bed ready and waiting."

"A real bed?" Rita teasingly questioned. She looked among the crowd for her uncle Sam before turning back to Julie. "Where's Uncle Sam? I can't imagine that he'd miss the race. He isn't sick, is he?"

Julie patted Rita's arm. "You worry too much. I said we'd catch everything up at home. Come on." Julie motioned to Rita, but she held back.

"Really, it sounds great"—Rita sighed—"but first—"

"First come the dogs," Julie interrupted and laughed. "They always come first," she added, linking her arm with Rita's. "Oh, by the way," Julie said with a wink, "Mark came in fifth."

———※———

Rita's dogs were taken in crates to the airport, but not before she gave each one a heartfelt thank-you. Dandy seemed to sense that he'd done quite well and jumped up and down in his harness until Rita finally calmed him down. She stood watching the transport truck disappear down the road, when she felt familiar hands on her shoulders.

"Hi, Seventeen," Mark's deep voice called out in the silence.

Rita turned quickly. At least calling her Seventeen wouldn't require an explanation. "Mark! I wondered where you went. Thanks for the help with the dogs. I still can't believe I really finished the race."

"No problem," Mark replied, acting as though their earlier conversation had never taken place. "I did want to point out, however, that you weren't there to greet me as I crossed the finish line." His teasing nature was infectious.

Rita couldn't help but grin. "I know, Number Five. I guess next year I'll just have to rectify that problem."

"Next year?" Mark questioned with a chuckle. "What makes you think I'll let you come next year?"

"What makes you presume that you'll have any say?" Rita's determined look made Mark back down with a laugh.

"I guess we can discuss it later," he added.

"Everyone keeps saying that," Rita replied and picked up the bag of things she'd decided to keep with her rather than ship back home. "I'm staying with my aunt, Julie Curtiss. I'm sure you'd be welcome to drop over."

"Maybe I will," Mark answered. "We'll see."

———#———

Rita followed her aunt Julie up the long shoveled walkway, grateful that she'd finally be able to take a hot shower and sleep in a real bed.

Julie unlocked the door of her two-story house and ushered her niece inside; the pungent aroma of flowers filled the air.

"Umm," Rita said, putting her bag down on the entryway floor. "It smells like a florist shop in here."

"It should," Julie replied and led Rita to the living room, where flowers and potted plants graced every tabletop.

"They're beautiful!" Rita exclaimed. "Where did they all come from?"

"Sam's funeral," Julie said softly. "He died the day you started the Iditarod."

Rita dropped quietly into a nearby chair. "Dead? Uncle Sam is dead?"

Julie pulled off her heavy coat and cast it aside. "Yes. I know it's hard to believe. I wish there could have been an easier way to tell you." Julie couldn't help but sympathize with the great shock her niece had just been dealt. August hadn't handled it any better when Julie had telephoned him with the news.

"It's hard for me to accept because it feels as though he's right here. His things are still here. His guitar still sits in its case against the wall. His reading glasses are still on the table over there," Julie said and pointed.

"Wha—what happened?" Rita asked as tears spilled down her cheeks.

"He died in his sleep, Rita." Julie smiled. "We'd had a wonderful evening with friends and had come home to discuss you and the race. Sam bet you'd place in the top twenty and, sure enough, here you are. Then we climbed into bed, talked some more, and held each other close. When I woke up in the morning, he was gone."

"You talk about it so calmly," Rita sobbed. "I don't know how you bear it."

"Sam's not all that far away," Julie answered. "He's not gone forever... he's just waiting in heaven."

Rita nodded. "But you're here, Aunt Julie."

Julie smiled and eased back against the chair. "Yes, that is the hard part. I must wait and join him later. But you know, a long time ago, when I traveled the old village trails as a public health nurse, Sam often had to wait for me here at home.

"I remember how hard the separation was and how eagerly I would hurry home to be with him again. Sam always kept a light burning for me in the window. . .it was our way of letting the other one know that we'd not forgotten them." Julie got up and crossed the room. She pulled back heavy drapery to reveal a small lamp. Its soft glowing bulb burned as a bright reminder that Sam was not forgotten.

"I know that Sam's burning one for me in heaven," Julie said, with a single tear touching her wrinkled cheek. "I'll make my way home when the time is right."

Rita rushed to her aunt and held her. "Oh Aunt Julie, I'm so sorry he's gone. I loved him a great deal. He always made me laugh." Her voice broke into sobs. "I'm sorry that I'm not offering you comfort. . .blubbering as I am."

"It's all right, Rita. I miss him too. I didn't say it was easy. But at least I know where he is."

Rita nodded and pulled back and wiped her eyes. "Aunt Julie, I asked Jesus to be my Savior." The sudden revelation seemed fitting.

Julie's face lit up with such joy that Rita thought she would shout. "I've prayed that you would. Now you don't have to worry about death. Not Sam's or mine, or even your mom's or dad's. You'll see us again in heaven, and you don't need to fear life or death."

Rita shook her head. "I want it to be that real to me, Aunt Julie, but. . ."

"But?"

Rita led Julie to the sofa, where both women dropped wearily.

"But, I don't feel anything really different. Oh, I think I feel peace. You know, the kind of peace that you get when you stop fighting something and give in. You're still not sure you understand what you're getting yourself into, but you feel better in just having done something."

Julie laughed. "Oh Rita, I do understand. Let me assure you, God is very much alive and working in your heart. Your salvation is quite real."

Rita shook her head. "I want to believe that. I said the words and I believed them true. It's just that I don't know what comes next. Doesn't that sound stupid? I mean, here I am, a church kid who spent a lifetime involved in Sunday school and Bible memory contests, but I don't know what to do next or how to find out."

Julie took Rita's hand in her own aged one. "Rita, God loves you. You understand this, don't you?"

"Of course," Rita replied.

"No, I mean," Julie reemphasized the words, "God loves *you*, Rita. God loves Rita Eriksson."

Rita's puzzled look caused Julie to continue. "God knows you better than you know yourself, Rita. He formed you in your mother's womb and molded you into the person you became. He patiently waited for you to turn back to Him and, because He loved you, Rita, He gave you a way back through Jesus. You can count on that way to be real, and even though you can't see the bridge that Jesus' sacrifice gave you, it's there.

"It's that old issue of trust," Julie continued. "God has given many promises in the Bible. You don't have to worry that some are true and others aren't. God didn't allow the Word to be created for some kind of show. It's genuine and real, and it offers you all the guidance and hope that you will ever need. You must have the faith to accept God's gift and live for Him."

Rita nodded slowly. "I guess my faith is very weak."

"No, Rita," Julie said, squeezing Rita's hand. "It's just newborn. It's tiny and small but very much alive and surprisingly strong. Give it time and it will grow as you feed on the Word and rest in the Lord. Now," Julie said as she glanced at the clock on her wall, "catching up on everything else will wait. You need to go to bed. Come along."

Julie showed Rita to her room and gave her a kiss on the cheek before closing the door. Rita shed her coveralls and dropped to her knees. "Oh God, thank You for Aunt Julie. She's such a strong and wise woman. I want to know You like she does and I want my faith to grow." Rita started to get to her feet but stopped. "And, Lord, please help her not to be lonely without Uncle Sam. Amen."

Chapter 15

The next day Rita answered the door of her aunt Julie's house while her aunt prepared breakfast in the kitchen.

A young man stood holding a white box and clipboard. "I have a delivery for Rita Eriksson," he said as he studied the paper.

"That's me," Rita replied and signed for the delivery. She tipped the delivery man and went back to the warmth of her aunt's kitchen.

"Just what we need," Rita mused, "more flowers."

"Who are they from?" Julie questioned as she loaded the table with more food than she or Rita could possibly finish.

"I don't know," Rita replied and opened the large box. Inside was a stately looking white Stetson hat. "Well, what do you know," Rita gasped, staring at the hat.

Julie peered over her shoulder. "We've better use for that than flowers. Who's it from?"

Rita couldn't speak for a moment. She knew full well who the hat was from, but it would be impossible to explain to Julie. "Here's the card," Rita finally replied. "It says, 'Congratulations, Texas Rita. What's so far-fetched about—'" Rita fell silent as she glanced over the words that followed.

"What's so far-fetched about what?" Julie inquired, joining Rita at the table. "And what's with the Texas Rita stuff?"

Rita shook her head. The gift was from Mark, and he wanted to know what was so far-fetched about their planning a wedding. How could Rita explain that to her aunt?

"It's nothing, Julie," she said and put the card in her pocket. "It's from Mark, and he's just giving me a hard time because I once mentioned wanting to move to Texas."

"He's a good man, Rita." Julie's words were true and Rita knew it full well.

"I know," she finally murmured and waited for Julie to pray over their food.

Julie sensed Rita's reluctance to discuss the matter anymore. Instead, she prayed a short blessing and offered her niece breakfast.

Rita felt relief to see that Julie was willing to drop the matter. Now, if only she could avoid Mark. There was no way she'd be able to face him and discuss anything rationally.

———※———

There were several parties and presentations at which Rita would have to be present. Of course, she could always feign being sick, but that would go against her newfound principles. Besides, it would no doubt bring Mark to her side, and in the privacy of her aunt's home, Rita knew it would be more than she could bear.

Rita made plans for her trip back to Anchorage amid meeting her obligations in finishing the formalities of the race. There was a party she was to attend that would honor all those who'd run the race. Julie had agreed to accompany Rita, but on the night of the party, Julie was sick in bed with a bad cold.

"I'll be just fine, Rita," Julie chided her niece. "You go to the party and have fun. I'm just being cautious with myself, knowing how easily I seem to contract pneumonia."

"But I could stay here and take care of you," Rita said, nearly pleading. She was desperate to stay out of Mark's reach.

"I wouldn't hear of it. You've earned your laurels. I insist you go and party with your friends and have a good time. I'm sure if you called

Mark at the hotel, he'd be more than happy to come escort you to the party," Julie added.

"Yes, I'm sure he would be," Rita said and walked to the door. "That's what I'm afraid of."

Julie chuckled and covered it with a cough. Rita knew her aunt was good-naturedly trying to help her to see the good side of Mark's interest. Rita just shook her head, however, and went to get ready for the party.

———— # ————

The evening passed without mishap, and Rita was beginning to have confidence that she just might avoid Mark, when suddenly he was at her side.

"I'd like to have a moment of your time," he whispered in her ear. Taking hold of her hand, he added, "If you aren't too busy."

Rita trembled at his touch and her eyes darkened to ebony.

Against her will, she looked up and saw the determination in Mark's face.

"All right." She barely got the words out before Mark was leading her down the corridor to the coat-check room.

"Let's walk," he suggested and called for their coats.

Rita felt her stomach turn flip-flops when Mark helped her on with her coat. She heard an inner voice that told her to run back to the safety of her aunt's house, but her legs refused to move.

"Are you ready?" Mark questioned, seeing that Rita was rooted in place. "You ought to have a good hat," he added with a grin.

It pulled Rita from her stupor. "I have one," she said with a smirk, "but my boots don't match."

Mark laughed heartily. "We'll have to rectify that." Outside, the town was still overrun with visitors and extended race parties. Mark led Rita down a quiet side street and off to a more secluded part of town. Rita sensed Mark growing more serious.

"I've wanted to talk to you for days, but you were avoiding me,"

Mark began. "I figured out if I didn't force my hand I'd have to wait until we got back to your folks' house, and I didn't want to wait."

Rita didn't even look up. She shuffled along at Mark's side waiting for the rest of his speech.

"I don't know why you are having trouble facing me, Rita." Mark's words weren't what Rita had expected.

Her head snapped up and the independent spirit in her won over. "I'm not having trouble facing you," she lied.

"You sure you want to stay with that story, ma'am?" Mark questioned, sounding every bit the law official.

"No, I. . .well. . . ," Rita stammered. "So I was avoiding you. What of it?"

Mark laughed out loud and pulled Rita with him. "Come on, let's have some coffee. I know a quiet little place."

Rita soon found herself seated with Mark as the only guests of the small café. Mark ordered them coffee and continued his conversation as though nothing had caused any break in his thought.

"Why are you avoiding me, Rita?"

"I don't know," she managed to answer. Her cheeks were flushed and her stomach churned. Why couldn't he just drop the subject and talk about something else?

"I think you do know," Mark pressed. "I think you know how I feel about you and I think you feel the same way."

"I don't know what you're talking about," Rita replied and turned her attention to the coffee that the waitress had just brought.

"I've come to care a great deal about you, Rita. At first, I thought it was just because of my loyalty to August, but that passed real quick," he said with a grin. "I love you, Rita."

The words were bold and without hesitation, no teasing and not a hint of sarcasm. Rita nearly spit out her coffee at the declaration. Her eyes opened wide and her mouth dropped open. How could he say something so important with no more warning than that?

"You what?" She thought she'd only questioned Mark in her mind, but the words vocalized themselves aloud.

"You heard me," Mark replied patiently. "I love you. Furthermore, I want you to be my wife. I want us to get married right away, even before we go back home."

"I don't believe this," Rita gasped. "I can't believe that you're saying any of this."

"Would you like me to get down on one knee?" he teased.

"I'm serious," Rita said in an offended tone. "How can you joke at a time like this?"

"I'm serious," Mark said, moving from the chair to put one knee on the floor.

"Get up," Rita said between clenched teeth. "Get up before somebody sees you."

"I won't get up until you say that you'll marry me," Mark restated.

Rita wanted to run, but instead tears came to her eyes, and before she could control them, she was nearly hysterical. Mark got up and quickly offered her his handkerchief.

"I'm sorry, Rita," he said softly. He sat back down and waited for Rita to regain control of her emotions.

"No," Rita whispered. "I'm the one who's sorry. You're a good man, and I can't imagine why you would continue to care about me after all that's taken place between us."

"The past is gone," Mark offered. "I don't hold anything against you, and I hope you don't hold anything against me."

"I don't," Rita said, shaking her head. "I just can't deal with all of this right now. I don't know what I feel or think. I was just trying to understand Christianity and where I stood with God and now this. I can't do it, Mark. I can't deal with you and God at the same time."

"But you've resolved your relationship with God. I was there, remember? I know that you've got a lot of questions, but they'll all get answers in time." Mark paused for a moment, still feeling disbelief for Rita's display of emotions. "I know you care about me. No, I'm certain you love me," Mark proclaimed.

Rita dried her eyes and held back the torrent of new tears that threatened to flow. "I'm glad you're certain, because I don't know what I feel."

They sat in silence for several minutes before Mark surprised them both and got to his feet. "I do love you, Rita. There will always be a place for you back home. I'll be there and you'll know where to find me. Just remember this," he added with a gentle smile, "I'm not the kind of man who gives up. I'm very patient and I can wait you out. Someday you'll come to me and I'll be there with open arms just for you, Texas Rita."

He threw some money down on the table and walked from the café, still carrying his coat. Rita stared after him in wonderment. He wasn't mad or, if he was, he held it in so that not a single trace made itself known to Rita.

She marveled at his confidence and peace. "How could he be so certain of his feelings?" she whispered. Yet, even as she questioned his actions, Rita knew in her heart that he was right. She did care for him. She did love him. But how was she supposed to deal with those feelings?

Rita left the café and took the long way back to her aunt's house. She had to think things through, and in spite of the cold, Rita took her time pondering the situation.

"Aunt Julie was right," Rita muttered aloud. "I'm afraid to trust Mark, just like I was afraid to trust God." She fell silent and wondered if perhaps she was still afraid to trust God.

"It's all so new to me, God," she whispered to the night air. "I know that I'm supposed to have faith and to trust, but You know that doesn't come easy for me. Now Mark is asking for the same thing. He wants to marry me, Lord. What am I supposed to do?"

She approached the Curtiss house and caught sight of the light in the window—Sam's light, Julie's light. The reminder of a love that had lasted through childbirth, death, wars, and all that came from the process of living.

Rita thought of the way Sam would look at Julie. There had always been so much love in his eyes, and Rita had marveled at it even as a teenager. How could anyone ever share a love like that and make it last a lifetime?

Rita looked up to the skies as if hoping that some celestial answer would be written across the heavens. Could it be possible that Mark loved her in the same way that Sam had loved Julie? Was it possible that Rita was throwing away her only chance for that kind of love?

She made her way quickly into the house and nearly ran up the stairs to get to her aunt's room. A light from beneath the door gave Rita all the prompting she needed.

She knocked lightly and called, "Aunt Julie, are you still awake?"

"Come on in, Rita," Julie answered. "What's going on?"

Rita left her coat in the hall and crossed the room to her aunt's bed. "I need to talk."

Julie smiled and patted the bed. "Have a seat and tell me what's on your mind."

Rita lost no time. "Mark asked me to marry him."

Julie clapped her hands together. "How wonderful!"

Rita frowned. "I told him no."

"You did what?" Julie questioned.

"I told him no. Oh Aunt Julie, I can't marry Mark. I don't know how I feel about him. One minute I think I love him; the next minute I don't think I even know the meaning of the word." Rita threw up her hands. "How can I promise to love and cherish someone, when I'm not even sure what it means to love."

"But Rita," said Julie, "you've known what it is to be loved and to love. You've had your family and friends—"

"No," Rita interrupted. "I never felt loved by any of my friends. I always kept them at arm's length. It was my fault, but, Aunt Julie, I never let any of them get close enough to love them or for them to love me."

"But your family," Julie protested, "they love you and surely you love them. You love me, don't you?"

"Of course," Rita replied. It hurt so much to think her aunt might question her love. "You've always been there for me. You've always loved me."

"Well then, what is it?" Julie continued. "Your mother and father love you. Your brothers and sisters love you. How can you say you don't know how to love or be loved?"

Rita hung her head. "I hardly know my brothers and sisters."

"Whose fault is that?" Julie questioned sternly.

"I know it's partially my fault," Rita admitted. "But some of it is their fault."

"You can't deal with other than what you, yourself, control. Your anger and alienation toward them is where you must begin. Let go of the past and the distances that separated you. When you get home, why not write each of them a long letter. Tell them how you feel. I think you'd be surprised at their response," Julie suggested.

"What about Mother?" Rita finally braved the question.

"What about her?"

"She never wanted me, Aunt Julie. I heard her say it. She can't love me if she didn't even want me." Rita broke down.

"Talk to her, Rita. Talk to her and let her explain. I know Beth loves you, and I know it hurts her when she believes, by your actions, that you don't love her," Julie said, holding her arms open to Rita's sobbing form.

Rita fell into her aunt's embrace like a small, hurt child. "I want her to love me, Aunt Julie. I want my mother to love me."

"Child, she already does. Give her a chance to show you," Julie said in a calming way. "Give them all a chance, Rita. Your mother, God, Mark. . .let them show you how important you are to them. Let them love you."

Chapter 16

A nchorage looked almost foreign to Rita. She realized how little attention she'd paid the town before the race. After living there for five years, she'd taken it for granted. Now, looking out from her hotel window, Rita found herself wishing she could be back in Tok.

For over an hour she watched as the townspeople hustled to beat the clock. Traffic moved at a quick clip along the busy, inner-city streets, while pedestrians fought competitively for their right to cross intersections.

Store windows sported huge signs that called the public inside to late winter sales and discounted prices. It was all so busy, so noisy, and completely out of sync with what Rita had just been doing for the last year.

Rita was surprised to find that she missed the quiet of her woods and the vast openness of rural life. She missed the dogs and the roar of the wind through the trees. Even the northern lights would be difficult to see through the harsh city lights. Rita longed for home.

"What am I going to do now?" she whispered to the city. "I don't belong here and I want to go home. But should I go back?"

And what of Mark? her heart questioned. He loved her and she knew she loved him. Dare she give up her independence and tear down the walls that separated them? Dare she return his love as openly as he gave his?

A knock at the door brought Rita back to reality. She crossed the room, opened the door, and found her parents on the other side.

"Mom! Dad!" squealed Rita. She embraced them both at once and missed the look of surprise they shared over her shoulder. "I wondered when you were going to get here. How are you? How are the dogs?"

"Fine to both questions," August said with a laugh. "If I didn't know better, I'd say you missed us."

"What makes you think you know better?" Rita questioned. "I did miss you, and I'm very glad to see you here. In fact, I have something important to tell you both."

August and Beth steadied each other. With Rita it was hard to tell what she might have in mind. Over the years they'd learned to take her declarations in stride and knew better than to try and anticipate what their daughter might say.

"Come and sit down," Rita said, taking them to a small table. "There are only two chairs, so I'll sit on the bed."

Her parents nodded and moved almost apprehensively to the chairs. Rita swallowed hard and tried to think of just the right words.

"I did a lot of thinking out on the trail," she began. "I know the reports of my foolishness have already reached the papers and television, so I realize how worried you must have been. I want to apologize for not calling you, but I had to think through a great deal."

August and Beth hung on their daughter's every word. They had worried about her. Worried that her stubborn pride would claim her life and remembered having to sit by and wait until news of their youngest confirmed that she was safe.

Rita paused for a moment. She still had a touch of pride that worried about her mother's reaction to her declaration of faith. If Beth reacted smugly, Rita just knew she'd run from the room. Steadying her nerves, Rita continued.

"Mark found me when I'd just about given up hope of going on. I'd lost the team and things looked pretty bad. I'd managed to make a windbreak by packing snow, but I knew I couldn't last long without my gear and the dogs. Then Mark showed up and everything turned around. That night we talked a lot and I came to be sorry for the problems my stubbornness and independence have caused."

"What are you trying to say, Rita?" August asked.

Rita drew a deep breath. "I guess I'm trying to apologize for the way I've acted in the past. I gave up my pride and accepted Christ as my Savior." She waited and watched Beth for the reaction she feared, but the only thing she saw were the tears in her mother's eyes.

August nodded. "That must have been the hardest decision you've ever made."

Rita was amazed at the peace that settled over the room. She had been so sure of how her parents would respond that she'd literally spent hours deciding how she, herself, would react.

"It was," Rita finally replied.

Beth wiped away the tears in her eyes but remained silent. Rita thought there was a gentler look to her mother. Was it Rita's decision to accept Christ that made her so? Or was Rita just truly seeing her mother for the first time?

A knock sounded at the door, and Rita hesitantly answered it. There was still much more she wanted to say, especially to her mother. She didn't like the idea of an interruption.

"Yes?" she questioned the hotel employee who waited on the other side.

"Is Mr. Eriksson here?"

"Yes, I'm August Eriksson," August said, coming to stand beside Rita.

"There's a gentleman in the lobby who wishes to speak to you. I believe he's a reporter," the man responded.

August shrugged his shoulders. "Don't know what he'd want to talk to me about, but let's go. I'll be right back."

Rita felt almost relieved that her father had something else to do. She had really wanted to talk to her mother in private. Closing the door behind her father, Rita went back to the table.

"I'm glad we'll have a few minutes alone," Rita said, as she took the seat vacated by her father.

"You are?" Beth questioned in surprise.

Rita nodded. "I wanted to ask you to forgive the way I've treated you all these years. I know I was wrong and only acting on hurt and bitter feelings. It was wrong and, despite the fact that you never really wanted me, it wasn't fair to punish you the way I did."

Beth looked as though the wind had been knocked from her. She sat with an expression of complete shock on her face. "What makes you say that I never wanted you?"

Rita felt the tears well in her eyes. "I overheard you. You told my sister that I was such a difficult child to get close to and figured it was your punishment. I heard you say that you never expected to have another child and, in fact, never wanted another child."

Silence hung between the two women as Beth tried to rein in her emotions. "It's true I never planned to have another child after your brother Edgar. He was, after all, nine years old when you were born." Tears streamed down Beth's face. "I wish I could explain those words. No, I wish I could take them back," Beth whispered.

Rita ached at the sight of her mother's brokenness. In the past, she'd thought on more than one occasion of throwing her mother's words in her face. Somehow, Rita thought it would offer satisfaction or compensation for the pain her mother had caused. Now, it just offered Rita grief and sorrow.

Rita started to speak, but Beth waved her off. "Please, let me finish," she said. "I need to tell you all of it."

Rita nodded and sat back, waiting for her mother to speak.

"I planned to finally spend time with your father," Beth began. "I hoped to dogsled with him or to at least have more time to just be alone with him. We'd never known a time in our marriage when there weren't children and, after twenty-some years of marriage, I intended to get to know him better as a man and husband, rather than a father.

"I found out I was pregnant after thinking that I was going through the change. Mind you, I was happy to be going through the change. My days of having babies were through as far as I was concerned. So, just when I had resigned myself to move into another stage of womanhood, I found that nothing had changed at all. I was pregnant after a nine-year break and it was devastating."

Rita tried to hide the hurt she felt, but she couldn't. Her eyes betrayed her misery, and Beth suddenly realized why all those years had been lost between mother and daughter.

"The story doesn't stop there, however," Beth continued. "I hadn't realized how much I'd distanced myself from you until one day your oldest sister was remarking on the crescent-shaped birthmark you had on your upper thigh. It was like a slap in the face. You were a year old and I didn't even realize you had a birthmark. Suddenly, I started to understand that I'd pretty much given you over to your sisters. They saw you as a chore and not a new baby to play with. They fed you, made clothes for you, changed you, and I surrounded myself in the pretense that I was busy with one project or another and that the experience was good for them.

"Little by little you worked your way into my heart," Beth said with a sad smile. "I found myself watching you. You were such a good baby. So quiet and content. I never had to listen to you fuss, and you were never sick. By the time you were a toddler and then old enough for school, I'd come to love you quite dearly. But the damage, of course, was done. You and I hardly knew each other. For the rest of your life, try as I might, I could never say the right thing or do enough to make it up to you. You never gave me an inch, and I can't really blame you. I didn't deserve an inch." Beth fell silent, trying to determine just how she would say what needed to be said.

Rita cried openly and remembered the lonely little girl who longed for a mother's comfort and instead found disinterested siblings at her side.

"I am so sorry, Rita," Beth sobbed. "I don't deserve for you to forgive me, but I love you so much and I can only beg for you to give me the mercy that I didn't show you."

Rita moved her chair back and stood up. Holding her arms out, she whimpered like a tiny, hurt child, "Momma, I love you!"

Beth threw herself into the arms of her child. The years of pain were cast aside as if they were old, useless coats in springtime warmth. The two women cried long and hard in each other's embrace. Fearful of letting go. Not wanting the moment to pass.

When their tears subsided, Rita was the first to speak.

"I could never understand what I'd done so wrong that no one loved me or wanted me around. I used to lie in bed and one minute I would think of horrible, awful things that I wanted to happen so that I would have my revenge. And the next minute, I'd push it all aside, knowing that I'd gladly give anything I owned to feel loved by you."

"How you must have suffered," Beth whispered. "I can never take that back. I can never make it up to you."

"You don't have to," Rita said, feeling the weight of her misery lifted. "I know now that if I forgive you, then I must let go of the past. That little girl is grown now, and we have a future together. Dad told me that his only real worry about leaving this world was that you and I would be alone. Now we can be there for each other. We can start all over."

Beth took hold of her daughter's hands. "I'd like that, Rita. I'd like a chance to put the ugliness aside and start fresh."

"Then that's what we'll do," Rita said and embraced her mother again.

Neither of the women heard August when he returned. When they pulled away laughing, he was there by the door with tears in his eyes.

"Daddy!" Rita exclaimed and held her arms open to him.

August crossed the room, hugging both Beth and Rita to him. "Dare I hope that this means you two have put aside the past?"

"Better than that," Beth replied. "We finally understand the past between us and we're going to forgive it and forget it. Aren't we, Rita?"

She looked into her daughter's dark eyes. Eyes so much like her father's that Beth never failed to see August when she saw Rita.

Rita smiled. "We sure are. We have a lot of lost time to make up for."

"Does that mean you'll move back home?" August asked.

"I don't know. I want to get on with my nursing career, but I've come to realize after being home this last year that I don't belong here in Anchorage. I think I'd like to settle down in Tok for a while. Of course, it will all depend on finding a job."

"I'm sure you could work for one of the local doctors," August suggested. "We'd love to have you back home, and that way you and your mom could spend more time together."

"Mom isn't my only concern," Rita said gravely.

"What is it, Rita?" Beth asked in a worried tone.

Rita pulled away from her parents and went back to the table, where she slumped into the chair. "It's Mark."

"What about him?" her parents asked in unison.

"I don't know where to begin," Rita said honestly.

August sat on the bed, while Beth joined her daughter at the table. "Just tell us what's wrong," August said.

"I'd love to," Rita admitted. "But I'm not exactly sure what really is wrong."

"Is Mark the reason you don't want to move home?" Beth questioned.

"Yes and no," Rita replied. "Mark told me he loved me and asked me to marry him."

Beth and August exchanged a smile. They thought Mark would make a fine choice for their daughter and didn't hide their obvious pleasure.

"How do you feel about Mark?" Beth asked.

"That's my real dilemma. I know I love him. I just don't know that I'm ready to get married. Allowing people to get close to me is something I'm not very good at. I'm not sure I could do justice to Mark's love." Rita's voice was shaky as she continued. "I guess I'm afraid."

Beth reached out and patted Rita's hand. "Committing yourself in marriage is something you should be very sure of. I will tell you this much, however. Most everyone is afraid of the magnitude of marriage."

"What am I supposed to do then?" Rita questioned. "I mean, I do love him and I don't want to lose him—"

"Why not give Mark credit?" August interjected. "He knows his own heart and he's a good solid thinker. Why not share your apprehension with him and take it one step at a time. I have a feeling Mark will know how to handle the situation."

Rita raised her eyes to her father. "Do you think he will think less of me for my confusion?"

"I don't think it's possible for Mark to think less of you," August answered with a laugh. "He's got it bad for you, Rita. I think if you told him to walk to the moon and back, he'd do it."

"But don't take advantage of him," Beth added. "He's a good man, and he deserves to be dealt with in an honest manner. Just talk to him, Rita. If you still have any doubts, work through them and take your time. And Rita. . ." Beth paused, almost fearful of her next suggestion. "Pray about it. Spend a great deal of time in prayer, and I will too."

Rita nodded. "Of course," she whispered. "I should have thought of that, first thing. Trusting God is something else new to me. I guess I have a lot to learn."

"Don't worry," August said. "God understands all of that, and He'll guide you through. Just trust Him for direction, Rita, and when you're afraid, trust Him even more."

Rita couldn't help but smile. "Mark told me about the verse in Psalm 56 that says, 'When I am afraid, I will trust in you.' It seems like a most appropriate verse for me."

Chapter 17

Rita stayed with friends in Anchorage until May. She felt that she needed the time away from everyone in order to sort through her conflicting emotions. She had mailed Mark a brief but poignant letter that offered no promises but allowed a glimpse of her true feelings for him.

She mostly spent the time in prayer and searching however. She had determined that it would be foolish to move to Tok without a job. Because of that, Rita gave it over to God and mailed her résumé to all of the area doctors in the small town.

"If God wants me in Tok," Rita had proclaimed, "He will provide me the means to support myself."

When a job offer came at the end of April, Rita was nearly stunned by her answered prayer.

"It was what I prayed for," Rita admitted to her mother on the telephone. "I guess I'm still so new at this that I didn't really expect an answer."

"Well, I have another answer for you," Beth replied. "Your father has built a small cabin for you about fifteen minutes away. It's closer to Tok than our place, but close enough to home that you could just hike over if you were of a mind to."

Rita shook her head. It seemed fairly obvious that God wanted her in Tok. "That would make it just under thirty minutes into town," she surmised.

"That's true," Beth answered. "If you don't mind, we'll start fixing it up for you. You know, a few touches of home. We can take over your old bedroom stuff and put in some new touches as well."

"I don't know what to say, Mom."

"Just say yes, and we'll all get to work." Beth's words were Rita's final straw. She knew God's destiny for her would take her north.

"Yes," she replied into the telephone receiver. "I'll take the train to Fairbanks when the tracks are open for the tourist season. That will be May fifteenth. Can you meet me?"

"You bet," Beth replied, not hiding the joy in her voice.

That left only one unspoken problem. Mark.

As if interpreting the silence, Beth braved a question. "Do you want me to tell Mark that you're coming home?"

Rita started to say no and then changed her mind. It would be fairer to warn Mark of her impending arrival. "Yes," she said softly. "Tell him my plans. I don't know that he cares anymore. I sent him only one letter, and he never wrote back. But, I'd still feel better if he knew."

"I understand, and I will let him know." Her mother's words offered a bit of solace.

"Mother?" Rita questioned. "Do you think he still cares for me?"

"Do you want him to?" Beth asked.

After a difficult pause, Rita spoke. "Yes, I do. I really want him to still love me."

"Then give it over to God," Beth suggested, "and trust Him for the rest."

"You're right, of course," Rita murmured. "It's really a matter of trust."

———— # ————

Rita was glad for the long train ride home. The miles offered her twelve hours of contemplation time before she would arrive in Fairbanks. For most of the trip, Rita rode the train in the area between cars. She opened the upper portion of the door and allowed the chilled May air to assault her face. The cold felt good and the fresh air seemed to clear her mind.

As the scenery rushed past her, Rita found herself praying. "God, You know my heart even when I don't. This time, I feel that I truly love Mark, but I don't know if he still feels the same way about me or not. Father, I know I must leave this matter to You. Help me not to take it back and work it for my own will rather than Yours. Amen."

The ride lasted from eight in the morning until eight at night, passing through miles of Denali National Park. It even afforded Rita a picturesque glimpse of Mt. McKinley before the clouds moved in and sheltered the summit from view.

From time to time the forest gave way to glimpses of small towns. Railroads always seemed to approach towns from the backside, Rita decided. It appeared to be just the opposite of the highway on which she'd driven north a year earlier.

When she caught sight of the DEW line, America's Defense Early Warning system in case of Soviet attack, Rita knew that she was nearly to Fairbanks. She mentally calculated the plans from there. They would no doubt stay overnight, given her parents' dislike of traveling the highways after dark. That would make it at least noon tomorrow before she'd actually make it home. How much longer after that before she could see Mark and talk to him?

When the train pulled into the station, Rita put her concerns of Mark aside and rushed to greet her parents.

"I'm so glad to see you both," Rita exclaimed, throwing herself into their arms. "It's good to be home."

"Well, nearly home," August laughed. "You don't mind staying over tonight, do you?"

Rita laughed. "No, I already had that planned. Did you get the things I sent by air express?"

"They're safe and sound in your new cabin," August replied.

"My new cabin," Rita repeated. "It seems so strange to know that

I'm now a homeowner."

Beth laughed and gave Rita a squeeze. "You're going to love it. I just know it. You should have seen the way your father and Mark worked to finish it."

"Mark helped?" Rita questioned. Was that an air of hope for something more in her tone?

"Mark nearly built it himself," August answered honestly. "I can't move like I used to. Gerald came over, and he and his older boys offered a hand as well. It was a real family affair once your mother started adding the homey touches."

"Well, well." Rita's tone made her pleasure evident. "It's going to be hard to stay over, knowing all that awaits me."

"It'll be just like Christmas," August said with a smile. "You'll have to wait until morning to unwrap your gifts."

"Like Christmas, eh?" Rita questioned teasingly. "Then we can get started at four o'clock in the morning, right?"

August and Beth rolled their eyes. "Some things never change with kids," August laughed. "Come on, we'd better get you fed and to bed if you plan to get started that early!"

———— # ————

Rita didn't get her parents up at four. She relished the soft mattress of the hotel bed and lingered there until her mother announced that they were going down for breakfast without Rita if she didn't get up.

She could hardly sit through breakfast while thoughts of Mark pressed her to hurry. When they were finally headed home, she couldn't help but count the landmarks and towns. Minutes seemed to drag by, while Rita barely heard the things her parents had to say.

By the time August finally pulled down the dirt road that led to the Eriksson homestead, Rita was gripping the door handle in anticipation. Home had never looked so good to her.

"I drew you a map," August said, coming to a stop beside Rita's car.

"I know you want to head right over, but you could stay a spell."

"That's true," Beth added, getting out of the car. "I'd be happy to fix you lunch and—"

"Thanks anyway," Rita interrupted.

Beth and August laughed. "Go on, then," August said. He put his arm around Beth and, for the very first time, Rita felt the warmth of the love they shared. She'd once questioned what her father could have possibly seen in her mother. Now, however, Rita thought she was coming to understand.

Rita glanced around, wondering if Mark was working with the dogs. Beth read her daughter's mind and shook her head.

"He's not here, Rita. He's getting your dogs settled at the new place."

Now Rita was even more motivated to see her new home. "I'll see you later." She grinned and jumped into her car.

"Don't speed," August called out to his daughter. "Remember where that got you before."

"I do," Rita said, remembering it fondly. "It found me the man I intend to marry!"

August shook his head and waved her on. It was good to know that his youngest had finally found happiness. Better yet to know that she'd finally found peace of heart and soul.

---#---

Rita glanced only briefly at the map. From her father and mother's earlier description and directions, she knew without the paper just where she was going. She crowded the speed limit as closely as she dared and finally found her turnoff just as her patience was wearing thin.

The dust sprayed out behind her car as Rita moved closer to her cabin. She rounded the final bend to face a huge banner with bright yellow letters strung across the road. As she approached the cabin, she found that banners were flying everywhere. WELCOME HOME, they read.

Across the front porch of the huge cabin, another banner in multiple colors reiterated the message. Rita felt her heart pound faster.

Were the banners her parents' idea or Mark's?

Parking the car, Rita got out and stopped. She looked around her, just trying to take it all in for a moment. The clearing set out before her held not only the cabin but a partially finished shed. From behind the house, Rita could hear the dogs raising a ruckus. They knew their mistress was finally home.

She searched the area for some sign of Mark's motorcycle or truck. Surely he hadn't tended the dogs and left. If he had, did that mean he no longer cared for Rita in the way he once had?

Rita felt a gripping despair come over her. Maybe her anticipated homecoming wasn't what she'd hoped for. Maybe Mark's kindness and work had been done out of his partnership status with her father. Maybe Mark wouldn't want to see her. After all, he'd never even acknowledged her letter.

Rita swallowed hard. Whatever happened was in God's hands. She had to trust Him and count on Him to make the way for her life. Breathing a little easier, Rita stepped forward to explore her new home.

She hadn't taken more than two steps when the unmistakable sound of a screen door opening caught her ear. Looking up, Rita found Mark coming out of the cabin. He walked to the edge of the porch and stood at the top step.

Rita stopped and appraised him for a moment. His expression was masked from revealing whether their reunion was a welcomed one or something that he was merely tolerating. His brown eyes were serious, and Rita felt their warmth as his gaze penetrated her fears.

The wind in the trees broke her concentration and Rita turned momentarily. She looked back quickly, half expecting Mark to have moved or done something that would indicate how he felt. Instead, he said nothing, did nothing. What did it mean?

Chapter 18

Mark's words came back to haunt Rita. She remembered in Nome when he told her, *"Someday you'll come to me and I'll be there with open arms just for you."*

Here I am, Rita thought to herself. *Now where is the open-armed welcome that he promised?*

Mark had played his game long enough. When a grin spread across his face, he couldn't help but fulfill his promise to Rita.

Rita ran across the yard and up the steps to where Mark's open arms waited. "I've missed you so much!" she exclaimed as his arms tightened around her.

"You have no idea how hard it was for me to leave you in Anchorage and wait here," Mark replied. "Thought you might have even headed off for Texas."

"I was afraid you wouldn't care anymore," Rita said, lifting her face to Mark's. She needed to see in his eyes that her fears were unfounded.

"I told you that I'm a very patient man," Mark whispered. "Although you very nearly made me a liar. It's a good thing your dad had this cabin project in mind, or I'd have never been able to get through the weeks."

"Oh Mark," Rita said, burying her face against his chest. "I love you and I'm so sorry for making you wait so long to hear me say it."

Mark pressed his lips to the top of Rita's head. Kissing her hair, he whispered, "The wait was worth it. All things in God's timing are worth waiting for."

Rita released Mark and stepped back. "The loneliness was incredible. I thought of you constantly and all I could imagine was that my foolishness had put you out of reach forever. I was truly afraid that I'd lost my dreams of happiness."

"You're the only dream that has ever mattered, Rita," Mark said with a grin. "And let me tell you, my time up here alone has given me an awful lot of time to perfect that dream."

Rita found Mark's sense of humor contagious. "I did some dreaming of my own," she admitted. "About a tall, broad-chested law officer, who saved my life and stole my heart. You've always been a part of my dreams, Mark. And you always will be."

"Then you'll marry me?" Mark asked for the second time.

Rita stepped forward and put her arms around his neck. "I would be most happy to marry you, Mr. Williams. Positively delighted!"

"Promise?" he said, raising a questioning brow. "You aren't going to change your mind and replace me with another Iditarod dream, are you?"

Rita laughed out loud. "Not hardly, Mr. Williams. You are caught, hook, line, and harness. No Texas or race or cowboys or frozen wilderness is gonna stop me. You're stuck with me, like it or not."

"I like it," Mark said, lowering his lips to Rita's. "I like it very much." He kissed her tenderly while Rita melted against him.

When he lifted his lips, Rita sighed. "I'm going to like this too. I can tell."

Mark surprised her by taking her hand and pulling her with him to sit on the porch step. "This is going to be new for both of us. We've both been used to independence, and we've both lived our lives without real concern for the decisions we make. Now, however, we'll have to consider each other in every choice we make."

Rita nodded. "It won't be easy to change our lifestyles overnight."

"We'll no doubt have our moments when we're not very happy

with one another," Mark added.

"True," Rita replied. "But if we're honest with each other and careful to work through those times, maybe we won't have to spend too much time in strife."

"It's going to be a lot of work," Mark stated.

"You sound like you did when you were training me for the Iditarod." Rita couldn't help but laugh. She saw the amusement in Mark's eyes.

"Marriage is going to be even more work than the race," Mark answered. "And a whole lot more dangerous."

Rita questioned his words. "Just what do you mean?"

"I hear you don't cook too well," he laughed. "I might be in for some strange cuisine. Then there's mending and sewing."

"Whoa!" Rita called out. "I'm a nurse, remember? I have a job that I hope to do and I enjoy working in medicine. You have the kennel and the dogs. I don't see any reason why we can't work together and trade off on the cooking and cleaning."

Mark rubbed his chin thoughtfully. "All right," he said in a teasing tone. "I suppose that's fair enough. But I draw the line at mending clothes. I'm no good at it. I can mend harness and rigs with the best of them, but I can't even sew on a button."

Rita laughed. "Me neither. I can stitch up wounds though. Does that count?"

Mark put his arm around her. "Maybe your mom could sew on the buttons."

"Maybe," Rita mused, "she could give us sewing lessons."

They fell silent, enjoying the brilliant sun and the warmth that filtered down to thaw the earth.

"What about dogsledding?" Mark asked suddenly.

"What about it?" Rita questioned.

"You plan to race anymore?" Mark's question took Rita by surprise.

"It all depends," Rita replied.

"On what?" Mark asked her. Now he held the puzzled look.

"On you." Rita grinned.

"Me? What are you talking about?"

"You asked me back in Nome, 'What makes you think I'll let you come next year?'"

Mark laughed and squeezed Rita's shoulders. "I guess I did at that. But, seriously, do you want to race again?"

Rita nodded. "I thought it was wonderful. It was everything I dreamed it would be."

"You suppose marriage will be the same way?" Mark's question caused Rita to think.

"I know it will, Mark. It's the best of all possible dreams, and even my goal of racing the Iditarod will never be as great as the goal of making you a good wife."

"You'll be a good wife, Texas Rita," Mark said, dropping his arm to take her hand. "There may be other Iditarod dreams, there may even be other races, but there is only one you—"

"And one you," Rita interjected.

"And together, we'll make the dream a reality," Mark whispered. "With God, we'll work to make a good life together. A life founded on Him."

Rita covered Mark's hand with her free one. Maybe it wasn't such a bad thing to give yourself over to another person, after all. Especially when that other person was God's very best answer to all your fondest dreams.

JOIN US ONLINE!

Christian Fiction for Women

Christian Fiction for Women is your online home for the latest in Christian fiction.

Check us out online for:

- Giveaways
- Recipes
- Info about Upcoming Releases
- Book Trailers
- News and More!

Find Christian Fiction for Women at Your Favorite Social Media Site:

 Search "Christian Fiction for Women"

 @fictionforwomen

ABOUT THE AUTHOR

TRACIE PETERSON, Often called the *"Queen of Historical Christian fiction"*, Tracie Peterson is an ECPA, CBA and USA Today best-selling author of over 120 books, most of those historical novels. Her work in historical fiction earned her the Lifetime Achievement Award from American Christian Fiction Writers in 2011 and the Career Achievement Award in 2007 from Romantic Times, as well as multiple best book awards. Throughout her career, Tracie has also worked as a managing editor, speaker of various events and teacher of writing workshops. She was a co-founding member of the American Christian Fiction Writer's organization and has worked throughout her career to encourage new authors. Tracie, a Kansas native, now makes her home in the mountains of Montana with her husband of over 40 years.